# BEYOND
## THE TRACKS

# MICHAEL REIT

Published by Michael Reit.

ISBN (Paperback): 978-3950503326
ISBN (Hardcover): 978-3200075573

Cover design, illustration and interior formatting:
Mark Thomas / Coverness.com

*To everybody who told me to keep going, despite my many attempts to quit and start an 'easier' story.*

# PART I

BERLIN, GERMANY
NOVEMBER 1938

# CHAPTER ONE

The blood-red swastika banners dominated Berlin. Draped across storefronts, houses, or taking over entire buildings, they demanded attention. Oranienburger Straße was as busy as ever this frosty afternoon, and Jacob Kagan deftly maneuvered through the stream of people on their way to the U-Bahn. He approached the New Synagogue, its gold-domed roof a proud symbol of defiance amidst the sea of Nazi symbolism.

Jacob nodded at one of the men standing guard in front of the building. "Everything okay today, Hans?"

"No trouble," Hans replied, shaking Jacob's hand, "if you don't count the Hitler Youth over there. But we can handle them." *Just like you always handled us in class*, Jacob thought wryly. He felt sorry for Hans, who had recently lost his job having taught at the same school for almost ten years until the new government decided Jewish teachers were no longer welcome. Now he spent most of his time keeping away trouble from the largest synagogue in the city.

Across the street, five teenagers in dark green uniforms handed out flyers. A common sight these days, they were generally harmless unless drink was involved – which often ended in pub brawls.

Jacob shook his head. "I'm sure they'll get bored soon enough and move on."

"I'm not so sure." Hans scratched his beard and puffed vapor into the air. "They've been here all day." One of the youngsters, who must be no older than twelve, stopped an elderly lady walking past. His face was flushed, and he gesticulated wildly. She responded calmly, took one of his flyers, and gently pushed the boy out of the way.

"They give everybody a flyer," Hans said, while Jacob frowned. "Everybody but us."

"I'm sure you fellows are not the most popular people on this street," Jacob said as he gestured to the other members of the synagogue standing watch.

"I've never cared about being popular, Jacob. Most people hurry by, their gazes firmly on the pavement in front of them—occasionally, the odd man will give us a dirty look," Hans said with a shrug and a wry smile. "It's business as usual. Speaking of which, how's the pharmacy doing?"

"Business is surprisingly good!" Jacob answered. "I've been out delivering all day. People will always need medicine, even if they won't be seen in our store anymore."

"Some of the lucky ones," Hans said. "Glad to hear it—your father has always been good to the community."

"Papa does his best navigating the restrictions. Some of our suppliers are wary, so we need to be creative." He looked up at the clock across the street. "I'll see you later, Hans. I have a few more packages to deliver before dark."

Jacob merged into the growing stream of people heading south toward Kreuzberg – all the while his fists were clenched.

It was dark by the time Jacob made his last delivery to a long-term customer, Herr Müller. He had been especially happy with Jacob for delivering his medication and saving him a trip to the pharmacy. Jacob turned from Spittelmarkt back onto the main thoroughfare of Leipziger Strasse—the street was alive with activity. Streetcars occupied the middle, their bells clanging to shoo careless pedestrians out of the way, while commuters paused to shop before making their way home.

Jacob hurried through the street and turned a few corners. He was late for his meeting with Ethan, his lifelong best friend. It didn't take him long to open the door to the Augustiner, a tavern just a few streets from his home.

He looked around for Ethan as the door closed behind him. The Augustiner was one of the few places in Berlin where Jews were still welcome, and as a result, it was packed every night. Tonight the warm, smoky air enveloped Jacob like a comfortable blanket.

Jacob spotted Ethan at a small table in the corner. Jacob pushed his way through the packed room, and Ethan stood up to hug him. Jacob was usually the tallest person in the room, except when Ethan was around.

"You're a bit late—nothing like you," Ethan said, flashing a broad smile.

Jacob took off his coat with a grin. "Are you trying to grow a beard?"

Ethan proudly scratched at his two-day stubble. "I think I'll look very respectable in a few weeks."

"Not until you take care of that mess on top of your head," Jacob said. Ethan's hair was especially wild today.

"These curls? Never!"

A waitress set down two large mugs of beer, catching Ethan's eye, the pair smiled at one another before she headed back to the bar.

They lifted their mugs, took their first sips, and set them down at the table. Ethan looked around the tavern – taking in a group of middle-aged men who were laughing loudly.

Ethan's face turned serious. "Do you remember when we would go out on Saturday nights, and walk into any bar we liked?"

Jacob nodded. "Nowadays, this is as good as it gets."

"I miss those days, Jaco."

Jacob looked around and thought nothing of the elderly couple at the table next to them, sharing a plate of pickled sausage and a small carafe of red wine in silence.

"What will be next?" Jacob asked. "Changes are taking place all around the city. Did you hear about that young boy who was attacked by the Brownshirts last week? They beat him almost to death in front of a crowd. Nobody did anything."

Ethan nodded. "And people losing their jobs. How long has it been since your mother left the school?"

"She hasn't set foot in there for over five years now. She used to go to school happy every day, and now she just sits at home."

They were silent for a moment.

Ethan stood and picked up their empty mugs. "I think we should have another one. There's not much we can do about it all tonight."

Jacob watched his best friend navigate his way to the small bar. Ethan was right—there was nothing they could do. The Augustiner was one of the few places where people could pretend everything was still normal.

Ethan returned with two foaming pints he placed on the table. "Right, Jaco. Here's to not speaking about politics, Nazis, or other shitty things for the rest of the evening." He raised his mug.

Jacob clinked Ethan's mug and took a sip of his own. Ethan met Jacob on the first day of school when they were just six years old. An older boy pushed Jacob in the playground, and Ethan had come to his rescue. Ethan suffered a black eye in the scuffle, but the boys had been inseparable from that day onward. Now both twenty-one, they were as close as ever.

"Oh, great." Ethan's expression darkened. "Not these guys."

Four men walked into the bar, wearing the characteristic brown shirts of the *Sturmabteilung*. One of the men pushed aside customers at the bar, causing an elderly gentleman to lose his balance, though someone caught him just in time.

The other people at the bar quickly made way for the heavily-built men. Jacob shook his head and looked down at his beer. "That's the first time I've seen Brownshirts in the Augustiner!" He took another sip to suppress the anger building up inside.

"You think we can take them?" Ethan asked with a twinkle in his eye.

Jacob set his mug down. "Are you kidding? There's four of them."

"So? I'm sick of these guys showing up everywhere and acting like they can get away with anything."

Ethan never walked away from a fight, but he was pushing it now. Jacob turned back to the bar and sized the men up. They were clearly drunk; perhaps this wasn't their first stop tonight. It was an open secret that the Brownshirts served as Hitler's personal riot squad, bringing violence and destruction wherever they went, although they were not officially recognized by the government.

The Brownshirts brought their beers into the main room, where most of the people kept their eyes on the group, anxious to see what they'd do next. All the tables in the Augustiner were taken, someone would need to make way.

The largest one spoke up: "Any Jews in here?"

A hush fell over the room as people averted their eyes and focused on their drinks.

Jacob looked at Ethan, whose face had further darkened. Jacob felt his anger bubbling over and heard himself say, "Right here."

The men turned toward their table. One of them cocked his head. "How about you get up, then?"

The other men laughed, and they took a few steps in Jacob and Ethan's direction as the people around them held their breath.

Ethan was the first to react. "We're okay here, but perhaps you want to knock another old man off his legs?" he nodded toward the bar.

The larger man scowled. "What did you say?" He stepped closer to Ethan, who stood up from his chair. Jacob did the same.

"You heard me. Nobody wants you here. Everybody was having a grand time until you stank the place up." Ethan gestured across the room, where the stunned patrons were looking back at him.

The largest of the Brownshirts was taken aback for a few seconds, then quickly regained his posture and lunged at Ethan with surprising speed.

Ethan side-stepped and easily dodged the blow. He landed a punch to the side of the man's head, and he went down like a sack of potatoes.

This only enraged the others.

The smallest of the three turned to Jacob, who managed to avert the man's first attack but didn't expect the off-hand blow that connected with his shoulder as he crouched down.

*Bring it on—I can dodge your slow punches all night.*

7

The attacker was panting and snarling. "Hit back, you *kike*," he slurred.

Then came the moment Jacob was waiting for. His opponent stumbled into one of the tables and lost his balance. Jacob's fist connected firmly with the man's face before a satisfying crack followed. The man grabbed his face while he crashed down onto the table, glasses shattering around him as he slumped to the floor.

Jacob turned to see Ethan holding his own against the two other men—waiting for the perfect time to strike.

Suddenly, the tavern door burst open, and more Brownshirts piled into the Augustiner, pushing their way through the thick crowd. Jacob counted at least five.

"Ethan!" he shouted, pointing at the door. "Time to go!"

His friend gave him a quick nod. The two Brownshirts still blocked Ethan's path out of the corner, so he took a step toward them and feinted an attack. Both men took the bait and swung wildly. Ethan ducked, and two quick stabs to the ribs doubled the men over. He kneed one in the face and the other in the groin, leaving them in pain, twisting on the floor.

Ethan skipped over them and joined Jacob. "Okay, now what?"

Jacob looked to the door and saw to his surprise that the new Brownshirts hadn't gotten much closer. The people in the Augustiner had blocked their path, forming a human wall.

"Quickly, over here!" One of the barkeeps waved from the side of the bar.

Jacob and Ethan hurried toward the man, deftly avoiding the overturned tables. The barkeeper lifted the bar and indicated the door behind it. Just as they passed, the elderly gentleman who had been almost toppled earlier placed a weak hand on Jacob's shoulder.

"If only more people stood up to them, we wouldn't be in this mess," he said.

Jacob smiled as he hurried through the door Ethan had left open behind the bar. The cold evening air hit his face as he stepped outside. Ethan was already halfway down the deserted alley, and Jacob rushed after him.

# CHAPTER TWO

It had been a while since Jacob and Ethan had been in a fight. Fortunately, the previous night's damage was restricted to a few bruises, and Jacob wondered how their opponents had spent their day. It felt good to put some of the Brownshirts in their place and get away with it.

Jacob opened the door to the pharmacy as he returned from the last delivery, his father busy at the counter, helping a regular customer pick up her prescription.

"Jacob! What took you so long?" The handful of customers in Kagan & Sons Medicine turned to look at Hermann Kagan—a small, stout man. "You only needed to cross Kreuzberg! It's been more than an hour!"

Jacob gave the customers a reassuring smile and went behind the counter to hug his father.

"I'm here now, safe and well," he said, grinning as Hermann tried to wrestle free from his grasp.

"Wonderful. Now let me go!" Hermann protested as Jacob released him. He was no match for his much taller and stronger son, and it was an odd sight—the pharmacist and his son jousting behind the counter. An elderly lady at the counter smiled knowingly.

Jacob casually tossed his bag behind the counter. "Any more deliveries?"

"No, we're done," Hermann said as he handed a small bag of medicine to the elderly lady. A modest bell clanged as the door closed on her way out.

Jacob watched as his father rang up orders for the last customers. Hermann had taken over the pharmacy twenty years ago from his father, who had built it from the ground up, and the business soon thrived. Then Hermann had worked hard to grow it into one of the largest pharmacies in the city.

"Jacob, can you help carry these to the back?" His father pointed to some boxes next to the door.

Jacob took them to the empty storeroom behind the counter—getting a steady stream of medication to the pharmacy was tough.

They stepped outside, and Hermann locked the door. It was already dark, and a chill hung in the air. Their neighbor, Herr Wagner, closed the door to his law office as well.

"Did you hear about vom Rath?" Wagner looked concerned.

Jacob tensed. "Is he still in the hospital?"

Ernst vom Rath, a diplomat, was shot inside the German embassy in Paris a few days ago. A young German-Jewish man named Herschel Grynszpan was arrested on the spot and admitted to the shooting. According to the newspapers, his original target was the ambassador, but he had not been present. Vom Rath had been in critical condition since, and the story dominated the German news.

Wagner shook his head. "He passed away a few hours ago. Goebbels was just on the radio." He checked the lock on his door. "He's calling it a Jewish attack on Germany."

Jacob looked at his father. Hermann's face was ashen in the glow of a street-lamp.

"Goebbels said the Jews should feel the anger of the people," Wagner continued. "I'm sorry, Hermann—I don't know what that means."

The words were a punch in the gut to Jacob.

"Hitler was looking for an excuse," Hermann said, his bottom lip quivering, "and the Grynszpan boy has given him the perfect excuse."

Wagner nodded. "They're talking about bringing him back to Germany to make an example of him, whatever that means."

Jacob had a good idea what it meant. His father looked like he'd aged ten years in the past few seconds. "Let's go home," Jacob said. "There's no sense in staying in the cold."

Wagner nodded and walked solemnly off in the opposite direction. Jacob and his father set off along the cobblestoned street, all the shop windows now dark. They passed the *Berliner Gasthaus*, one of the few places where light shone from behind the windows. A few tables were occupied, the people enjoying simple suppers of sausage and bread.

"I'm worried about Goebbels," Jacob said, breaking the silence. "Do you think this means they'll make us close the pharmacy?"

Hermann shook his head. "I don't know. There's no telling what they'll do. We've been lucky to stay open so far, I guess."

"We'll just have to wait and see what happens the next few days," Hermann continued. "There's not much we can do about it."

They walked home in silence, each lost in their own thoughts.

Jacob's mother always made sure there was a hearty meal waiting for her men at the end of the day. Elsa Kagan cleared the empty plates from the table, and Jacob followed to help her wash the dishes in the small kitchen.

The Kagans lived in a modest house that had been in the family for generations, and while they could certainly afford to move to a larger home, they preferred to stay in Kreuzberg. Elsa always said the house had the sort of character which couldn't be bought. Jacob agreed; there were so many memories here that he couldn't imagine living anywhere else.

"Just hand me those, Mama."

Jacob rinsed the plates before plunging them into the scalding water. His mother joined him at the sink and started drying the dishes while Hermann sat down with a newspaper and switched on the radio. Goebbels' voice boomed from the speakers.

"I hope they keep him there," Elsa said. "Who knows what will happen if he's handed over to the Nazis. I doubt there will be a trial at all."

Goebbels was calling for reprisals after the assassination of Ernst vom Rath and added that the German government demanded the extradition of Herschel Grynzspan from France.

"He'd probably receive a one-way trip to an SS basement," Jacob said. Rumors about the makeshift prison under the SS headquarters circulated Berlin, those unfortunate enough to earn an unsolicited invitation were never heard of again.

"It's such a shame. The boy must've been so desperate to do what he did," Elsa said, placing the dry plates in a cupboard.

Jacob drained the water and dried his hands with a small towel. "This gives the Nazis more incentive to blame all of us, even though we had nothing to do with it."

He put the towel down and yawned. "I'm going to go upstairs and study a bit."

Hermann smiled. "I should have the exam for you next week."

Jacob stopped. "Herr Lughart at the university came through?"

"He did. He's smuggling the latest exam out for you."

Jacob saw his mother smile. Even though he wouldn't be able to formally take the exam, this was as good as it got these days.

"I'll be ready, although this first book is quite tough," Jacob said as he bound up the stairs with a spring in his step. He closed the door to his room. He wasn't just going to be ready; he planned to ace the exam.


Jacob awoke in the middle of the night. It was dark, and it felt like he'd slept for only a few minutes. His eyes needed a few seconds to adjust to the darkness. He squinted at his watch on the bedside table—one in the morning.

He switched on the night light and got out of bed. Rubbing the sleep from his eyes, he felt his senses switch on. He heard angry voices outside and smelled smoke. He quickly dressed and opened his bedroom door. His father stood in his nightclothes in the hallway, a surprised look on his face.

"What's going on, Jaco? Is there some kind of protest outside?"

"I don't know, but I smell smoke."

Jacob raced down the stairs and looked out into the street. A dozen or so people stood outside, the small bakery across the street was ablaze. Angry bursts of fire shot from the bakery window, smoke billowing from all sides of the building.

Hermann appeared next to Jacob. "Oh no! Midas must've had an accident. Let's help him put out the fire." He went for the door before Jacob stopped him.

"Wait," Jacob said, a hand on his father's arm. "Look at the people around the bakery."

Their neighbor was frantically pleading with the growing crowd to help him fight the fire. The people didn't move as the baker rushed between his burning bakery and a well, carrying a small bucket. It was useless; the fire had engulfed the shop.

"It doesn't look like an accident," Jacob said.

One of the men said something to Midas, prompting a chorus of laughter from the others. Midas looked distraught and ceased his attempts to put out the fire. The crowd stood by idly as the flames consumed the building.

"We can't just stand here and do nothing," Hermann said, opening the door to the street. Jacob followed him, and they rushed toward their neighbor.

A few paces down the street, a jewelry store had its front window smashed, and several looters were running away, dropping necklaces as they went.

On the other side of the road, two men doused the front of a small butcher shop in gasoline while another man held a blazing torch. The men stepped away from the shop window, throwing the now-empty jerry can on the ground. The man with the torch casually lobbed it at the window, and the fire roared to life with a loud whoosh—the butchers was engulfed in flames within seconds.

Jacob looked around, their peaceful street transformed into a war zone.

*What's wrong with these people?*

"They're targeting Jewish businesses!" Hermann said, fear rising in his voice.

*Papa is right, but what about*—"I'll check on the pharmacy," Jacob said, rushing back to their home to grab the keys from just inside the door. "You stay here with Mama and don't go anywhere. Lock the doors!"

His father nodded and disappeared back inside the house.

Jacob ran down the street, reaching the intersection with the larger Gitschiner Straße. The mayhem was even worse here, with half the buildings on fire. A large man took a loose stone from the street and launched it at a shop window. The window exploded into a thousand pieces. Further down the street, a group of firemen stood working a large hose. Jacob was relieved; maybe they could salvage some of the damage?

As he got closer, he overheard who he assumed was the owner of the store, pleading with the firemen.

"But my building is burning down. Please help me!"

"I'm sorry, we can't," one of the firemen said. "We're only here to make sure it doesn't spread."

The plumes of smoke increased, obscuring the view of the surrounding buildings as pieces of stone crumbled down haphazardly.

Jacob ran on for another five minutes, almost to where their pharmacy was located. He braced himself as he thought of the mess he'd find there. *If a crowd were looting the pharmacy, there wouldn't be anything I can do about it.*

As he turned the corner, he was relieved to find the pharmacy untouched. The street was relatively quiet, and there were no fires, but there were plenty of people outside their homes. A young girl not much older than seven looked up at Jacob with big, frightened eyes. She wore but a nightgown, and her mother kept her close. A man stood next to them, holding a shovel, scanning the street with an air of defiance.

Jacob reached the pharmacy, where Herr Wagner stood outside the door to his offices. He saw Jacob and motioned him to come closer.

"It's madness," he said, his eyes wide with fear. "They're destroying the city."

Jacob nodded. "I ran across town, and there are fires everywhere. People are looting shops, grabbing whatever they can. I haven't seen any fights yet, but it can't be much longer."

"They're only attacking Jewish businesses, though," Wagner said. "Looks like Goebbels got exactly what he wanted."

"I can't believe this is a spontaneous reaction. Do you think it's the SS?"

"Maybe, or the Brownshirts, more likely. I saw some men in uniforms giving orders. Most of them are wearing normal clothes, though." An explosion on the next block rocked the ground, and they instinctively ducked.

A large group of men appeared from around the corner. They carried torches and jerry cans and shouted at people to get out of their way. Jacob counted at least twenty of them.

"Out with the Jews!"

Jacob looked at Wagner. He'd turned pale, his gaze fixed on the men.

"Trouble's here," Jacob said. The man across the street tightened his grip on the shovel. Jacob tried to get his attention, but the man was too focused on the group. The girl hid behind her mother, only her face peeking out.

The group reached the small family's house and stopped.

"Look at the brave one," one of the larger men in the front said. He flashed a sinister smile and held his arms out wide. "What do you think you're going to do ?"

The homeowner didn't respond but just looked at the brute and clenched his jaw.

"Get out of the way," the man said, stepping forward. "Don't give me a reason to hurt your little girl there."

Behind him, a man took a bottle from his backpack and filled it with gasoline from one of the jerry cans.

"You want to be a homeless *kike*?" The first man flashed a dirty, toothless grin "or a dead one?" He held up the bottle menacingly and struck the first match. The flame didn't hold, and the man cursed.

Jacob looked around the street—most people had fled into their houses.

*We can't just leave them to fend for themselves.*

He took a step toward the family across the street. Before he could take another, he felt a firm hand on his shoulder.

"You can't help them, Jacob." Wagner's eyes showed concern as he shook his head. "Look at those thugs—there's no reasoning with them."

Jacob tried to shake off the older man's grip, but Wagner was adamant.

"If you walk over there, they'll burn down the pharmacy as well. Not to mention what they'd do to you. You're a Jew, Jacob. Don't give them an excuse."

Jacob felt his eyes sting as he struggled to control his anger. *I can't just stand here and do nothing.* At the same time, he knew he couldn't take on twenty men on his own. *If only the man backs down, maybe it won't be that bad.*

The little girl started to cry. The sound pierced the evening sky, and her father looked over his shoulder. It was the first time he took his eyes off the group.

"It will be okay," he said softly as he put down his shovel to gently stroke her hair. "These angry men think we're going to hurt them, but you know that's not true, right?"

She sobbed and buried her face against her mother's skirts. The mother looked up at her husband with pleading eyes.

He shook his head. "I can't let them destroy our house. It's all we have."

The man grabbed his shovel and swung it at the man holding the bottle, smashing it to pieces on the street. The man roared with pain, and for a moment, everybody was too stunned to react as the sweet smell of gasoline spread.

The group recovered quickly and descended on the man like a pack of hyenas. He managed to get a few swings in, stepping back while they approached. He could only keep them from him for so long, and it was only a moment later he was pinned down on the ground.

Jacob saw the flash of a knife and looked away.

The leader of the group called out: "Stop, don't kill him!"

The man holding the knife paused and looked up at the leader in surprise. The man on the ground was a mess, his face bruised and bloodied. Despite this, defiance still shone in his eyes.

"Get him up," the leader said. "And get his wife and kid away from the house."

The man was dragged away; the girl left crying as her mother tried to comfort her. She shielded her daughter and clawed at the men approaching them. Outnumbered, the men pulled her and the child away from the house. They were left next to their husband and father, whose breathing was labored and shallow as he struggled to sit upright.

"I've decided it's better to have you see your house burned to the ground than to kill you here," the leader of the group said. "Besides, there's a better place to send you than kill you." He grinned and lit the rag hanging out of one of the bottles. The thugs smashed a window using the homeowner's shovel and stepped out of the way.

The leader threw the bottle into the house, which instantly engulfed the small front room in fire. The house turned into an inferno within seconds.

Jacob felt the heat on his face from the other side of the street. He could only watch as the small house crumbled in front of them.

"Okay, that's enough. Take him to the police station." The large man pointed at two strong men to pick up the homeowner, who'd passed out.

They dragged him away and left his wife and daughter in front of their now-smoldering house. They looked stunned.

"Where are you taking him?" the wife asked the group leader, who was walking away. She held her sobbing daughter close.

He looked at her with contempt. "He'll be in one of the jail cells nearby, along with the rest of you scum. You can go with him if you want—I don't care." He walked on, the group following him and ignoring the woman on the ground.

Jacob looked on in shock as the men passed him chanting Nazi anthems with outstretched arms. Most of them were in their early twenties, although he also spotted a few teenagers amongst them. Their eyes were full of menace, satisfied with the damage they'd wrought.

Wagner tugged at his shirt. "Keep your head down, Jacob," he whispered. "It looks like they're passing by our shops."

The men appeared to have sated their lust for blood for now and moved away. Relative peace returned to the street. Jacob stood in a daze. The pharmacy had survived this attack, but he felt the next wave of violence was just around the corner – would he suffer the same fate as the young father?

Wagner looked at him and took control. "I know it feels wrong, not doing anything just now. But we couldn't stop them. You know this, right?"

Jacob nodded absently.

"You need to get home and stay inside," Wagner said. "This can't go on forever, and you can't protect the pharmacy on your own. Keep yourself safe."

Jacob looked across the street, where the mother and child were wrapped in blankets.

*He's right. I'm just as much a target.*

He regained his senses and looked Wagner in the eye.

"Now go home, Jacob. I'm going to do the same. Avoid the main streets, and don't stop until you're inside."

Jacob shook Wagner's hand before turning back toward the city center, the dark sky overcast in smoke.

The Berlin streets were in pandemonium. People were dragged along by mobs of young men as trucks holding bound men zipped around the streets. This was no spontaneous uprising.

Jacob's only option was to keep moving and pray he wouldn't run into any of the groups he'd seen earlier. If he kept his head down, his chances were pretty good. So far, the people he'd seen hauled off were trying to defend their property. He pitied them; they didn't know what they were up against.

He suspected the Brownshirts were behind the attacks. They were the only group in Berlin that would exert themselves at these tasks with such zeal. The SS was just as despicable, but they were too organized and proud to plunder and loot.

Jacob avoided the main throughways, but he needed to cross Oranienburger Straße and pass the New Synagogue to get home. When he got there, the street was swamped, shattered glass lined the pavement.

He stepped over the large pieces of glass and hoped his boots would stop any smaller bits. Something was going on in front of the New Synagogue. He spotted a row of about twenty people who'd hooked arms and formed a human wall. Jacob was unsurprised to see Hans standing in the middle of the group.

Opposite them stood a much larger crowd, some armed with clubs and knives.

The groups were in a deadlock. Those people protecting the synagogue were content keeping the thugs at bay. Bystanders waited to see what would happen next. The sound of broken glass signaled that one of the ornate windows of the synagogue had been smashed.

A large man wearing a dark red coat stepped forward, Jacob could see a large scar on his cheek, his face blotted with rashes.

"We're burning down your synagogue," he said in a quiet, raspy voice.

Jacob couldn't place his accent, but he wasn't from Berlin.

"You can get outta the way or burn with your holy building," he continued.

A number of the younger men in front of him shuffled their feet. They looked to Hans, who stood tall in the middle of the group.

"You have no authority—you can't bully us," Hans said, his face hardening. "I've dealt with people like you all my life, and I'll be damned if I let you destroy our synagogue without a fight."

The man held Hans' gaze while he stepped toward him. "I was hopin' you'd say that." He leaned toward Hans, and their noses almost touched.

Hans was unfazed, and the men stood frozen for what felt like an eternity.

After everything Jacob had seen earlier today, he knew Hans wouldn't blink first.

"You'll have to go through me to get to the synagogue." Hans took a step toward the man, forcing him to step back. His courage emboldened the people around him, and they moved forward, too.

The man in red recovered quickly. Behind him, the larger group became restless as they clenched their weapons tighter.

Out of nowhere, the man lashed out at Hans, but Hans ducked, and the man hit nothing but air.

"You shoulda moved," the threatening man growled. The men behind him took this as their cue and poured forward.

The scene was horrific. The bloodthirsty crowd of thugs cut through the Jewish barrier with ease. Some of the younger men guarding the synagogue got a few punches in, but the fight was unfair. The men attacking knew what they were doing, expertly cutting and stabbing at essential spots on the defenders' bodies. Some of them were cut down and trampled as the men moved on to their next victims. Jacob watched on helplessly—there were too many people between him and the synagogue.

It ended as quickly as it started.

The coppery scent of blood hung in the air as Jacob searched for Hans amongst the fallen people. He was aghast to see him on the pavement, a large pool of blood forming around his body. Hans's breathing was shallow, his eyes rolled back in their sockets. Jacob instinctively began pushing through the crowd to help his friend, but hands clutched at him, and one voice came through sorrowfully: "Wait—or you'll end up just like them."

The thugs stepped over the bodies, ignoring the victims' pleas for help. They carried their jerry cans toward the New Synagogue, people nearby unable or unwilling to stop them.

"Just move the jerry cans into the place," the man with the scar said. "It'll burn faster, and they're not going to stop us anymore." He pointed at the heap of people sprawled on the ground.

Just as they opened the doors to the synagogue, there was a commotion in the crowd. A uniformed policeman marched straight to the entrance.

Jacob recognized Otto Belgardt, a well-known lieutenant he knew as a friendly and dedicated officer. He was the first uniformed policeman Jacob had seen all night.

Belgardt looked in horror at the scene. He stopped one of the men carrying a jerry can to the entrance of the synagogue.

"What do you think you're doing? Get that gasoline away from the building!" Belgardt barked. The young man stopped, a flash of uncertainty crossing his face.

Jacob felt hopeful. *Is someone finally going to put a stop to this mayhem?*

Belgardt went up the steps, pushing past the other men. "All of you, stop this nonsense right now!" he shouted at the group drenching the New Synagogue in gasoline. "Don't you know this is a protected building? You're all breaking the law!"

The men turned to their leader, who stood in front of the main door holding an unlit torch.

"Move along, cop," said the man in red. "You got no power tonight. You know who we are, dontcha?" He struck a match and held it to the torch, which caught fire immediately, its hungry flames consuming the gasoline. That encouraged his men, who turned back to their work and ignored the police officer.

Belgardt looked unfazed. He calmly opened his jacket and unclipped his gun. Effortlessly, he cocked the hammer and aimed it at the man with the unsightly face—the scar now a deep shade of red, betraying his anxiety.

"Perhaps you'd like to reconsider my authority now?" Belgardt said. He moved closer to the door of the synagogue, keeping his pistol aimed at the leader.

Fear crossed the man's face and quickly spread to his companions, who put down their jerry cans.

A few of the younger attackers shirked away, trying to blend into the crowd.

*Good.*

Belgardt reached the top of the stairs and was only a few steps away from the leader. His aim was fixed on the man's chest. "I suggest you get out of here now. You've done enough damage for one night."

The larger man looked angry, but Belgardt was the one with the gun.

"This isn't over," the man said, walking away from the synagogue.

"You know we work under the Führer's own say, dontcha?" He spat on the ground.

Belgardt didn't budge, the barrel of his gun following the man down the stairs. "I must've missed the part about destroying national monuments."

The man snarled at him one last time and disappeared into the crowd.

Jacob rushed forward to check on the injured people, especially Hans, as the crowd dispersed now that the fight was over. He scanned the faces of the people on the ground; some of them no longer moving as he made his way up the steps. Fire trucks screeched to a stop in the street, the firemen quickly extinguishing the torches the men had left behind.

He found Hans propped up against the side of the synagogue. He was relieved to see his old teacher looking a little better than before.

"You see? We can stop them—we just need to have faith"—he burst into a violent cough, and a fireman handed him some water.

"Take it easy," Jacob said. Hans looked horrible, his face swollen and his left eye completely shut. Hans' clothes were stained with dark crimson patches of blood, but his good eye shone brightly.

The fireman gave them a thumbs-up. "You're going to be fine, but you need to get yourself checked by a doctor soon." He moved on to a young man next to Hans; hands gripped tightly to his side—it looked like they'd cracked a few of his ribs.

Jacob gently patted Hans on the shoulder. "That was both the bravest and most foolish thing I've ever seen you do."

Hans smiled. "Somebody had to stay here until the police finally showed up, no? You boys gave me practice in standing up to ruffians."

"I think Belgardt is one of the good ones—I haven't seen any other police out on the streets tonight."

"He IS a good one," answered Hans with a nod toward the policeman, who hadn't moved from his post, his eyes scanning the street. "He's checked on us a few times a day while we were out here the past two weeks. Even sent the Hitler Youth away on a few occasions. I'm sure he's not very popular with the brass."

Jacob looked around. "The streets have been taken over by gangs of thugs."

"It's the Brownshirts, no doubt. They might be wearing regular clothes, but I recognized a few of them."

"You saved the synagogue tonight, Hans. Don't you think you should see a doctor? There have to be plenty of them still willing to help you." Jacob looked around. "You're going to be okay here?"

Hans nodded. "Of course. It'll take more than a few cowards to get me down. Is the pharmacy okay?"

"It was when I was there a little earlier, but who knows?" Jacob shrugged. "Anything could happen tonight. I'm going to check on my parents."

Jacob walked wearily down the stairs. The Oranienburger Straße was a little less crowded, the shattered windows the remnants of the destructive wave that had passed through earlier. In the distance, the first rays of the rising sun struggled to make their way through the smoke.

# CHAPTER THREE

Jacob and Hermann were up early to check on the pharmacy. In the pale morning light, Berlin resembled a battlefield. The streets were littered with glass; broken windows a testimony to the night's destruction. They stopped in front of the smoldering remains of the butchery. A large pile of debris blocked their passage through the narrow street.

Hermann shook his head, stepping over a large wooden beam. "This must've come down when the building collapsed."

"Look at the others," Jacob added. He pointed at the adjacent buildings, which had only minor smoke damage on the walls. "You can see where the fire brigade focused its efforts."

They continued past a small jewelry store, which had an extra barrier in front of its shop window. The looters had been unable to smash the window but did vandalize the building with paint—*Jude Raus. Jews out.*

As they silently walked on, they saw the same words in red paint on buildings across the city.

They headed next to the offices of Hermann's boyhood friend Lars Brixen. Hermann peeked his head around the corner. "Lars, you must be the luckiest man in Berlin today!"

Lars looked up, a sad smile on his face. The door was open, and they stepped inside. "I suppose I am!" He hugged his friend and shook Jacob's hand. "I'm mostly relieved, though. Did you see what they did across the street?"

Hermann nodded, looking out the window, creases of worry across his forehead. "There's nothing left." They'd celebrated their bar mitzvahs a week apart, but Lars had never practiced his religion openly. In fact, most people didn't know he was Jewish.

"Are you on your way to the pharmacy?" Lars asked with concern.

"We are. But we're not hopeful," Hermann said. "Jacob was on the streets last night. The pharmacy was untouched when he left, but—"

"—only because the thugs were distracted by a family across the street," Jacob finished, then told Lars about his night.

Lars shook his head. "They left my office alone because I don't have a big sign out front. I'm sure if they'd known this was my place, I'd be picking up the pieces as well. Or worse. I'm not sure I could've stood by watching them destroy my life's work."

He picked up his keys from the desk. "Let's walk to your place."

Jacob saw the looks of determination on the faces of the local community as they walked. These were bakers, butchers, and shopkeepers, whose only 'crime' was being Jewish.

As they turned onto the street of their pharmacy, it looked like all others they'd passed through that day—covered in shards of glass and wood splinters. In front of the pharmacy, their neighbor, Herr Wagner, was busy with a hammer. The Kagan pharmacy was housed in a beautiful, large building with an impressive entrance. The windows were covered with bright red paint—miraculously, only one had been smashed. Jacob suspected the iron safety curtain had deterred the looters from trying to get in through the windows.

As they got closer, they saw why Wagner was there.

"How did they destroy a door like this?"

Hermann entered through the opening where the door had been. Jacob followed him, and as he had expected, it was a mess inside. The shelves were empty but for a few packages. The floor was covered in empty wrappers and broken containers – the looters had stuffed as much medicine into their pockets as they could carry.

Behind the counter, the cabinets had been broken open, the shelves hanging out haphazardly.

Hermann said hopelessly, "Well, they've taken everything." He walked into the storeroom and picked up one of the boxes Jacob had brought in the day before. As he turned it upside down, only a few small packs of aspirin fell onto the floor.

Jacob walked through the store, inspecting the rest of the damage. "They just went for the drugs—nothing has been destroyed. In a way, I think we're lucky."

Lars was outside inspecting the windows, and he came in to report: "It's a miracle they didn't smash all the windows. The paint will come off easily. It's going to take a lot of cleaning, but you could be back in business in a week or two."

Jacob scratched his chin. "Even if we fix everything and replenish supplies, might this happen again?"

"That's a good point, but what are we going to do?" Hermann asked, closing the drawers behind the counter, inspecting the broken locks.

"Let's help Herr Wagner get the door fixed and see what we still have left," Jacob answered. "Even if it's just a few things, it's still better than nothing."

They placed everything of value in the storeroom, fixing the lock with a spare Lars brought from his offices. They used whatever scrap material they found to board up the door as well as they could.

Jacob and Lars were scrubbing paint off the windows when two city officials showed up along with two grim-faced policemen.

"Are you Hermann Kagan?" one of the officials asked Jacob, looking at a ledger in his hand.

Jacob dropped his sponge in the bucket next to him. "No, that's my father—he's right there"—he pointed at Hermann, who was coming outside with a fresh bucket of water and soap.

"What's going on?" Hermann asked, placing the bucket on the street. Lars stopped scrubbing and walked over as well.

"Your license to run this pharmacy has been revoked." The man with the ledger spoke without emotion, placing a mark on his piece of paper.

Hermann's countenance dropped, and Lars looked incredulous. Jacob was the first to recover.

"What do you mean? We've run this pharmacy for over sixty years."

The man with the ledger looked up, forming a scowl. "And now you don't anymore. Orders from the city council."

"But we own the building," Jacob said, glaring at the man.

The man with the ledger held Jacob's stare. The policemen behind him stepped closer. "According to this document, the building is now owned by the city of Berlin." He handed an official-looking document to Hermann, who stared at it shell-shocked.

Jacob took the document and quickly scanned it, frowning. "The building is taken as part of repayment to the state?"

The official shrugged.

Jacob was incredulous. "Repayment for what?"

"For the riots. You did hear Goering's announcement earlier today, right?"

Jacob looked at the man in confusion. *What announcement?*

The man continued: "All damages are to be paid by the Jewish community." He waved his arm at the street behind him.

"What's going to happen to our pharmacy?"

"I don't know, and frankly, it's none of your business anymore. Take your belongings and get out."

Jacob shook his head. "This can't be happening."

One of the police officers stepped forward. "Get your stuff—you have five minutes, then we lock the pharmacy."

The three men put everything they could in a few boxes. Hermann insisted on taking most of his prized collection of medical books. Apart from that, there wasn't a lot they could take after the looting. Hermann, Jacob, and Lars stepped out of the pharmacy, the police officers shutting and locking the door behind them.

The city officials left without another word.

"What now?" Hermann asked, deflated, and standing in front of the shop.

"I'm sure it's all a big mistake," Jacob said with little conviction. "There's only one place to go to get this fixed."

The square in front of *Rotes Rathaus*—Berlin's city hall—was packed.

"There must be at least two hundred people here," Hermann said.

People were angry and desperate. A large group of uniformed policemen blocked the building entrance—City Hall wanted to avoid any confrontation. A man with a megaphone stepped outside, carefully staying behind the police cordon. He looked uncomfortable as his eyes darted about warily.

"May I have your attention for a moment?" he ordered the crowd. He fumbled with a piece of paper. "Due to recent events, the Rathaus will remain closed today. We have a lot of things to take care of, and we will not process any public petitions today."

The people around Jacob looked confused as angry murmurs spread through the crowd. His father looked at him with resignation in his eyes.

"That's hardly a surprise," Hermann said. "This way, nobody can complain about losing their business."

A woman standing nearby overheard him. "Did you lose yours as well?" She didn't wait for his answer. "They took our bakery this morning. We thought we were lucky because we're a little out of the center. It wasn't set on fire, and we only needed to repair the front windows."

Jacob nodded. "About the same as our pharmacy. The city officials showed up when we were cleaning up."

"They told us the bakery was taken as a repayment for the riot," she said, the pain visible in her eyes. "But what did we do? It was Goebbels' criminals smashing up the city. And they only attacked our houses and shops. Our neighbors couldn't stop it, either."

"I don't think anybody could've stopped it," Jacob said. "There were too many of them." He recounted what had happened with Belgardt in front of the New Synagogue.

"One of the few good ones, I'm afraid," the lady said.

The man with the megaphone finished his announcement, but by now, nobody was listening to him anymore. They were talking amongst themselves, sharing the same worries Jacob and his father had. Some people were dissatisfied with the statement and shouted at the man, who was on his way back inside.

"How are we supposed to feed our families? You took our businesses!" A heavyset man pushed forward. He was only a few steps from the cordon of police before they stepped forward in a single line, forcing the man back.

The rest of the crowd pushed forward. "This is wrong!" one shouted, and another called out, "It was the Brownshirts who destroyed our city and businesses! Why do we have to pay for it?"

The man with the megaphone hesitated and signaled to the policemen before he disappeared inside the building.

The policemen took out their batons.

"Move back and disperse!" one of them shouted at the crowd. "Go back to your homes. You heard him—the Rathaus is closed!"

Jacob remained at the back of the crowd until Hermann tugged at his jacket.

"Perhaps it's time to leave, Jaco."

At home, Jacob and Hermann found Elsa pouring a cup of tea for Ethan at the Kagans' kitchen table. Jacob told them about the pharmacy being taken by the city as Hermann sat down heavily next to his wife.

"It gets worse, Jaco," Ethan said, getting up from the table. "They're arresting people all over the city."

"Arresting people? What people?" Jacob asked, dreading the answer.

"Our people."

Hermann looked at Elsa, who just shook her head.

"They're arresting guys our age. It started during the night, but they're rounding up people as we speak," Ethan continued. "Our neighbor's sons were picked up last night."

"By whom?" Jacob asked.

Ethan sat down and put his hands on the table. "The Gestapo, mostly. Nobody's told where they're taken."

Jacob sighed. "If the Gestapo took them, they could be anywhere."

Elsa spoke up. "I heard it's Sachsenhausen. The SS is also involved."

"Isn't Sachsenhausen meant for communists and political dissidents?" Jacob asked. *They're not sending regular people there, surely?*

"All I know is that they won't tell our neighbors anything. They don't even have to give a reason for taking them."

Hermann stood up and poured himself a glass of water, waving off Elsa's tea offer.

"If the Gestapo and SS are involved, I wouldn't be surprised if they're sent to Sachsenhausen. They're worse than the Brownshirts—they're just a group of thugs. The SS is the law, as far as Goebbels is concerned." He looked outside; the last rays of sunlight reflected off the pavement. "I'm worried the police aren't involved."

"They seem to be mere bystanders these past few days," Jacob added. "It feels like a coup."

Ethan picked at a splinter on the table, and silence fell for a while, all four of them staring into space.

Jacob broke the silence. "So, now what? They've taken the pharmacy from us; they're arresting innocent people everywhere. What are we going to do?"

"We're going to sit tight," Hermann said. "There's nothing we can do. Surely when the city hall opens again, we can get this fixed." There was little confidence in his words.

That night, parts of Goering's speech were broadcast on the evening news. The Kagans listened to their radio, shocked by what they heard.

"Did he just say all Jewish business will be taken over by Germans?" Elsa said, her eyes wide.

"Aryan Germans," Hermann corrected. "We're as German as everybody else."

They turned back to the radio—Goering could be heard clearly.

"The fundamental idea in this program of elimination of the Jew from the German economy is for the Jew to transfer his property to the state. All business owners will be compensated."

Hermann scoffed. "So much for that. They just took our store!"

Goering's voice droned on in the background. "But, because there are too few Aryans to take over all the stores, we have to find another solution. We will liquidate these businesses, as there is obviously no demand. This is all perfectly fine."

Jacob looked at his father, who'd gone pale. *This can't be happening. This isn't real.*

Loud cheers went up in the background. Goering proceeded to lay out his plans for the factories of Germany, moving away from the stores. Hermann switched off the radio.

They sat in stunned silence. The family wouldn't get the pharmacy back—that much was now evident. Goering finished stating that all insurance money from the damages of a few nights before would not go to the former owners but to the German state.

Hermann looked around the table. "We're ruined."

Jacob had a sleepless night. He tossed and turned, expecting a truck to stop outside their house, SS men breaking down their door and taking him to an unknown camp.

But they never came, and he got up early to find his parents already at the kitchen table.

"You couldn't sleep, either?" Hermann asked. His father had the morning newspaper in front of him, and his mother poured him a cup of coffee.

Jacob shook his head. "I thought about what we can do, but I have no solution." He took a sip of the steaming hot coffee, which did little to calm him.

His parents exchanged a look. Jacob raised an eyebrow.

"We need to consider leaving," Hermann said.

Jacob looked at his father. "Leave Berlin?"

"Leave Germany."

Hermann slid the newspaper toward Jacob. "Here's an overview of all the new rules the government will put into effect. They're all related to us."

Jacob looked at the front page. It confirmed what they'd heard the previous evening. All Jewish businesses were to be sold to Aryan-Germans—stores, factories, any ownership—but that wasn't the worst of it.

"One billion marks?" Jacob looked up at his parents. "They're holding us responsible for the damages of the past few days?" He was incredulous.

His parents remained silent as Jacob read on. The government had decreed that the damages were to be paid back by all Jews in Germany.

Jacob put the paper down. "This is madness!"

Hermann scratched his chin. "I'm not allowed to run any kind of business anymore. And nobody will hire us to work for them, for fear of reprisals."

Jacob saw the determination in his father's eyes. *He's made up his mind.*

"We still have some money and jewelry," Hermann continued. "We'll need to use that to get out of the country. There's no other option."

"So, where will we go?" Jacob asked.

Elsa looked at him. "We can't move east—Poland hasn't accepted any refugees for a few months now. And Austria is out of the question."

Jacob nodded. "I wouldn't be surprised if the situation is just as bad there, too many Nazis since the unification."

"We'll have to look west—we might still have a chance in the Netherlands," Hermann said. "Amsterdam has lots of Jewish businesses."

"And it'll be temporary," Elsa smiled wearily "until people come to their senses."

Jacob listened to his parents, who'd clearly thought this through. The new decrees must have been the final push. There was nothing left for them in Berlin. Their pharmacy had been their life, and his father was right—they wouldn't be able to get new jobs.

"When do we leave?"

His parents looked at him. "Today," they said together.

# CHAPTER FOUR

While Hermann and Elsa packed their belongings, Jacob sprinted to Ethan's house. He learned Ethan's family had toyed with the same thought, and it hadn't taken much persuasion to get them to join them. They agreed to meet at the station and were hopeful they'd be able to take a train out of the country together.

When Jacob returned home, his parents were ready, holding only a suitcase each. They had packed only their most valuable belongings. Jacob carried a suitcase containing jewelry and money packed among a few articles of clothing. It was heavy, but he didn't mind.

Hermann and Elsa wore their best clothes, looking as respectable as possible—and not like poor refugees—for when they got to the Dutch border. Jacob wore his usual jacket to keep warm. They looked like a family going on holiday.

"Here we go, then," Hermann said, closing their front door with a loud thud. He pulled at the door, making sure it was well secured. Satisfied, Hermann lifted his large suitcase and took Elsa's as well, despite her protests.

It was a short walk to Berlin's Lehrter train station. A weak mid-day sun battled its way through the thick clouds. The cobblestone streets were quiet, most people staying inside on this cold Sunday afternoon.

They passed many shops with boarded-up windows. Some of the owners hadn't bothered, and their once-impressive storefronts had been quickly reduced to ruins. Jacob wondered what would happen to these stores; would the Nazis consider them interesting enough to sell to Aryan storekeepers, or would they just let them be?

As they neared the station, the street traffic increased.

"Looks like we're not the only ones trying to leave," Hermann said, pointing at the streams of people congregating at the entrance. They looked very similar to the Kagans, carrying only bare essentials in their small suitcases and backpacks.

Inside, a cacophony greeted them. The spacious main hall was packed, and hundreds of voices bounced off the high ceilings. The queue for the ticket booths snaked through the building.

"We'll have to get in line with all those people. There's still plenty of time before the evening train," Hermann said.

Elsa frowned. "Do you think we'll be able to get a ticket? There are hundreds of people in the queues."

"Maybe they're going somewhere else," Jacob said, with hope.

The three of them joined one of the queues. The man in front of them turned.

"Where are you going?" he asked, his face friendly.

Hermann answered, "Away from here, but it doesn't look too good."

The man shook his head. "No, I've been standing in this spot for over half an hour. They say all trains are full."

"But everybody stays in the queue?" Jacob asked, peering down the line. Indeed, there was little movement in front of him despite all the ticket booths being manned.

"We're hoping there might be extra trains or book tickets for later in the week. So far, we've heard nothing about it yet," the man said, wrinkling his forehead. "But we've nowhere else to go, so we might as well see if anything changes here."

Jacob looked at his father. Hermann looked worried, although he was doing his best to hide it.

"What do you think, Papa?"

"Let's wait and see if anything happens. This man's right—there's nowhere else to go. This is the only station with trains to Amsterdam."

The man in front of them overheard. "Did you say Amsterdam? Forget about that. The Dutch have closed the borders."

Hermann looked up. "Are you sure? Where did you hear that?"

"They'll only allow people with valid visas to enter. If you don't have one of those, it's a big gamble. I've heard some people managed to get in based on special skills," the man said, frowning. "Some also got in by walking across the border, but let's say they're not waiting for us with open arms. Can't blame them, after the situation with Poland."

Jacob turned to his father. "We don't want to be left stranded on the border. Look at what happened to the Polish and German Jews stuck in no man's land. Nobody cares about them."

Before Hermann could respond, an announcement boomed through the station hall: "Please be advised there are no more seats on any of today's trains. Ticket sales for tomorrow's trains will go on sale tomorrow morning. There will be no advance sales."

With that, the hopes of hundreds of people were dashed. The Kagans looked at each other.

"Have you ever heard that before? No advance sales?" Hermann looked bewildered.

Jacob shook his head. The crowd in front of the ticket booth wasn't moving. People were happy to settle in for the night to be the first in the morning. The man ahead of them stepped out of the queue.

"It's still early," Elsa said, looking toward the ornate clock in the middle of the station. Its hands showed it was just past noon. "I don't think we can stay here for the entire day and night."

Hermann agreed. "No, and even then we're not sure of a ticket, I'm afraid."

"What about the border situation? What if we can't get in, even if we get a ticket?" Jacob asked.

"We'll need to take our chances," Hermann said, his face determined. "It can't be as bad as that man said. There are plenty of Jewish people in the Netherlands that will vouch for us. Besides, we're bringing a lot of valuables to the country. We can support ourselves and find new work."

An argument erupted at the front as Jacob watched a young man jump the queue just as the attendant was about to close his window. Jacob craned his neck to see what was going on. More people in the front moved closer.

"Look!" the man shouted, "I saw you sell tickets to those people over there earlier!" Jacob could see the veins in the back of his neck pop out. "They weren't in the queue, and I was! So what happened?"

The attendant remained calm. "Those people were picking up tickets they'd bought earlier."

"So you are selling tickets in advance? Why can't we buy tickets for tomorrow?"

"I don't know—I only follow the rules." The attendant tried to close the little window, but the young man blocked it with his head and shoulders, and the attendant now had an angry young man in his face.

The crowd inched closer to the window booth.

The attendant got some support from his colleagues, who managed to push the young man away and slammed the window shut.

This only angered the man further, and the people behind him, too. They pounded on the glass, the sound reverberating through the station hall. More people joined in, frustration in their eyes.

Suddenly a dozen men wearing black uniforms strode toward the commotion. Swastika armbands prominent on their left arms, two silver S's in the shape of lightning bolts on their collars. They were part of the SS and walked with the confidence of men who had nothing to fear. A number of them grinned as they passed the Kagans.

*How did they get here so fast?* Jacob thought. *This is not going to end well.*

They took out their steel batons without prelude and swung at the first people in the group, who hadn't seen them coming and were hit from behind. The SS men didn't discriminate as men and women went down, some of them not even screaming but merely slumping to the floor.

Panic quickly spread as the unarmed people in the front realized what was happening. Some of the younger men tried to fight back and got a few punches in until the well-trained SS men took them down.

The man who had started it all was still at the window. He watched in horror as the group of SS soldiers approached. He made a run for it and pushed a couple of older people out of the way as he knocked over some queue barriers.

Two of the SS men in the front saw him running away and quickly followed.

"Halt! Stop that man!" one of them shouted through the crowded hall. But most of the people in the station were Jewish and not about to help the SS. The young man was now close to the exit, and though the SS men were gaining on him, it became clear they wouldn't catch him before he reached the doorway.

One of them stopped and drew his pistol. His compatriot turned and quickly moved out of the way.

A shot rang out.

People screamed and dropped to the floor; everyone's eyes turning to the sound of the shot. Jacob was on the floor, too, his hands covering his ears.

The first shot missed its target but not its purpose—the young man paused, his face a mix of surprise and fear.

The SS soldier adjusted his aim and issued another shot.

The young man's knee exploded with a sickening crunch. He fell to the floor, his body twitching. Blood and bones sprayed on the floor around him, and he screamed in agony, clutching the wound with both hands.

The entire station went quiet but for the screams from the man on the floor. All eyes were on the two SS soldiers casually walking toward the stricken man.

The soldiers got to the young man, scowls on their faces.

"Not running away anymore now," said the taller one with the pistol as he kicked the young man's knee, causing him to wail even louder. The smaller SS soldier poked his boot into the wound. The young man writhed away, trying to shield his ruined leg. The soldier kicked him again, this time in the ribs.

"Get on your knees." The smaller SS men dragged the man up, his cries piercing the air as he was forced to support his weight with just one knee. The other leg dangled next to it, the young man supporting himself with his arms.

The larger SS man cocked his pistol, the sound echoing through the station hall. People gasped when he placed the barrel against the young man's head.

*Surely they're not going to execute him in public? Not even THEY are capable of this, right?* Jacob looked at his father, who had turned pale.

"Perhaps we need to make an example out of you," the larger man said, speaking up so everybody could hear him. "Next time, when you think about starting a riot in public, they'll remember what happens." He looked around menacingly.

The young man raised his chin. His face was wet, sweat dripping down his hair. He looked scared and muttered something through clenched teeth.

Jacob couldn't hear what he said, but he saw the SS soldier grin. He looked away, waiting for the sound of the shot ending it all.

The shot never came. The soldier pulled his gun away, and the man collapsed on the cold marble floor.

"I have a better purpose for you! We'll take you to Sachsenhausen, where you can live the rest of your short, sorry life in agony," he said. "Yes, that's what we'll do! But don't worry—you won't be alone. All your friends over there will come with you." He pointed at the people on the floor near the ticket booth.

Jacob felt a chill running down his spine. *So the rumors about Sachsenhausen are true.*

The other SS men nodded approvingly. They pulled the people in the cordon to their feet, or simply hoisted them when they were unable to stand up.

The two SS men dragged the wounded man to the entrance, where more SS uniforms poured in. Four large trucks waited outside. Those near the ticket booths were hauled toward the exit and thrown into the backs of the vehicles when they didn't—or couldn't—comply with the soldiers' orders. Family members of the people in the trucks pled with the soldiers and were told to back off or join them. A number of the people got in the vehicles voluntarily, clinging on to their loved ones.

They had started their day hoping to get on a train away from trouble and ended up in the back of a truck heading toward a grim future.

Jacob turned back to his parents, who looked equally shocked by what they'd just witnessed.

"We need to get on a train today, no matter what," his father said. "If the SS is in charge now, there's no saving this city."

In the afternoon, normalcy returned to the station. Trains left Berlin in all directions with German efficiency. There was no trace of the violence the SS had inflicted a few hours earlier. The blood had been cleaned up quickly, and passengers with tickets glided through the beautiful station.

Most of the people who'd been in the queue with the Kagans found places to rest in the hall, trying to make themselves as comfortable as was possible in the circumstances.

Jacob volunteered first to hold the Kagans' place in line. He sat on the floor behind a young family hoping to travel to Denmark. The father told him he had family there who would be able to take them in.

The previous animosity toward the attendant in the ticket booth hadn't spilled over to the people now in the queue. Most of them were calm and resigned to the long night ahead.

Hermann hadn't given up on getting on a train today. The last train to Amsterdam was due to depart at eight in the evening. Jacob had watched his father scurry around the station hall all afternoon. It was now five, and Hermann pushed his way through the queue, gesturing enthusiastically at Jacob.

"Come with me," he said, keeping his voice down—he looked excited.

Jacob followed his father, leaving his spot in the queue. "What did you do, Papa?" He had to take an extra step to keep up with Hermann as they crossed the hall.

Elsa was waiting for them, their bags neatly stacked next to each other. She was also smiling.

"Come on, what's going on?" Jacob asked, but his father was still not answering his question.

"Your father managed to get us tickets for the train to Amsterdam tonight," Elsa said, her eyes sparkling.

Hermann smiled. "I got lucky. I thought our best chance would be to check with the people working near the ticket inspection. Turns out an old friend works at the ticket office. You remember Claus Berger?"

Herr Berger had come to his father to ask if there was anything he could do to help his terminally ill wife, and Hermann secured some powerful painkillers to ease her pain. The doctors didn't believe she'd last longer than a few days, but she miraculously recovered.

"Herr Berger hasn't forgotten what you did for him then?" Jacob asked.

"Oh, no. I was talking to some of the ticket inspectors over there," Hermann pointed to the entrance to the tracks, "when Claus came over and asked what was going on. As soon as I told him we needed to get to Amsterdam, he said he'd arrange something for us."

He held up three pieces of paper. "He came back with these."

"That's great," Jacob said, inspecting the tickets. "What will we do when we get to the border?"

"Claus said there should be no problem for us. We have German passports and money, so we should be okay." Hermann looked confident, the tickets giving him new-found belief.

His mother added, "The most important thing is we're leaving Berlin tonight. Let's have something to eat before we go."


The Kagans sat in a small restaurant, a few streets from the station. They'd secured a corner table near the window. The place was busy, and the solitary waiter had a hard time keeping up with the orders. He rushed from the kitchen to the tables while juggling the drink orders.

Jacob looked around the restaurant. It was a homely place, with candles on all the tables. The other patrons looked a lot alike—suitcases stacked next to the tables, and people seemed a bit on edge.

Hermann caught his look. "Looks like they all have the same idea tonight."

"I wonder if they all have tickets as well," Elsa added, her face lined with a frown.

*She's worried about other people, even now.*

The waiter placed three plates of sausages and sauerkraut on the table before disappearing back into the kitchen without another word.

The tangy smell of the sauerkraut reminded Jacob how hungry he was; he hadn't eaten all day and dug in. *It could be a while before I have this again.*

As they ate, Jacob's thoughts turned to what was ahead. How would they be greeted at the Dutch border? And did Ethan get tickets as well?

"I'm sure we just missed him," Hermann said, wiping his mouth on a napkin before setting down his cutlery. "Ethan always finds a way—you know that."

Jacob wasn't so sure. "Not everybody can be as lucky as we are, Papa. I doubt we would've had a ticket if you hadn't run into Herr Berger. The queue for tickets wasn't moving, and I doubt anything has changed. There will be hundreds of people waiting for tickets." He used his last piece of sausage to scoop up the remaining bits of sauerkraut and pushed his plate away.

Elsa put her hand on his arm. "Ethan will be fine. Your father is right—he'll make it work." She looked at the waiter, who hastily cleared their plates and left the bill on the table. "Looks like he wants us to leave."

Hermann nodded and placed some banknotes on the table. "We need to get to the station anyway—we don't want to be late."

As they crossed the short distance to the station through the slippery streets—the drizzle had turned into a light rain—Jacob wondered when he'd be back. This was home. There were memories on every corner, and he couldn't imagine living anywhere else.

They waited as a streetcar passed them before crossing the tracks toward the station. In the darkness, the station looked imposing—its main entrance flanked by a series of small archways on both sides. The building appeared to glow as light filtered through its large, ornate windows and the arched glass ceiling. Its beauty was tarnished by the abundance of red and black Nazi banners draped over its façade. It was a stark reminder of why they stood in front of this building, carrying their lives in a few suitcases.

Entering the main hall, Jacob saw a familiar head of curls bobbing through the crowd. Ethan was purposefully running toward them. He looked flustered, but Jacob thought he saw something else on his face. *Is that a smile?*

It didn't take long for Ethan to notice them in his rush to the exit.

"Jaco!" His face broke into a wide grin.

*This must be good news.*

Ethan reached into his coat pocket and produced three pieces of paper. "I got them! I got the tickets for tonight's train."

Jacob felt a wave of relief wash over him. His best friend had indeed found a way.

"But how did you fare?" Ethan asked Hermann, his face suddenly serious as he realized he didn't know. "Did you get tickets as well?"

Hermann nodded and smiled, producing their own set. They compared the identical tickets—for the eight-o'clock train.

"How did you manage that?" Elsa asked.

"I got here about an hour ago and didn't see any of you," Ethan started, catching his breath. "So I queued at the ticket booths for a few minutes, but it was clear nothing was happening there. There was one clerk, but he wasn't helping anyone."

Jacob nodded. "It's been like that the whole day." He told Ethan about the SS violence earlier.

"So that's why the trucks were driving off. I did see those, and it was eerily quiet when I got here," Ethan looked thoughtful for a moment. "Anyway, I realized I wasn't going to get a ticket that way, so I walked to the inspection area and asked one of the men if there was any way to get on the train. He told me to bugger off if I didn't have a ticket, and no, there was no other way than by queuing."

Jacob exchanged a look with his father. *We were so lucky.*

"On my way back to the queue, a man approached me. He asked if I needed a ticket to Amsterdam tonight." Ethan smiled. "It was odd because whenever I think of a ticket scalper, it's a shady person, but this man looked very respectable. He somehow had a whole stack of tickets, and I bought these off him."

Elsa looked worried. "That must've cost a pretty penny."

"Sure, and I worried if they were legitimate, but he even provided the original receipt." Ethan held up another piece of paper, which was dated a week before.

*They must've known something was about to happen.*

"But after comparing them with yours, I'm sure these are fine," Ethan said with a smile.

The station clock chimed, and Ethan looked up. It was seven o'clock.

"I'd better get going if we want to make this train. It'll be a bit of a rush, but we'll make it. Papa and Mama have everything packed. I'll see you in an hour!"

With that, Ethan ran off into the darkness outside.


The area around the platform bustled with activity. The lucky few who held tickets for the night train all waited near the empty tracks. The platform was brightly lit, in stark contrast to the darkness of the tracks leading out of the station. Anxious faces looked into the night, waiting for the last train.

The Kagans queued at the ticket inspection, and the line moved at a snail's pace. Jacob stood on his toes, trying to get a view of the platform. A barrier was set up between them and the platform.

"The train's not here yet," he said. "I count at least two hundred people on the platform, so it must be a large train."

Hermann looked behind them, the queue growing. "I wonder if all these people have tickets, or if they're hoping to squeeze through."

"I doubt anyone will sneak through," Jacob said, nodding at the ticket inspectors. There were at least twice as many as in the afternoon. Beside them stood official-looking men, and a large number of policemen hovered around.

Getting closer to the front, Jacob noticed the officials were checking all sorts of documents, not just tickets. His father frowned. "Looks like customs is involved as well," he said and frowned. "Can you see what they're checking, Jacob?"

Some people were allowed to move to the platform directly. Most, however, had to step aside and open their luggage. They were guided to a row of large tables, where officials ordered them to take out their valuables. On the other side of the tables, stern-looking men methodically inspected the goods.

Without fail, they'd shake their heads at the papers and point at the valuables. Jacob couldn't hear what was said, but the travelers all looked aghast.

"It doesn't look good," Jacob said, keeping his gaze on an elderly couple trying to reason with the official. The inspector scowled at them, shaking his head and pointing at a single silver necklace. The elderly man pointed at his train ticket and passport. The official didn't budge and called to a nearby policeman, tossing the necklace into the suitcase and shoving it to the elderly couple across the table. The policeman took them back behind the barrier, away from the tracks. The man was arguing with the police officer as they passed the Kagans and were roughly pushed behind the barrier. *They're not going anywhere tonight.*

"Next!" It was the Kagans' turn. They handed their tickets to an imposing inspector who took them with an air of indifference.

Despite this nonchalance, the man took his time inspecting the tickets and passports. It felt like an eternity before he handed them back.

"Your tickets are fine. Follow him for inspection of your luggage." He handed their passports to the young customs officer who had appeared beside him.

Jacob looked at his father, who merely nodded. The Kagans moved past the barrier, keeping their suitcases close as the customs officer pointed them to an empty table.

"Open your suitcases and put valuables on the table." The officer looked no older than twenty and spoke with a thick country accent. His shoulders were straight, and his piercing blue eyes exerted authority. *Probably got this job for being a model Hitler Youth.*

"Hintzer!"

The young man turned to one of the senior men calling him from the other side of the hall.

"Help us carry this to the trucks," the man said, pointing at a large crate filled with all sorts of jewelry.

Hintzer nodded. "I will be back in two minutes. I expect all your valuables to be ready for inspection."

Jacob turned to his parents. "We need to buy our way out of the country," he said in a hushed voice. "That couple just now had too few valuables and were sent back to the station hall." He nodded to two men on the other side of the tables, now busy inspecting a large pile of gold jewelry.

They nodded their heads approvingly as they took the entire pile and placed it in one of the empty crates behind them. The travelers looked nervous until one of the customs officers handed them their passports and waved them toward the tracks.

"We've got a lot more than what they just handed over," Hermann said. Jacob could see his father calculating what was needed to get them through. Hermann looked down the line, the inspectors moving on to tables a bit further from them.

"Put all of our money in your pockets before that boy returns. Elsa, place all of your large pieces of jewelry on the table—it should be enough."

His mother unpacked her jewelry, her eyes damp. Jacob felt sorry for her; most of the items had been in the family for generations.

"Put the rest in your pockets, Mama. They haven't searched any of the women. I can hide some of the coins in my socks"—Jacob pointed at their rare old coins. He knew the collection was his father's prized possession, and the coins could easily fit in their clothing.

Hermann nodded and handed the small pouch to Jacob. He quickly took out the coins, looked around, and when he was sure no one was looking, pretended to tie his shoelaces. Jacob slipped the coins into his socks and shook his feet a little—no sound. *It will have to do.*

Hintzer returned just as they finished placing most of Elsa's jewelry on the table. It was a sizable collection—the highlight a small golden pendant with a ruby surrounded by diamonds. The young officer looked approvingly.

"You're not poor, are you?" he asked, more a statement than a question. He looked at Jacob, his youthful eyes narrow and suspicious. "Is this all? You're not keeping anything from me?"

Jacob held Hintzer's gaze, determined not to look weak. "This is all of it."

Hermann stepped forward. "I have only a few marks in my pocket." He placed a small pile of bills next to the jewelry.

Hintzer lifted an eyebrow at Jacob. "No more money?"

Jacob made a show of checking his empty pockets, turning them inside out.

Hintzer moved forward and patted Jacob down, starting with his shoulders. Jacob swallowed as Hintzer's hands moved down. The coins had already slid down his socks and were now near the soles of his boots. Hintzer double-checked the pockets of his pants, then moved toward his feet. His hands were around Jacob's ankles, and he paused. He looked up at Jacob, his expression showing annoyance. *Please don't ask me to take off my shoes.*

"What have we here?" asked one of the inspectors, holding the pendant up to the light.

Hintzer snapped to attention. "I think these Jews are carrying some pretty valuable things out of the country, sir." He handed the passports to the other man.

His superior took the documents absently. His eyes fixed on the ruby. "Are their passports in order?"

"Yes, Lieutenant Dietrich."

"Tickets?"

"They're good—bought here in Berlin."

Dietrich put down the pendant and looked at Hermann. "This is very valuable. What is your occupation?"

"I'm a pharmacist."

"That makes sense. I guess you're not a pharmacist anymore," Dietrich said with a grin, drawing a chuckle from Hintzer, eager to please. "You are aware of the departure tax for leaving Germany?"

Hermann shook his head. "I wasn't until we arrived here."

Dietrich's grin widened as he sifted through the pile of jewelry, inspecting a silver ring.

"Did you check their bags, Hintzer?" Dietrich asked, pointing to the suitcases on the floor. There was little more than clothing left in them.

Hintzer hesitated, losing his confident posture just for a moment. "Not yet, sir. I was helping with the full crates just now."

Dietrich nodded. "Have a quick look then. They might be hiding something."

Hintzer rummaged through the suitcases while Dietrich turned the jewelry pieces over in his hands. After a few moments, Hintzer announced he'd found nothing.

"Well, I guess this will do," Dietrich said to Hermann, gesturing to one of the men behind him. "Take this to the crates over there."

He handed the passports back to Hermann, while Hintzer swept all of the Kagans' valuables off the table and took them away. Dietrich waved the Kagans toward the platform in a dismissive manner. "Consider your departure tax paid." With that, he walked to the table next to them, already eyeing the next pile.

Jacob breathed a sigh of relief. They closed their suitcases without another word and walked toward the platform. Jacob feared they'd be recalled at any moment and wanted to get as far away as possible.

As the train pulled in, the sound of hundreds of hopeful voices rose in anticipation.

The train was an old steamer, the engine letting out a heavy sigh as it ground to a halt. The impatient crowd started opening the doors even before the train had stopped. Within seconds the platform resembled a beehive. People pushed each other out of the way and used their suitcases to wedge themselves on board ahead of everybody else.

Jacob looked at the mayhem in front of them and gritted his teeth to say, "Let's get on the train."

His father was pale—the stress of the last days was getting to him—a stark contrast to the man who ran a pharmacy a week before.

Hermann nodded, holding Elsa's hand. She'd been silent, but Jacob knew losing most of her prized jewelry had shaken her. His mother didn't care much about worldly possessions, but the heirlooms handed down for generations were an exception. She looked with empty, expressionless eyes at the people pushing and shoving. Jacob had to get them moving quickly.

"Stay close to me—I'll get us on the train," Jacob said, taking his father's suitcase. His parents followed him, his mother holding onto his shoulder and Hermann shielding her from the back. Scanning the different entries, Jacob noticed one crowd at the end of the train appeared more civilized, with no pushing, shoving, or shouting. A large man stood in the door opening, lifting suitcases on board. A mother with a young child approached him, and he gently lifted the girl onto the train while her mother climbed on board.

Jacob moved to the orderly queue and checked the station clock. More than fifteen minutes before departure. It shouldn't be a problem for them to get settled in time. Another family boarded, and the Kagans were now just a few feet from the train steps.

"Let's go," Hermann said as he let Elsa pass first. Jacob helped his mother and looked in the direction of the ticket inspectors. They were still checking bags and making sure no one could leave without paying their departure tax.

"Looking for Ethan?" Hermann asked, following Jacob's gaze. "There are too many people waiting to get through for everybody to get here in time."

His father was right. Jacob tried to count the people standing on the other side of the barrier, but he was too far away to distinguish their faces. There were probably around a hundred or so behind the barrier.

Jacob stepped aside to let a young family pass. A mother held a baby close to her chest, wrapped in heavy blankets. Jacob saw the determination in her bright blue eyes and smiled at her. She smiled back, but there was no mistaking the sadness in her expression. Jacob hoped she had somebody waiting for her in Amsterdam.

"Why don't you go and find a good seat with Mama?" Jacob said. "I'll catch up with you in a few minutes." He turned, scanning the platform for Ethan.

Hermann nodded and climbed the short steps. "Don't do anything crazy—just get on the train in time. I'm sure Ethan is already on board."

"I'll be right there."

Hermann disappeared inside the car, and Jacob looked up at the clock. Ten minutes to go.

The chaos of the first minutes was replaced by a trickle of people coming through the checkpoint and hurrying toward the open doors. Jacob walked in the opposite direction.

It was clear he'd underestimated the number of people on the other side of the barrier. Around the corner and out of sight from the train, two to three hundred people waited. Behind them, the station hall was empty, as everybody congregated near the barrier for the last train of the night.

Between those people and the ticket inspectors, a squad of SS formed a human barrier. Their aggressive stance left no doubt why they were there. They carried sidearms, a few holding automatic rifles.

Their presence was enough to stop anybody from sneaking through the inspection post.

Probably only twenty people were left waiting for their bags to be checked, and the queue moved quickly.

The train's whistle shrieked in the background. Five minutes left. *What's taking them so long?*

As if on cue, a familiar face appeared as Ethan navigated his way toward the wall of SS soldiers, his parents following. He handed their tickets to one of the SS men, and after a surprisingly quick inspection, two of the men parted to let the Weissmans through.

Jacob felt a wave of relief. He whistled toward his friend. Ethan saw him, and his face lit up.

"We'll be right there—hold the train!" he shouted across the platform. Ethan's father carried a single suitcase, and his mother had nothing but a small picnic basket. Ethan had a duffel bag slung over his shoulder. They looked hurried but relieved.

Jacob smiled and pointed at the clock. "Hurry!"

The Weissmans were the last people to go through the inspection. They opened their luggage, and Jacob saw the same surprise he'd felt earlier appear on their faces. Ethan's mother rummaged through a side pocket inside the suitcase and produced a golden necklace. From a distance, Jacob judged that was enough, for the inspector motioned for her to close the case.

Jacob looked at the clock. Three minutes to go—they should be able to board the train just in time. He relaxed a little.

A shot rang out, the explosion deafening, echoing around the high ceilings of the station hall. It silenced everybody in the station as they turned toward its source.

Time appeared to stand still as Jacob did the same. He saw a very young SS soldier standing a few steps out of formation, his pistol pointed at the crowd and a faint trace of smoke rising from the barrel. The soldier's hands trembled, confusion on his face.

Looking through a small gap in the wall of soldiers, Jacob could make out a small boy on the marble station floor. He lay on his back, a pool of blood already forming around him. The boy clutched his stomach as he tried to stop the life rushing from him.

Even from a distance, Jacob saw the boy fading quickly.

The SS men stepped forward as one, falling in line with the shooter. They pointed their weapons at the crowd.

The faces in the crowd showed a mix of anger, desperation, and disbelief, unsure what to do next.

Ethan stood with his father's suitcase in his hand; his eyes betraying no emotion. His mother looked pale and fragile, her hands in front of her mouth. Ethan's father, Levi, had wrapped his arm around her.

On the platform, the shrill whistle of the conductor announced the last call before departure.

The whistle sparked something in the crowd. The group moved toward the boy on the floor. His face was as pale as snow, the crimson pool around him no longer spreading. His eyes were closed, his hands resting on the sides of his body, no longer clutching his stomach.

The soldiers remained impassive as they sized up the restless crowd.

Jacob had seen too much violence in recent days. They had to leave now and quickly. He looked at Ethan and jerked his head toward the train.

"Go!" he mouthed as Ethan pulled his parents toward the train.

Another impatient whistle from the train. One minute left. Jacob spun on his heel and sprinted toward the train, Ethan and his parents only a few paces behind.

"Keep going," he shouted at Ethan. "This is not going to end well!"

Ethan caught up with him, despite carrying the bulky suitcase. "We'll make it for sure—the train is right there." He urged his parents on, and they breathed heavily as they struggled to keep up.

They crossed the empty platform, running to the first set of doors—

Ethan pulled on the handle, but nothing happened. The people inside looked at them through the windows with wide eyes.

Behind them, another shot rang out.

Jacob looked over his shoulder. The crowd had charged the soldiers. More shots were fired. Panicked shrieks filled the air.

"Jacob! We have to go now!" Ethan brought him back to his senses.

*The train. We have to get on it.*

The train started creeping forward, slowly picking up speed.

Jacob ran ahead and pulled frantically at the next set of doors. They remained shut. Ethan's parents caught up with him, and his mother doubled over as she gasped for air.

"Easy, Mama," Ethan said, supporting her while they moved down the train cars.

Jacob banged on the doors and windows. People tried to open the doors from inside, to no avail.

A burst of automatic gunfire erupted behind them. They ducked instinctively, and Ethan's mother screamed. Jacob expected to feel the impact of a bullet at any moment.

He turned and saw the SS soldiers retreating. Their backs were to them; their focus was on the crowd pressing toward them.

A few brave men still came at the soldiers—the train was their last chance. The SS men held firm, reloading their rifles.

Some cars ahead of them, a head poked out of a door on the train. One of the conductors must've heard them.

"Over here!" he shouted. "Hurry!"

The train's engines roared as more steam was forced through. To Jacob's dismay, the train was speeding up.

He looked back and was glad to see Ethan and his parents on his heels, their faces red from exertion.

Behind them, the SS soldiers finished reloading their weapons.

"Come on, we can make it!" Jacob shouted. They were still faster than the train, but it wouldn't be long before the open door was out of reach.

Jacob reached the door, and the conductor stood in the doorway, holding out his hand. The jump was small, but Jacob felt his heart in his mouth as he jumped headfirst into the small gangway. He landed with a hard thud but turned immediately to see Ethan running parallel to the door.

Ethan threw the suitcase through the open doors and continued running alongside the train. Jacob moved to the door opening near the conductor. He saw Ethan's parents struggling to catch up. They were almost out of platform space, the front of the train pulling clear from the station. They had less than ten seconds to get on board.

"Run! You're almost there!" Jacob shouted.

He looked at the conductor. "Is there any way to open the other doors?"

The man shook his head. "Not unless we use the emergency handle, and there's no way I'm doing that after what just happened back there."

Jacob understood. If they stopped now, nobody would get out of Berlin tonight.

Ethan and his father were level with the door. His mother was almost there. Both men refused to leave her behind, waiting for her to catch up before they'd jump.

Using her last bit of strength, Ethan's mother launched herself forward, level with the door. The conductor didn't hesitate and grabbed her arm. Jacob stood next to him, grabbing her other arm as she jumped.

Ethan's father immediately followed, and they tumbled into the back of the galley.

Ethan sprinted next to the train, his face turning a dark shade of red, his coat flapping.

Just before the car cleared the platform, Ethan flew in. He landed face-first in a pile of suitcases in the back of the galley.

As the train pulled out of the station and into the darkness, there was no mistaking the sound of automatic rifles exploding into life behind them.

# PART II

## WESTERBORK,
## THE NETHERLANDS
## JUNE 1942

# CHAPTER FIVE

"I guess it's going to be another sunny day," Jacob said to Ethan as the morning sun warmed his face. They pulled a small hand cart along a gravel road lined by oak trees.

Ethan nodded. "I'm glad van Drunen sent us out this morning. It's been a while. I was starting to get a little bored, to be honest."

They were lucky the camp's head cook had picked them to run errands whenever he needed something special. It meant a brief respite from the place they'd called home for almost three years now. It felt like a lifetime ago, but Jacob remembered their escape from Berlin vividly.

The journey had been long, and people in their train car had been nervous. The train had stopped numerous times, and each time Jacob expected SS soldiers to pull everybody from the train cars and haul them off to the dreaded camps they'd heard about—Sachsenhausen, Dachau.

When they finally crossed into the Netherlands after two days, Dutch border guards escorted them off the train, where buses waited to take them to different refugee camps. The Kagans and Weissmanns were placed in a small working village in the north-west of the country. The Dutch were wary of the newcomers and had little interaction with them. But Jacob was happy to be away from Germany, where they had heard things had only gotten worse. They were well taken care of in the village, with plenty of food and simple jobs to keep them occupied.

With growing numbers of refugees entering the Netherlands, the Dutch government decided to build a centralized camp. In October 1939—almost a year after they'd fled Germany—Jacob, Ethan, and their families arrived at Camp Westerbork. Located in the east of the Netherlands, it was a dreary place built on desolate plains. They were some of the first people there, and in the following weeks, another five hundred refugees arrived—mostly Jewish Germans scattered around the Netherlands. They spent their time plowing the bare plains into cultivated fields for farming and expanding the spartan facilities—every barracks had little more than a single washbasin and a small kitchen with one burner to share among seventy inhabitants. It was up to the new residents to make the best of their new home. They were relatively free to run the camp, and the Dutch authorities encouraged them to improve their surroundings. They received financial support from Jewish refugee organizations, and little by little, the camp resembled something of a village.

When the Nazis invaded the Netherlands in May of the following year, things quickly changed. Military police now controlled the strictly marked boundaries of the camp—inhabitants were no longer allowed to go out and about freely. Roll calls were introduced in the morning and evening. Jobs were assigned, and any letters had to remain unsealed—open to censorship before they could be sent, and messages received were read, too.

The influx of new arrivals had also halted—the Netherlands was no longer a refuge from Nazi reign. But the previous week, a group of about 500 Dutch Jews had arrived in Westerbork, bringing the total camp population close to 1100. Jacob had been surprised to see the newcomers—Westerbork had housed only German and Austrian Jews until then.

"What do you think of the new arrivals?" Ethan asked, interrupting Jacob's thoughts.

"They're very different from us. It's a good thing we've picked up some Dutch."

While inhabitants like Jacob and Ethan performed many of the camp duties—Hermann worked in the camp hospital while Elsa and Ethan's father worked in the little school—they all reported to the Dutch administration. Most of the officials spoke only halting German, so Jacob, Ethan, and their families made sure to pick up the Dutch language quickly.

"The Dutch keep to themselves, but I overheard a few during breakfast," said Ethan. "They thought I couldn't understand them, and they spoke quite freely." His expression was grim.

"So . . . ?" Jacob asked as he looked around, taking in all the sights, sounds, smells, and even the slight fatigue of their trek. It had been a while since they'd been on one of these errands; he wanted to appreciate the freedom.

"Well, it seems they were rounded up in the middle of the night. From what I heard, it sounds like they're Dutch communists."

*So, political arrests*, Jacob thought. *It makes sense—the Nazis do the same with their political opponents in Germany.*

"It seems like they're all from Amsterdam," Ethan said. "I think they were put on a train in the middle of the night and got here the next morning, and then we saw the trucks that brought them to the camp."

"Just like Berlin," Jacob murmured. Despite the warmth of the late-morning sun, he felt a chill run down his spine.

Ethan didn't respond, and they walked along the road in silence. A million thoughts raced through Jacob's mind.

After a few minutes, the unmistakable sound of an engine in the distance drew their attention to a small tractor approaching, its engine straining to pull the weight of whatever was in its trailer. Ethan and Jacob moved out of the road so the tractor could pass.

Soon they recognized the driver—Jan Steen, an amiable local farmer. He slowed down and stopped next to them.

"Morning, Ethan, Jacob," he said in Dutch. "Another special delivery for the camp today?"

"Quite so," Jacob responded. "We're on our way to pick up some spinach from the market."

Jan smiled. "You should get a good price for that, there's plenty this year." His face turned serious. "I heard you have some new arrivals in

Westerbork? We were told to stay off the roads last week and, well, news travels fast."

Jacob's ears perked up. *Does he know more about what's going on?*

"Apparently they're from Amsterdam," Ethan said, beating Jacob to the question. "Have you heard anything about that?"

Jan leaned a little out of the tractor seat. He looked uncomfortable. "Between you and me, we've seen a lot of German soldiers around the city recently. Everybody in town is talking about it—there are lots of rumors flying around."

"Like what?"

"People say they want to take over the camp."

"Really? There's nothing of real interest for them there. It's just us trying to survive," Jacob said. *What would they want with our little camp?*

"As I said, it's only rumors, and I agree with you—there's little going on here, anyway," Jan said. "All I know is that there was talk of changing the camp status from refugee to something else, but nobody knew what, exactly."

"If we're not refugees, what are we?" Ethan looked alarmed.

"I honestly don't know—I'm only telling you what I've heard." Jan looked keen to change the subject. "But I must be on my way; I need to deliver these in town." He pointed at the trailer filled with radishes. The engine roared as he switched into first gear and hit the gas.

"I'm sure it's nothing!" he shouted over the engine. "Nothing ever happens around here anyway!" He pulled away from them and continued down the road.

Jacob and Ethan stood next to their cart as the tractor disappeared.

"That doesn't sound good at all," Ethan said, his brow furrowed.

Jacob agreed. "We need to find out what's going on. Nothing good can come from Nazis invading the country. But I didn't figure anything would change in Westerbork. It's a boring little town, and they must have bigger things to worry about."

"Let's get back and see if anybody has heard anything," Ethan said. "Peter will know—don't you think?"

Peter played football with them, and because his father worked in the camp administration, he often knew camp news before anyone else.

Jacob replied: "Let's get that spinach and hurry back."

Ethan picked up the handlebars of the cart with a groan, and they moved down the road with new urgency.

It was an hour before dinner when Jacob and Ethan approached Peter's small house on the camp's perimeter. Most of the people in the camp lived in barracks while the Dutch workers commuted from nearby villages every day.

Peter's father helped run the camp with the Dutch commander, Jacques Schol. Funding was limited, and they had to find creative ways to feed the five hundred—now a thousand—souls in the camp. He did a good job, and there was hardly any trouble.

Since there were no gates inside the camp, Ethan and Jacob walked straight to Peter's front door.

"I'm sure he knows more," Jacob knocked on the door. "We just need to make him comfortable enough to talk to us about it."

"Let's hope his father shares some of the news at the dinner table," Ethan said.

The door opened, and they were glad to see Peter's face. He was tall and lanky, like many of the Dutch men around Westerbork. His blue eyes shone brightly.

"What's up, guys?" He looked happy to see them.

"We're just taking a walk around the camp before dinner," Jacob said. "You want to come along and build up an appetite?"

"Sure, why not?" Peter closed the door behind him.

They walked along the perimeter of the camp, marked with a modest fence. Vast cultivated fields stretched to the horizon, a small pine forest the only break in the dreary landscape. A small group of camp inhabitants worked the fields in the distance, hunched over in the dirt.

"How is your father?" Jacob asked. "I haven't seen him around the camp much recently."

Peter kicked a small pebble. "He's been rather busy. The administration in Amsterdam has asked him to come down quite a bit. Something appears to be up." He looked uncomfortable, fumbling with his hands.

"The Dutch government, or the Germans?" Jacob asked.

"Both, I think. Father says the Germans are more involved than usual these days."

Ethan and Jacob exchanged a look. *This sounds like bad news.*

"How so? Come on, Peter, tell us more. We're stuck in the barracks and only hear things when somebody in town talks to us. Even that is becoming harder" he pulled at the star patched on his shirt. "People are starting to avoid us. We only get to talk to the shopkeepers and the occasional farmers we see on the way to and from town. We're completely cut off," Jacob said, his eyes pleading.

Peter's eyes shot around, inspecting the area around them. "Okay, okay," he said, slowly walking on and motioning them to follow him. They were far from the camp entrance, in a spot where the ground was muddy and uncultivated.

"It's not good," he started. "What I gather from Father—and mind you, he doesn't speak a lot about this—is that the Germans are going to take over the camp soon. You must've seen them walking around the camp the past few weeks, right?"

Jacob and Ethan nodded. *So it's true.*

"This week they've started sending people from Amsterdam to work in Germany. They're Dutch Jews, and I've heard they're selecting mostly men. I don't know what for, but I think they need more manpower for the war effort."

"That makes sense, but what does that have to do with us?" Jacob asked.

"The work details are just part of what's going on in the larger cities. A friend in Amsterdam told me they're rounding up entire groups of people in the city. He said German troops, together with Dutch police, block off entire streets at night. They load people up in trucks, and off they go."

"Just like some of the ones who arrived last week," Ethan said.

Peter took a short moment to gather his thoughts before continuing. "This has been happening in only a few cities so far. When I asked Father about it, he said he'd heard the Germans have plans to extend the policy to the rest of the country. The round-ups are done on a small scale, but you can tell they're working toward something bigger."

Jacob looked up. "They can't transport people on a larger scale," he noted. "Only a few hundred at a time can travel on the trains."

"That's what it seems like. They need a central place where they can bring them before transporting them onward in batches to these work camps." He pointed to the barracks behind them. "I think Westerbork is going to be that place."

They were silent as Peter's chilling words sank in.

Jacob broke the silence. "It all sounds very familiar, doesn't it? It's what happened when we left Germany—the SS raiding houses and public places and trucking people off."

"And it was never random. It was always us Jews," Ethan said as he began pacing around. "But what can we do? We don't know if this is really going to happen, or if it's just rumors."

"Wishful thinking. You know they could do the same here," Jacob said. "It makes sense to expand this camp. Look around you—there's plenty of space, 'cause we're in the middle of nowhere. And Commander Schol, with our help, has already set up the basic needs for this camp."

Peter was solemn. "I think we need to accept there are going to be changes. Father hasn't said anything about having to leave this post, so I guess that's a positive thing. Maybe the Germans won't completely take over—Westerbork is run quite well as it is, don't you think?"

Jacob was unconvinced. "They haven't been visiting without reason. Those perimeter walks make more sense now. They're scouting the area."

"I honestly don't know any more than what I just told you," Peter said, his hands up.

They were interrupted by the sound of an engine approaching the main gate. Peter's father was returning with the commander.

"It's almost dinner time," Peter said. "You should head back to your barracks to make sure you don't miss out. I'll see if I can learn anything more. I'm sure Father has news from his meetings today. Let's meet tomorrow morning—after roll call."

Ethan nodded. "That makes sense. We'll have a supply run to one of the farmers in the morning, so maybe you can join us."

"Let's do that. Hopefully, I'll have some better news tomorrow."

Ethan and Jacob rushed back to the barracks, hoping there would still be some food left for them.

Jacob was up early with a steady stream of people on their way to the sanitary block. Despite the camp's growth, these facilities hadn't been expanded—getting a shower meant getting up extra early to beat the queues.

The toilets were not what most people were used to. Wooden planks were bolted to the walls, with circular holes intermittently placed a few feet apart, over a steady stream of water running below, washing their excrement away. It was relatively hygienic, but there was absolutely no privacy. New arrivals usually took a few days to get used to the arrangement, but eventually, nature found its course.

Outside, Jacob bumped into Ethan, and they headed toward roll call together. He looked tired, with bags under his eyes.

"Some of the older people said a large group of German soldiers was on their way to the camp. I think they spoke to some Dutch people from the villages, but you never know if they're telling the truth."

"—Or where they got their information," Jacob added. "I'm sure their surrender to the Germans hasn't made their lives easier, either."

"I guess so; it adds up with what Jan and Peter said."

They approached a sandy clearing amidst the barracks. It was immediately clear this was going to be a day unlike any other. Every morning, all camp inhabitants assembled for a head-count. Jacob and Ethan would then report to the kitchen to see if they were needed for a supply run. For most other people, it meant another day of scattering around the camp to find someone to debate with or play cards with tattered handmade packs.

Today, the entire camp police force surrounded the area, somber and stern-faced. A small platform was erected on one side of the clearing, and several senior policemen hovered closely.

Ethan and Jacob looked at each other.

"Does this seem odd to you?" Ethan asked. "They're never out in such force for roll call."

The policemen looked a little nervous. At the front, Max Willems, the police commander, paced back and forth, occasionally barking something at the growing crowd. The atmosphere was electric—people were chatting, trying to find out what was going on.

"I'm more worried about the platform surrounded like that."

Ethan nodded. "I guess we'll find out soon enough. I'd better make my way over to my side."

"Sure, I'll see you at the kitchen later."

Ethan disappeared in the stream of people, then Hermann and Elsa approached their son.

"What's going on up there?" Jacob's father asked, inclining his head toward the platform.

"Don't know—we're all wondering the same thing."

A shrill whistle ended their speculation. People stopped talking, and all turned toward its source.

A tall man emerged from the crowd, the Dutch commander, Jacques Schol. He walked purposefully to a spot in front of the platform, exuding confidence. Schol was well-respected within the camp, and, like most of the Dutch command, fair in his treatment of the Jewish inhabitants. Although he never openly spoke about it, people knew he was fiercely anti-German. When the Germans invaded the Netherlands, he'd tried—unsuccessfully and unknown to the Germans —to evacuate Westerbork's residents to the United Kingdom. They'd wound up stranded in the north of the Netherlands and had had to return to the camp. Jacob had nothing but respect for the man, and he knew most of the people around him felt the same way.

Schol mounted the platform and looked around. The roll call area was now silent, a thousand pairs of eyes looking up at Schol.

"Good morning. Before today's roll call, I have a short announcement to make," he started solemnly.

"From this afternoon onward, there will be some changes in the camp. The duties of Herr Willems' team will be handed over to German command."

The commander of the Dutch police shifted uneasily and adjusted his glasses.

"Unfortunately, this changing of the guard also applies to the entire administrative staff, including myself. The Germans will bring in a new camp commander, who will arrive shortly. I will help the new commander settle in, but then I will take my leave."

People looked at each other. Jacob saw the disbelief in his mother's eyes, while his father just shook his head, looking down.

"While I can't assure you everything will remain the same, I've been told that all camp facilities will remain as they are. The school will remain open, work details will continue, and the hospital will be stocked. They've given me assurances that life in Westerbork will remain as it has been."

Soft murmurs spread as the crowd became more restless. *Nobody's buying this.*

Schol shifted uncomfortably. It looked like he was having trouble believing his own words. The murmurs increased, and Schol had to shout to finish his speech.

"Roll call will continue as usual, reporting here every morning. It will be handled by the new German command from tomorrow onward."

With that, Schol stepped down from the platform, and what had started as a civilized, organized roll call had turned into an anxious mob.

Some tried to keep a brave face, but they all knew better. Everywhere the Nazis had gone, life had changed for the worse. Jacob had seen it in the few towns around the camp. The Dutch didn't complain openly, but he noticed the little things. People went quiet when German soldiers entered stores or markets.

The policemen decided enough was enough and moved in, blowing their whistles. Their calm but firm demeanor spread over the group, and people came back to their senses. They seemed to realize there was nothing the Dutch police could do about the changes. Roll call started and, on the surface, life in Westerbork returned to normal for at least one more day.

Jacob and Ethan stepped into the kitchen, navigating the narrow passages between the stoves and prep stations, steering well clear of sharp knives and boiling cauldrons.

"Jacob!" shouted the burly head cook, Paul van Drunen. The giant man was not just tall, but also boasted massive shoulders and a belly that left no doubt about his food inspection skills.

Jacob and Ethan liked van Drunen, especially as he always found a way for them to get outside the camp.

"What's for dinner?" Jacob asked, pointing at a large pot.

Van Drunen smiled. "Potato soup with a bit of chicken"—he lifted the lid and sampled the broth—"Hmm, could use a bit more salt. Good thing we have plenty of that." He added a generous amount to the soup. "The thing is, I need some more supplies from the market. The camp commander wants to welcome the Germans with something special, so I need you to buy some decent meat."

He handed them the camp order form, and Jacob quickly inspected it. They were never given actual money, but the form guaranteed payment for the shop.

Ethan peeked at the order as well. "That's a lot of steaks. How many are you expecting?"

"They didn't tell me the exact number, but probably between fifty and a hundred Germans today and tomorrow," van Drunen said, replacing the lid on the large pot. He turned up the heat and stepped away from his stove. "You should get on your way—I need time to prepare before they get here."

"You got it, chef," Jacob said. "We'll be back before you know it."

They grabbed a large duffel bag each and left the kitchen. Outside, the sun was making a steady ascent in the blue sky, rendering Westerbork slightly less dreary than usual. Jacob had become used to the grey, overcast skies of the Netherlands—two sunny days in a row was a real treat.

"It might not have been good news this morning," said Jacob, "but at least we get to escape the camp for another day before the Nazis arrive. I doubt they'll allow us to carry on with this job."

They took the main camp throughway, a sandy path that cut straight through the camp lined with simple, green barracks on both sides. That morning, it was even busier than usual, with people converging near the barracks' entrances to wait on their rickety chairs and stools.

When they got to the main gate, they were surprised to find it locked.

"This must be the first time it's been closed during the day, right?" Ethan said.

Jacob nodded and walked toward one of the guards smoking a cigarette. He didn't recognize him, which was odd, because after passing through here almost every day for three years, he'd come to know most of them.

"Morning—could you open the gate for us? We need to get some supplies from town."

The guard took a long drag from his cigarette. He exhaled slowly and pointed to the gate.

"Nobody's going out today," he said, dropping the cigarette butt and using his heel to grind it into the sandy ground. "Commander's orders. Until the Germans arrive, you're all staying put." He turned away from Jacob.

"I think you'll want to make an exception for us," Ethan said.

The guard turned back with a frown.

"Oh yeah? Why's that?"

Ethan nearly shoved the order form into the guard's face.

"Because you're going to have some very pissed-off Germans tonight if they don't get their steaks after their long trek here. And right now, our kitchen has zero steaks. You want to be the guy that ruins their first dinner in the camp?"

Another guard approached from the other side of the road. It was Jean, one of the friendlier guards in the camp. Jacob raised a hand in greeting.

"What's going on, Henry?" Jean asked, looking at his colleague. He nodded at Jacob. "Hey Jaco, how are you?"

"All good, Jean—we just need to run an errand for van Drunen."

Henry handed the paper to Jean, who took one look at it and shook his head.

"Come on, Henry. I know you haven't been around for long, but surely you know Jacob and Ethan are exempt from these orders. If van Drunen wants to cook our new German friends a steak dinner tonight, I'm not going to stand in his way."

He returned the papers to Jacob and waved his hand toward the gate. "Go on, don't just stand there," he said to Henry. "Open the gate for them."

Henry shrugged and raised the barrier.

"Maybe you can bring us an extra steak or two as well, huh, Jaco?" Jean asked with a wink.

Ethan and Jacob left the camp behind, both happy to be away for a few hours. The beautiful weather lifted their spirits.

"You know you can be a little too cocky at times, right?" Jacob said, kicking a small pebble down the sandy road.

Ethan grinned. "I don't know what you're talking about."

"That guard might have been a bit of a slowpoke, but you probably shouldn't pull that stunt with the Nazis coming in. We were lucky Jean was there, or we might still be there, trying to convince him to let us out."

"Yeah, well . . . We're here now, right? Plus, I'd rather risk a small argument with someone like him—what's his face?—Henry—than with van Drunen. Imagine coming back without steak and having him storm out to the gate?"

Jacob laughed. "It wouldn't have ended well for him!"

"Sure, but he wouldn't have been too happy with us, either. So, in the end, we did ourselves *and* Henry a big favor."

"You think they'll replace everybody in the camp staff?" Jacob asked. It had been on his mind since the morning roll call.

"I was thinking about that, too," Ethan said, forming a small frown. "They said the camp command would be replaced, so I guess that means all the Dutch police will be out. But I can't imagine they're sending cooks from Germany, right?"

"We're doing most of the manual work already. I mean, we all clean the barracks and toilets ourselves, and run the hospital and school—so maybe there can't be too much of a change."

"I'm not so sure about that. Don't you remember Berlin? I'm sure it's only gotten worse now that they're invading other countries," Ethan said. "I can't see anything good coming from them taking over Westerbork."

The church tower of the village rose in the distance as they got closer.

*What will the Nazi arrival mean for my family?*

Jacob's future felt uncertain. He doubted he'd be allowed outside the camp, and he wasn't even sure van Drunen would stay on. At least he was young and able-bodied, so perhaps he could volunteer for other work?

*There's no sense speculating. We'll know more soon enough.*

They arrived in town and headed straight to the butcher shop. At the entrance of the little store, the pleasant aroma of freshly cut meat hit their nostrils. There was nobody behind the small display, and Ethan hit the bell on the counter.

A freckled face peeked through the doorway to the back room.

"Oh, hey, guys! What do you need today?" It was the butcher's son, Alfred, a gangly teenager.

Jacob handed him the order form. "I hope you have enough to supply the new camp command tonight."

Alfred studied the paper, his eyes widening. "You need a hundred pieces of steak? Let me check with my father. I doubt we have that much."

He disappeared into the back room, leaving Jacob and Ethan to look around. The meat in the display looked fresh, but the variety wasn't impressive.

"Seems business is pretty slow," Ethan said.

Jacob nodded. "I don't think the occupation is doing the Dutch any favors."

Alfred returned with his father, who wore a bloody butcher's apron and held a large knife. His face was puffy, and the small glimmer of sweat on his forehead suggested they'd interrupted him during some heavy-duty work. Nevertheless, he smiled.

"So you boys need a whole lot of meat," he stated, rather than asking. "I'm afraid I won't be able to supply you with a hundred steaks. There simply aren't enough cows around here to produce that amount of fine meat. Also, I don't think I'd be able to sell the rest of the beef to anyone. On the other hand, all those Germans coming to Westerbork sounds like it might be good for business—"

Jacob let the insensitive remark pass. "What could you supply, though? Anything else in your freezer that we can use for tonight's dinner?"

The butcher nodded. "There's plenty of pork chops in the freezer. You can take those, along with maybe thirty steaks? It'll be cheaper, too."

Jacob looked at Ethan, who nodded. "It's better than nothing, and a whole lot better than what we get served every day."

"I'll wrap them up for you. Give me about fifteen minutes, and they'll be ready."

"Thanks—we'll grab some fresh air and be right back," Jacob said.

They stepped outside to the narrow cobblestone street. Winding through small alleys, they ended up at the village square, where small benches surrounded a modest fountain. Four were occupied, but they sat down on the last free one.

The square fronted the small city hall, outside of which were many green jeeps.

Ethan stretched out on the bench. "What do you think—German military?"

Jacob stood up and crossed the small plaza while Ethan remained on the bench and watched his friend with interest.

Jacob peeked inside. The car was empty but for a pack of cigarettes on the passenger seat.

"Find anything?" Ethan sat on the bench; his long legs stretched out.

"Not really. Military, but nothing inside." He sat down next to his friend. "Perhaps the new German command?"

"Most likely. Let's wait and see if they're almost done in there. We still have a bit of time to wait for the meat, anyway."

They sat on the bench, and Jacob looked at some of the people around them. They also kept an eye on the entrance to the city hall.

The pair didn't have to wait long, as a young man in a black uniform stepped out the front door. He held it open, and almost immediately, a group of about twenty men in similar uniforms streamed through the opening. Even from a distance, Jacob could spot the arrogant strut of men who didn't have a care in the world.

*Oh, shit.* Jacob swallowed hard and looked at Ethan, whose face had gone pale.

The men quickly got into the cars and revved their engines on the square. The people on the benches turned up their noses in thinly veiled contempt, while the vehicles sped away in a cloud of exhaust fumes and dust. When they turned the corner, the only sound on the square was that of the fountain gently splashing.

"Please tell me those aren't the uniforms I think they are," Jacob started. He felt his throat constrict.

"No. It was definitely them."

Jacob was appalled. "When they said new German command, I didn't think it would be them."

"I know."

An elderly couple on the next bench had overheard. "You two are in the camp down the road?"

They nodded.

"We've seen those soldiers driving around town quite a lot recently," the man continued, while the woman next to him shook her head. "They're always in and out quickly, running their business over there."

"They're not real soldiers," Ethan said. "I've seen them in Berlin when we still lived there. They're the absolute scum of the Nazis, and that's saying something."

The man looked at him in surprise. "They look like soldiers to me, with their fancy uniforms."

"Are they always so many?" Jacob asked.

It was the woman who answered this time. "No, normally it's just one or two cars. This was different."

Jacob looked at Ethan and got up. "Let's get the meat and get back. I have a feeling they'll be waiting for us at the camp."

They walked toward the butcher's shop in silence.

Back at the camp around noon, the friends knew something had changed. The same guards manned the gate as before, but they appeared nervous. Even Jean seemed rattled as he quickly closed the barrier behind them.

"Hurry up, guys. The Germans are here, and they've made it clear nobody leaves today."

"How many?" Jacob asked.

"I don't know, we've had around ten jeeps arriving throughout the morning."

"Were they all SS?" Ethan had stopped and stood next to Jean.

Jean looked Ethan straight in the eye. "It appears so, from what I've seen."

Jacob saw sympathy in the guard's eyes. He wasn't as oblivious to the German army ranks as had been the people they spoke to in town.

"Just keep your head down, guys. I'm sure you'll know more soon. We're shipped off tomorrow morning, or so we've been told. Now get that bag to the kitchen—I'm sure van Drunen is anxious to get started."

They practically jogged down the camp's main road.

"Is it just me, or is it strangely quiet here?" Ethan asked, looking around. "Where is everybody?"

The sun was at its highest point now, and a gentle breeze made it rather pleasant outside. People would typically be out, playing cards and gossiping on such a beautiful day.

They passed the school, which was dark and empty inside. "You're right—the kids should still be in classes now."

They entered the kitchen through the back door, spotted van Drunen and handed the duffel bag to him.

"Pork chops?" He frowned as he inspected the cuts. "It'll have to do."

They turned to leave, but he stopped them. "Oh—Jacob, Ethan— you won't have to come in tomorrow. Work details are scrapped. Orders of the Germans, of course."

"What does that mean for us?" Jacob asked.

"I don't know." Van Drunen looked uneasy. "There will be lots of changes. I've had to tell many of the people working in my kitchen they won't have to come in. I don't know how I'm going to prepare the meals without them. We'll find out tomorrow, I guess."

*How are the Germans going to replace the entire kitchen staff?*

"So they haven't told you anything either, then?"

Van Drunen shook his head. "All I know is I have to report to the command post tonight after we've finished dinner. I assume they'll tell me what will change, and we can go from there. Sorry, guys, I can't tell you anything more. But know if it's possible, I'll try to get you back on my team. Now, I need to get to this welcome dinner for our new commanders."

He turned away, reaching for some large skillets. One of the kitchen hands walked over with knobs of butter, and van Drunen resumed cooking mode.

They left the kitchen and walked through the seemingly deserted camp.

"I suppose it's best to check in the barracks and see what people know," Jacob said.

"Not really anything else to do. It stinks that we've lost our jobs, huh?"

Jacob nodded. "The changes have started. But maybe it's just a reshuffle."

Ethan gave him a sad smile. "If only that were the case—but I doubt it. I appreciate your optimism."

Jacob found his parents on their beds in their quarters in barrack number ten. Only a few of the barracks in Westerbork had these private compartments for families. As some of the first inhabitants, and due to Hermann's position in the hospital, they were fortunate to have been allocated their own space. It was sparsely furnished—hardly more substantial than a bedroom in their home in Berlin. His parents shared the bottom part of their bunk bed—with Jacob in the top bed—but at least they had some privacy. Most people were housed in the barracks without any compartments, and bunk beds were lined up along the length of one large, open space.

"I didn't expect to find you here this early," Jacob said to his father as he sat next to him. Hermann usually spent his entire day in the hospital, only retreating to the barracks for dinner, before making a last round in the evening.

"Everybody was dismissed from their jobs when the German commander arrived late in the morning."

"What about the patients?"

Hermann shrugged. "I don't know. It's not too bad at the hospital now, and some of the Dutch nurses are still around. They should be fine."

Despite his father's stoic demeanor, Jacob could see he was worried. The wrinkles on his forehead were a little deeper, and his cheeks were flushed. He knew better than to press this issue and changed the subject.

"So, what happened after I left? I saw SS soldiers and officers in town. I assume they're here now?"

His father nodded, but it was Elsa who answered. "They arrived throughout the day. I think there are about fifty, maybe sixty of them now."

"Are they all SS?"

"Yes"—she paused—"I was helping out in the school library when they came in during the lunch break and told us to send the children back to the barracks and close the school for the day. A few of them waited at the entrance to make sure we locked up. I've never seen the school cleared so quickly."

"The same happened in the hospital," Hermann chimed in. "They stormed in and told me to leave. They allowed me to finish bandaging a patient, but then they escorted me out. I was only half-way through my rounds, but they didn't care. They said they would take care of the patients. I can't imagine them doing anything helpful for the people in the hospital."

There was a soft knock on the door. Dr. Brunner—the lead doctor at the hospital—entered the room. He had arrived in Westerbork around the same time as the Kagans, and he and Hermann had spent their time in the camp improving the conditions. Although it was still a far cry from a proper hospital, they had a functional operation going, and there were always beds available for those in need. The

Dutch government had been surprisingly generous with medical supplies.

"Sorry to disturb you, but I just wanted to let you know everything in the hospital is okay," he said to Hermann.

Hermann looked up with relief. "Did you speak to the nurses?"

Brunner shook his head. "No, I went back. I've been running that place for over three years, and I wanted to know what was going on."

Jacob thought that was both brave and foolish. He'd seen what happened to people who crossed the SS in Berlin and doubted they'd have much respect for Brunner's credentials. To them, he was just a Jew.

"I was stopped by a soldier guarding the door. Can you imagine that? Nobody in there is going to try to escape from those conditions to the barracks," he said with a thin smile. "But never mind that. I told the soldier I was in charge of the hospital and needed to check on a few patients in critical condition."

Hermann sat up. "We don't have any patients like that now, though, do we?"

"No, indeed, we don't. But we do have a lot of patients that require proper care. I certainly don't trust those soldiers to provide it."

"Did he let you in?"

Brunner sighed. "No—he was adamant about his orders. When I told him people might die because of this, he shrugged and told me to get back to my barracks. I tried reasoning with him, but he said I'd have a lot more to worry about than those patients if I didn't leave. In the end, that's what I did."

He looked downcast for a split second before continuing with vigor: "However, as I left, the nurses—Vera and Evelien—also left the building.

"They were on their way home to the village, and I waited for them as they walked toward the gate. They told me the SS aren't interfering with anything going on inside the hospital. They carried on their duties as if nothing had changed."

"So, all the patients are okay?" Hermann asked.

Brunner nodded. "Yes, they're all in good shape. And as far as the girls knew, they will still be coming in tomorrow."

That was the first good news Jacob had heard all day—maybe the changes wouldn't be that drastic after all.

"Do you think you and my father will be allowed to return, Dr. Brunner?"

"The new command didn't bring any medical staff, so I really don't know who else could run the hospital. We need some sort of medical care. I think they're simply taking stock of what's going on in the camp today, and they will give us our old jobs back tomorrow morning." Dr. Brunner looked confident.

Jacob looked at his father, who seemed a little less shaken than he had been a few moments before. Dr. Brunner's news had lifted his spirits, and Jacob wanted to believe he was right.

# Chapter Six

The sun struggled to break through a dense layer of clouds, spreading a strange hue over the packed roll-call area. As Jacob moved to his place, he saw black-uniformed SS guards everywhere, patrolling the grounds and inspecting the inhabitants of the camp. Each had a sidearm strapped to his belt.

"How many of them do you think there are?" his father asked in a low voice.

Jacob made a quick calculation. "No more than twenty in SS uniform, but look at those men on the outside perimeter."

Encircling the area was a large group of men in uniforms Jacob didn't recognize. These men didn't have sidearms but were armed with batons instead.

"There must be fifty of them," Hermann said. "I've never seen them before. What kind of uniform is that?"

Jacob held up his palms. "I'm sure we'll find out soon enough."

Another platform had been set up with a Nazi swastika banner flying behind it. A large SS officer mounted the platform and stood behind a microphone. They hadn't wasted any time setting up a speaker system.

The man tapped the microphone, the sound attracting the attention of everybody on the field.

"My name is Deppner, and I'm in charge of this camp from today," he started. His blond hair was perfectly styled—the image of the ideal German soldier. On either side of Deppner stood a host of SS commanders, their eyes fixed on the crowd.

"As you know, the Dutch command has left after setting up an adequate camp structure. But Westerbork is bound for greater things, and needs our expertise to expand beyond what we have today. All of you will be part of this new camp."

People looked confused, and some whispered to their neighbors.

"We will start expansions of the living quarters immediately—the current capacity is inadequate," Deppner continued, ignoring the murmurs from the crowd. "All of those who volunteer for these construction works will find their lives a lot more meaningful, and they will be rewarded."

Jacob raised his eyebrows. *Meaningful? Do we have a choice?*

"I've also noticed the administration run by our Dutch predecessors was suboptimal. Therefore, everybody will be required today to report any special skills they have. This will help in designating proper work assignments. After roll call, everybody will report to the administrative building."

Deppner paused for a moment, looking up. More than a thousand pairs of eyes looked back.

"As for the rest of the details, the roll call will continue every morning and evening. You will obey any order from my men, as well as from our support from the Dutch military police." He gestured to indicate the men on the perimeter.

*Military police. Perhaps it wouldn't be that bad if the Dutch were still involved?*

Deppner nodded at one of the men next to him, and the man stepped forward and shouted a command in German. As one, the SS soldiers moved toward the people in the field and shouted at them to move toward the administration building.

The Dutch military police were also on the move. They positioned themselves along the main road, blocking access to the barracks.

Jacob had trouble processing what was going on. Used to an orderly roll call, they were now herded as one massive flock of sheep. He didn't immediately move, and the pressure of the crowd pushed him along as he lost sight of his parents.

The SS guards were disciplined. They guided the group but were experienced enough not to walk amongst them, herding them along the road running through the middle of the camp.

Outside the administration building, rows of tables were set up, each one equipped with a large stack of forms and manned by a clerk. Jacob counted ten tables.

The SS shouted at the people to form orderly lines. Before long, ten queues snaked through the camp. The processing began, and Jacob felt like he'd arrived at a new camp. He felt his stomach grumble, but he knew breakfast was still far away.

The next morning Jacob managed to get to the latrines before most other people and had a very early breakfast in the communal canteen. He was halfway through his simple meal of bread and a small slice of cheese when Ethan joined him.

"Morning, Jaco. How did you sleep?" Ethan put his small plate down across from him.

Jacob reluctantly took another bite of his stale piece of bread. "Not too bad. I was exhausted yesterday. The processing took forever. By the time I was done, it was already well past mid-day. How did you fare?"

"Well, I told them I was a skilled carpenter with experience in construction. So they asked me if I wanted to volunteer for the building work. I told them yes."

"Me, too. The lady taking my details said it was the best way to get some extra meals. She practically recruited me to the construction crew," Jacob said. "But you don't have any carpentry experience."

"I know how to hold a hammer and jam a nail through a piece of wood. Besides, how many of the people in here do you think have actual building skills?"

Ethan finished his last bite, wiped his mouth on his sleeve, and got up. "Let's go and report for work, shall we? I'm quite curious to see what they'll make us do."

"You seem very enthusiastic to work for the SS. What gives?"

"I just want to know what's going to happen next," Ethan said.

They walked the short distance to the administrative building, where a large group of people of all ages waited. It was immediately apparent these weren't necessarily the strongest men in the camp. It looked like everybody who had the chance to get into the construction work detail—and get more food—had volunteered.

Jacob didn't see many familiar faces as he scanned the group.

"How many of these do you think actually have more experience building stuff than we do?" Ethan asked in a low voice.

Jacob shrugged. "As long as everybody is willing to try, I don't really care. Many hands make for light work, right?"

Ethan looked unimpressed. "As long as I don't have to do all the work because they have no idea what they're doing."

Jacob tried to count the people around him, but it was hard. They were moving around, and a constant stream of new faces meant the group grew quickly. He guessed there were anywhere between 200 and 300 men.

"So, what happens next?" Ethan asked impatiently. "Are we too early?"

"I'm sure we'll get started soon."

More people joined, and there were now a good 300 men assembled. It didn't take long until the doors opened and five men in SS uniforms stepped out, all lower-ranking officers. Behind them, a larger group of Dutch MPs lined up.

One of the men carried a stack of papers and double-checked them before raising his hand—the group went quiet.

"Good. That's how I like my workers to be," the officer said in German. His name tag read Muller. "Silent and obedient."

"You've all volunteered for this job, and we've created work details for the different tasks to be carried out," Muller continued. He stood tall, upright, and had no trouble looking the men in the eye. "Based on your skills, you will follow one of my colleagues to different parts of the camp."

"You will report here every morning at 6:30 sharp. Make sure you've eaten, as you won't have time for that during the work. Failure to report will have severe repercussions." He emphasized the last word by pausing and looking at the group for a few seconds. The men remained silent.

"Now that we've got that covered, one more thing: some of you will be working outside the camp perimeter. You might think you're free. You'd be wrong. Any attempt to escape will be met with the same repercussions I spoke of earlier." He patted the pistol in his hip holster. "I trust I don't need to explain myself further."

Jacob glanced at Ethan, who kept his gaze firmly in front of him.

"Other than that, we expect all of you to carry out your work in a professional manner. You will be working on the great *Reich's* future, and you should feel honored to be given this opportunity. Now, I will read out the work assignments. When your name is called, step forward and join the group at the front."

Muller filed through the stack of papers and proceeded to read out the first names. The first group would place barbed wire and dig a moat around the perimeter. Jacob looked at Ethan and frowned. *Barbed wire is new.*

The first, and largest, group left with plenty of military police in tow. Jacob and Ethan's names were called in the last group. They were informed they'd work on expanding the housing Deppner had mentioned earlier. They would be building new barracks.

As the seventy followed their SS overseer, the man was keen to impress them with the importance of the task ahead. Jacob and Ethan were near the front of the group, so they overheard him speaking to one of the Dutch policemen:

"Once we're done with all the expansions, we'll be able to house more than double the current population. This will be important for the Reich, as we need more hands to help out in the war effort in the east," he said, his face beaming with pride. He didn't get more than a polite nod from the policeman, who looked uncomfortable.

"Double the population?" Ethan murmured to Jacob. "I wonder where they're going to get those people. Surely they're not shipping people off from Germany to come work in Westerbork, right?"

One of the men walking alongside overheard. "Of course not," he said. "Haven't you heard about the way they're treating the Dutch Jews? They've become the same second-class citizens we used to be in Germany. The ones we have in the camp now are political dissidents, but I hear they're rounding up normal people as well."

Jacob remembered what Peter had told them a few days ago. "I think it's likely they—or at least a large part of them—will join us soon enough. I just wonder how they think they're going to house double the number of people here without expanding the grounds. I didn't hear Muller mention anything about extending the camp perimeter, right?"

"Well, there's still plenty of space on the east side of the camp, where we play football. And he did say we'd be expanding the existing ones."

"Expanding sounds more like stuffing more beds in there," the man said.

*People wouldn't be happy, but the SS wouldn't care much about that.*

They walked to the far north-eastern corner of the camp, but stopped at the sandy area that still bore the scuffs of the most recent football game.

The SS man leading their work detail, called Schröder, ordered them over, holding a map of the camp. It had the current layout but also showed where the new buildings were to be built. The expansion required ten new barracks. The hospital was also set to be expanded. *Maybe they do care about our health?*

"We'll start with the buildings closest to the main road," Schröder shouted from the front. He didn't have a microphone, so he raised his booming and authoritative voice to get through to the men in front of him. His heavy build added to the impression of power.

"It's important we get these buildings up as quickly as possible. We have new prisoners joining the camp in two weeks—"

A small shock went through the group. *Prisoners?* Jacob heard murmurs of disbelief around him. Some of the men shuffled on their feet. It was the first time they had been addressed as prisoners.

"—and we'll need places for them to sleep," continued Schröder, unfazed by their reaction. "The current barracks will be expanded, but there won't be enough space for everybody. I want to get the first of the new buildings up within three days. Most of the material arrived at Hooghalen train station last night. We'll need to collect it there. For now, all of us will walk there and load up the supplies. I expect to have the foundation of the first building in the ground by the end of the day."

The murmurs increased, and somebody in the back spoke up: "Three days is mighty fast for a whole building—do we have any building plans available?"

Schröder turned his head sharply. "Step forward, whoever that was." His tone was hostile.

The sound in the group died down instantly; nobody moved.

"Step forward, now."

Again, there was no movement. At that point, one of the MPs in the back stepped into the crowd. He pushed his way through the ranks and grabbed by the arm the man who'd spoken up. He marched forward, pushing the man out in front of him.

Schröder dismissed the MP with a curt nod and turned to the well-built man. His shoulders were straight, and he looked at the SS man without fear.

"So you're questioning whether this group of men can accomplish building those barracks," Schröder said.

It was a smart move, separating the man from the group this way.

"Not really," the man said. "I just wanted to know if we have anything to go by. I'm an experienced builder, and I've never seen a building erected within three days before, let alone without a blueprint."

Schröder looked thoughtful, weighing the words of the man carefully. But then, his demeanor changed. His tone became milder. "So, you've built before. What's your name?"

"Olivier Fischer—and yes, I ran a construction company near Rotterdam before coming here."

The group watched in silence.

"Well then, Fischer. I think we're in luck"—he smiled and addressed the rest of the group—"It looks like we've found the group leader for this project."

Fischer looked puzzled.

"We should use all experience we have available," Schröder

explained, "and you're the perfect candidate to make sure we reach our goal not only today but also for the rest of the project."

"You want me to lead this group?"

Schröder nodded. "I couldn't think of a more capable man. And the most important thing is, you stepped forward and took your responsibility!"

Schröder had played him perfectly, Fischer's eyes narrowed as it dawned on him what it all meant.

Schröder clapped his hands sharply. "Well then, let's get the materials from the train station. That will give Herr Fischer some time to think about his approach—a third of you will stay to help unload."

With that, he turned and walked toward the gate, the chosen number of the men following him, prodded along by the Dutch MPs.

The walk to nearby Hooghalen was familiar to Jacob, but it had been a while since many of the men had left the camp. The village had a small train station with just two tracks. As far as Jacob knew, not many regular trains passed by. But today, a freight train and a dozen tractors with flatbed trailers awaited them. The local farmers had been recruited to help, and Jacob recognized Jan Steen next to his tractor.

The military police stood nearby, keeping an eye on the proceedings. Jacob saw a few of his fellow campmates looking around nervously. He hoped none of them were thinking about escaping. Apart from the MPs, he also spotted most of the SS soldiers holding their rifles at the ready. *They're leaving nothing to chance.*

Jacob's group was assigned to the last freight car, one stacked with wooden planks they were told to unload onto the flatbeds behind the tractors. The farmers would drive to the camp where another group had stayed behind to unload everything.

It quickly became evident that most of the men were in pretty bad shape. Some of them dropped their planks after the first few steps. Jacob and Ethan had no such trouble and easily carried two planks at a time.

Because they were a large group, their weakness did not matter; the first tractors rolled toward Westerbork within fifteen minutes. The German soldiers mostly looked on, but in some cases, they decided the men needed some extra encouragement. A few of the older men had trouble keeping up, and one soldier, in particular, enjoyed drawing attention to this.

"If you can't keep up, maybe you need to go back to your barracks, old Jew-man," he said as he walked toward his next victim.

The man ignored him and walked on, dragging a particularly heavy wooden beam. He huffed and puffed, his face red from exertion.

The SS soldier followed him. "You're holding up the entire line. You'll need to get fitter if you don't want to be a useless waste of space in the camp. We have no use for the weak."

The other soldiers laughed. "We have excellent facilities in the east for people like you," one jeered.

The man got to the flatbed and struggled to lift the wooden beam. Jacob had just finished loading his own pieces and turned around to help.

"No, no—he'll need to do that all by himself," the soldier said, grinning.

The man took a deep breath and—in an impressive show of strength—managed to tilt the beam at an angle. The people around him stopped and looked on. The beam cleared the top of the high pile as he gave it a mighty push. With that, the piece of wood slid onto the top of the pile. The man sighed loudly and rested his hands on his knees, his breathing short and unsteady.

The soldier looked surprised and, for a second, didn't know how to react. Then he caught himself and gave the man a single sarcastic clap.

"Well, well, you managed it in the end. Now get back to work—you're not even halfway through the morning. No time to rest!"

The man straightened his back. His face showed pride and a hint of defiance as he walked back to the train.

Jacob caught up with him.

"Are you all right, sir?" Jacob asked.

"Don't let them break you," the man said, looking tired but proud. "We need to keep going and do what they say. It's the only way to survive."

They spent the morning unloading the train. With the help of the farmers, the job turned out to be tough but manageable. Nobody tried to escape, and they returned to Westerbork in time for the midday meal.

Outside the canteen, the group joined the long queue of people waiting for their meager lunch. Jacob and Ethan stood in line, exhausted and anxious to get some food before starting their afternoon shift. The sun had slowly crept overhead as they had worked that morning, and while they had had some relief from the clouds, these were quickly clearing.

"It's going to be a grueling afternoon," Ethan said, looking up at the sky.

Jacob nodded while he kept his eyes on the people in front of him, and the line slowly crept forward.

"Do you think we'll be able to get a new building up within three days?" Ethan asked.

"Doubt it, although our group looks pretty strong. I kept an eye on them during the unloading, and nobody really struggled. Even the old man who was picked on seemed to be doing all right."

They got to the front of the line and were handed a bowl of watery soup. Jacob got lucky with a small piece of potato floating in the broth.

"You're part of the work party outside, right?" asked the woman behind the pot of soup.

They nodded.

She handed them an extra piece of bread from a separate pile. "Need to keep your energy up, they tell us."

They took the bread gratefully and sat near one of the barracks, savoring the brief respite and the sun on their faces. The food was as tasteless as usual, but they wolfed down the bread and slurped their soup with relish.

"You know, I think we might have a chance with building the barracks anyway," Ethan said, scanning the crowd. "That man who was appointed our group leader, what's his name?"

"Fischer, you mean?"

"Him, yes. If he is the experienced builder he claims to be, he might find a way for us to work together. There are plenty of strong men in our group."

Jacob took another bite of his bread. "If you look at it that way, it might work. Also, I don't think the quality of the current barracks is especially high. Ours has mismatching doors that don't quite close, and cracks in the walls everywhere."

"Exactly. If they want us to work fast, we just need to make sure the building is livable. It doesn't have to be a castle, right?"

"Did you hear that—the 'excellent facilities in the east'?" Jacob asked. It had been on his mind ever since that morning.

Ethan shook his head. "I saw something was going on, but I was too far away to hear. Must be referring to people sent to Germany and Poland." He cradled his soup bowl in his hands, tilted it toward his mouth to finish the last bit, and then wiped his mouth with the back of his hand. "It's nothing new, though, is it?"

Jacob looked doubtful. "I don't know. The way he said it, it sounded more ominous."

"I don't know what to say, Jaco. It sounds like they've got big plans with this camp, so let's take it one day at a time. Life hasn't been too horrible here so far, and I'd rather not find out firsthand what they're doing in the east if you know what I'm saying."

"It still doesn't feel right, but you're right—there's nothing we can about it now." Jacob noticed most people around them were heading back to work. "Let's see what Fischer came up with."

They arrived at the worksite to find Olivier Fischer hunched over a large piece of paper. Most of the men in their group were still eating or trying to find a bit of shelter from the scorching sun. The clouds had cleared, and the temperature was rising steadily.

Jacob and Ethan approached Fischer, who was busy drawing lines across the sheet of paper. A few other men looked on, but Fischer was engrossed and didn't pay them any attention.

*He looks a lot younger than I thought.* Jacob estimated him to be in his early forties, his tanned face devoid of wrinkles. His large hands drew straight and sharp lines across the paper, forming the unmistakable shape of a building.

Some of the men suggested improvements, but Fischer ignored them. Beads of sweat glistened on his forehead, and he seemed oblivious to his surroundings.

*He knows what he's doing.*

Ethan saw it too. "Even I can follow what he's trying to indicate with the lines."

Fischer was setting up a fundamental blueprint—it was important the men around him understood the primary purpose rather than get lost in the details.

Fischer put his pencil down and stepped away from his makeshift table of stacked wooden planks. He wiped the sweat from his brow and inspected his blueprint.

Jacob approached him. "Did you figure it out?"

Fischer nodded. "I think so. They gave me that list." He pointed at a piece of paper. "It lists all the materials we unloaded this morning. Schröder told me this is just the first shipment to get us started, and that we'll need to find a way to build the first three barracks with that pile."

"It's nothing fancy"—he raised his pencil hand to scratch his temple —"just wood, nails, and some hinges for the doors."

"They asked you to create the design?" Jacob asked.

"Yep—Schröder made it clear he didn't care how we got the barracks erected, as long as they're ready in about two weeks from now. He also mentioned they each needed to be big enough to house 200 people." He scratched his chin. "I think it's possible with this setup."

"You can count on us."

Fischer sized them up with a curious gaze and nodded approvingly. "I can use all the help I can get."

There was a small scene in front of them, where the men waiting around parted to let Schröder through. He took large strides toward the table before inspecting the sketch.

"That looks pretty good, Fischer," he said, following the paper's lines with his fingers. He hummed a little, his eyes darting back and forth like a rat's as he took in the details.

From close range, Jacob observed Schröder. He'd seen some of the SS men in Berlin let themselves go, enjoying their privileged lives a little too much. Schröder certainly wasn't one of those—he looked fit and alert. None of the puffy red cheeks of some of his colleagues.

"Very well, then," Schröder pronounced. "It all looks in order on paper. Let's see how you'll get this group of men to work for you and get it done." The men in the work detail had inched closer to get a look, and looked keen to see whether their German overseer approved.

"How long until we have the first building up?" Schröder asked, loud enough for the others to hear.

Fischer took a while to think about it while the other men looked at him expectantly.

"If everything goes well, it should be ready within five days."

Schröder looked at him for a second. Jacob could see his eyes shooting back and forth between Fischer, the stockpile, and the blueprint as he pondered a response. He rubbed his wrists.

"Wasn't I clear enough about the timing?" he asked. "We need to have the first three buildings up in two weeks. If it takes five days each, there's no way they'll be ready."

Fischer's expression didn't change, and he remained collected as he answered: "It's the best estimate I can give you now. I set up this plan in two hours, and we've never done this before. It might take three days— or it could be five or six. All I know is that the faster we get started, the better it'll be. The good thing is that we have plenty of hands, and there should be enough supplies for the first buildings."

The crowd stirred a little, but most of them nodded their support.

Schröder looked around and sensed the change in energy. *He must realize the men have faith in Fischer.*

"All right, then. I'll give you the benefit of the doubt. Your plan looks in order, and you're right—you have a lot of men who seem willing to work for you."

Fischer nodded, his fierce, bright eyes never leaving Schröder's.

Schröder addressed the men: "Fischer will brief you on how we'll get the barracks set up. Remember, if they aren't all ready in two weeks, we'll have a big, big problem. We have a lot of new people joining us, and they'll need places to sleep. If you fail, I'll be sure to let them know you couldn't supply them with a dry place to sleep. If the buildings aren't done by then, you'll join them outside."

This got the attention of the men, who looked eager to get started.

"All yours, Fischer. I'll be back to check on you later," Schröder said before leaning in a little closer.

"I'll check in here every morning and evening to see how things are getting along. If I even suspect you're taking me for a ride, you'll be on the first transport east." Schröder added the last threat in a hushed voice, which Jacob and Ethan did not miss.

Schröder turned and stomped off back to the administration building. The MPs stayed with the group, but Schröder would spend his afternoon in the comfort of his office.

Fischer blew out a long breath before turning to Jacob and Ethan. "There's no way I can keep an eye on all these men on my own. I'll need some help."

Ethan responded before Fischer could even ask. "Just tell us what to do."

Fischer smiled and looked at Jacob, who nodded.

"I think the best way to do this is to have three groups who all have their own particular tasks. Ethan, you'll make sure supplies are always available. I'll tell you what we need, and when we need it. Jacob, you will assist me."

"I can do that, sure." Ethan had a sparkle in his eye.

The groups set out, and within minutes the new build-site turned into a hive of activity. Fischer was everywhere, inspecting the construction site and making sure the material was up to scratch. Ethan's haulers efficiently supplied the required material for Fisher and Jacob's men to work with.

They spent the rest of the afternoon laying the foundation and finished just as dusk set it. The men were clearing away their tools when Schröder arrived.

"I'm sure you have some good news about today's progress," the tall German said as he approached Fischer with a scowl across his face.

"We finished laying the foundation for the first building," Fischer said as he walked away from the tool shed with Schröder in tow.

Fischer led him around the build-site, and for the first time, Schröder looked impressed as he inspected the foundation.

"If it weren't for these two young men over here, we wouldn't have been able to get this done so quickly," Fischer said, signaling for Jacob and Ethan to join them.

Schröder gave them a quick once-over but didn't speak to them.

"Very well. Not a bad start, but I expect to see much more tomorrow." He motioned toward Jacob and Ethan. "Since you seem important to him, I'll make sure you hold the same responsibility as he does."

They looked at him, not sure what to say. This appeared to please him as he smiled. "If you do well, it will look excellent for you. If you fail? Well, things might not be so good."

He didn't wait for an answer. Instead, he took out an expensive-looking pocket watch. "Better get going, gentlemen, or you'll miss your dinner. You'll need all the energy you can get for tomorrow. Bright and early—I expect you here at 5:30 am sharp to go through your plans for the day."

Jacob heard Ethan balk next to him.

*Five-thirty? I thought we were supposed to start an hour later.*

Schröder left them standing there.

Fischer recovered quickest. "I'm sorry he's placed the responsibility on you now, as well."

"Apart from the early start, it's not too bad," Ethan replied. "Most of the men in the group are quite willing to work hard. Right, Jaco?"

Jacob's eyes were fixed on Schröder as he walked away and caught up with some soldiers on the main road. He appeared to say something funny, as they all laughed, and Jacob turned back to Ethan.

"I don't even mind the early start that much," Jacob said. "I'm more worried about getting everything built quickly enough. But you're right —the men are fine. Not all of them are strong enough to spend a whole day working, but they're willing."

Fischer nodded. "We didn't get to pick and choose, but we'll manage. There is so much to do, and we can give the older ones some lighter work. Let's head back and get something to eat. Schröder was right about that—it will be busy tomorrow, and an early start will help."

They turned onto the main throughway where tired men joined them from all sides of the camp. It had been a strenuous first day under the new command.

"What about the plan he was talking about?" Jacob asked Fischer. "Do you know how to get the rest of the buildings up?"

"Leave that to me. I've got it all up here"—Fischer tapped the side of his head—"I'll draw up some more detailed plans, but we'll have most of the building up in a few days."

Jacob was curious about this man who took control of the build-site with such authority. He carried himself with confidence, and while his face betrayed that he was just as tired as the rest of them, his broad shoulders were pulled backward, his back straight.

"How did you end up in Westerbork, Olivier?" Jacob asked.

"The same way most people got here. Before the war, my company thrived. I built houses everywhere in the west of the country, and there was plenty of work. When the war started, it didn't affect me much. Houses still needed building. But when the Germans invaded, things changed." He paused and looked at Jacob. "I'm sure you've noticed that as well, right?"

"Sure—we could tell from the time we spent outside the camp and the things we heard from the local people. But Westerbork has remained pretty much the same in the time we've been here. So what changed for you?"

"A few months after they invaded, I was told I couldn't continue my own business any longer."

*That sounds familiar.* Jacob remembered vividly.

"So you just packed up and left?"

"We had no choice. My business was officially closed, but I managed to get by doing the odd chore for people. I mean, things still break down, and houses need repair. Those jobs kept me going, fed my family, until one day last month, I was caught by one of my competitors. He reported me to the authorities." Fischer sighed as he continued. "It was then that we were told to pack our bags and be ready to leave the city the next day. My wife and I didn't know where to, but the next day we were on a train to Westerbork."

They walked on in silence for a while. Passing the camp's perimeter, they noticed tight rows of barbed wire had replaced the simple fences. There were also the beginnings of the moat.

A little way ahead, a stack of wooden planks was piled up near the fence.

"That's odd—there's no way we could fit another barracks there," Fischer said as they walked toward the pile. There were no more than a few meters between the barracks and the fence; the wood stacked neatly in between.

Fischer inspected the pile and frowned. "This isn't enough to build barracks, even if there were enough space." He walked around the heap and lifted one of the planks. It was a lot longer than the ones they were using for the barracks. "If I had to guess, I'd say it looks like they're building a watchtower here," Fischer said. He looked down the fence. "Look, there's another pile."

They walked the short distance to the other stack.

Sure enough, the material at the corner of the fence was the same quantity as what they'd just seen.

"This is starting to look more and more like a prison," Ethan said.

Jacob was late for dinner but managed to get a small plate from van Drunen in the kitchen. He walked back to the barracks and found his mother chatting outside along the way. She saw him approach and smiled a big smile as she excused herself from her conversation. They walked to their barracks, where it was relatively quiet and sat down in their private room. The weather outside was still warm, and many of the others had chosen to stay outside.

"You look tired," she said as she sat down. "What did they make you do today?" She studied Jacob with concern.

He brushed her worries aside. "It wasn't too bad. We're working on building new barracks on the other side of the camp."

She nodded. "I spoke to some of the others just now, and anybody who can hold a hammer is in construction. The SS are really set on expanding this camp as quickly as possible."

"We need to finish the work within two weeks, they said. I'm sure new people will be arriving before that," Jacob noted, leaning back onto his bed. He suddenly felt drained. "Did you see Papa today?"

"Yes, he had a quick break just before midday. He's been busy in the hospital."

"Has his work changed at all, or is he still helping the doctors?"

His mother nodded and smiled. "Of course, they recognized his value. All the doctors are still working there, and they made sure everybody else stayed on as well. Your father was very relieved to be able to do his rounds again this morning. But why don't you ask him yourself?"

Jacob followed his mother's gaze and saw his father in the door opening. He looked sharp in his neat, checkered shirt and brown pants. His hair was combed back, and the only thing missing was his pharmacist's coat. He preferred to leave that at the hospital, especially in the warm weather. His face broke into a wide grin.

"So nice that we're all here quite this early," he said, sitting next to Elsa. "It's been an odd day."

"How come? Changes in the hospital?" Jacob asked.

"It's almost business as usual, apart from the SS making their occasional rounds. No, it's more about what's going on outside. They're expanding the hospital. I saw work crews carrying material in all day. Actually, I heard them more so than saw them. It's not good for the current patients."

Jacob nodded. "It makes sense. There will be lots of new barracks, and I suppose more people in the camp also means more sick people. The standard of the new barracks is hardly going to help." He told his parents about the construction. His father listened silently, but Jacob could see he shared his concerns about the quality of the new buildings.

"They appear rushed with the hospital as well," Hermann replied. "From what I've seen, the SS have big plans. Dr. Brunner told me they're building two new wards. There are even rumors about dental facilities being installed. Incredible, don't you think?"

Jacob was surprised. Why would the SS care about the health of the prisoners? He mentioned the other expansions around the perimeter.

Hermann didn't have an answer. "I didn't see any of the barbed wire, but I did hear about the watchtowers. I guess it makes sense if they're bringing more people into the camp, though."

"It's going to be more crowded, and we'll have less space," Jacob said. "The barracks we're building are still in the normal perimeter of the camp. I don't think they're moving the fences." Jacob looked to his mother. "Are you allowed to keep your job at the school?"

Elsa nodded, her eyes lighting up. "We were all allowed to stay on. Levi, too."

"Just like the old days—is Salo still around as well?" Jacob asked.

Salo Carlebach was one of the younger teachers in the school, and the children adored him. He even spent his time playing games with them after school.

"He sure is," Elsa said, still smiling. "The school wouldn't be the same without him."

Jacob opened a drawer and found the book he was looking for.

Hermann asked, "Some more studying?"

Jacob smiled. He was glad his father had insisted on taking some of his medical books when they fled Berlin. The evenings in Westerbork were quiet, and he enjoyed continuing his make-shift studies to become a pharmacist.

"Once you've finished those chapters, you should come to the hospital. Perhaps you can put some of the theory to practice—we can always use some extra hands." Hermann lay down on the bottom bunk with a groan.

"I'd like that very much," Jacob said as he climbed up to his bunk, opening the textbook. He fell asleep half-way through the chapter.

It was still dark when Jacob met Ethan and Fischer outside the administrative building the next morning. Only a few other men were there, probably with the same summons from their SS overlords.

"I heard they were still drinking and smoking in their houses late into the night," one of the men said. He had oddly large ears, making his head look smaller than it was. "But, of course, they make us appear here before the crack of dawn." He spat on the ground.

A larger man gave him a reproachful look. "Watch out what you're saying. The walls have ears. You don't want to get in trouble with them."

The men around him nodded and murmured their assent.

"It's true, though, isn't it? We're just waiting around for them." The man with the large ears wasn't backing down and looked around for support. When he found none, he walked away to sit on a nearby bench on his own.

Jacob shook his head at the man's grumbling. Even within the

Jewish community in the camp, some people would have no problem sharing this information with the SS. Many people were evicted from their houses in Berlin, based on anonymous tips. He'd learned to keep his mouth shut and trust no one but Ethan and his parents.

Ethan gazed at him knowingly. "What do you think the odds are on that one getting transferred away somewhere pretty soon?"

Jacob looked at the other men in the group. He knew a few of them, but a lot were new, like Olivier Fischer. He shrugged. "You never know who you can trust around here, right? Better to keep to ourselves."

"Olivier seems like a good guy, though, wouldn't you say?"

Fischer was talking to some of the other men, peering over some hastily drawn-up plans. He looked animated and genuinely interested in what the other men had produced.

"I think he's one of the good ones, and he seems to trust us as well," Jacob said. "It's good to make some more allies. In two weeks, we'll need to be ready for a lot of new people. And you never know what they're going to be like."

One of the men overheard them. "The new people? They're all Dutch Jews."

They looked at the man who'd spoken, a bit older, wearing ragged clothes, and from his sturdy build, it was clear he'd always worked with his hands.

"Where did you hear that?" Jacob asked.

"Our German handler was quite happy to talk about everything that is going to change. We're working on the barbed wire, and he was overseeing the work. I asked him what else was done, and he told me about the other construction work going on." His left eye twitched every few seconds. "He told me they're rounding up all the Jews in Amsterdam and sending them to Westerbork."

"All of them?!" Amsterdam had one of the largest populations of Jews in the country. Even with the new barracks, they would have too little capacity.

"That's what he said. He said it didn't matter where they were from —eventually, all of the Dutch Jews would make their way through Westerbork."

Jacob and Ethan exchanged a look. "He said *through* Westerbork?" Jacob asked.

The man nodded. "That's what he said—there's only one way to go from Westerbork, and that is to work in the camps in the east."

"He said they'd go to the east?" Ethan asked, his face lined with worry.

"No, no. You know they like to drop hints and leave us to think about it." He looked at them with a curious expression. "Don't tell me you're not getting the same half-baked information from your overseer?"

Jacob shook his head. He didn't trust the man with the twitchy eye. Ethan raised an eyebrow.

"He didn't, actually. But thanks for telling us about this. We'll keep our eyes and ears open as well," Ethan said.

Before the man could respond, they were interrupted by the sound of boots crunching the gravel. They knew what that meant before they saw the troopers approaching, Schröder in the lead. This time he wasn't cracking jokes. They all looked a little haggard. Perhaps the story about a late-night with beers was true. Apart from that, the men looked just as imperious as they had the previous days. Their uniforms were freshly pressed, and they sported shiny boots.

Ethan also noticed. "I bet they got someone to shine their shoes overnight," he whispered to Jacob.

The soldiers stopped in front of the administration building, and the Jewish crew assembled around them.

"Happy to see you're all here on time, gentlemen," Schröder said evenly. He didn't appear to be suffering any side-effects from the night before. "We'll meet here every morning at this time. All of you will give us an update on how things are progressing, and if this is satisfactory, you'll be able to get on with your day, starting at roll call, of course."

Schröder scanned the group, briefly making eye contact with Jacob. He thought he saw a glimpse of recognition, but the SS man moved on quickly enough. *He probably didn't remember yesterday's chat. All the better, I don't want to be singled out.*

"Right—let's get an update from the work crews," Schröder said.

"Fischer, how about you start with the situation with our new barracks? The first one will be done later this week, yes?"

Fischer responded in his usual calm manner, using his latest sketch to show his approach for the next few days. The men crowded around, and even the soldiers were impressed by his preparation. Jacob saw it annoyed Schröder, who looked like he'd hoped to catch him out.

It took half an hour for all crew leaders to provide their updates. After that, Schröder dismissed them, and Jacob and Ethan caught up with Fischer. They'd just heard about all the planned expansions for the camp. There hadn't been any mention of why the expansions were done, other than the increased capacity. Nevertheless, the extra security measures worried Jacob.

# CHAPTER SEVEN

The next two weeks were much of the same. Early starts, roll calls, and days of hard work with little rest. Jacob went to bed exhausted every night, only to rise earlier than everybody else. Despite the harsh conditions, he felt himself getting stronger every day. He made sure to stay on the good side of the people handing out food, and it helped that he knew many of them.

Olivier Fischer gave Ethan and Jacob more responsibilities on the worksite, and by the end of the first week, they'd managed to get the first building up. It was the most basic building Jacob had ever seen. Despite their best efforts, the material provided meant the walls creaked, the flooring was uneven, and the loosely hinged doors made the building very susceptible to the elements. The most important thing was some sort of shelter for the prisoners scheduled to arrive in a good week's time. Schröder had inspected the building and had been pleased.

In the first few days, Schröder had stomped around the build site, inspecting and questioning everything. He'd ridden Olivier hard, but the man had somehow managed to keep his composure. He had an explanation for everything, and Schröder couldn't pick at any faults. As a result, Schröder stayed away from the build site after that, happy to have the MPs oversee the prisoners. He'd show up every morning and evening to check on the progress, but he spent most of his time indoors. That was fine with Jacob, who felt nervous whenever the SS man was nearby.

The third barracks had been the easiest to finish. With all the experience from the first two, they finished it in record time. The crew was finishing the building's interior, where large bunk beds needed to be installed. With three beds stacked one above the other, Jacob didn't envy the future inhabitants.

"You ever saw a triple bunk bed before?" Olivier asked, appearing next to Jacob and slightly startling him.

He shook his head. "It doesn't look comfortable, but the beds look solid enough. I wouldn't want to be in the top bunk."

Olivier walked past the rows of beds. His trained eye spotted every possible mistake as he silently inspected the work. The space between the bunks was small, and people would have to squeeze between the beds to climb up.

"There must be more than two hundred beds in this one alone. That's at least three times as many as the current ones," Jacob said while Olivier crouched down near one of the beds, bolted down to the floor.

"I know, but those are the specs they needed. You can be sure that they'll need all these beds, though."

"Did Schröder tell you when the first new people are expected?" Jacob asked.

Olivier looked at him with a smile. "What do you think?" He started walking back to the entrance of the building. "Of course he didn't. All he cares about is the building staying upright and having these bunks installed."

He patted one of the beds, or what was supposed to be one—there were no mattresses or blankets. They'd been hastily constructed with the same wooden planks they had used to build the walls and had small pieces of steel on the bottom to bolt the beds to the floor.

They stepped outside, and the bright light hurt Jacob's eyes. The sun had been a blessing and a curse in the past two weeks. They'd been fortunate not to have had any rain, which would've delayed their progress. Nevertheless, the sun had burned down relentlessly, and quite a few of the men had collapsed. Most of them were taken to the hospital, where Jacob's father was waiting to help treat them. A few fights had broken out during the construction, as tempers flared in the hot weather.

Jacob took in the warmth of the sun, its rays feeling a lot better now that the hard work was done. They were lucky the Dutch military police didn't care too much and often just stood around chatting among themselves, smoking cigarettes, and keeping a very loose watch.

"It's time to eat, Jacob," Olivier said. "Let's get our men out, so we're the first to get back. We might be lucky and get some good portions. And then we'll finish the last building in the afternoon. The beds look fine, and as soon as the lights are up, we'll be done."

Jacob looked back at the build site as they walked to the canteen. He was proud of what they'd accomplished in only two weeks. The buildings weren't perfect, but considering the material they'd had to work with, they weren't half bad either.

After dinner, Jacob joined his father on his rounds through the hospital, pushing a cart with small cups filled with pills.

"This will give you a much better understanding of what you're reading in the books," Hermann said, as they entered a large ward. It was tranquil—most patients had just eaten and either napped or read— it was comforting to see books.

The work at the construction site sapped most of Jacob's energy, and he hardly read more than a few pages before falling asleep each evening. His father had noticed. *Probably wants to encourage me.*

They approached an older man in a bed near the window. He didn't look too ill and smiled as they approached.

"Ah, Hermann, this is the son you always talk about?" The man spoke with the raspy voice of someone who'd smoked his whole life.

Hermann smiled and patted the man on the shoulder. "This is Jacob. He's training to become a pharmacist as well."

The man nodded at Jacob. "How's life outside? You look strong and healthy, so they must have you working hard?"

"I'm in one of the construction crews. It's tough work, but I like being outside."

"Not much working outdoors if you succeed your father," the man said with a wink.

Hermann handed him a small cup from his cart—the man pulled a face but took it anyway.

"Whenever I take these, I always need to run to the bathroom right after. But your father says they're good for me, so I just put up with it." The man swallowed the pills without any water.

They handed out a few more cups to the other patients in the ward before turning back into the hallway. It was quiet, and the distinct smell of the disinfectant hung in the air.

"That was the last ward for tonight," Hermann said as he pushed the cart along. "The most important thing about this job is making sure people are taken care of. It doesn't matter if that's in our own pharmacy or this hospital. That man we just spoke to—when he came in, he wouldn't take those pills."

"Why not?"

"He was convinced they would kill him. Instead, he thought if he only drank watered-down tea, he'd be fine. He's a character."

"How did you get him to take them anyway?"

Hermann smiled. "Let's just say the alternative I gave him was a lot worse. He's much better now."

They parked the cart in the medicine room, and Hermann locked the door. It reminded Jacob of their evenings in Berlin. They would lock up the store in much the same manner. His father looked at him, and Jacob could see he was thinking the same.

"I need to see if Dr. Brunner is still in—I think we're running low on aspirin," Hermann said. "Deppner hasn't been too concerned about refilling the medication since he took over."

*No surprise there.*

"Why don't you go ahead to the barracks?" Hermann continued. "I'll be there in half an hour. Hopefully, Dr. Brunner has a solution."

Jacob confidently navigated his way through the maze of hallways to the exit. He was glad to have the pharmacy books. The construction work kept him occupied during the day, but he wanted more. Life was on pause in the camp, and he wanted a life after this—when the world came back to its senses.

"Whoa, watch where you're going there!" exclaimed a nurse in Dutch while she swerved out of the way just in time.

"I'm so sorry," Jacob responded automatically in the same language. "I was all caught up in my own world." Then he became aware of her.

"It's okay—it's a good thing I wasn't carrying anything sharp. Not this time, anyway," she said, looking up with a smile.

Her bright green eyes were hard to miss as they contrasted perfectly with her curly brown hair. Jacob hadn't seen her in the camp before—and he was sure he'd have noticed. She was probably a couple of years younger than he.

"Again, I'm sorry," he stammered. "It's been a long day."

She studied him for what felt like an eternity before she answered. "I'm fine, thank you. It wasn't *that* bad." To his surprise, she held out her hand. "I'm Agnes. I started last week."

Jacob shook her hand and managed to mumble his own name.

"I don't mean to be rude, but what's that accent I hear? You're not Dutch, but you speak my language," she said.

*Who is this forward young woman?*

"I'm from Berlin, but I've been in here for almost four years now," he said, slowly recovering his confidence. "It's an easy language to pick up."

She grinned. "Perhaps you can tell the other Germans? They seem to have a different conclusion."

Not everybody made the same effort to learn the local language. Even before the SS took over Westerbork, all official communication was done in German. It made sense, as nobody in the camp spoke anything but German. And most in the camp had little to do with the Dutch. That changed when the Dutch Jews had arrived the previous week. A chasm was already forming between them and the German-speaking inhabitants.

She studied him with curious eyes.

*She's very confident, nothing like the girls back home.*

"So what are you doing in the hospital? I haven't seen you around before," Agnes asked.

"Hermann Kagan is my father, so I came to see him."

"I know Herr Kagan! He's been so helpful in getting me set up here. So, are you a pharmacist as well, then?"

Jacob shook his head. "I've always worked in our store in Berlin, but I'm not qualified. Not yet, anyway."

"Not yet?" She cocked her head, a few strands of hair bouncing around her face.

"My father is teaching me the basics. We had our first practical lesson tonight."

Her eyes lit up. "That's amazing! Does he teach a class or something?"

"It's just me."

She seemed to hesitate for a moment before speaking, her voice rising an octave or two. "Do you think there's space for another student?"

He smiled, but before he could answer, she continued:

"I was in my second year to become a nurse when the Germans invaded. That's when I was no longer allowed at school. I would love to join your class."

"I'll ask him tonight. I wouldn't mind having some company."

A smile spread across her entire face. "That's great, Jacob! I'm already very grateful to work in the hospital—I've really missed learning about medicine and taking care of people. In a way, coming to Westerbork has allowed me to do what I've wanted to do all along. It's weird that I have to be locked up for that, huh?" She looked at the clock on the wall next to them. "Speaking of that, I need to get going. Hopefully, I'll see you in class soon?"

With that, Agnes strode down the hallway.

Jacob shook his head and made his way out of the hospital. As the fresh air hit his face, he wondered what his father would say. It wasn't common for women to be pharmacists—but what *was* normal these days, anyway? Agnes could use the classes to become a better nurse—that would help everybody in the hospital.

*I hope he says yes.*

Jacob spent the next day helping Olivier fix some problems in the new barracks. They tried to cover the cracks as best they could—what was a pleasant breeze in the heat of summer would be brutal in winter—and made sure all the lights worked. The barracks were as good as they were going to be.

In the evening, Jacob and Agnes walked together out of Hermann's shared office, which served as their makeshift classroom.

His father had been excited to hear of her interest, and they'd spent the previous two hours rehashing the basics. Unsurprisingly, Agnes had had no trouble keeping up—Jacob suspected she'd covered all of this before, but she had been too polite to mention it.

"I know it's just the first class, but it's all coming back to me now," Agnes said. She looked happy as they left the hospital. "Your father is an excellent teacher."

"He likes to talk about his work," Jacob said with a smile. "Plus, my mother is a teacher, so I think she's given him a few tips here and there."

Agnes shook her head. "It's not just that. You can tell he enjoys teaching us about it. Especially you."

"Back in Berlin, we all kind of assumed I would take over the pharmacy the way he did from his father. It's partly why I enjoyed working there so much—one day the place would be mine, as long as I worked hard enough. That future looks very far away now."

"Don't give up on it. This can't last forever, right? And as long as we're here, we can learn from him." Agnes looked at him with determination.

They passed the barracks Jacob had finished the previous day. He pointed out the rickety buildings.

"You managed that in two weeks?" Agnes looked impressed.

"Yes, but they look better than they actually are. They're drafty, and there's very little space."

"So now that you're done with that, what's next?"

He sighed. "We have to report to our SS overseer tomorrow morning. He said we'll get new orders there. I don't know what that means."

"Maybe there's more construction work? I think they did bring in new supplies today, didn't they?"

Jacob shrugged. "I'll find out tomorrow. I don't want to think about it too much yet. So what was your life before Westerbork like?" he asked, leading her to a bench. "I know you were studying to become a nurse before the Nazis invaded, but that's about it."

She sat next to him and smoothed her skirt. "I spent my entire life in Amsterdam, and I always knew I wanted to become a nurse. My father was a doctor, and he encouraged me to go after my dream. We were always comfortable, and I never doubted I'd become a nurse. I have a younger sister, Yvette. She's a year younger, so we're very close."

She paused and rubbed her eye before continuing.

"When the Nazis invaded, everything changed, as for many of our friends. My father lost his job—he was no longer allowed to practice medicine. We have a large Jewish community in Amsterdam, and we managed to support each other. I guess you could call it an underground support network. That's what kept our family from going poor or hungry. When someone got sick, my father would help them, and they would help us if we needed something they could provide."

Jacob listened to her as they got up and walked back toward their barracks. It was close to dusk, and they'd need to be inside soon. Apart from the lights on the guard towers, there was little illumination at night.

"At first, the network was mostly supporting, but as restrictions increased, it changed into something more partisan. Talk of fighting back started."

"Like a resistance?" Jacob asked. He'd heard stories of the Dutch resistance before, but those were always second-hand.

She nodded. "They started small—spreading illegal pamphlets and forging documents. But it didn't take long before it escalated to violence. While my father never talked about it, we'd have nightly visits by wounded men he helped. We were always told to stay in our room, but Yvette and I knew what was going on."

"You must've been proud of him."

"Yes, but we were also scared. You need to understand many of these people were arrested and then simply disappeared. We were always frightened the same would happen to us. And one night, it did."

She swallowed hard before continuing.

"It was a night like any other when we heard the rap on the back door. It was our signal that someone needed my father's help. Yvette and I were already upstairs when my father opened the door. This time, though, something was different. Instead of the quiet footsteps we'd become accustomed to, we heard heavy footsteps. Although we couldn't see them—we were in our rooms—we heard them. They spoke in harsh, German tones. My father had been betrayed."

Jacob gasped. "Someone from the resistance had sold him out?"

"That's what we think." Agnes nodded. "Yvette and I hid under our beds, and when they came upstairs, we held our breath and hoped they wouldn't find us. It was the best thing we could think of."

"And?" Jacob held his breath as the sun disappeared behind the barracks as they slowly walked on.

She shook her head. "It didn't work. They knew we were there—whoever had sold my father out had told them about us as well. We were all hauled off in a truck. As we barreled through the dark Amsterdam night, my parents told us not to speak to anybody, as they were sure we'd be separated. They were right. As soon as we got to the police station, they were taken to another truck. That was the last time I saw them."

A tear rolled down her cheek before she turned to him.

"And I didn't speak. I kept silent all along, through all the interrogations. They told me I'd join my parents on their journey to the east if I didn't tell them about their activities. But I never spoke. That's when someone must've decided to take pity on Yvette and me because, after three days in an Amsterdam police cell, we were put on a train to Westerbork."

*It could've so easily been a train further east,* Jacob thought.

"I don't know what to say," Jacob started. "I'm so sorry."

She wiped her eyes. "You're the first person I've told, Jacob. Nobody knew about this, but Yvette and me."

"You can trust me, Agnes. Your secret's safe." His heart ached for her.

"This is me," she said as they stopped in front of one of the women's barracks. "Thanks for listening. It helped to share this with someone."

She stepped closer, and to Jacob's surprise, she hugged him. "See you in class tomorrow."

As he watched her disappear inside the building, he felt a warm, tingling sensation in his chest. For the first time in a long time, he walked down the darkening camp with a spring in his step.

# CHAPTER EIGHT

Jacob and Ethan stood with Olivier Fischer at their usual morning inspection with the SS overseers. They had finished the barracks the previous afternoon, but Schröder told them to report regardless. The rest of the detail leaders were also there. They'd made it a habit to be early, just in case the SS decided to make life hard for them.

The building was dark as always at this time of the morning. For the first time in weeks, a slight drizzle came down, and the men huddled up under the eaves, tense and reeking in badly-laundered and suddenly-damp clothes.

"Did anyone not finish their assignments?" Olivier asked as they waited. They all shook their heads, unsure of their purpose this morning.

They didn't need to wait long. Schröder showed up, with only two other men in tow. The morning briefings were typically attended by all SS overseers in charge of a work detail. *Something is off.* Jacob looked at Ethan, who nodded. *He feels it, too.*

Schröder was dressed for the weather, wearing a long, black overcoat and a traditional SS army cap. As they got closer, Jacob was surprised to see the men with Schröder were Dutch MPs.

"What an absolutely horrendous morning," Schröder growled as he spat on the ground. He turned to the group—the men had wisely moved away from the building to allow him some shelter. They now stood in the rain, the small drops slowly soaking their clothing.

"You're probably wondering why you're standing here this morning. After all, all the construction was finished yesterday," Schröder pulled the collar of his coat, "though barely in time."

Jacob resented his tone. They'd worked more than twelve hours a day to get everything done.

"But your job doesn't end there," Schröder continued. "We know you're capable men, and we know you can lead."

Jacob frowned, Schröder never handed out compliments. He hadn't been violent, but Jacob always felt the man's fury burned underneath the surface. Jacob's crew hadn't been victims to his wrath, but some men had misplaced parts of a watchtower and got an earful.

Schröder scanned the faces of the men while he took off his gloves. He rubbed his hands together.

"We need men like you in the camp organization. You know your way around. You know how people are supposed to behave. And most importantly, you're strong. The new prisoners will come in large numbers, and they need to be contained—controlled, even."

The men looked unsure. Something was not quite right.

"—Which is why, when the newcomers arrive tomorrow, you'll be there to receive them and guide them to the registration. We're expecting nine hundred men from Amsterdam. They'll arrive at the Hooghalen station and will walk here to be processed."

Schröder pointed at the group, slowly moving his finger from left to right. His face broke into an ugly smile.

"Well, don't you understand what this means? It means you'll stay around here, unlike the men arriving tomorrow!" His voice rose an octave. "While everybody else needs to prove their usefulness to Deppner again, your positions are safe! And it's all because you've done such a great job for me."

The men remained quiet while Schröder stuffed his gloves into his pockets. The drizzle turned into proper rain, and Jacob shivered.

"You, gentlemen, have been selected to be the first Jewish *Ordedienst*—order squad—of camp Westerbork."

Jacob and the other men selected entered the roll call area in silence, led by Schröder.

They passed their fellow camp inhabitants, who were already in their assigned positions. The SS insisted on perfectly straight lines, people getting out of line meant getting beaten back into their place. Jacob saw his parents in their barracks group. Hermann gave him a puzzled look while Elsa grabbed her husband's hand. She looked dismayed as Jacob passed them. He gave them his most reassuring smile.

Jacob was surprised to see camp commander Erich Deppner at the front. He feared the cut-out Nazi commander, in the few instances he was seen around the camp, he was cruel or just ugly.

Deppner's Dutch was quite good, so he was the perfect candidate to take over Westerbork. It was rumored he'd executed several Russian soldiers in one of the POW camps in the Netherlands during his earlier postings. Jacob had heard he'd botched some of the initial executions and had to deliver the fatal neck shots himself.

This morning Deppner stood looking over the group of prisoners, which was odd—roll call was usually carried out by underlings. As they got closer, Jacob saw Deppner's face was puffy, and his eyes a little red, probably not from a lack of sleep.

They got to the front, and Schröder turned around. "Line up facing them," he said, pointing to their fellow camp inhabitants.

*What's going on?*

Jacob and the other two dozen men did as they were told. More than a thousand faces looked back at them, devoid of emotion. He saw plenty of the men who'd worked in his crew as well. Some of them gave him a nod or a thin smile. Most just looked straight ahead. Nobody wanted to risk the attention of the SS.

To Jacob's left, Deppner stood only a few paces away. The camp commander picked up the microphone.

"As you know, a lot of work has been done recently to improve camp conditions." His voice boomed through the speakers and ricocheted off the surrounding barracks. "The new barracks will allow us to house more people here while keeping the good conditions you've become accustomed to."

Jacob flinched. The new barracks were horrible, barely shelter from the elements.

"We will use these new barracks right away. Tomorrow, a group from Amsterdam will arrive. There will be almost a thousand of them joining us."

The crowd gasped. This would double the population of Westerbork. Jacob tried to keep an even expression, watching Deppner from the corner of his eye.

Deppner smiled as he enjoyed the shock going through the people in front of him. "Yes, it is a large number. And now that the expansions are done, we'll reassign work duties. After breakfast, everybody needs to report outside the administration building. We will assess your skills once more and assign new duties."

A thousand new people was madness. Even with the expanded barracks, there wouldn't be enough space for everybody to have a bed.

Deppner wasn't done yet. "The men standing to my right have done a fine job making sure everything was finished in time." He glanced over at Jacob's group before continuing. "Because of this, they are an important element of our camp organization. From today onward, they will assist us in running Westerbork efficiently. You will listen to them when they tell you to do something."

He held up a white armband with the letters "OD" on them. "These men make the Ordedienst, and they will make sure the new people joining us will be handled smoothly," Deppner emphasized the last two words. "It is important you follow their instructions at all times."

Jacob felt all eyes on him. The looks on the faces changed. Some were no longer blank but had turned—hostile? Or was it envy? He couldn't tell—he had trouble meeting their gazes. Deppner and Schröder had deliberately placed him and the other new OD men opposite the other people of the camp. The armband was another way to set them apart.

He looked at Ethan, standing next to him. He too scanned the faces and turned to Jacob with a fearful look in his eyes.

The newly-assigned men of the OD stood in one of the smaller rooms of the administration building. They wore their new uniforms, handed to them after roll call. The dark green overalls had an almost military look. To make sure they didn't look too sharp, the German command had made sure the uniforms fitted poorly, in stark contrast to the intricately tailored uniforms worn by the SS. The OD were only Jews, after all.

Jacob had never been inside the building before. He was surprised by its simplicity and basic furnishings. From the outside, he had always imagined there would be nice, comfortable offices. Instead, it was sparsely furnished with only the bare essentials. The desks were neatly positioned in the middle of the room. A wooden desk chair provided little extra comfort, and only a few of the desks were equipped with typewriters. He assumed most of the men working here simply made do with pen and paper.

Deppner stood in front of them, flanked by Schröder and two SS officers Jacob had never seen before. More than twenty men in the small room made for a tight fit, and the prisoners curled into a semicircle of two rows. Jacob studied Deppner and realized the commander looked even more rugged from nearby. He had missed a few spots shaving, which gave him a haggard look.

The SS commander took a sip of water while he leaned on one of the desks.

"I want to make it very clear you've been selected for the OD because we believe the people in the camp trust you."

Jacob caught a whiff of alcohol on Deppner's breath.

"The large number of new people coming into the camp means we need to expand the current organization," Deppner continued. "This is why we're selecting more people to join the OD in today's selection, and people who will assist in the administration and the kitchen." He waved his hand dismissively. "You get the picture."

"The point is, we expect you to set the example, just like you did at the construction sites. We need you to keep order, and we need you to be our eyes and ears in the camp. When someone misbehaves, you tell us. When someone steals something, you tell us. When you hear of somebody thinking of escaping or anything like that, you tell us."

He took a step away from the desk and drew closer to the group. He inspected the men in the front row one by one. When he got to Jacob, he paused.

"What's your name?"

The smell of alcohol was now unmistakable, and Jacob breathed through his mouth.

"Jacob Kagan, sir."

"Very well, Kagan. You sound like you're from Germany, by the accent. Am I right?"

"Berlin, sir."

Deppner's face lit up. "A fine city, and a proud symbol of our nation's greatness, wouldn't you say? I grew up near Berlin myself, and I miss it. This small country is nothing like Germany. Hell, even Amsterdam is tiny compared to Berlin. So little to do around here, especially in this backwater camp."

Jacob simply nodded.

"Any others here from Germany?" Deppner asked, looking around the group. About half of the men raised their hands tentatively.

"It's good to know our OD has a fair bit of German influence then," Deppner said with a smile. "Even if it's Jewish."

Schröder and the other SS men laughed. "For Jews, they're not too bad," Schröder said. "Especially that one over there," he pointed at Olivier Fischer. "He drew up the plans for the new barracks. I didn't think he'd manage it, but somehow we have three big new barracks."

Olivier stood motionless and looked at Schröder without emotion. It had become his default expression whenever Schröder addressed him.

Deppner cocked his head at Olivier. "Is that true? You drew up the plans yourself?"

"I did." His expression didn't change as he looked straight ahead.

The commander stepped closer, but Olivier didn't flinch.

"So, if something's wrong with the barracks—if they collapse, say— you're the person responsible?"

Olivier raised his eyebrows slightly. "With the material and time we had, I believe we've done the best job possible. I don't see why the buildings would collapse. The people living there won't be too comfortable, though. But you're probably already aware of that—sir."

Deppner grinned and turned to Schröder. "This one's pretty confident."

Schröder nodded. "People will follow him. He's got the respect of the group. He's perfect for the OD."

From the expression on Olivier's face, Jacob knew his friend was calculating all outcomes.

Deppner turned back to Olivier. "In that case, I think we've found the leader of this OD. You'll be responsible for these men."

He walked back to his spot at the desk and picked up a stack of papers. He leafed through them and picked one out.

"The group arriving tomorrow. I have their details here. There will be around nine hundred Dutch Jews from Amsterdam. They've been marked for the first transport, which will also leave tomorrow."

Jacob wasn't sure he'd heard that correctly. *Leave tomorrow?*

Deppner sensed their surprise. "Yes, this camp will no longer be a refugee camp but a transit camp. We are now responsible for sending Dutch Jews to the work camps in the east."

Jacob felt his skin crawl. It all made sense now—the paltry conditions in the new barracks, the watchtowers, and the barbed wire. The people arriving wouldn't need too much comfort if they were only transiting through. But for how long would people generally stay? Surely they couldn't transfer everybody at once?

"While they'll have a long journey ahead of them, we'll make sure they're well prepared for the journey. The kitchen workers will prepare sandwiches enough for them—I think this will have them working through the night."

"Also, Schröder, let's make sure we set up enough tables to process all the people coming in tomorrow. And I'll inspect the existing men in the camp at today's selection myself—I want to make sure we keep the useful ones."

Deppner tossed the stack of paper on the desk. "That will be all. Schröder will work with you on the details for tomorrow." He looked at the men. "Let it be clear that I expect full cooperation from you all. Any problems, and you and your family, if you have family, will be on the next transport to the east. This job is yours only for as long as you are useful to us. Don't think for a moment that you're special."

A chill traveled down Jacob's spine.

Deppner's face broke into a wide smile. "But I'm sure you'll all do a fine job. Dismissed."

Schröder cocked his head toward the door, and the new OD of Westerbork marched outside for the first time.

"Deppner had a long night again, don't you think?" Ethan asked as they walked toward the small assembly hall to set up the next day's registration area.

"I've heard he usually opens his first bottle of beer a little past noon," said Jacob, "and doesn't stop until late into the night."

It was crowded around them as several work crews carried more construction material around the camp. They huffed and puffed as they struggled with the heavy planks.

"They're continuing with the expansions tomorrow, I've heard," Ethan said. "Apparently, Deppner wants more barracks built."

Jacob was surprised. "Wouldn't they need Olivier for that? Or us?"

"I don't know—perhaps our new job is more important." Ethan shrugged. "Either way, I'm happy not working in construction anymore. How hard can this new job be?"

Jacob wasn't so sure about that. It all started with the baggy uniform—it felt wrong in many ways. An ill fit, but even worse—Jacob felt dirty. He'd seen the looks on the faces at morning roll call.

"People might think we volunteered for this," Jacob ventured. "They might think we're on the Nazis' side."

Ethan dismissed his worries: "It won't be that bad—we'll make it clear we're still on the same side."

Arriving at the assembly hall, they found a group of fifty people waiting for them. Jacob recognized only a few. Two Dutch MPs approached them.

"Are these people here to help set up the registration area?" Jacob asked.

One of them nodded. "Yeah, you're the OD in charge?"

"I guess so," Jacob said, looking to Ethan, who nodded.

"Good, because they've been waiting here for over half an hour now, and getting restless. They're your problem now. Just let me know when you're done." The MP walked off and lit a cigarette, disinterested.

Some of the crowd looked at Jacob and Ethan with interest. There were no hostile glances, but they certainly stood out in their green uniforms among the others in their ragged clothes. The only thing they had in common with the other residents was the Star of David sewn onto their breast pocket. Jacob was still one of them, despite his new position. *Maybe they will see it that way, too.*

"Let's split up the work," Ethan said to his friend. "Let's each take half of the group and start setting up the tables and chairs. We can then take the whole group to the administration building and pick up all the paperwork and typewriters."

Jacob nodded and clapped his hands sharply, which got the attention of the people in the room. A crowd gathered around, fifty pairs of expectant eyes looked in their direction. Jacob explained how they would set up the tables, and without too much delay, they started to shift around the furniture.

It took less than half an hour to get everything in place, and after fetching and distributing the paperwork from the nearby admin building, they were done well before dinner. They inspected the area one last time—enough registration forms and a typewriter on every table. Processing a thousand people in this confined space would be a challenge, and they'd be held responsible if it didn't go well.

Then, with a word of encouragement, Jacob dismissed the people. None of them had made any trouble, but they had kept their distance.

"Maybe you're right," Ethan said as they walked back to their barracks to wait for the dinner line to die down. "They did seem distant."

"They would only speak when spoken to," Jacob agreed. "Even James, who never shuts up—he seemed quiet today."

"Quiet to us, sure. He was chatting happily with the others," Ethan said with a frown. "This OD position is going to be a curse, isn't it?"

"I've been thinking about it. We'll be doing the SS' dirty work, for sure. We're policing our own people. But there could be an opportunity to make a difference in a good way, too, you know."

"How so?"

"Think about it," Jacob urged. "Nobody in the camp is going to be closer to the German command than us. We'll have new people joining us tomorrow, for sure—there's no way the twenty of us can guide a thousand people from the station to Westerbork. And with more of us, there's more opportunity. As part of the OD, we'll hear all the news first."

Ethan looked at him. "Go on."

"Take today. Deppner flat-out lied about the people coming in tomorrow. Everybody in the camp thinks they're going to be around for a while. People are worried about a lack of space, a lack of food. Then he tells us we'll transfer them to the east the same day. The same day, Ethan!"

He lowered his voice as a group of SS soldiers passed them. One of them gave the two ODs a funny look.

"Look at the Jew police," one called. "How's the patrol going, boys? Ready to send them on their way?" The group burst into laughter and walked on.

Ethan squatted by the stoop of his barracks, gesturing to Jacob to sit on the step – scowling in the direction of the soldiers once their backs were turned.

"Forget about them," Jacob said, taking a seat. "What I'm trying to say is, we keep up the facade of helping the SS, but at the same time, we try to help as many people around us as we can."

Ethan had a sparkle in his eye. "I like your idea. But we'll have to be very careful. I fear that not everybody in our group will feel the same way. Some of them are quite happy to cuddle up to the SS."

Jacob nodded. "I know. I trust none of them. Well, Olivier has his heart in the right place. Let's see how he handles the new duties."

Ethan's eyes were alert. "We could keep an eye on people who need a little extra food, or who might need some more medical care."

Jacob added cautiously, "Let's see what happens tomorrow. We'll keep an eye on the way our fellow ODs handle the incoming prisoners.

By then, we might know who to trust or who is just in it to save his own skin."

Ethan stood, a signal he was ready to go inside for a rest. "I imagine there will be plenty of chaos as well. I mean, handling so many people in one go? That's got to be a challenge, even for the SS."

A few young boys banged open the door on their way out of the barracks, almost knocking Jacob off the stoop. They were loud until they spotted the two and then averted their eyes and quickly trotted off.

Ethan gave Jacob a look of concern. "They seem afraid of us."

"I know," said Jacob. "Can you believe how much our lives have changed? Less than five years ago, we spent our evenings in the Augustiner. Now look at us, patrolling for the Nazis in a faraway camp."

"Not even years—it's just hours since we changed roles!" Ethan shook his head and opened the door to the barracks. "I'm going to try to get an early night after I eat. We'll have a busy day tomorrow, I'm sure." He disappeared inside.

Jacob walked onto the main street. The afternoon rain had turned the sandy road into a muddy slough that tugged at his boots with every step he took.

His mind wandered back to Deppner's morning briefing. The man's mood swings worried him. He wondered if the stories about the executions of the Russian POWs were true. After seeing the man up close today, he had little doubt. The hairs on his arms pricked up. He had a feeling things in Westerbork were about to take a turn for the worse.

Jacob met Agnes outside the camp commissary after dinner. He handed her a piece of chocolate as they walked down the main road. It was a lovely summer evening, and he was glad they had a night off—his father needed to help Dr. Brunner prepare for the hospital for the next day's transport. Deppner had told them to be prepared for the men arriving to need medical care.

Agnes took a bite of the chocolate. "This is good—how do you afford it? The prices in the commissary are crazy!"

"I have my connections." He grinned.

They turned off the main road and passed Barracks 35—the orphanage. Children played outside, and Jacob kicked a ball back to them. He wasn't surprised to see Salo Carlebach amongst the children. The young teacher walked over to Agnes and Jacob with a smile.

"I'm so happy the sun is still out at this hour. Keeping them inside when it rains is probably the toughest part of my job," he said.

"You always know how to keep them entertained," Jacob said. "My mother says you work wonders in the school, even with the ones she has trouble controlling."

Salo shook his head dismissively. "I just like making them happy. I'm lucky they still let me take care of a class after the SS took over."

Agnes stood by, watching the children playing. Two small ones approached and now clung around Salo's legs, tugging at his pants.

"Have you met Agnes before?" Jacob asked, introducing her. "She works in the hospital with my father."

She smiled and held out her hand. "Lovely to meet you, Salo."

The children pulled at Salo's legs, and he pretended to almost fall over. They squealed in delight and called for help.

"We'll have to become more acquainted later, Agnes," Salo said as he struggled to stay upright—two more children joined the quest to pull him to the ground.

*Salo likes her, too. It's obvious why she became a nurse—people are drawn to her.*

As Jacob and Agnes walked on, they heard Salo collapse—the children now piling on top of him.

"I guess there are some characters in this camp, after all," Agnes said, pulling her hair back into a bun she secured with a pencil from her pocket.

"Salo's a great guy. He's been here for years, and he's had a big hand in setting up the school. The kids adore him, as you can tell."

They wandered a while longer and then sat down on a small tree stump near the camp's edge. Beyond the now completed moat and fence, there were only long stretches of fields.

"When we arrived at the camp, most of this wasn't here yet. We had to cultivate those fields ourselves, and we built most of the barracks. We thought this would be a temporary home," Jacob said, gazing into the distance. "And now I'm part of the squad that has to transfer people through this transit camp."

Agnes sat up. "Transit camp?"

He told her about Deppner's briefing earlier.

"So those people will be marched here, processed, and then sent back to the station?"

Jacob nodded. "That's the plan. And I don't think it's going to be a one-off. Those barracks we built aren't good enough to house people for longer than a few days. They're nothing like what you and I sleep in. I'm already cursing this new job."

Agnes stood up and paced between the edge of the moat and their spot, careful to stay away from the edge. Stepping too close would draw the attention of the guards in the towers—they would shoot without warning, Deppner had ensured them.

"Do you know where they'll be sent?" Her bright eyes were full of concern.

"No. This has never happened before. Deppner said they're going to work camps."

"Do you believe him?"

"The only work camps I knew of when I was still in Germany were brutal. I'm sure it hasn't gotten any better over time," Jacob said.

She sat back down next to him. They sat so close, their knees touched.

"I'm going to make sure those sent to the hospital tomorrow get the best possible preparation for their journey, wherever it is," she said. "It's the least I can do." She looked at him with determination.

He smiled at her. "That's also what Ethan and I decided—we're going to make their journey as comfortable as possible. I've heard some of the other men in the OD talk about how they're going to impress the SS. They seem genuinely excited about helping out. That worries me."

She put her arm around his shoulder, and his heart skipped a beat.

"You want to help people; maybe you can do some good as well. It might not be all doom and gloom."

He nodded. "Let's get through tomorrow. I'm sure you'll do an amazing job in the hospital as well."

"Not just me. I'm going to make sure we're ready for them. We can at least make it bearable in this camp."

They sat in silence, and Jacob silently cursed as the sun crept toward the horizon. He didn't want this evening to end—nor did he want the dawn to come.

# CHAPTER NINE

The barracks were unusually busy when Jacob awoke the next morning. It was a little past three-thirty, and Hermann stood next to him, fully dressed.

"Time to go, Jaco—everybody needs to assist with the new arrivals."

*The new arrivals.* The night had allowed him to forget about them for a few hours, but he was wide awake now. He dressed quickly and ran toward the canteen, where he skipped the queue and grabbed a bread roll from a massive pile.

Outside the administration building stood a truck, its engine puffing. Its headlights formed a cone of light illuminating a small scene of the frenzy of activity going on within the dark camp.

Jacob jumped aboard and found most of the other men already there, sitting in silence. Ethan gave him a sad smile from across the truck. The space was tight, and he saw lots of new faces. Their initial group of around twenty had expanded to well over fifty men.

"Cutting it close, Jacob," sounded Olivier's voice from the darkness in the front. Two more men hastily jumped in before the truck started moving.

Riding through the dark, empty countryside, the men had only the constant hum of the truck engine to disturb the quietness. There was no other traffic, and they reached the station within ten minutes. For Jacob, they were the most peaceful minutes of the past month.

Hooghalen station was quiet, with no curious locals hanging around as they had the last time they'd come for the train. Getting off the truck, they saw the SS regiment was already there with Schröder and Deppner waiting on the station platform. Dutch military police flanked both sides of the tracks. SS soldiers stood every few meters, forming a wall of power where the train would arrive.

Schröder and Deppner were talking animatedly—both looking flustered. They seemed to disagree on something, but it was Deppner who had the final word. Schröder looked up and called Olivier over, and he, in turn, motioned for Jacob and Ethan.

They walked to where the two Nazis towered over them from the platform.

"The train will arrive in ten to fifteen minutes," said Deppner crisply, in contrast to his presence the day before. "You will escort them to Westerbork. Our men will walk with you, so don't think of doing anything stupid." He pointed at the SS men standing nearby.

"The prisoners need to come with you peacefully. There will be something for them to eat at the camp," Schröder added. "That should be ample motivation for them to keep moving."

Jacob had seen the mountain of sandwiches back at the camp and knew they would have to make the journey twice that day, but he bit his lip. *How difficult would this be?* The SS men stood by, wielding their rifles.

"On our way to the camp, we want you to motivate these people. They've been traveling all night, so they'll be tired. Make sure we get to the camp without any stragglers. We need them at roll call by noon."

The sun slowly crept its way to the horizon, its first beams lighting the sky blood-red. The OD stood in silence, their eyes focused on the tracks. Before long, the approaching train could be heard in the distance. It didn't take long for it to chug into the station at a snail's pace.

Through the windows of the passenger cars showed the haggard faces of the people from Amsterdam. As the train stopped, the doors opened, and they piled out of the second-class carriages, desperate for some fresh air. It was clear some had been standing the entire journey. They carried small suitcases, although some had had the foresight to pack light, with only a backpack.

Jacob pitied them—they had no idea what awaited them. They had probably been torn away from their houses just yesterday, then packed onto a train to an unknown destination.

The new arrivals looked around, some with hope in their eyes. For a short time, the small station came alive with the hum of voices—men, women, and children enjoying the relative freedom of the station platform after their long trek.

That sense of freedom was quickly broken as the SS blew their shrill whistles, herding them off the platform. Jacob fell in line and guided them up the road. Although the sun had started its steady ascent, the rays did nothing to dispel the chill that went through his body.

The walk to the camp was slow. Jacob kept an eye on the people from his side of the road, while Ethan was in the front, chatting away with some of the younger men. Jacob tried to keep his distance from the arrivals when a man approached him.

"Say, where are we going?" he asked in Dutch. The man looked quite respectable; he studied Jacob inquisitively. Jacob noticed he didn't have the dead-tired look in his eyes that some of the arrivals did. He carried a small suitcase, but it didn't slow him down—he was able to keep up with the pace set by the SS.

"The camp is called Westerbork," Jacob answered in Dutch. "You must've heard of it, right?"

The man shook his head. "I haven't. Is it a labor camp?"

*How can he not know about Westerbork?*

"I wouldn't say that," Jacob replied. "It's been a refugee camp for over two years—before the Nazis took over." He nodded toward the SS men around them. "Now, we listen to what they say."

The man looked Jacob up and down. "I guess that's why you're helping them—in your green uniform."

Jacob felt stung. "It's not by choice, you know. Nothing we do in the camp is by choice."

The man stepped back from Jacob, raising his hands in protest. "Hold on—I didn't mean to offend."

Some of the people around them had overheard and looked over.

"Then you should keep your mouth shut and keep walking. You'll soon learn it's better to keep your head down," Jacob said, his voice rising more than he intended.

The man looked startled and stepped away, blending back into the crowd. Others averted their gaze and carried on. Jacob felt the adrenalin flowing through his veins and was startled when he felt a hand on his shoulder. It was Olivier.

"Are you alright?" He looked concerned. "Not like you to fall out like that."

Jacob shook his head. "He just got to me—accusing us of helping the SS because we're part of the OD."

"They have no idea what our lives are like," replied Olivier. "When I was still on the outside, nobody told me about Westerbork. As far as the Dutch are concerned, it doesn't exist. We don't exist."

They walked on, the words sinking into Jacob with every step.

"These people, they're from Amsterdam. They don't know about some small village in the east of their country, much less care about it. But remember, Jacob, they're not the bad guys. They're simply ignorant."

Olivier was right. The people marching alongside them were the condemned—names on a list to feed into the Nazi war machine in the east.

Olivier put his hand on Jacob's shoulder and gave him a little tug. "Remember that next time one of them gets under your skin. They're simply tired, and you're just another uniform escorting them to an unknown place. Some were probably with their families yesterday. Imagine getting ripped away from your house to be put on a train, then getting off here."

He spread his arms in an arc, indicating the surroundings. "I'd be cranky, too, you know? It takes a while to get used to this dreary landscape."

Jacob nodded. Olivier had a knack of putting things into perspective. He always found a way to connect, and it was no surprise the German command had appointed him the head of the OD.

The watchtowers of the camp appeared in the distance, as commotion broke out at the front of the group. Two young men had broken away and made a run for a small pine forest nearby. Everyone stopped to watch. Unfortunately, they also drew the attention of the SS and the Dutch MPs.

The distance between the road and the woods was at least two football fields, and Jacob knew the forest was too small for them to hide in—if they made it that far. Some of the younger men were cheering them on, oblivious to the danger.

Instead of chasing the men, the SS soldiers closest to the escapees drew their rifles. Jacob had a flash of nausea as he remembered them placing wagers on who could shoot the most birds while they were practicing outside the camp—they were accurate shots.

*They'll never make it.*

The first shot rang out, silencing everybody on the road. The two men sprinting in the field paused for a second—hesitating momentarily before stumbling on over the soft, muddy ground that sucked their feet into the ground.

*They're nowhere fast enough to get out of range quickly enough.*

More shots rang out as four soldiers lined up. The escapees were only halfway through the field.

It surprised no one when one appeared to lose his footing mid-sprint. His friend turned around and held out his hand. He tried to help the fallen man up, but he'd injured himself in the fall. He signaled for the unhurt man to go on alone.

Another shot pierced the air. Almost immediately, the man who still stood fell to the ground. His cry of pain reached the group with a slight delay, making surreal the scene in front of them.

There were now two stricken men in the field. It wasn't clear whether the man who'd been hit was still alive, but there was no movement.

Schröder—who'd been leading the march from the front—now stood with the shooters. He looked out into the field.

*Those men aren't going anywhere.*

The group was still quiet, and now all eyes were on Schröder. The German considered his options and then signaled for two of the soldiers to go into the field.

He turned to the group as the men jogged into the field. "Let this be a lesson for anybody who thinks they can escape."

The soldiers approached the fallen men, and one of the men cried out in fear as the Germans reached them. The Dutchman tried to wriggle away from the soldiers.

The soldiers looked back at Schröder, who simply nodded. It was almost imperceptible, but it was enough. They drew their pistols and pointed them at the two men.

The man on the ground held his hands up trying to shield himself. It was hard to watch, but like everybody else, Jacob was unable to look away.

Four shots pierced the silence before the soldiers jogged back to the group.

Schröder signaled to a small group of ODs to go into the field and collect the bodies.

"Off we go, then—we're almost at Westerbork," Schröder said matter-of-factly.

The rest of the march was done in silence. The only people talking were the soldiers, congratulating each other on a job well done. The Dutch MPs kept their distance.

Schröder walked in the front, on his own, his posture a little slouched.

As they passed through the camp gates, people stopped what they were doing and gawked at the endless stream of tired people. Jacob caught the sympathetic looks. Most people had once been like those now entering the camp.

Jacob found it easy to guide them to the roll call area. The shooting had dampened every spark of resistance. Everyone kept their heads down, putting one foot in front of the other.

Jacob and the other ODs lined them up on the field.

Schröder took the microphone and explained they would receive their share of food only after they'd registered. Some of them grunted, prompting almost immediate shushes from the men nearby. Jacob approved—they understood the need for obedience.

"When you've registered and had something to eat, you will report back here immediately," Schröder said. "We will then assign you to your barracks."

Jacob bit his lip. *Liar.*

The registration area teemed with activity when Jacob arrived behind the group. He was surprised and impressed to see the new arrivals patiently joining the queue, which stretched far beyond the assembly hall. Looking at them, it was clear why there was little trouble between them. The trip to Westerbork had exhausted them physically as well as mentally.

He threaded his way through the line and into the building. The rows of tables they'd set up the evening before were now manned by the administrative staff. Curiously, these people were also prisoners of the camp who had been just as fortunate as Jacob to receive new assignments. A group of SS officers oversaw the registration. Schröder was nowhere to be seen, nor Deppner.

*They must be enjoying their lunch.* Thinking about food made Jacob's stomach grumble, but he knew it would be a while until he'd have his share.

Ethan caught up with him.

"If this is what we're doing for the rest of our time here, I might well volunteer for a transport to the east myself," he said, pale and a little breathless.

Jacob looked at his friend, aghast. "Don't be ridiculous. This is nothing compared to the horrors you'll find in the east, and you know it."

"People getting shot in the middle of a field? You think it gets worse?" Ethan exclaimed, louder than he should have.

Jacob shushed him. "Keep your voice down. And yes, it will be worse in Germany. At least here they have to keep up the facade somewhat. The Dutch are already hostile against the Nazis. I'm sure this was an incident they'll want to avoid in the future."

Ethan looked unconvinced.

"Did you not see the way Schröder behaved after the shooting?" Jacob asked, his voice low and darting his eyes around. "It almost seemed like he regretted what happened. He wasn't his usual confident self."

Ethan shook his head. "I didn't pay a lot of attention to Schröder afterward, to be honest. I just wanted to get away as quickly as possible."

The assembly room was orderly, and the people processing the registrations efficient. There was a low hum of voices, but considering there were more than sixty people in the room at any time, it was oddly quiet below the sound of the typewriters clacking away.

They looked at the group of prisoners in the room. They were of all ages, sizes, and postures. Some looked like they did manual work, while others had the delicate builds of office workers and shopkeepers. Every so often, children clung onto their parents, their eyes darting around the room in shock and amazement. The only thing connecting the people here was their Jewish background. The Nazis didn't discriminate beyond that.

Jacob took his short lunch break to detour past the hospital. He nodded at one of the nurses walking through the corridor who returned his greeting but hurried on. The hallway was quiet, but looking into the rooms, he could see the beds were full.

"Look who graces us with his presence in the hospital." It was Dr. Brunner, a smile on his face. "You must be looking for your father."

*Or Agnes. Was she on duty?*

"Do you think he'll have some time for me? The wards look very crowded."

Dr. Brunner nodded and frowned. "Some of the people that came in today went straight to the ward—they were in a pitiful state. But you already know that."

"They traveled through the night, and some are quite frail. I suppose they're better off staying here in the hospital for as long as possible," Jacob said.

"That's what I would want, but Deppner is coming in later to check on them. From what I've heard, he wants to have most of them out of the hospital today. They're just here to recover from the trip." Brunner looked concerned. "I don't see the rush—it's either here or in the barracks—but I'll see what happens when he gets here."

*So he doesn't know, either.*

"From what I saw," Jacob said carefully, "they need all the rest and attention they can get. Where can I find my father?"

Dr. Brunner looked lost in thought. "Ah, yes. He's in the wards in the back. Just down the hall."

They went their separate ways, and Jacob pondered Dr. Brunner's words. It was odd that Deppner had gone to the trouble of sending people to the hospital. He intended to get them through registration and back to Hooghalen, after all. Why would he care about their condition?

His thoughts were interrupted when he walked into one of the wards, where people were resting quietly. He spotted his father in the back. Hermann was checking an older man's heartbeat, and Jacob waited until he was done.

"What a pleasant surprise," Hermann said, taking off his glasses. "What brings you here?"

Jacob gently guided his father to the hallway. "The people that came in today—did you attend to any of them?" He kept his voice low.

"I did. Most should be back on their feet in a few days." He breathed on his glasses and rubbed them clean with the back of his sleeve. "Why do you ask?"

"I just spoke to Dr. Brunner. He said Deppner wants them out of the hospital later today. Have you heard anything about that?"

His father looked thoughtful. "Deppner? I've never seen him in here before. But it's not entirely unusual. The SS comes in almost every day. They like to disturb the peace and show who's in charge of the hospital."

That was what Jacob had expected. Deppner would insist all would go on tonight's transport. He made a decision.

"Papa, the people who arrived today—they're not going to stay in the camp."

His father looked at him calmly. "I know—they're going to the work camps in a few days, right?"

"Not in a few days. We have to escort all of them back to the station this afternoon. Those in the hospital will have to come with us. That's why Deppner is coming."

Hermann's expression changed as his face creased with worry. "Are you sure? Some of them could barely make it to the barracks, let alone back to the station."

"Why do you think Deppner is coming here? He wants to make sure this is done. He's taking care of this one himself."

His father's face fell. "I suppose that makes sense. But what use are they going to be in a work camp in this state?"

"I don't think they care too much about that at this point. He just wants to get the correct number on the transport."

Jacob checked the time on the wall clock. He'd been away from his post for almost half an hour now. He needed to get back.

Hermann looked like he was considering his options.

"I'm going to find Dr. Brunner and see what we can do about this before Deppner arrives," Hermann said.

*It will have to do.* Maybe the medical authorities could delay the men's departure.

He said goodbye to his father and quickly exited the hospital. On his way back to the assembly room, he saw a cohort of soldiers led by Deppner was heading for the hospital. Jacob hoped his father was ready.


The queue at the assembly hall was almost gone when Jacob returned. He found Ethan inside, looking rushed.

"Was there still some food left?" Ethan asked as Jacob caught up with him.

Jacob realized he hadn't eaten. "I don't know—I went to the hospital instead."

Ethan looked surprised.

"To see Agnes?"

He shook his head. "No, I wanted to see what happened to the people who were sent to the hospital after coming through here." He looked at the last people coming through the door. "Sounds like they'll be on the same train as these people."

"No matter their state?" Ethan asked with concern. "Some were practically carried in."

Jacob nodded. "Deppner is in there now, checking on them. Dr. Brunner and Papa are going to try to keep as many of them here as they can, but we both know that will be hard."

Some of the registration desks were now empty. The clerks sat idle, unsure of what to do next. Olivier walked in, spotted Jacob and Ethan, and headed over.

"We're all done here," he said. "Schröder wants us at the administration building right now. Looks like we're heading out again."

Jacob was aghast. "Already?"

Olivier shrugged. "They won't waste any time if they don't have to. Let's go."

They made the short walk to the administration building, where the rest of the OD waited outside. Schröder stepped out of the building, as if on cue.

"Registration's done, so we're going to ship them back to the station, where a new train will arrive in two hours. I want to be there as quickly as possible. This time, let's make sure we don't have any repeats of what happened this morning." Schröder looked agitated, his face flushed.

*He's rattled. Did the executions in the field do that?*

The men were ready to return to the roll call field to finish the day's gruesome business when Schröder spoke up:

"One more thing—the registration showed the shipment of this morning was too low."

*Shipment?* Jacob frowned. He felt a familiar, uncomfortable feeling building in the pit of his stomach.

"That means we'll need to send some of the people from our current population along with the newcomers. About a hundred men have been picked to join today's transport," Schröder said.

A small wave of panic flowed through the group. While the OD had been promised they were exempt from the transport, they knew anything could change in an instant. Schröder sensed the unrest and signaled for them to calm down.

"You need not worry. You'll escort these men to the train along with the new arrivals. You might know some of them, as they were selected by Deppner this morning. With them, we have fulfilled the quota for today's transport."

Schröder descended the steps from the building and walked toward the roll call field. Olivier indicated for the group to follow. Jacob felt a heavy burden—who would they find waiting for transport? Would he know any? Walking beside him, Ethan was lost in his thoughts, a distant look in his eyes as they both flowed with the group and approached the group of a thousand condemned waiting for them.

The roll call area was noisy. The new arrivals' spirits appeared to have been lifted somewhat by the sandwiches and milk. Many had found a spot to sit down, and they chatted as they waited for the Germans to return. Along the perimeter of the field, the Dutch military police stood guard. SS soldiers in watchtowers kept a close eye—their long-range rifles at the ready.

Some of the people had regained a bit of color in their faces. He overheard a group talk about the possible barracks they'd be assigned to —they were much like Ethan and himself.

He stood on the side of the field with Ethan as they waited for Schröder to make his way to the front. Deppner stood, tapping his foot impatiently. Jacob saw him snarl something at Schröder, who deferred and stood next to the commander.

Jacob scoured the field and spotted the group of men who'd been part of the current population, gathered in a back corner of the area.

"Looks like they're keeping to themselves," Ethan said, nodding at the men. "I don't recognize anyone right away—do you?"

Jacob peered at them, but it was hard to make out all the faces. "No, nobody jumps out at me."

"Odd that they're sending the older men to a work camp, huh?"

Ethan was right. Jacob had expected to see some of the stronger men to be sent along, but the youngest he spotted were in their late forties.

They were interrupted by Deppner's voice booming through the speakers:

"There's been a change of plan. You will not spend the night in this camp but will transfer directly to the work camp you've been assigned to," he said.

A wave of surprise tore through the crowd. They looked at each other in confusion. Some were too tired to respond and stood there with blank faces.

Deppner carried on without acknowledging the restlessness in front of him. "You will set off to the station right away. And remember that any attempt to break away from the group will be punished."

*I'm sure we won't have to worry about that.*

The group set out along the main thoroughfare, the original hundred from the camp in front, followed by those from Amsterdam. Jacob was relieved to see none of the exhausted faces from the hospital among the group. Men, women, and children stood on the side of the sandy path as the procession passed. The silence was deafening, interrupted only by sobs from some of the women.

Jacob felt for them. Some of those men who had been in Westerbork for a longer time were leaving their families behind.

Hermann stood on the side of the procession. He looked sad as Jacob approached.

"I couldn't save them, Jaco. When you left, Deppner forced all of them out of the ward. A truck will bring them to the station," he said.

*No relief for them, after all.* "You did your best, Papa. I'll try to make their journey as comfortable as possible."

*Even though I don't know how.*

As the front of the group reached the gate, one of the women could no longer control herself. She dashed toward one of the men, who stopped as she fell into his arms. They stood still as the rest of the group silently passed by. Her wails cut through the silence as the man tried to keep a brave face, but soon both of them were shaking.

Jacob heard some shouting from across the group, but it didn't register. He was jolted out of his daze when two men from the OD pushed their way toward the couple. One shouted something at Jacob in anger. The other man barked at the woman to "get away."

The couple had blocked out everything around them. They gazed into each other's eyes, tears streaming down both faces. The man spoke softly as he stroked her face.

The moment was brutally interrupted when the two ODs reached them. One grabbed the woman by the shoulders, causing her to trip and fall. This caught the attention of the people around her. As one, the entire procession behind the woman stopped.

The OD men didn't notice. "Get moving—you have a train to catch," shouted the taller of the two, exuding power.

The prisoner ignored him and rushed to the side of his wife. He tried to help her up, but when he reached out to grab her hand, one of the ODs used his baton to lash out at his arm. A crack was heard as he struck the elbow. The man yelped in pain as his arm hung limply at his side.

The woman shrieked; some of the prisoners helped the woman up as she trembled.

The ODs were still focused on the stricken man and hadn't noticed the other prisoners closing in around them. When one of them lifted his baton again, the group stepped in his way.

"Get out of the way, or you'll have some of the same," the OD said as he waved his baton menacingly.

They didn't back down. "There is nothing you can do to us that the Germans won't do in their work camps," one of them said, as he looked at the ODs calmly.

The incident had developed into a stand-off. The two ODs were outnumbered—for now, but back-up would be on the way soon enough. The prisoners had nothing to lose.

"You should be ashamed of yourselves working with the Germans for a little bit of extra food," the large man sniped at the ODs. "You're betraying your own people, and now you're attacking them as well." He spat at their feet.

The tall OD wanted to lash out, but his colleague stopped him. "Look around you."

Ahead of them, a small gap formed in the procession as the rest of the group marched on.

Jacob wanted to stay away from the scene, but he also knew he needed to be careful. It would be only a matter of time until the SS noticed the hold-up. He decided to act before things got worse, and he stepped toward the group.

Jacob gently nudged people aside, keeping his baton firmly tucked away in the pocket of his pants. He didn't want to give them any reason to think he was on the side of the two thugs. The ODs were no longer confident, and their stances more defensive now. Relief spread on their faces at Jacob's approach. He ignored them and knelt near the injured man.

"Are you okay? Is it broken?" Jacob asked. At first, the man recoiled at the sight of another OD in uniform, but when Jacob held up the palms of his hands, the man relaxed somewhat. Jacob tried to be as non-threatening as possible. He inspected the man's arm.

"It looks like one of the bones in your arm is broken," Jacob said, as he gently massaged the man's arm at different points.

The man cried out when Jacob applied a bit of pressure. He'd seen his father do this many times.

"You're in no state to be in a work camp," Jacob said. "Let's see if we can get you to the hospital."

Up until this point, the two other ODs had waited, but with the situation seemingly under control, they regained some confidence.

"If you think this one if staying here, you've got another thing coming," said the tall one, with a scowl. "He was holding up the entire transport. When we told him to move on, he resisted. It was self-defense."

Jacob felt a pang of anger. "I saw exactly what you did. You attacked an unarmed man and his wife without provocation."

The man took a step toward Jacob. "So you're on their side, huh?" He waved at the people around him. "Not the best side to pick, wouldn't you say? They're heading out today, and we'll still be here tomorrow."

Jacob took a step closer to him and lowered his voice: "Threaten me again, and I'll find you and your friend over there. You disgust me. We're supposed to help these people, not injure them."

Their argument was broken up as a group of ODs, and SS soldiers appeared. The gap in the procession had attracted their attention.

"What's going on here?" one of the soldiers asked. It was quite the scene—the injured man on the ground and three ODs squaring up to each other.

Jacob and the other OD backed away from each other. The other man took the initiative:

"He was holding up the group. We told him to move on, and he attacked us. In turn, we had to defend ourselves."

His friend nodded while Jacob shook his head.

*Disgusting liars.*

The soldier's eyes narrowed. He looked at Jacob. "Is that what happened?"

Jacob looked the soldier in the eye. "No, they struck him down from behind, unprovoked, and broke his arm. He's of no use in the work camp now, thanks to those idiots." He nodded toward the two other ODs, whose eyes shot fire at him.

The soldier paused momentarily while he considered his options.

"You—on the ground—get up," he said to the stricken man.

The other men helped him up, and he stood in front of the soldier. His left arm dangled. The soldier reached out and roughly pulled on his arm. The man stifled a cry of pain, which sounded like a growl instead.

The soldier let go of the arm and turned to Jacob. "Looks fine to me. He'll go on the train as planned, and he'll be inspected by a real doctor at the work camp."

*What? He can't be serious!*

"But—" Jacob started.

The soldier interrupted him. "Shut it—I said he's fine. Or do you want to take his place?" He looked at Jacob menacingly.

Jacob turned away as the soldier addressed the group: "Enough of this nonsense. The train is waiting for us, and we can't have more delays. Let's go!"

Slowly, the procession started moving again. They caught up with the rest, and it wasn't long until the last of them left through the gates. Jacob walked on the side of the road in a daze but kept an eye on the stricken man. His face had gone deathly pale, and he needed support from the people around him. He would be of no use in a work camp.

The two attacker ODs walked on the other side of the group. Every time Jacob looked across, their eyes were on him, full of hatred. He would need to watch his back.

After a slow two-hour journey, Jacob's group reached the station without further incident. A long freight train was at the station, its engine purring gently, sending small puffs of smoke into the sky. Behind the locomotive were twenty cattle cars. The people around Jacob continued hesitantly.

*This can't be right. Where are the passenger cars?*

"This must be the wrong train, right?" A woman asked as she approached Jacob. Her tired eyes looked at him, expectantly.

There wouldn't be any other trains arriving today. They had a very uncomfortable journey ahead of them.

He shook his head. "I'm sorry, it looks like this will be your transport."

Her face fell. "Shipped off like cattle—this is what it's come to now."

As more people arrived, the group became restless, and the tension rose a few notches. Despite carrying a baton, Jacob felt exposed, as the OD and SS were vastly outnumbered. He looked around and saw the SS had picked up on the change in energy as well.

The soldiers had two significant advantages over the crowd—they were armed, and they were well-rested.

Schröder started shouting orders at the soldiers and looked for the head of the OD.

"Fischer, get over here!"

Olivier Fischer moved toward the officer.

"I need you to fit forty men in a car," said Schröder. "As soon as it's full, shut and lock the doors."

Fischer looked at him, perplexed. He checked the size of the cars from a distance. "They're never going to fit."

Schröder impulsively lashed out at Fischer, who ducked just in time. "Don't tell me what can't be done. Get them on the transport—we have a schedule."

Schröder was already on his way to the train, shouting at everybody wearing a uniform.

Olivier turned toward Jacob, his face contorted with rage.

"Olivier, what's going on?" asked Jacob. "Are we really going to put them in those cars?"

"I know. It's inhumane," Olivier said. "But nothing surprises me anymore. Let's try to make them as comfortable as possible. And Jacob —try to keep your dignity and let the SS do the dirty work. Try to keep them calm."

*Easier said than done.*

Jacob looked at the people herded around the train—the SS had done a stellar job in tiring them out so much that very few had any spark left.

The SS men opened the doors and started pushing people toward the cattle cars. The first few stepped up easy enough, adequately motivated by the rifles aimed at them from a small distance. The soldiers shouted and hustled, and soon the OD was helping to get the people boarded. Some of them were so tired or crippled they needed to be lifted into the cars.

They were about halfway done when Jacob heard the sound of a truck approaching. *That must be the people from the hospital.*

The truck drew the attention of the people waiting to board. They paused, and all eyes were on the truck. It stopped close to the back of the train, its engine hissing as the motor shut down.

Deppner descended from the passenger door. The commander looked haggard, his eyes scanning the situation. The angry look on his face got the SS men moving again as they continued pushing the prisoners into the cars.

Jacob helped some older men board the train but kept one eye on the truck.

The driver opened the tarp, and two SS soldiers jumped out. The next image was hard to process. Coming down the steps of the truck was a young boy, no older than eight. He clutched a brown teddy bear in his arms, along with a small backpack. One of the soldiers helped him down and pushed him toward the train.

More children of all ages followed, none older than fifteen.

The children looked lost as they gathered near the truck. A small girl looked at the train—her curious eyes focused on an almost full car. The German soldiers tried to cram some more men into the car, but it was impossible. After a few tries, they gave up and shut the door with a loud clank. They locked the door and moved to the next car.

Faces peeked outside through the barred windows, trying to get some fresh air by sticking their noses through the bars.

The girl turned to a larger boy next to her and asked him something. The boy shook his head.

*He doesn't know what they're doing here, either.*

Olivier and Ethan appeared next to Jacob. They looked solemn, and Jacob knew what was coming.

"We need to get those kids into the last car," Olivier said. He swallowed hard but kept his composure. "I need it done with compassion, so I'm sorry, but I need you and Ethan to do it. You're the only ones I know will look after them properly."

"Those are the orphans from Barracks 35, aren't they?" Ethan said as they walked toward the children.

"It looks like it. What use could they possibly have in a work camp?"

They reached the group and noticed that the kids were quite calm. They hadn't been alone in the truck. Jacob spotted Salo Carlebach speaking to them. He was telling them they were going on a trip and they should all stay together. Jacob felt a stab of pain in his chest.

Once the SS had unloaded all of the children and closed the truck, they lit cigarettes and took a break. They paid the group no further attention.

Salo looked around with trepidation—but then smiled when he saw Jacob.

"Of all the people I'd hoped to see here, you were top of the list," Salo said, with relief.

Jacob gave him a sad smile. "What's going on?" he asked. "Why are you here with the children?"

Salo sighed before he answered. "The kids were taken out of their classes only an hour ago. Deppner himself came to the school and demanded the orphaned children report outside the school. I was teaching a math class when I heard the commotion in the hallway."

Jacob nodded. The school building's walls were paper thin. A curious man like Salo would always hear whatever went on in the other rooms.

"When they were lined up outside, I asked Deppner what was happening. He said he needed to send more people to the work camp, and these children would do just fine.

He pointed at one of the smallest—a girl no older than five. She nervously held onto an older girl's hand as her eyes scanned the area. She was clearly overwhelmed by her surroundings.

"What did Deppner say about that?" Jacob asked although he knew the answer.

"He said there's a place for children there as well. A larger school and better facilities. He would send them there right away, and they needed to hurry. That's when I said I wouldn't let them go on the long journey on their own. So here I am."

Jacob admired his bravery. He wasn't sure if he'd have done the same, with so much uncertainty about where they were going.

"So, what happens next?" Salo asked. He looked at the children waiting patiently. Some of the older kids were listening in.

Jacob swallowed hard. "I need you to help us board all of them in that car." He pointed at the last car in the row. It was empty, and an OD stood guard to make sure nobody else boarded.

Salo looked resigned. "There's nothing we can do about it. We're going to the east. Hopefully, life will be somewhat better there." He turned to motion for the kids to follow him.

Jacob escorted the small group alongside Salo. Despite the chaos, the young man looked confident. He needed to be, for if he panicked, the children would surely follow. They reached the train, and Jacob helped lift the small children into the car. The older ones climbed in on their own.

A couple of cars ahead, a group of men stopped boarding. They looked on as the kids were lifted into the train car. One of the OD men told them to keep moving, but more and more of them stopped getting on the trains. The silent protest spread to the front of the train. Within seconds, the children's car was the only one with movement.

Deppner was talking to some SS men near the middle of the train when he noticed the boarding had stopped. His face registered surprise before it made way for anger. He shouted at the people closest to him to get on the train. They ignored the SS commander—further fueling his rage.

The shouting got the attention of the other groups, and their silence made way for murmurs of protest as the people were horrified to see the young children joining them for the journey.

"Why are we taking them if we're going to a work camp?" one shouted.

Some of the people in the train cars tried to open the doors. They were locked in, yet this only increased their efforts to get out. A few of the train cars started to rock back and forth.

Jacob saw the looks of confusion around him. The children were still getting onto the train, but they were also curious about what was happening.

A couple of men from the train car next to Jacob's walked over. They stood in front of the door and blocked the children boarding.

"They're not coming with us," a large man said, crossing his arms in defiance. His eyes were cold as he looked at Jacob. Another man stood next to him while a third started unloading children from the car.

Jacob stood helpless. There was little he could do against three determined men. He tried to reason with them.

"I don't agree with this, either, but if you keep this up, he's going to send in the SS men with their rifles," he said, looking over at Deppner. "It won't end well for you—you've seen what they're capable of."

Salo stood next to Jacob. "Listen to him," Salo said. "He's one of us, looking out for us."

The larger man scoffed at him. "One of us in a uniform like that, helping them ship us off to devil knows where?" He spat on the ground close to Jacob's feet. "I don't think so. He's just as bad as the SS, that turncoat."

Before Jacob could respond, a scuffle broke out further up the train. Deppner had sent some of his men in, forcefully trying to push people into the cars. To Jacob's horror, several ODs were helping a little too enthusiastically.

The group wasn't about to go willingly, and they pushed back as one. It was clear the SS weren't going to out-muscle them. Shouts of encouragement roared from those in the car next to theirs as they further pushed the soldiers back.

"Looks like your overlords have a problem," the man in front of Jacob said with a smug look. Meanwhile, the children were getting off the train, looking around in confusion.

Deppner wasn't going to stand by idly. He saw his plan falling apart. SS soldiers from all around the train ran toward the scene. Some prisoners on the platform tried to unlock the closed train cars but were beaten back by the OD standing their ground.

The German commander stormed to the front train car with Schröder in tow. The group was pulsating, SS soldiers tangling with the Jewish men and women who used all their might to push away from the train car.

Deppner pushed through the group. He grabbed the first person in front of him—a young boy no older than sixteen—and dragged him away. The boy protested, but Schröder was right behind them, kicking him in the ribs. He coughed and stumbled along as Deppner pulled him along by his hair.

The German commander reached an elevated position near the middle of the train. He said something to Schröder, who forced the boy on his knees.

Jacob held his breath. He remembered the stories about Deppner's ruthlessness with the Russian prisoners of war.

Deppner unholstered his sidearm. Realization dawned on the face of the boy. He tried to get up, but Schröder forced him back on his knees, kicking him in the groin for good measure.

Those in the scuffle still hadn't noticed what was going on. Deppner casually raised his weapon and pointed it at the boy's forehead. The boy cried and pleaded for his life, but Deppner's face was devoid of emotion. His cold eyes were focused on his target.

A loud bang exploded through the air. Time slowed down as everybody turned to the source of the sound. Deppner stood with his arm still outstretched, holding the weapon. The boy's body lay motionless on the platform, a small red spot on his forehead.

Defiance deflated from the group in an instant. The hooting from the cars stopped. The group at the front no longer pushed back but stood frozen. Some of the children started crying.

Deppner holstered his weapon and raised his voice. "I think that was enough for today. We need the rest of you in Germany—get in the cars."

Jacob felt sick. *Three executions in a day!* The men around him were silent but made no attempt to board the train.

Deppner clapped his hands and addressed his SS men in German: "Anybody who refuses to get on gets the same treatment." He pointed at the body next to him, a small puddle of blood forming around the boy's head. "The train leaves in fifteen minutes."

The SS broke the silence and took a different approach. Instead of trying to push people into the cars, they stepped back. They held their weapons at the ready and shouted at the prisoners to get into the cars. Some of the ODs started pushing, adding to the rougher ODs' eager efforts, and the men boarded the train.

The soldiers hadn't reached Jacob's car yet. The men near him were all Dutch, and they probably hadn't understood the last part of Deppner's message. Some of the children tried to climb into the car, but they were stopped by the large man who'd defied Jacob earlier.

Jacob translated for them. "You don't want to end up like him, do you?"

There was indecision in the man's eyes. "It doesn't matter. We're going to die anyway."

"You're going to decide for everybody here?" Jacob asked shrilly, becoming flustered. "You don't know where the train is taking you, and neither do I, but I can guarantee you that if you stand here and do nothing—even if you don't otherwise resist—they'll execute you."

A couple of soldiers made their way toward them, and some of the men got restless.

"We should listen to him," one of them said. "There is nothing left for us here, anyway." This got murmurs of approval, and some of the others stepped up into the train car.

Emboldened, Jacob pushed on. "Don't let these children witness another execution—it's not worth it."

The soldiers were now at the car next to them, prodding the people onto the train.

The big man finally gave in and climbed aboard. He didn't look back at Jacob but started lifting children aboard the train.

Within fifteen minutes, the train was loaded without further incident. The cars were locked, and more than a thousand souls were stacked like cattle within them.

Jacob caught up with Ethan near the end of the platform, where the OD gathered beside the last few cars. The train engine was building up steam, and everybody stood aimlessly by the tracks. The people in the cars were silent.

"They must be exhausted from the past two days," Ethan said.

Jacob looked in front of him. "They left their houses as men, and they're shipped off to the unknown like animals."

"Did you see how some of the ODs enjoyed their work today?" Ethan asked, keeping his voice low.

Jacob recalled his incident with the two men earlier. "A little too much, yes. That might become a problem for me when we're back in the camp."

"Don't worry—we're on your side. We'll talk to Olivier later."

Their talking was interrupted by the shrill whistle from the train, which started moving at a snail's pace. As the last cars crept past them, Jacob forced himself to look at the faces behind the iron bars. *I hope they know I had no choice.*

# Chapter Ten

In the following months, life became routine in the camp. New people arrived all the time and trains to the east left several times a week. Jacob and Ethan continued their work with Olivier in the OD.

A few months after the messy first transport, Deppner was replaced. No reason was given, but one day he simply packed up and left. Rumors floated around that the German leadership disapproved of his harsh methods. Even though the SS were ruthless, the situation in Westerbork with Deppner had shocked even the German command. The Dutch population also played a small role in this. The people around Westerbork kept their eyes averted from what happened inside the camp—as long as there was no apparent violence. The execution had set more of them against the Germans, and this resistance wasn't helping the Nazi program. So Deppner was replaced.

The new commander, Dischner, wasn't much better. Quick to anger, he enjoyed punishing prisoners for the smallest of infringements. He lashed out with little provocation and—even more so than Deppner —reeked of alcohol from early in the morning. Dischner only lasted a month before he was replaced by a man called Bohrmann, who kept to himself. Jacob had hardly seen him in the three days he'd been in charge so far.

Jacob and Olivier, each with a large bag slung over his shoulder, walked along the new train tracks that had been completed earlier that month. There was no need for escorts to Hooghalen, as the trains now stopped directly in the middle of the camp.

"I hate this part of the job almost as much as the actual transport," Olivier said as he picked up a crumpled piece of paper. He inspected it and put it in his pocket.

After each transport, a few of the OD were sent along the tracks to collect discarded items. People dropped notes and even some valuables in envelopes, hoping these would be found and somehow make their way to friends or relatives. Depending on who found the items, they were either smuggled out of the camp or confiscated.

"At least we can help get some of these messages passed along," Jacob said.

Jacob's bag of valuables was light, which cheered him—less for the SS to paw through—and he'd also stuffed a few notes into his pocket. He'd make sure these reached the underground mail service in the camp.

When they returned to the camp, it was clear something was off: the people were all crowded outside their barracks. In the chilly October weather, most would stay indoors; overcrowded as the barracks were, they still provided the best shelter from the cold. Jacob and Olivier exchanged wary looks as they crossed where the tracks now ran parallel with the road. The camp population had renamed it the Boulevard of Misery. On departure days, families clung onto each other as the SS and OD mercilessly loaded the cattle cars bound for the east.

Jacob looked up. The guards looked down from looming towers onto the hive of people.

"What an odd situation," Olivier said, his eyes also drawn upward. "They're usually keen to draw their weapons and cause a bit of a scare. Something has everyone spooked."

They proceeded through the crowd. So much had changed since the very first transport in July, only three months before. There was no repeat of the riot like the one at the station, and new arrivals now spent at least a few days in the camp. Despite his many faults, Deppner had seen that rushing them through only worked against him, so he established the few days' residence.

Of course, the threat of being put on one of the transports always lingered. It was a simple matter to add someone to a transport with the train tracks running directly into the camp.

Jacob and Olivier reached the administration building, where a small group of ODs stood outside. They were surprised to find Arthur Pisk amongst them.

When Deppner left, Olivier had been happy to give up his position when the new commander wanted new leadership, and Pisk had volunteered. His status as an Austrian Jew elevated him somewhat. Now Olivier simply did as he was told. Despite his drop in rank, he was still a highly trusted member of the OD, and Pisk often consulted him—not out of friendship but for expediency. That meant Olivier was still very well-informed about what was going on in Westerbork.

"Took you quite a while," Pisk said, tapping his watch and stroking his thin mustache.

Olivier ignored the reprimand and smiled pleasantly as he answered Pisk: "We wanted to make sure we collected everything."

"When you've emptied those bags, I need you to report to the small assembly hall. There are some changes we need to discuss. Make sure you're there in half an hour," Pisk grunted, then dismissed them with a wave.

After they emptied their bags and the contents had been properly registered, they headed toward the administration building.

"Pisk looked a bit cocky there, don't you think?" Jacob asked.

Olivier looked at him in surprise. "Doesn't he always? He's an arrogant bastard, that one."

"It's sad, really, that he wields so much power. He's chummed up to the command a bit too much, thinking that will save him—he's just as Jewish as us."

"That's not the way he sees it. He has the commander's ear because he's as ruthless as the Nazis. I think he enjoys his job—have you seen him on deportation days? He barely disguises his enthusiasm," Olivier said.

"It makes me sick to wear the same uniform," Jacob said.

They walked past a group of women near one of the barracks. Agnes was among them, and she greeted them with a smile.

*Such a beauty.*

"Hey, you," she said affectionately to Jacob, giving him a quick peck on the cheek. "Hi, Olivier."

"Hi, Agnes—good to see you. How is everything in the hospital?"

"It's crowded, but we're managing. It's a bit surreal, really—we have more medicine here than we did on the outside." She turned to Jacob. "Do you know what's going on in the camp? Everybody's been told to stay near their barracks."

"I've been away; I was hoping you might know more."

She shook her head. "Not really. All I've heard is that a large group of Germans came into the camp this morning. They arrived in jeeps and went straight for the commander's house. Other than that, I don't know."

Jacob frowned. "We must've missed them."

"People are drawing their own conclusions. Everybody has a different story. Most seem to think there is a high-powered Nazi here to inspect the camp. Others say they're here to change the camp. Some people are even saying the camp will be closed, and we'll all be sent to the east." Agnes looked worried.

Jacob frowned. "I haven't heard anything about closing the camp. Besides, it makes no sense—the tracks are brand new and took a lot of labor to build!"

This appeared to calm Agnes somewhat. "I know—I'm just telling you what I've heard. I think people are going crazy because nobody really knows."

"Have you seen Ethan?" Jacob changed the subject.

"Not today, no. Otherwise, I would've asked him about what's going on." She looked thoughtful. "I think he's supposed to be in the barracks on the other side of the camp. He said there were problems with overcrowding. Something about fights breaking out."

*More fights. They're keeping him busy.*

The SS had shipped a lot of new people into the camp, cramming them in the new barracks. Most inhabitants complained about the poor standards, but their complaints had fallen on deaf ears.

"We'd better get going, or we'll be late for the meeting. If there's any news, we'll find out over there," Olivier said, sensing trouble.

"See you tonight," Jacob said as he gave Agnes a quick hug.

"Don't forget—we're doing advanced dosing with Dr. Brunner tonight. Better be prepared!" She smiled as she walked back to the other women.

Jacob felt Olivier's eyes on him as they walked down the main street.

"You've become close these last weeks," he said, smiling.

"Ever since I met Agnes, I have a reason to get up in the morning again," Jacob said. "She's smart and cares about people."

"I'm happy for you two—it's great to see something good in this camp."

They arrived at the assembly hall just in time. A few other men wearing the same green uniforms hurried in after them. The 200 men squeezed into the airless heat. Most talked softly; there was no sign of any SS yet.

Pisk stood at the front, facing the rest of the group.

*Of course, he wants to make sure everybody sees him as one of the SS.*

Jacob spotted Ethan at the front and pushed his way through the crowded room toward him.

"Did you find anything interesting along the tracks?" Ethan asked.

"Not really—just a few notes." He looked around the room—nothing was happening just yet. He lowered his voice. "But what's going on in the camp? When I got back, it was complete chaos."

Ethan nodded. "Nobody knows. Some fights broke out in the new barracks, but I was able to get them to hear reason." He grinned.

"Agnes told me you were sent over there," Jacob said. He looked his friend up and down. "But you look fine—nothing big happened?"

"No, it was a small scuffle. One of the younger guys tried to take a new bunk when he thought someone wasn't coming back. When the other guy came back, he didn't want to move."

Having so many people in too small a space was always going to bring irritations.

"But that's not why the rest of the camp was so heated, is it?" Jacob asked.

"Of course not. Early this morning, a group of German trucks and jeeps entered the camp. The trucks were only here for an hour or so and then left. Some people said they saw the SS unload weapons, but you know how it goes—they're just guessing." Ethan shrugged.

Jacob nodded impatiently. "And?"

Ethan looked thoughtful before continuing. "Well, the jeeps are still there in front of the commander's house. Apparently, there was another SS commander in one of the jeeps."

"Another commander? That doesn't make sense. There are only fifty SS soldiers here. They would never send a second commander."

Ethan looked at him with a curious look. "Well, you know that can only mean one thing, right?"

"Another change of the guard?" Jacob frowned.

*Bohrmann has only been here for a few days. Would they replace him already?*

"Fights like this morning are becoming more common. And when that gets out to the command in Germany, they don't like it. They want people to go quietly."

They were interrupted as Pisk launched his unmistakable whistle from the front, piercing everybody's ears. He'd picked up that annoying habit since taking over the OD. Ethan silently mimicked the head of OD, pursing his lips as he caught Jacob's look.

A group of SS men in full uniform marched in, led by Bohrmann. His face was as passive as Jacob had seen it every time he'd spied the man, and Jacob wondered whether he had any feelings at all. Following the large German was Schröder, who had risen to second in command.

The role hadn't changed Schröder much. He was still heavily involved with the OD but spoke mostly to Pisk, who was happy to relay the orders to the rest of the OD and pretend they came directly from him. Most of the OD despised him, but for different reasons—some of the men wanted his position and waited for him to slip up. Others simply hated him for his cruelty. Jacob and Ethan belonged to the latter group. Pisk enjoyed the misfortune of others a little too much. He was always the first of the OD to take out his baton.

Nevertheless, Jacob and Ethan were stuck with Pisk, and they tried to keep a neutral approach. As some of the first prisoners in Westerbork, they had a slightly elevated status themselves. Pisk never gave them an especially hard time.

As Bohrmann and Schröder silently took their positions, another four SS men walked in.

"Must be the men from the jeeps," Ethan whispered.

They settled next to Schröder. One of them had the stripes of a commander, like Bohrmann. He looked out of place among the rumpled OD: his face neatly shaven, every single hair combed back, and his tie immaculately knotted. He looked alert, in contrast to the haggard men around him.

"Thank you all for coming," the tall officer said. Jacob immediately recognized the crisp Bonn accent. "I'm Albert Gemmeker, and I'll be relieving commander Bohrmann from his position."

The group didn't react—they simply looked on with interest.

"I know you've been through a lot of changes recently, and I've heard of the recent unrest in the camp," Gemmeker spoke calmly, and Jacob was surprised by the respectful tone with which he addressed them.

"I'm also told you've had an important role in the running of this camp so far, and I intend to keep all of you in your current positions. Together, we can make sure this camp is run well, and that the people in the camp are treated with the dignity they deserve."

Schröder shifted on his feet. It was an involuntary movement.

*He looks very uncomfortable with this.*

Gemmeker pretended he didn't notice and continued: "We'll make some changes in the next few weeks, and you'll be informed about what we expect from you. Trust me when I say things will get better. That will be all for now."

Jacob and Ethan filed out of the room with the rest of the OD.

"That was really odd," Ethan said as they stepped outside.

Jacob nodded. "He almost seems like a decent Nazi."

"What do you think it means?"

"I have no idea, but let's see what he does. He can't be worse than the other commanders."

Ethan looked unconvinced. "I hope you're right."

A few days later, Ethan and Jacob found themselves summoned to the crowded assembly hall. Pisk stood in front of them, holding a stack of papers. That meant only one thing—there would be another transport the next day—Jacob dreaded the days when Pisk walked in with a transport list. Pisk would have one for every barracks. Each OD was responsible for keeping the peace within the barracks, and Jacob had been assigned to one of the older barracks, in which he knew most people. He'd been glad to have few of his charges transported, as most people there worked in the camp administration and hospital, which exempted them from the transports. Recently, however, he'd been the bearer of bad news more often. Ethan was in charge of one of the newer barracks. Apart from the occasional fight, he didn't have to intervene too much. The men, women, and children in his barracks lasted hardly longer than a week before making the journey east. Although the job was tough on Ethan—he often had long lists—he managed quite well by keeping his distance. Jacob wasn't sure he could do the same job.

"I bet he enjoys this part of his day most of all," Ethan said as they followed the small queue toward the Austrian. There were many people in the line, and Jacob and Ethan were in no rush to get to the front.

Jacob nodded. "He loves the power."

They got to the front of the queue and took their lists from Pisk, who hardly acknowledged them. They didn't have to look closely to see Ethan had the tougher task, as always. His list spanned two full pages of numbers and names. "There's no one on here that I know. These are just names to me."

"Unfortunately, I know quite a few people on my list." Jacob pointed out some names, and Ethan nodded.

They walked out of the hall and went in different directions without another word. They'd see each other soon enough, but they preferred to deliver the bad news as quickly as possible. People would need to prepare for their journey the next day. Jacob hated it when families were torn apart, and Westerbork was flooded with tears.

An hour later, Jacob stepped out of the camp commissary and onto the windy Boulevard. After delivering the terrible news to the people designated for the morning's transport, he needed some time to himself. The Boulevard was deserted—most people preferred to stay indoors and deal with the news in their own way.

The few people he ran into were either ODs or people on their way to their assignments—they were safe from the transport list for a few more days, at least.

Jacob had a spot in the back of the camp, just out of the wind where one building addition butted up against another.

Agnes and Ethan sometimes used it, too, or joined him there, but he spent most of his time alone here—they knew not to disturb him after he had to deliver the transport news.

He sat down on a large rock and unwrapped the chocolate bar he'd bought in the commissary. One of the small advantages of working in the OD meant he got paid a meager wage to use in the small shop. He closed his eyes and tried to forget where he was. He took another bite of his chocolate and remembered better times, sitting at the kitchen table at home in Berlin. His mother would have a steaming hot pot of tea ready as he came home from school. There would be chocolate cookies, and everything would be all right.

He was brought back to the present by the sound of rapid footsteps approaching.

"Jaco! I thought I'd find you here!"

He'd recognize that voice out of a million.

*Agnes! Something is wrong.*

He opened his eyes and found her standing in front of him. Her big eyes were red and puffy—she looked worried.

*Something is really wrong.*

Jacob jumped up and took her hand. "What happened?"

"She's on the list, Jaco," she exclaimed before collapsing into his arms.

He caught her as she sobbed and shook—he'd never seen her like this before.

"Who? Tell me, who's on the list?" But he knew.

Agnes choked up, and no words came out as she looked at him with panic in her eyes.

"Calm down, Agnes. Then speak to me," he said as he stroked her cheek.

She took a deep breath and swallowed hard before answering—tears now streaming down her face.

"Yvette," she managed to squeeze out in a croaking voice. "My sister is on tomorrow's transport."

"There must be a mistake," Jacob said, although he knew better. *The transport lists have no logic. It's only about reaching the numbers.*

She shook her head. "No mistake. We were in our barracks just now when it was announced. The OD put the list up at the front and left.

*Coward. He didn't even have the decency to tell them in person.*

"We've been through this so many times now, and we were never on the list. My job in the hospital keeps me safe, and as far as we know, the kitchen staff is happy with Yvette. But when we went to look," she sat down as she choked back her tears, "Yvette's name was on there." Agnes buried her face in her hands. "What are we going to do, Jacob? I can't lose her, too—she's the only family I have left."

Jacob sat down and put his arm around her. She put her head on his shoulder, and he felt her shaking.

*I need to fix this.* His mind raced in a million different directions.

They sat like this for a minute—Jacob stroked her hair.

She looked up, her eyes pleading. "Is there anything you can do?"

"I don't know. I think there are only a few people in the camp who can change anything on the transport list."

"Who?"

"Gemmeker. But there's no way we can reach him, so that leaves people a little lower down. Do you know anybody in the administration?"

*Maybe we can bribe someone there.*

She shook her head. "I don't think anybody in the administration is in my barracks. I only know people in the hospital."

*The hospital. Of course.*

He sat up a little straighter. Agnes looked at him with a glimmer of hope in her eyes.

"The only way we can get Yvette off the transport is if she's too sick to travel. Dr. Brunner has the authority to keep people in the hospital, right?"

She nodded. "I think he's defied the Nazis a few times, but—" Agnes hesitated and looked uncomfortable before continuing.

"But what?"

"It hasn't always worked. I remember Deppner came in a few times to check on the people, and he simply selected people he thought looked good enough for transport. Dr. Brunner protested, but in the end, there was little he could do."

"But Deppner is no longer here. Has Gemmeker ever done this?"

Without hesitation, she shook her head. "Never."

"Then I think it's worth a shot. But there's no time to lose. Let's go to the hospital and speak with Dr. Brunner." He was on his feet and already on his way when he noticed Agnes hadn't moved. She looked unsure.

"What if he doesn't want to help us?"

*That's ridiculous. Of course he'll help us.*

He walked back and crouched down in front of her. "You work for him; he knows my father and me. Dr. Brunner is a good man. He does whatever he can to keep people off the trains."

"But Yvette isn't really sick. I don't know what he can do."

He held out his hand. "But we must try, regardless. Come with me —let's find him."

Agnes took his hand, and he gently pulled her up. "We're going to make this work, Agnes. I promise."

She nodded.

*I sure hope I can keep this promise.*

As they ran toward the hospital, Agnes never let go of his hand.

The run had done Agnes good—she looked focused. It reminded Jacob why he liked her so much—she cared deeply for the people around her and wouldn't give up after a setback.

They entered the hospital, and Agnes navigated them through the hallways. She greeted a few people along the way but didn't stop.

"Do you want to do the talking?" Jacob asked as they neared Dr. Brunner's office.

Agnes nodded. "Yes, but I appreciate you being here. He also respects you and your father. Hopefully, he'll know what to do."

They got to the doctor's door, and Agnes knocked without hesitation—the only sign of nerves was her foot gently tapping on the floor.

Jacob strained his ears for any sound from the other side of the door. *It's too quiet.* Normally he'd expect to hear footsteps approach or the doctor calling out for them to come in.

Agnes turned to Jacob. "I don't think he's here." She looked anxious.

Jacob tried the door handle—locked.

A nurse approached. "Can I help you with anything?" She looked stern until she recognized Agnes, and a smile appeared on her face. "Oh, hi, Agnes. I didn't expect to see you here—you're off today, aren't you?"

"Mimi, I'm happy to see you," Agnes answered. "Do you know where Dr. Brunner is?"

The nurse nodded. "He was called away to the administration about an hour ago."

Agnes looked disappointed.

*If Dr. Brunner can't help us, maybe Papa can.*

"Do you know if Herr Kagan is still in?" Jacob asked Mimi.

She nodded. "Yes, he volunteered to stay until Dr. Brunner is back, in case anything urgent came up. Ah, now I recognize you. You're his son, right?"

"Yes." *We don't have time for chitchat.* "Is he in his office?"

"He should be."

Jacob took Agnes's hand. "Let's go."

"Thank you, Mimi," Agnes said as they raced down the hall—Hermann's office was just around the corner.

"We can't wait for Dr. Brunner, but I'm sure my father can help us as well."

Hermann's door was open, and Jacob was relieved to find him at his desk studying a chart. He looked up and smiled when they walked in.

"What a pleasant surprise—what brings you here?" He put the chart down and took off his glasses. That's when he saw Jacob and Agnes weren't smiling. His eyebrows shot up. "What's wrong?"

"Yvette is on tomorrow's transport, Papa," Jacob said without preamble. *There's no time to sugarcoat this.*

Hermann looked aghast and stood up in alarm. "I'm so sorry to hear that." Hermann had taken an interest in Agnes in the past few months —she had been an excellent student in their classes—and Hermann had become somewhat of a father figure to her.

Agnes managed to stay composed, and she sat down across from his desk, Jacob beside her, and Hermann sat down again himself.

"We need to find a way to get her off the list somehow," Agnes said. "And we think her best chance is to be admitted into the hospital."

Hermann looked at them curiously.

"If we can convince the SS she's too sick to travel, she gets to stay here, right?" Jacob asked.

Hermann grabbed a pencil from his desk and paced the small office. He spun the pencil between his fingers.

Agnes looked to Jacob, and he nodded at her. *He's considering it.*

Hermann turned back to them. "We've tried this a few times before. You know about this, Agnes."

Agnes nodded.

"And we've mostly failed. The SS gets the numbers handed down from Berlin, and they have to make these quotas on the transport. If someone can walk, they normally go on the train."

Agnes looked downcast.

"Are you saying it's not possible, Papa?"

Hermann shook his head. "It's not impossible, but it's very hard. For Yvette to stay, she needs to be brutally ill, and that's hard to fake."

Agnes sat up. "Hard, but possible?"

"There's one thing we can try, but it's very risky," Hermann said, as

158

he took a book from a small shelf next to his desk. He started leafing through it and quickly found what he was looking for.

"Yes, this is it," he said as he pointed at one of the pages. Agnes and Jacob looked at it and didn't understand what Hermann meant.

"This is a mix of medicine we use to clear someone's stomach. Look at this warning at the bottom."

"This purgative will make your sister very, very ill," Hermann said as he closed the book. "It should be enough to convince the SS that she's unfit for transport."

Agnes looked worried. "Isn't internal bleeding dangerous?"

Hermann nodded. "Yes, and that's the risk we'd need to take."

Agnes looked at Jacob. "What do you think?"

Jacob answered without hesitation. "I think we need to try it. But it's Yvette who will need to decide."

Agnes slowly nodded. "How do we proceed?"

"If you wait here, I'll get you the pills, and then you need to get your sister to take them as quickly as possible. The effects should appear within an hour, and then you need to bring her here quickly."

"Okay, let's do it." Agnes still looked worried, but there was conviction in her voice.

"I'll be right back. But Agnes, don't forget one thing"—Hermann took a deep breath before continuing—"She will feel absolutely horrible —make sure she knows this."

Agnes swallowed hard. "She'll do whatever is needed."

Hermann nodded and rushed out. Agnes sat down and looked at Jacob—her eyes darted around his face.

He sat down next to her. "It will be okay. Papa knows what he's doing."

It didn't take much to convince Yvette to take the four small pills. She was terrified of being put on the transport.

"I'll do anything that gives me a chance," Yvette had said before swallowing the pills in one gulp.

That had been over an hour before, and they were now on their way back to the hospital. Yvette was already feeling weak—her face was pale, and she had trouble moving by herself. Jacob and Agnes supported her as they stumbled down the Boulevard.

"Keep going, we're almost there, sis," Agnes said as Yvette breathed heavily.

*She's trying to suppress nausea. Papa wasn't kidding about this being painful.*

"If you need to throw up, just do it," Jacob said. "You already look pretty bad. I don't think we'll have trouble convincing the people in the hospital you need to be admitted."

"I'm alright—let's just get there," Yvette said as she swallowed hard.

As they entered the hospital, Agnes called out to two nurses walking in the hallway. They turned around and rushed toward them.

"Agnes, what happened to her?" The older of the two asked. The other nurse took one look at Yvette and hurried off.

"We don't really know—she was okay a few hours ago, but when I got back to the barracks, she started to turn pale," Agnes said, her eyes showing concern. "I'm glad you're here, Sarah."

*She's a good actress. I would believe her, too.*

Sarah nodded. "Can you walk?"

At the point, Yvette's knees buckled, and Jacob had trouble keeping her on her feet. They sat her down in one of the chairs near the entrance. She sat hunched over, her hands on her knees.

The other nurse returned with a rolling stretcher. "Let's get her in a bed, and I'll call one of the doctors." She turned to Jacob and Agnes. "We'll look after her—you can wait here if you like."

Agnes shook her head. "I'd like to join you if that's okay."

"Of course you can come," Sarah said.

Jacob helped Yvette onto the stretcher. She looked even paler than before and breathed in short gasps.

*How much worse is it going to get? Did we give her too much?*

Sarah and the other nurse started rolling Yvette down the corridor. Agnes turned back to Jacob. Her expression was stricken.

"Whatever we did, it worked. I hope this is the worst of it," she whispered. "I've never seen my sister like this."

Jacob nodded. "For sure. But there is no way they'll put her on the transport in this state."

"I don't think so, either. Thank you."

"Go with your sister—make sure she's okay."

She gave him a quick kiss. "I'll catch up with you later."

He watched Agnes hurry after her sister and smiled to himself. Yvette might feel horrible now, but no doctor would send her on transport tomorrow.

Jacob stood in the middle of the platform. The sun wouldn't be up for another hour, but the harsh artificial lights made the area around the train as bright as day. He was early, and the other ODs joined him in small groups. They were mostly quiet, but for the chattering few who seemed excited about another deportation. Other than that, the only sound was the soft humming of the locomotive, patiently waiting for the day's cargo to arrive.

Ethan appeared at his side. "Another big transport today. Pisk said around two thousand."

"They've been ramping up the numbers," Jacob replied.

"How is Agnes? She must be relieved."

Jacob nodded. Their plan had worked. Yvette had spent the previous evening hunched over a bucket, and the doctors had been very clear—she was in no state to go on the day's transport. When Yvette had finally fallen asleep from exhaustion, Agnes had come to find Jacob and bring him the good news. She had been beyond relieved, and they'd spent an hour together before she had to go back to her barracks.

"I just hope this doesn't mean she'll be on the next transport once she's better," Jacob said. It had been on his mind the whole night.

"We'll find a way to keep her here, Jaco. Let's just get through this transport first."

Jacob and Ethan had been assigned to keep order on the platform, along with a group of twenty other ODs. There were also plenty of SS men hovering around when the first of the day's condemned prisoners appeared on the far side of the platform, led by an OD. It was always the same sad sight. Men, women, and children with nothing but a small bag or suitcase, shuffling toward the train of cattle cars.

All along the perimeter stood other ODs, making sure there were no curious onlookers. Not that there are many of those—people fortunate enough not to be selected for transport stayed in their barracks.

It didn't take long for the usual organized chaos to ensue—not everybody boarded the train voluntarily, and there were plenty of ODs ready to shove them into the cars. Some of the older people had trouble climbing up, and they were assaulted by baton-wielding ODs until they somehow managed to crawl into the car or were helped by other unfortunates already in there. It never failed to disgust Jacob.

It took about fifteen minutes for the first cars to fill up. The ODs rolled the doors shut and locked them in place, making sure to stay clear of the barbed wire wrapped around the cars. They wouldn't be opened until they reached their destination. This train would go for the Polish camp of Auschwitz-Birkenau, a journey of more than two days. The faces of the people peering out of the small barred windows were always the same—fearful and desperate. They didn't know where they were going, but their surroundings had already rapidly deteriorated since leaving their barracks that morning.

Jacob and Ethan had little to do—no one was attempting a last-minute escape. Jacob looked around as more of the doors slammed shut. Almost all prisoners were now in the cars, but a few looked emptier than usual. That was odd—they normally had too little space by the time the final people boarded.

"What's happening over there?" Ethan pointed to the back of the Boulevard. A group of people—no more than thirty—approached from the back of the camp. They walked slowly, carrying small bags, just like the other people who were now in the train cars. Some of them wore white clothes, in sharp contrast to the darkness around them. At the front of the group walked Arthur Pisk.

*Oh no.*

Jacob's heart dropped.

As the group got closer, he saw people in the back pushing wheeled stretchers—and walking alongside one was Agnes.

Jacob jumped down from the platform and rushed toward the group. He knew there would be trouble later, but he didn't care.

*What is Agnes doing here?*

The group had reached the now-deserted ramp. The people in the cars were quiet—only a few whispers could be heard—and the only movement came from the group coming from the hospital. Two dozen looked a little ill, but they had been able to make the short walk from the hospital on their own. Some of them coughed and wheezed, but they were nowhere in the precarious shape of the five people on stretchers.

Pisk looked at Jacob as he approached the group. "Help us load these people in the final cars."

"Are we sending these sick people off on transport?"

"Yes—now get on with it," Pisk said, his eyes narrowing. "We're behind schedule."

The big Austrian brushed past Jacob, shouting at the other ODs to help load the final people. Jacob felt anger rising inside him.

"Jaco, it's okay."

*Agnes.*

She stood in front of him, her eyes soft. Next to her, two nurses pushed a stretcher toward the train. Yvette lay on it, her eyes closed, her face pale as snow.

Agnes took his hand and pulled him along, following her sister as the nurses gently pushed the stretcher up the ramp. Yvette wasn't moving.

*This can't be real.*

"What happened? They took her off the list." His eyes shot between Agnes and Yvette's stretcher rolling along the ramp.

Agnes nodded. "Everything was fine when I started my shift this morning. I went to check up on Yvette, and that's when I was told she was back on the list. Apparently, there was a mistake in the calculation for the original list, and they needed to add people at the last minute."

"And they took them from the hospital?" Jacob felt dizzy as they passed the closed train cars, following Yvette. There was only one open car left ahead of them.

"It was the easiest way, everybody's already registered there, and they decided to take a random selection of people. Dr. Brunner tried to keep them, especially the ones that couldn't move, but the SS stuck to their list."

Jacob looked at Agnes as they walked down the ramp. She wore her nurse's uniform and carried a small backpack. She looked composed, her eyes bright and alert.

*How can she be so calm when she's about to lose her sister?*

They reached the open train car, and the nurses—with help from the people inside—carefully lifted Yvette into the car. She still didn't stir as the people inside the car placed her on a makeshift mattress of hay.

Agnes caught Jacob's look. "We sedated her just before we left to make the journey more tolerable. It should be enough for the next 24 hours."

Jacob nodded. The ramp was empty as most ODs had made their way down—there was no one else to load into the train. Jacob turned to Agnes.

"Do you want to say goodbye before I close the door?"

She nodded and took his hands. There were tears in her eyes now, and her hands felt cold.

"Yes, but it's not Yvette I have to say goodbye to." Her voice was uneven, and she squeezed his hands.

In the background, the shrill whistle of the train pierced the silence —it was departure time.

"I can't abandon her now, Jaco. She's the only family I have left. I'm going with her."

Tears streamed down her face, and Jacob felt his eyes sting. His knees buckled, and he felt a sharp pain in his chest.

"Agnes—please don't do this," he said as he tried to compose himself.

She put her finger on his lips, then pulled him in close and hugged him hard. They stood like that for only a short time—Jacob heard boots approaching. Soon, they would close the door. Agnes broke the embrace, looked him in the eye, and gave him a final kiss before climbing into the car.

Jacob stood frozen on the platform. It felt as if he were looking down on himself, unable to stop what was happening. Agnes stood only a few yards away in the crowded train car—their eyes locked. Someone said something, but it didn't register. Just before the door of the cattle car was shut, the last thing he saw was Agnes mouthing her final goodbye—*I love you.*

# CHAPTER ELEVEN

A small stage was set up in the packed assembly hall, and all eyes watched a young woman and man acting out a scene. In the story, she walked the streets of Berlin while he tried to get her attention from a nearby terrace. Both of the actors were dressed in simple clothes, but she had somehow managed to find a fancy hat.

Ethan mumbled conspiratorially to Jacob, "We know how this story ends, right?"

Jacob nodded. They'd seen the play many times, but for most of the people watching, it was the first time. It would probably also be the last time. The weekly performances didn't get a lot of return visitors.

"Let's get some fresh air," Jacob said.

They left unnoticed through the back door. The play entranced the audience—it looked like the young man was about to gain the favor of the young maiden.

"It's a smart move by Gemmeker—these plays, don't you think?" Ethan asked when they got outside. The late May evening weather was pleasant—summer was on its way.

"The plays, the school, the hospital. He's doing a fine job keeping everybody in line," Jacob said.

After Gemmeker had taken over seven months earlier, life in Westerbork had changed dramatically. Gemmeker decided to proceed with as little violence as possible, and the hospital had even been expanded with several dentist chairs. One of his most popular decisions had been to use the assembly hall for plays on Sunday evenings.

People generally fell in line with the camp command and felt more at ease. Jacob and Ethan had less to do than before—and that suited them just fine.

"If only we didn't have the Tuesday transports, you'd almost think we were living in a normal village," Jacob said.

One thing that hadn't changed was the constant flow of trains going in and out of the camp. Gemmeker had further optimized this, and the transport lists were ruthless. By now, the regulars in the camp knew the trains were bound for labor camps in Poland. People who lost their wives, husbands, or children to these trains never heard from them again. Monday evening was dreaded, when the transport list was issued for the next day.

"This week will be a big one, I've heard," Ethan said. "Pisk said this will be the biggest train yet."

Jacob looked up. "How many?"

"Three thousand."

Jacob was shocked. They'd never handled such a large number before. "How are we going to fit 3000 people on a train? The ramp isn't big enough to handle that many cars."

They were silent as they walked along Boulevard. They reached the center of the camp and sat down on the large ramp running parallel to the train tracks, their legs dangling on the side.

"How much longer do you think we will be able to stay here?" Ethan asked.

"What do you mean?"

Ethan looked at his friend intently. "We've been here for almost four years. Most of the people coming through here don't even reach four weeks. We've been lucky, Jaco, but there's no way they'll let us stay here forever. The number of prisoners is going down every week. It seems like they're running out of people. With transports like this week's, the camp will be close to empty soon."

"You think we won't be needed anymore?"

His friend nodded. "The way they've set up the camp now means we're already quite useless. People feel relatively safe, and they've done a fine job making people feel like they're taking care of everybody. But you and I both know that nobody comes back from the east. It's a one-way ticket."

"They still need us to assist with the transports. It will be hell again on Tuesday," Jacob said. He looked down the ramp and envisioned the mayhem they'd have in two nights. Families torn apart, people volunteering to step aboard the train so they wouldn't lose their children. He'd seen it all, and it didn't get any easier.

His mind wandered to Agnes. She'd been away for seven months, and he missed her dearly. He clung onto the hope that she was surviving in one of the camps, but he also knew the conditions were brutal, and the odds were not in her favor. Despite this, he still went to the small post office in the camp every week, hopeful for a sign of life. He returned empty-handed every time.

He turned back to Ethan.

"We're some of the youngest, strongest men in the OD," Jacob said. "We've also been around the longest and know everything about this camp. I think we would be some of the last people to be sent on the transports."

Ethan nodded his head slowly. "I hope you're right. But it doesn't mean our family is safe forever. We've seen people who were deemed safe because of their role—and they were sent on transport just the same."

"And that's why we have to make sure we are useful. If they shrink the OD, we have to be at the top of the list to stay. I'm sure we can manage that."

Ethan stood up resolutely, like a mock-serious soldier. "I know we can. We'll survive, no matter what happens."

Jacob smiled and stood up next to him.

Ethan's expression soured. "But Jaco, remember what we said. If anything happens to either of us, we look after each other."

Jacob wrapped his arm around his friend. "We're in this together. We've made it this far, all the way from Berlin. Once the war is over, we'll still be standing, no matter what."

Ethan looked him in the eye and nodded. "We will. But at what price?"

Monday morning brought a familiar silence to Westerbork. Fear ruled the camp, and as Jacob made his way to the administration building, people averted their faces, afraid a look might land them a last-minute spot on the transport list.

Jacob didn't take it personally; he wasn't much safer than them. Ethan's words had shaken him more than he cared to admit. The camp population was shrinking every week, as was evident from the growing number of empty barracks.

Entering the building, he found the room full of ODs waiting for instructions. Most looked as if they didn't have a care in the world, and Jacob envied their simple thinking. Many of the men sided with the SS —it was the easiest route. Some fraternized with them, smoking cigarettes and occasionally sharing a drink. But it hadn't mattered when the OD had shrunk the first time. Men who considered their positions safe because of their German "friends" had been the first on the transports— they probably knew too much. Jacob had always kept his distance and his head down.

As Pisk started handing out transport lists, Jacob looked around for Ethan. *That's odd.* He was generally on time and should have been there by now. Jacob got to the front and took his own list. Pisk lifted an eyebrow.

"Where's your friend? I've got a big list for him," Pisk said, looking annoyed.

"I'm not sure—perhaps he got caught up at the barracks. But I can take the list and give it to him when he gets here," Jacob said, holding out his hand.

Pisk looked at Jacob with disdain. He held his gaze for a short while, then shrugged and handed the list to Jacob. "If anything's wrong with this list, I'm holding you responsible."

Jacob turned away from Pisk, who was already chewing out the next person. The head of the OD was in a foul mood.

He left the building and looked up at an overcast sky. The Netherlands was a dreary country with too much rain, too many clouds, and too little sun. Despite that, Jacob had come to like the Dutch people, both inside and outside the camp. He didn't get to spend much time outside anymore, but he enjoyed hearing the newcomers' stories. It sounded like the Dutch were still resisting the Nazi occupiers—stories of the underground resistance filled him with hope.

Jacob strolled toward his barracks. His list had only ten names—none of which he recognized. *Lucky, for now.*

The Boulevard was quiet. Most of the people in the camp were either at work or in their barracks. Mondays were like that. People stayed out of sight.

He looked at Ethan's list with a little gasp. A quick scan showed over two hundred names, and he sighed. Ethan had a very tough day ahead.

Nearing Ethan's barracks, he caught his friend rushing out the door.

"Where were you?" Jacob asked as he handed him his transport list.

"There was some trouble in the barracks. I needed to help out and completely lost track of time." He scanned the transport list. "I guess they weren't kidding about the large numbers."

Jacob nodded. "It's looking dreadful. I saw some of the other men's lists. That 3000 isn't much of an exaggeration."

Ethan shook his head. "And not many new arrivals, either. It won't be long until all the new barracks are shut down."

"We'd better go deliver the bad news. Sooner is better than later," Jacob said. "Good luck."

Ethan nodded, and they went their separate ways. Jacob pictured the faces of the people waiting in the barracks. They would be scared, everybody dreading to hear their name called out.

He saw some of the other ODs coming out of the other barracks. Their pained expressions bore the marks of having shared news of an unholy fate. Most were good men, just trying to survive like he was. Jacob nodded at one of them, and he returned the gesture. Jacob heard wails coming from the barracks just before the door closed behind the man.

Jacob reached his barracks.

*Here we go again.*

He took a deep breath and steadied himself before he opened the door, his face as neutral as possible.

The next morning Jacob and Ethan stood on the ramp lined with ODs and SS soldiers under the glaring sun.

All but one of the train cars in front of them were locked. Two ODs struggled to close the door. One of them put all of his weight into it, and the door slid into the locked position. An additional handlebar further secured it.

The people looking through the few small barred windows struggled to get fresh air, and Jacob pitied them. Some of them called out, asking for water. Others panicked in the extremely confined space.

Today's transport had been especially savage. When the train pulled into the camp, it was clear to everybody there was too little space. The cattle cars could typically hold forty people; today, they had crammed in closer to sixty people per car.

Ethan stood next to him, unable to block out the anguish of people pleading in the cars.

"I wish they would get moving already," Ethan said softly. "This is the worst part of it all—having to watch them watch us."

Jacob scoffed. "It's not about us. Imagine what they're going through in there."

"That's not what I meant. It's already horrible enough to have to do this, and this just makes it worse. Besides, there are way too many people in there. I doubt many of them will survive the journey."

Jacob had thought about that as well. Even if the trains stopped along the way—and they didn't—the doors wouldn't be opened. The signs on the side of the cars were very clear. The doors shouldn't be opened until the final destination. This train would go to a place called Sobibor—a name now as familiar to Jacob as Auschwitz-Birkenau and Theresienstadt.

The shriek of the whistle indicated the train was ready to depart, and the hairs on Jacob's arms stood up—they always did.

Slowly, the train started moving, crawling away from the camp like an iron snake cutting through the farm fields around them. The plumes of smoke from the locomotive intensified, and the sound of the rattling cars increased. The faces of those in the cars blurred, until the last car flashed past them and left them on the empty ramp.

As the last car turned the bend out of the camp, silence hung in the air for a few seconds. It was always like this. It was as if the men of the Ordedienst paid their respects to the people they'd just shipped off. But soon enough, everybody would step down from the ramp and return to their usual duties.

Today, however, things felt different.

"I need everybody to report to the assembly hall in half an hour," Pisk announced, his voice breaking the silence. "No exceptions."

Jacob and Ethan arrived early to find the room already packed with green uniforms. There were some SS soldiers in the room.

"What are they doing here? Can't be anything good," Ethan said.

*And why are they wearing their sidearms in here? And why is Gemmeker here?*

Jacob felt his palms turn clammy; the commander was rarely involved in the OD gatherings.

Pisk appeared at the front of the group with the same harried expression Jacob had seen earlier that morning.

"I'll get right to it," Pisk said. "The number of prisoners in the camp is going down. You've all seen this. As a result, we no longer have any need for the new barracks in the back."

The group remained silent, waiting for Pisk to continue. The head of the OD took a breath before continuing.

"Today's transport also saw one of our biggest shipments carried out well. This was a good job by everybody in this room. However, Commander Gemmeker has told me the population of the camp will continue to decrease."

Pisk looked around at the group. Gemmeker stood by him, waiting patiently for the Austrian to continue. Some of the other ODs' eyes darted around nervously.

*Can he just get to the point?*

"Therefore, we will further decrease the size of the OD. We no longer need this large a group policing the camp population. Our group will be halved. You will all report to me after this gathering, where some of you will be reassigned and informed of your new duties."

Jacob swallowed hard. He knew what reassignment meant. Ethan looked like he was about to be sick. Losing your spot in the OD meant the chances of your name appearing on the next transport list increased significantly.

Gemmeker spoke up for the first time: "For all of you, we will take into account what you've done for us in your time here. Know that we still need a strong Ordedienst in the camp. All of you are considered for this. Even if you're reassigned, you will find Westerbork is still a good place to be."

The commander's words did little to ease the palpable tension in the room. Gemmeker saw this as well, and he adjourned the meeting. They were told to report back in an hour. The men filed out of the room, most of them quietly talking amongst each other.

Jacob and Ethan walked over to one of the benches near the Boulevard and sat down without a word, watching the people passing by.

"Our chances of staying are pretty good, wouldn't you say?" Ethan broke the silence.

Jacob nodded.

"Your father is also an important part of the hospital administration," Ethan continued. "Your mother runs a classroom in the school. I think you'll be fine. I'm a little worried, though. My father should be okay as a teacher, but Mama is helping out in the kitchen most of the time, where they could easily replace her."

Jacob turned to his friend. "Don't think that way. You've been just as important to the OD as I have. There's no way Pisk will have forgotten about the both of us building up the new barracks—"

"—Which are now obsolete," Ethan interrupted.

# PART III

## SOMEWHERE IN GERMANY SEPTEMBER 1943

# CHAPTER TWELVE

Jacob woke to the sound of the train clattering along the tracks. The sun was doing its best to break free of the thick layer of clouds—not that the people in the train car could see. The small, barred windows offered little view and were too high for anybody to see anything without climbing up.

He shivered and wrapped his arms around his body. The car was not insulated, and Jacob's breath came out like a smoke plume in the frosty morning air. The only advantage of the packed car was the body heat radiating from other people.

In the semi-darkness, he looked at his father. Hermann was still asleep, snoring softly. Next to him, a mother and a teenage daughter were slumped against the side of the car.

He thought back to the day before when they'd left Westerbork in the afternoon. The platform had been crowded with more than a thousand people waiting for the train. He hadn't paid them any attention as he stood with his father and Ethan. His mother had miraculously escaped the list, as had Ethan's parents. He had no idea why they'd been spared, but he'd long since learned the transport lists were beyond all logic.

At first, Mama had insisted she'd come with them. It took all of his and his father's powers of persuasion to convince her otherwise. Leaving her behind had broken them. He didn't know if he'd ever see his mother again, but staying in Westerbork was still better for her than where he was now. Papa hadn't spoken since their departure.

Many of the Ordedienst had been on the platform. This time, however, they were the ones being shipped off. After Pisk's announcement that the OD force would be reduced, Ethan and Jacob were kept on for another four months. In that time, the transports had often exceeded two thousand souls, and Gemmeker had decided against trimming the OD too rigorously right away. But as the camp population and number of trains decreased, everybody in the OD knew it wouldn't be much longer until it was their turn to board the very trains they'd helped load—and that day had come the previous Monday.

Pisk had kept a small group of men, and most able-bodied men were placed on the transport this time. Jacob had spotted Olivier Fischer a few cars down. He'd tried to get his friend's attention, but it had been impossible to reach him or even signal him on the crowded platform.

The train had crept slowly through the Dutch countryside, and it took almost two hours until they crossed into Germany. It didn't help that the train had to stop several times along the way. The soldiers on the train wouldn't tell them why they stopped, and after a while, people stopped asking.

Jacob counted the people in his carriage. It was hard; everybody was packed close together. For some people, it had been impossible to sit down, and they'd alternated turns standing up, while other people found a cramped spot to sit. He estimated about fifty people crowded in the small space.

When dusk fell, the train had continued into the night. Despite the constant rocking of the train, he'd found it hard to catch any sleep. Ethan was in the car in front of him, but the din of the tracks made it impossible to communicate. Besides, what would he say? There was nothing to do but wait until they reached their destination. From the signs on the side of the train, he knew where they were headed—Auschwitz-Birkenau.

*Will Agnes be there? Is she still alive?* It had been almost a year since that morning on the ramp. His hopes had dwindled with every passing week without news. He had trouble remembering her face some days.

He felt some movement to his side and found his father looking up at him with puffy eyes.

"Do you know where we are?" Hermann asked in a croaking voice.

Jacob shook his head and replied softly: "I can't see anything, Papa. We rode through the night, so my best guess is that we're somewhere in western Germany. But it's impossible to see, and we haven't stopped at any stations. How are you feeling?"

"Like I've slept on the floor of a train," Hermann said, trying to readjust himself. Jacob tried to make some space, but he felt resistance from the woman next to him.

He tried to get up but instead stepped on the hand of another man who'd found a spot in front of him. The man grunted, and Jacob withdrew his foot.

Jacob felt the warmth of the sun on his face and savored it—a small comfort.

A shriek from the far side of the carriage interrupted the monotone sound of the clattering train. It jolted the man in front of Jacob, who stood up. Jacob did the same and was happy to stretch his legs. He felt cramps tightening in his calves and stretched to fight them.

The scream had come from a young girl sat on the floor—she was shaking, and her eyes were wide with terror. Next to her, an older man lay motionless. His face was ash-white—his eyes staring into space, devoid of any expression.

The girl tried to move away, but the people around her were too close to find enough space. She was horrified and kept her eyes averted from the dead man.

*He won't be the last.*

A woman in the middle of the carriage shook the man next to her. His eyes were closed, and the commotion hadn't roused him. She shook gently at first, but her eyes betrayed her worries. She poked the man and called his name, to no avail.

The people around the woman supported her as she burst into tears.

Jacob did a quick count and found at least ten people had perished overnight.

"We need to isolate the bodies," Hermann said, interrupting his thoughts.

Jacob nodded. "I know, but how are we going to do that? It's too cramped here. They won't open the doors along the way."

"Not even to get rid of the deceased?"

"They're instructed to keep the doors closed under any circumstances. I've seen it in the instructions for the transports. Once the doors are locked, they don't open until arrival at the camp."

Hermann looked aghast. "It's not going to be very respectful, but we'll need to collect the bodies and keep them in the corner of the car. I don't know how long our journey will be, but we need to keep as much space between them and us as we can, or nobody will make it."

Most people in the train car overheard their conversation. A tall man spoke up. "He's right. We need to pile the bodies in the corner over there. It will also give all of us a bit more space."

"Weren't you one of the doctors in the hospital?" the tall man asked Hermann.

Hermann corrected him: "Pharmacist, but I can't do anything more than keeping a distance between us and the bodies. We need to move them before they start to decompose, and we get sick from them."

Everyone worked together to move the bodies to the corner in the back of the car—they did so in silence, respectfully but with urgency.

The woman in the middle was the last person to part from her husband. She held onto his body.

Jacob gently nudged her. "You have to say goodbye to him now," he said.

She looked up, her eyes filled with sorrow. It broke Jacob's heart. He'd seen his share of grief in the past years, but the raw emotions on the woman's face struck him with new force in this moment.

"I can't leave him," she said. "He's everything I've got. I'd rather go with him than go on this journey on my own." She made no effort to move.

The other people in the car kept their distance as best they could.

Jacob spoke softly. "He will be right here in the carriage." He pointed to the area for the dead in the back of the car. "You can see him there, and when we get to our destination, you can bury him yourself."

The woman followed his pointing finger with glassy eyes. She wasn't really listening, but her grip on her husband loosened somewhat as she sat back and nodded.

Two men took that as a signal. They lifted the body and carried it to the back. The woman followed them. As they gently laid him down next to the other bodies, she sat down next to him. She turned her back to the rest of the prisoners and held onto his hand.

The rest of the morning crept by as the train droned on. People tried to catch some sleep, but the bumps and turns in the tracks made it almost impossible.

Jacob looked with affection at his father. Hermann had the uncanny ability to sleep just about everywhere, and his eyes were closed now. Hermann had achieved much in the camp—helping numerous people and keeping many of them off the transports. He and Dr. Brunner had tried their best to keep people in Westerbork. It was a cruel twist of fate that he was now on his way to the east himself.

Despite the horror of the dead, and even with people keeping their distance, it meant there was a bit more room for the living.

A man who'd helped them earlier squeezed through. "Some people over there aren't going to last much longer, either. Do you know if they'll feed us anything?"

Jacob's eyes went to the two buckets on the side of the car. One had a little bit of water left, and the other was rapidly filling with excrement. The smart ones had brought food for the journey, but not everybody had had that clarity of mind. The camp had long since stopped fortifying the transport prisoners with sandwiches.

"I don't know. But I wouldn't count on it," Jacob said. He checked his pocket for a piece of chocolate he'd managed to grab just before they left. "We'll be lucky if they stop and give us some water along the way."

The man looked at him. "You were in the OD before, weren't you?"

"I was." *There is nothing else to say about it.*

The man studied him. There was no anger in his face, no sign of malice. It was the one thing Jacob had feared after he'd been told he was no longer required. But he hadn't been attacked, and people hadn't treated him differently.

The man held out his hand. "I'm Bertho."

"Jacob."

"We know what you did when you were in that group," Bertho said as he crouched down next to Jacob. "I was in the camp for a long time, working in the kitchen. They must've thought I did a good job because they kept me there for over a year. I've seen my fair share of people come and go, and I've also seen many ODs."

Jacob sat silently, waiting for the man to continue.

"I could spot a good one from a bad one instantly. You may not have noticed this, but we all talked. We knew who to avoid, and which ones were okay. Can't say the same about the SS. They were all evil."

"They're the worst of the German army machine," Jacob agreed. "Most of them came from humble backgrounds and were sent to the SS training camps before they could think for themselves. They don't know any better."

Bertho scoffed. "Doesn't matter. They lack any form of human decency. But that's not my point. Some of your colleagues—if I may call them that—enjoyed their power. They abused it and hurt people for no reason. I've seen things in the barracks when they thought no-one was looking . . ."

*I could give you a whole list of names right now.*

"There were some animals, I agree," Jacob said. "But most of us tried to do our jobs with decency." He paused for a moment. "If they enjoyed cajoling people onto the trains, I'd make sure to stay well clear."

"And we noticed," said Bertho. "The rest of the people in the camp saw the difference. That's why you were left alone when you were no longer part of the OD. We knew you tried to help people, and so did your father. Some of the others didn't fare so well when they were part of the normal population again." Bertho looked at Jacob. "They had it coming. And now most of them are on this train as well, sharing the same fate."

They were silent for a moment, the rhythmic clanging of the wheels on the tracks the only sound.

"Some of the others say we're going to a place called Auschwitz," Bertho said, breaking the silence. "Do you know anything about that?"

Jacob nodded. "They say it's a work camp, but I also know nobody's ever come back from there."

"I spoke to some of the people coming in for deliveries to the kitchen. Dutch people from the outside."

Jacob's ears pricked up. "What did they say?"

"That the transports aren't actually going to work camps," Bertho said, lowering his voice to a whisper. "Sure, some people get to work for a while, until they're completely spent. But they have no use for children or old people."

"So then what?" Jacob was concerned now.

Bertho's face went solemn. He was silent for a few seconds before inching closer to Jacob. "They dispose of people."

"Dispose?"

Bertho nodded. "Too many people go into the camp, but nobody comes out. They've told me the smoke coming from the chimneys in the camp never stops."

Jacob was dumbstruck. He'd never heard of this before. The SS at Westerbork spoke about the work camps, and they admitted some people didn't survive the harsh conditions. "You're saying they're killing these people?"

Bertho shook his head and held up his hands. "Look, all I know is that people go into the camp, and that's it. They don't come back out. And honestly, what do they need children in a work camp for? They don't care about us. Look at the way they're transporting us. We're literally cattle to them."

Jacob couldn't argue with Bertho's logic. But he couldn't believe the Nazis were going through all this trouble to send people to be killed. The conditions at Westerbork had been quite good—why the hospital, school, and even the dental area later on?

His thoughts were interrupted by the screech of brakes and the train slowing down rapidly. Everybody in the car was now awake. Some of the bodies in the back shifted forward and were pushed back as the train jarred to a stop.

Jacob looked through a small crack in the car. They were at a small train station. He didn't recognize the name.

The German soldiers climbed down from their carriages and walked past the cars, smoking and laughing. Some sat down in the grass. The sun had completely broken through the clouds, and the soldiers basked in its rays.

Some people in the cars started shouting.

"Open the doors!" shouted a small boy in Jacob's car. Jacob wanted to tell him it was useless, but he couldn't muster the energy. Besides, there were too many people banging the sides of the car to get his point across.

Jacob pulled himself up to see through a crack in the door—one of the soldiers approached the car. He didn't recognize the man. He must've gotten onto the train during one of the earlier stops.

"Shut up—we're not opening the doors. But we can get you some water," the soldier said, keeping his distance from the door. "Is that what you want?"

That got the attention of the people in the other cars.

"Yes! Water! Please give us some water!" they cried out.

The soldier turned around and went into the station. The people in Jacob's car stopped shouting.

He returned with a bucket, and the faces of the people around Jacob turned hopeful. The people in the other cars also saw the soldier and shouted even louder.

The soldier approached Jacob's train car, and everybody squeezed forward.

"There's only one way to get us that water," Jacob said under his breath.

The soldier was now a few steps from the car—with some of the others gathering close by. The soldier looked back at them and smiled. "They wanted water, so I got them some ice-cold water."

He swung the large bucket back and forth with all his might. His aim was good, and the water rained in through the barred window. The people in the front were completely soaked. The rest of the water splashed onto the floor of the car. It quickly spread, even if some of the water leaked away through the cracks in the floor.

Jacob was just in time to get out of the way for the first splash, but his father wasn't as lucky—Hermann was soaked.

Outside, the soldiers roared with laughter. One of them took the bucket and ran back inside.

The sound in the other cars died down, and the people around Jacob shivered.

"Take off your clothes," Jacob said. "Wring them out and try to suck as much of the water as you can. We still have a long way to go."

He helped his father out of his wet shirt. "Try to get as much as you can, Papa. This is the best we'll get."

Hermann and Jacob took turns sucking the water from the dirty shirt. The others in the car did the same with their own soaked clothing. The water was foul, but it was better than nothing.

Outside, the soldiers had found more buckets and now doused the other cars.

Jacob took off his shirt and gave it to his father. "Wear mine, so you don't get too cold."

Hermann took it gratefully. "Do you know how much longer it will take?"

Jacob shook his head. "No, I don't recognize the place we're at. But I don't think it's Poland yet."

The train whistle shrieked. The SS stopped terrorizing the people in the cars and hastily jumped back on board as the train started moving again.

Jacob looked around the car, filled with shivering people. Most of them stood up, as the floor was still wet, but some of the older people crouched, regardless. They didn't seem to have enough energy to stand up. As the car hobbled along the uneven tracks, he feared for the cold night ahead.

The night was rough on everybody, and Jacob dozed in and out of sleep. The train car bounced up and down the tracks far more than it had at the beginning.

Jacob worried about his father—Hermann had started shivering early in the evening. As the sun went down, he developed a cough, which worsened during the night.

As the morning light hit the car, Jacob saw his father's condition had drastically deteriorated. His face was gaunt, and his eyes looked hollow—he'd aged ten years overnight.

"Try drinking a bit of this," Jacob said. as he wrung one of the shirts again. He squeezed a few drops of water as he held it above his father's mouth. Hermann struggled to open his mouth but managed to lick the drops off his lips. He tried to speak but only managed a rasping sound.

Jacob stroked his father's hair. "Save your energy, Papa—don't speak. Try to get some rest." It was perverse that he was giving his father medical advice. Hermann nodded and closed his eyes, his head finding support on Jacob's shoulder.

Jacob looked up to see some of the others pulling bodies toward the back of the train car.

Bertho leaned into him. "Another twelve didn't make it through the night," he said softly. His eyes were sad, but he looked strong and determined.

*At this rate, only a handful of us will make it to the camp.*

He felt his father's forehead—*burning up*! Jacob looked around the car. He thought about soaking his shirt in a puddle on the floor, but there wasn't a drop left.

Jacob considered taking a shirt from one of the people who'd died that night—to wring that out—but couldn't bring himself to do it. *Need to stay as far away as possible.*

Bertho looked at him. "What are you looking around for?"

"I need to bring his fever down," Jacob said.

The tall man didn't hesitate for a moment and took off his coat. He pulled at the bottom, where it was slightly unraveled. The piece of cloth gave way quickly, and he tore off a strip and handed it to Jacob. "Here, this should help. It's still a bit damp."

Jacob took it gratefully and tied it around his father's forehead. Hermann shifted a little, but he had already gone back into a deep sleep.

"Thank you—this could mean the difference between life and death," Jacob said.

"Anything I can do." Bertho wrapped his coat around his body. "I hope it helps your father."

It wasn't long until the train slowed to another stop. The deeper the train ventured into Germany, the more frequent the stops. They often halted on a side track as freight trains roared past.

They stopped at another small station, and the soldiers quickly jumped off the train. Most were posted between the train cars, and Jacob didn't think they could be much more comfortable than the people inside. However, they weren't crowded into the stinking cars, and they could use the bathrooms at the small stations.

The smell in the car worsened during their journey as some of the bodies started to bloat. The smell was unbearable. When the train moved, there was welcome ventilation, but even this didn't completely mask the lingering smell of death.

The bucket used for excrement was almost overflowing. Some of the men in the car had taken some of the clothes off the dead bodies and secured the bucket in one of the corners, to keep it from tipping.

Every time the train stopped—mostly alongside fields and small villages—people crowded under the small windows for air, pulling up to get a glimpse.

"Can you see where we are?" Jacob asked an adolescent boy whose friend was giving him a boost up to the bars.

"It says Świebodzin," the boy said, an odd look on his face. "That doesn't sound German at all."

Jacob sighed. *We're already in Poland. We could be in Auschwitz within a day.*

As he waited for the train to start moving, he heard a commotion in one of the other cars.

"Some of the soldiers are running back from the station to the car behind us," the boy said, straining to catch the scene outside.

"What's going on?"

The boy craned his neck to get a better look. "Some of them are running with their guns drawn."

The noise from the other car increased as men and women shouted for the soldiers to let them out.

People in nearby cars joined in, and the sound traveled through the entire train. People shouted and banged on the doors of the cars.

"The soldiers don't know what to do," the boy said. His face was flushed, and there was excitement in his voice.

A shot rang out. It was nearby—probably the car behind them. The noise in the rest of the train died down instantly.

The boy jumped down and shrank away from the window. Nobody wanted to look outside anymore.

Another shot reinforced the silence. A child started crying. The heavy boots of a couple of SS soldiers running past their car. Everybody held their breath as the soldiers slowed down.

They all breathed out as the sound of boots ebbed away. The soldiers inspected the next car—and the next.

Everything was silent on the platform. Although nobody saw what had happened in the next car, they all knew.

Before long, the train whistle announced their departure. Nobody talked anymore—they sat in silence and stared into space.

The last pretense of humanity was abandoned at the station of a small Polish town none of them had ever heard of.

In the silence of the car, Jacob took out his small chocolate bar, broke off a piece, and savored the bitter taste. He'd saved it for as long as possible, but his stomach was in full protest after almost two days without food. Their water supply had long run out, and he found himself squeezing every small drop of moisture from his clothes.

He looked at his father, who was now barely conscious. He took another small piece of chocolate and held it out to Hermann's mouth. His nose twisted as he picked up the scent. Hermann tried to open his mouth, but his muscles were too cramped.

Tears welled up in Jacob's eyes. His father was fading quickly. In Westerbork, Hermann had boarded the train without help. The man on the floor next to him wasn't even able to eat anymore.

Hermann's eyes were glassy, but there was a spark of recognition when they met Jacob's—there was a faint hint of a smile on his father's face.

Bertho remarked with tenderness, "That shower of water weakened even the strongest men."

Jacob wiped his father's forehead. He was still burning up, and Jacob didn't have any water left to cool him down. He took off the makeshift head compress Bertho had given him earlier.

"Has his fever gone down at all?"

Jacob shook his head. "If anything, it's gotten worse."

"I'm sorry."

Jacob changed the subject. "Do you have any family left?"

"I arrived in Westerbork with my parents, and because I was young and relatively strong, the Nazis decided I could help out in the fields and kitchen. My parents spent only two nights in Westerbork." Bertho looked downcast.

"Do you know where they were sent?"

He shook his head. "Nobody told me. You know how it was. If you weren't on the transport list, you weren't allowed near the train."

"You wouldn't have wanted to be anywhere near on transport days. It was hell," Jacob said. He still had nightmares of the faces looking at him as the train cars sped eastbound.

Bertho cleared his throat. "You know, Jacob, I've been wondering. Do you think there's a way to escape from this train?"

Jacob looked sharply at his new friend. He hadn't thought about that. "Not through the doors, I wouldn't think." The walls had small cracks, but they were sturdy enough, and it wouldn't be possible to force through a wall. "There's barbed wire around the outside of the car as well. Even if we could break through some of those cracks, we wouldn't be able to get through that."

Bertho looked tense. "I'm worried about where we're going. I think it might be worse than we think. What if they've decided they don't need us, and they simply execute us right away?"

"I still have a hard time believing they'd do that," Jacob said, though he had thought the same. "They need all the hands they can get in their war effort." *But what if he's right and there's no work camp?*

Bertho got up and pushed himself through to one of the windows and pointed at the bars. "What if we could move these?"

Jacob followed him. "It's the only place without barbed wire on the outside. But how are we going to get through those?"

Bertho boosted Jacob to give him some leverage. Jacob pulled on one of the bars and found little movement. He tried another, which gave way a little.

"I think we have a chance," he declared, and saw a spark of hope in Bertho's eyes.

The boys near the window watched them with interest. "But how are you going to get past the guards?" one asked. "Even if you get out, they're everywhere."

The boy was right. Every other train car had an extra compartment that served as a small guard tower. Jacob had seen during their stops that the soldiers carried long-range rifles.

Jacob tried the bars again and was encouraged by how much he could wiggle them. He used all his strength to pull on two of the bars. They moved, but he also felt they were sunk too deep into the foundation of the window. There was no way they'd be able to pull the bars out.

Bertho tried the same but gave up after two attempts. "They're too solid."

Jacob thought back to his work with Fischer in the camp. He'd seen how his friend had drawn up blueprints, always calculating the forces in play when setting windows or supporting beams for the new barracks. There were always weak spots in the design. Fischer said any structure had weak spots—you just needed to find them. Jacob was confident he could.

"Give me some time to think about this," he said. "The bars are giving way, so we have a chance. I just don't know what the way is yet."

Bertho's eyes lit up.

The boy on the floor was unconvinced. "What about the guards, even if you manage?"

Jacob looked at the youngster. "We'll cross that bridge when we get to it."

Jacob racked his brain. They had no tools, so the most obvious options were off the table. The window was broad enough for a man to fit through if even just a few bars were displaced.

His father lay next to him, his breathing shallow as his upper body jerked with every short breath he took. Jacob kept him as comfortable as possible with Bertho's coat. Still, Hermann needed food, water, and medical care. And judging by the speed of their journey, they couldn't count on any of those soon.

They were stuck on a sidetrack for what felt like an eternity. Every so often, another train would zip by. From what Jacob could see, these were military supply trains bound for the eastern front.

Darkness fell, and it appeared they would spend the night in the field, as the German soldiers sat by a small fire they'd kindled.

*We must be far into Poland if they're confident enough to build a fire and not worry about any British planes.*

Jacob smelled a stew cooking, and his mouth watered.

"Any brilliant ideas yet?" Bertho sat down next to him. He kept his voice down, as most of the people in the car were sleeping or trying to. The silence of the field made the train stoppage a welcome respite.

Jacob shook his head. "Not just yet. We need tools."

"We won't get any, so stop thinking like that." There was a hint of frustration in Bertho's voice.

"There's not much we can do in this darkness—better try to get some rest," Jacob said. "I'll think better after I've slept a few hours."

Bertho calmed down. "Sorry I snapped at you. I just want to get out of here. If this journey takes much longer, we might end up the only two people alive."

Jacob flinched, and Bertho realized his mistake. "I didn't mean it that way—of course, I hope your father recovers."

"It's okay—he seems at peace now. And to be honest, I'm not sure if getting to Auschwitz is going to be much better for him. If what you said is true, he won't be put to work anyway."

Bertho stood up. "I'm going to follow your advice. Hopefully, we can think of something tomorrow."

Jacob hoped Bertho was wrong about Auschwitz, but doubt gnawed at him. He'd seen so many people shipped off from Westerbork, never to be heard from again. People just disappearing in the endless stream of trains. He rested his head against the side of the car and drifted away in a restless sleep.

Jacob woke in the middle of the night. The train was moving again.

He took a small piece of chocolate out of his pocket and broke it in half. He checked his father's fever and knew something was wrong. His father's forehead was no longer burning—it was cool and clammy.

He was instantly awake and sat up, the piece of chocolate falling to the floor. He checked Hermann's neck. Cold. His hand went to his father's chest as he tried to find a heartbeat—there was none.

Jacob looked hard to see his father's face in the light of the moon overhead. Hermann looked like he was sleeping.

A tear rolled down Jacob's face. He was surprised he still had enough liquid in his body for tears. *Papa.*

In the darkness of the train car, he let his tears flow freely as he buried his face into his papa's chest.

# CHAPTER THIRTEEN

The light of the morning did nothing to bring the people in the car to life. Most of them opened their eyes but made no attempt to move from their spots. Jacob sat slouched against the wall of the car. He and Bertho had just carried his father's body to the back. Hermann wasn't the only one to perish over the night. A little under half of the people who had boarded the train in Westerbork were still alive. Most of them were young, some of them even younger than himself. Some of the older people managed to survive, but Jacob could see the journey taking its toll on the survivors.

He looked to the back of the car where his father's body lay. He looked peaceful. Some of the other bodies had already started to bloat, Jacob hoped they'd reach Auschwitz before his father's body befell the same fate.

All he wanted to do was curl up in a ball and grieve. But he knew he couldn't do that. He needed to find a way out now more than ever. He walked toward the window and studied the bars. He reached out and pulled on two of them. The movement gave him new hope as a thought struck.

"Bertho," he said, calling out for his friend who looked at him inquiringly. "We've been looking at this the wrong way."

Bertho gave him a puzzled look. "How so?"

Jacob tried to pull the bars toward them. "This doesn't work, right? You can see that the bars are fixed too deeply into the top and bottom of the window. Try it."

Bertho pulled on two of the bars. Very little happened.

"You see? Now try putting all your weight into one instead," Jacob said.

The tall man did so, pushing his legs against the wall for extra strength. It moved a little, but not enough for it to be forced out.

Bertho let go. "So, what's your point? That it's useless to force the bars?"

Jacob smiled. "Not by trying in the most obvious way. But we can use that movement in another way."

He positioned himself a little to the side of the window. He grabbed one of the bars and pulled it aside.

Bertho moved closer while Jacob continued to pull. "I think there's some movement," he said, excitement in his voice.

Two of the boys stood up and looked on as Jacob strained to pull the bar further to the side.

"I can feel some movement as well," Jacob said. He released the bar with a sigh.

"It didn't bend or anything," one of the boys said.

"Well, I only applied a little bit of pressure for a few seconds. Of course, it's not going to make a big difference. But it's steel, and if we continue on those middle bars, we might have enough space to crawl through."

Bertho nodded slowly. "I think you're right. But it will be slow, don't you think? Even if we take turns, it'll take too long for the steel to weaken."

"We need a lever," Jacob said. He scanned the car for anything useful. If only he'd smuggled some tools on board the car, but it was too late for that now.

"Jacob, what about these?" Bertho stood near a pile of abandoned jackets and pullovers. People had taken the clothing off the dead, but some were so dirty that nobody wanted anything to do with them.

"It's not a lever, but we could rip these to form ropes and pull on the bars together?"

*It's a good idea—we can pull on the bars from down here.*

The boys got up as well, keen to help.

Together, they picked the strongest sweaters and tied them together. They now held two make-shift ropes, which they tied to the same iron bar. Jacob gave his rope a hard pull and was happy to see it held firm.

"Now we need to pull on these as hard and long as we can," Jacob said. "It will take patience, but the bars will give way little by little."

Bertho was keen to get started and took the other rope as he signaled to one of the boys. "How about we pull on this one together?"

They set about the task with vigor. At first, it seemed like nothing much happened. After half an hour, Jacob checked the bars. Bertho and the boys looked on, short of breath and sweaty.

He inspected the middle of the bars, where they had exerted the pressure. He turned to his companions.

"It's working!" he said with a triumphant smile. "The space is widening."

They crowded around to see the results on their work so far. It encouraged them, and they continued with enthusiasm.

After they continued for another hour, Jacob realized the going was too slow. Their make-shift ropes kept slipping from their hands.

"If we had more grip, this would be a lot easier," one of the boys said when he tumbled backward for the umpteenth time.

Jacob agreed, but he didn't have a solution. Meanwhile, their work had attracted the attention of the rest of the car. Some people helped taking turns to pull on the bars so they could take a quick breather.

An older man stood next to Jacob, his eyes studying the rope. "I have an idea, but you might not like it."

"Try me."

"Normally, I'd say you should use water to get more grip on those shirts. But since we don't have any water, you'll have to make do with the only other fluids we have in here," the old man said, his eyes on the front of the car.

Jacob followed his gaze—the toilet bucket.

"That liquid is also highly acidic," the man continued. "So it might give you a small advantage with it biting into the iron."

"Every little bit helps," Jacob said, and he crossed the short distance to the bucket. The smell was horrible, and he pulled his shirt to cover his nose, which didn't help.

"You really want to do this?" Bertho asked, his nose crumpling.

"What he says makes sense. We'll be able to put force into it without slipping away the whole time."

Bertho nodded. "Then we'll do it. I want to get out of here, and if this speeds things up, all the better."

The bucket was almost overflowing—the liquid had a dark, almost black color, and small pieces of excrement floated on the surface. Jacob gagged as he crouched down and quickly turned his head away from the bucket.

Bertho handed him the two make-shift ropes. Without looking, Jacob plunged the ropes into the bucket. The smell intensified as he dunked the sweaters into the putrid liquid.

When he was sure the sweaters were completely soaked, he pulled them out. He dropped them on the floor and stepped away from the disgusting mess. He fought down the urge to vomit and hurried to the window.

He sucked in the fresh air, and the wave of nausea passed.

Bertho wrung out the ropes above the bucket. They tied the wet sweaters back to the iron bars. The rope held as Jacob pulled on it.

The two boys looked on with disgust-wrinkled faces.

"You still want to get out of the car?" Jacob asked. "Time to get your hands dirty."

Bertho laughed as the boys reluctantly wrapped the ropes around their hands. "It does feel easier to hold on to these," one of them said after a while.

They spent the rest of the afternoon and early evening working the bars as they alternated going to the bucket. Bit by bit, the space between the bars increased.

"I think we might be able to fit through these soon," Jacob said as he looked up.

Bertho grabbed one of the bars, and it moved freely. He nodded approvingly.

"If we keep going like this, we'll be able to squeeze through tonight," he said.

The two boys stood behind them. They were leaner than Jacob and Bertho, and their eyes lit up. *They could squeeze through even before we could!* They grabbed their pieces of rope and continued to tug at the bars with extra zeal.

Some of the other people in the car gathered around. The older man who'd helped them earlier smiled at Jacob.

"If I were younger, I would've done the same as you," he said.

"Without you, we wouldn't have come this far," Jacob said as he picked up the rope. They'd found that using a technique of fast, quick pulls worked best.

The man's face turned serious. "But what are you going to do when you get out?"

"I haven't thought that far ahead." In fact, he hadn't thought about it at all.

"Do you know anyone in Poland?"

Jacob shook his head and gave the rope another sharp tug. "We've passed a lot of villages and some smaller cities along the way. I'm going to take my chances with the people living there. Maybe I can hide in a barn for a while."

He tried to sound more confident than he was. What did the Polish people think about the Germans? *Probably hate them as much as the Jews and the Dutch do.*

The man walked to the bars and inspected them. "You'd better get your plan ready soon. At this pace, you'll need to decide whether you want to take the leap tonight or tomorrow morning—latest."

Jacob looked to Bertho, whose face was covered with sweat. His new friend hadn't hesitated for a second as they plotted their escape. He hoped Bertho was ready to take the jump with him.

The train didn't stop for the night. Darkness had fallen many hours before, but a full moon shone just brightly enough for a glimmer of light to shine into the car.

Most people were asleep or trying to. Jacob, Bertho, and the boys had worked through the evening and early night and now stood in front of the window.

"I think we've done it, boys," Bertho said. The moonlight hit his teeth as he flashed a triumphant smile.

"Give me a boost." Jacob jumped up and held onto the wiggly bars while the two boys held his feet. He looked out into a forested area as the train crawled by. The space between the bars was now big enough for him to stick his head and shoulders outside. He moved just enough so he could look down the car. He knew if a guard spotted him, the plan was foiled.

There was nobody to the front or back of their car. He made out the outlines of a small guard tower on the car in front of them. The orange flicker of a cigarette betrayed a guard's presence.

He jumped down. "There's a guard tower just in front, and it's occupied. He doesn't seem too alert, though."

Bertho smiled. "Why would he be? How many people escape from these trains?"

"We'll still need to be careful."

Jacob pulled on one of the bars, and it moved quite freely. "You see? If we apply constant pressure on both bars, there will be just enough space for us to wriggle through."

One of the boys spoke up: "That's all good for the first two people going through, but who's going to keep these in place after they've escaped?"

"We're going to need some help," Jacob said. "But first, I want to know if all of you are willing to jump. Getting out of the car is just our first hurdle. We don't know anybody in this country. Hell, we don't even know where we are right now. For all we know, the people here might sympathize with the Nazis."

Jacob saw three determined young men looking back at him. There was no doubt about their willingness to follow through on their plan.

"They probably don't have enough food to feed themselves, just like the people in the Netherlands," Jacob continued, making eye contact with all three.

"But it can't be worse than where this train is taking us," one of the boys said. "At least when we jump, we have a chance at making it. If we stay here, we know they're going to do whatever they want with us."

The other boy nodded. "I'm jumping."

Jacob turned to Bertho. He scoffed. "I'm all in. I have nothing keeping me here."

"Then it's decided. We jump tonight," Jacob said.

An hour later, they were ready. They had no belongings other than the clothes on their backs.

Jacob felt completely unprepared, but he knew there was nothing left for him in the train car. Ethan was only a car away. So near, yet so far.

*I will come back for you. I don't know how, but I'll find you.*

The group huddled in a small circle.

"I will climb out of the car first, then Bertho and then you two," Jacob said, pointing at the two boys. "Those men over there will help you after we've climbed through the opening."

He pointed at two older men standing nearby. They'd volunteered to keep the pressure on the bars so the two boys could climb through as well. The two dozen people still alive in the car looked on with interest. They were too weak or old to attempt the jump but didn't want to miss this bold escape.

"Once you're outside, there is very little time to wait. You'll need to jump off the train immediately, so the guards don't see you," Jacob said.

Bertho nodded. "Remember, they have searchlights, and they will use them. Also, we don't know how they'll react. They might stop the train or simply keep going. They will probably shoot at you."

One of the boys fumbled with his hands, Jacob could see he was scared.

*I don't blame him.*

"Don't think of anybody but yourself once you've jumped. We

might run into each other again in the future, but it's better to be on your own. A group of haggard-looking men like ourselves is bound to attract attention." Jacob looked at them. "Are you ready?"

They nodded, determination in their eyes.

"Then, we leave now."

The boys crouched down, and Jacob stepped onto their backs and lifted himself to the small window. The cold night air hit him in the face as he peeked outside. He shivered as he looked up. The moon had shifted a little, offering less light than before.

*Good—that will make it harder for the guards to notice us.*

"Good luck, Jacob," came Bertho's voice behind him.

He looked back one more time and smiled at him. Without Bertho, he wouldn't be where he was right now.

He steadied himself and took a deep breath. He pushed his head through the window, his legs dangling. The air rushed at his face with more venom than he'd expected.

This was the most dangerous part of the escape. If a guard noticed his head poking out, he'd be a perfect target.

He looked to the left where the guard post was—it was dark. Perhaps the guard was asleep? On the other side, he saw the silhouette of the cars behind them snaking along. There was no guardhouse on that side.

He felt queasy, and he suppressed a wave of nausea. He needed to push through, and there was only one way to go.

Jacob moved his hands from the bars to the outside of the car. He pushed himself forward and wiggled his shoulders through—one at a time. His upper body was now almost completely exposed.

While he hung outside, he felt the train slow down somewhat. Ahead, he saw train cars banking to the left. It meant they were going into a turn. This would be the perfect place to jump.

He used all his strength to squeeze his lower torso through the narrow opening. It was a very tight fit, but he managed. To the left of the window was the door. He managed to grab the door handle and hold onto it as he swung his legs through the opening, barbed wire dragging at his clothing. For a moment, Jacob felt himself drift as the wind caught his legs.

Then—just as quickly—he slammed into the door and struggled to find some narrow footing. The wind howled in his ears and tugged at his clothes. The clattering of the wheels was almost deafening. He gripped the handle a little tighter.

His heart thumped in his chest. The sound was louder than everything else around, yet he worried the guards might see him. He looked ahead as the car was about to go into the turn and braced himself for the jump.

He looked back at the window and saw Bertho's hands at the bars—his friend was on his way, but he also knew he couldn't wait for him.

Four cars to go until his car would be at the turn. He closed his eyes for a second.

*Keep breathing and count to five. You're almost there.*

"Halt!"

A shout in the distance interrupted his thoughts. He opened his eyes and turned toward the source of the sound as time appeared to slow down. A shadow moved in the guardhouse, and its small door opened. A soldier looked in his direction—but not at him.

*Shit. He's spotted Bertho.*

Jacob turned and saw the terrified face of Bertho peeking out of the window. His hands were already on the outside of the car, which meant there was no way back—he needed to push through.

The guard's eyes fixed on Bertho as he aimed his rifle—he pulled the trigger without hesitation.

The bright flash from the muzzle blinded Jacob, and he pushed himself closer to the door. The bang was muffled by the howling wind, but the impact of the bullet on the side of the train car was unmistakable.

Jacob turned to his friend and saw the shot had missed—Bertho frantically tried to wiggle free.

Jacob didn't hesitate. "Hurry up, Bertho! Push out and jump—we're about to go into a turn!"

Despite the other sounds, the soldier heard Jacob. Their eyes met, and Jacob saw surprise in the other man's expression. He seemed unsure what to do next—but only for a moment, as he swung his rifle in Jacob's direction.

*This is it, last chance.*

As the train banked into the turn, Jacob let go of the door handle and launched himself into the darkness.

A shot rang out, but he felt nothing as the wind carried him for a split-second. The next thing he felt was the cold, muddy ground crashing into him out of nowhere. He rolled on, trying to lower the impact, but felt a sharp pain in his shoulder.

He lifted himself, his shoulder protesting at every move. The moon had moved behind the trees, but he saw the outline of the forest ahead of him. He ran into the cover of the trees, cutting himself on branches along the way. Behind him, the train thundered on. Jacob kept running further into the woods.

He didn't know where he was going, but he knew he had to get as far away from the tracks as possible.

# PART IV

OŚWIĘCIM, POLAND
SEPTEMBER 1944

# CHAPTER FOURTEEN

Zofia tapped her foot impatiently while she reached for a stack of papers on her desk. Her eyes shifted to the door of her little office whenever someone passed in the hallway.

It wasn't like Antoni to be late.

She'd made sure to come in early this morning—she'd been the first clerk in. That allowed her to finish most of her tasks even before her colleagues walked in at nine. Not that the work in the public registration office required much effort on her part—it was the same every day. Zofia Zdrowak spent her days keeping track of the people living in the small city of Oświęcim. Ever since she could read, she'd helped her mother in and around the office, but when the Germans invaded their country, things had changed. For starters, they'd renamed the town Auschwitz, and all official papers now bore the German name of her hometown.

The registration office required more and more staff to track the growing stream of people arriving every day. When Mr. Oskar, her mother's boss, asked Zofia if she'd be interested in helping out, she hadn't hesitated. The work came naturally to her—she was good with numbers and had a keen eye for detail. She was fascinated by the endless stream of large ledgers and thick files brought in by stern-looking soldiers every day.

Zofia took another folder from the filing cabinet. She might as well keep going—people were late all the time.

As she sat down and opened the folder, she couldn't help but feel uneasy —she checked the clock again. It was half-past nine, and the people from the Auschwitz-Birkenau camp should be here by now. The German machine worked with pinpoint precision, and their transports were no different.

*Have they found out about our plans?*

She dismissed the thought immediately—Antoni would rather die than tell the Germans anything.

There was one other small desk in her office, and it was normally occupied by Antoni. He was interned in the camp just down the road. Every day, a small group of prisoners came down to the administrative building. These jobs were some of the most sought-after in the camp, as it gave a select few people a chance to work outside. Zofia knew that all other posts required strenuous manual labor in harsh conditions.

She found it impossible to concentrate and closed the folder. She stepped into the hallway, which was as eerily quiet as always, and walked to the front of the building, passing the open office doors. The Germans had made it clear the doors were to be open at all times. SS guards some-times patrolled the hallways and could ransack an entire office without reason. It meant people kept quiet but for the occasional whisper when they were sure nobody was listening.

Since no Germans prowled the hallway, she popped her head around the doorframe of the office furthest down the hall.

"Zofia!" a blond girl whispered. "You startled me."

"Sorry about that," Zofia smiled. "Just checking in on you."

Maria got up and hugged Zofia. "Were you in early? You look very awake."

Zofia nodded. "I needed to get some work done before everybody came in. You know how crazy it gets when the office is full, right?" She winked at Maria. "Nobody has arrived from the camp yet, have they?"

Maria shook her head. "I'm surprised—it's the first time this has happened since I started working here."

*So she's noticed it, too.*

"Do you think something happened?" Maria looked worried.

"You never know what goes on in there. But it could be a roll call taking longer than normal, or maybe they're having some transportation problems. Hopefully, they'll be here soon—I have a ton of work, and I can't finish it all by myself."

Maria looked thoughtful. "Let's wait and see."

"I'll leave you to it, then—let's go for a short walk around lunch, shall we? The weather is quite lovely today," Zofia said.

She returned to her work for half an hour before she was interrupted by a knock on her open door. That was unusual—most people simply walked in. She looked up to see a lanky boy in the door opening. He wore the familiar striped uniform of the camp and swayed on his feet, unsure what to do—hands in his pockets.

"Are you Zofia?" he asked—in German—with a voice deeper than Zofia had expected. His accent was unfamiliar to her, but certainly not Polish.

She nodded. "Come in—what brings you here?"

He took two steps forward but kept his hands in his pockets. It made Zofia a little uncomfortable.

"I was sent to help you with your paperwork today," he said. "I speak German and Hungarian."

*So he is Antoni's replacement.* "Do you know where Antoni is?"

The boy shook his head. "I don't know who that is. This morning I was taken from my barracks and told I wouldn't spend the day in the potato fields, but that I needed to board a truck into town. They told me you needed extra hands in processing the large group of Hungarians who arrived in the camp this week."

Zofia tried to hide her disappointment. She enjoyed working with Antoni, who'd helped her out for the past four months. But most of all, she worried about him and whether anything had happened in the camp. She wanted to ask the boy, but she first needed to find out whether she could trust him.

"First things first—what's your name?"

"I'm Denes, but most people simply call me Deni," he said. "I'm from Budapest, and I've always worked in my father's accountancy shop. I might be young, but I know how to work with numbers."

Zofia smiled, and he returned a shy smile. "Well, then we have one thing in common. Let's get you started."

They worked throughout the morning with Deni occasionally asking questions, but he picked up the work quite quickly. By midday, Zofia told him to take a short break and get something to eat.

He looked at her in surprise. "We never get breaks in the field, never mind food."

She was mortified. After the months working with Antoni, she had become accustomed to him knowing his way around their office. The small kitchen in the building provided everybody with a simple lunch. It was one of the reasons everybody wanted to work here—extra food was a lifeline afforded to the very few. The only thing camp prisoners couldn't do was go outside.

As she explained this to Deni, his eyes grew wide.

"Come, let me walk you to the kitchen," she said. "I'll introduce you to Olga, the cook."

The communal eating area was nothing more than a small room with a dozen chairs. It was empty—most people preferred to have lunch in their offices.

Zofia entered the kitchen without knocking, Deni in tow behind her.

The room was small, hot, and cramped. A large stove in the middle dominated the space—with cupboards and a large refrigerator flanking it. A diminutive woman furiously moved between the stove and a chopping board on the far side of the kitchen.

"Zofia, you're late today!" she cried. "I saved the best piece of the bread for you, but I almost thought you weren't coming." She didn't break her stride as she took the lid off a large pot, then stirred and sampled the liquid. "Excellent, if I say so myself. This is a pretty good soup considering what I'm working with here."

Zofia grabbed a piece of bread from the counter, then took a second piece and tossed it to Deni while she took a big bite. "I know—it's a bit of an odd day. The people from the camp were over an hour late, so we're trying to catch up."

In reality, there was little to catch up on. Deni had done good work, and they were well ahead of schedule.

"Olga, can you look after Deni? He's working with me and could use some of your home-cooked food. I'm heading out for a walk—just bread for me today."

Olga stopped just long enough to size Deni up. "Looks like he needs more than one portion." She pointed at one of the cupboards. "Grab yourself a bowl, and you can sample the soup."

Zofia smiled. Olga would make sure Deni ate plenty today.

She turned to Deni. "I'll be back later, but just eat as much as you can before I return, and we'll spend the afternoon finishing up the Hungarian files."

Deni needed no encouragement as he eyed the soup.

"Just leave him here, and I'll take care of him," Olga said, winking at Zofia.

Zofia and Maria sat on a bench outside town. They liked to take this walk on their lunch break when the weather allowed it. Today the sun shone brightly, and they looked out to the countryside.

"This place would be beautiful if it weren't for the camp," Zofia said, as she looked up to the dark sky, and suppressed a shudder.

Maria nodded. "The crematoriums never stop. I can almost taste the ash in the air."

"I don't think it's almost—I'm sure it's in the air."

Zofia took a bite from her simple sandwich. She'd managed to find a bit of cheese this morning and wrapped it in a handkerchief to tuck into Olga's bread. She savored the taste. Cheese was rare these days, and she was grateful for her mother's contacts. Somehow, she always found something special to break the boring diet of potatoes and carrots.

"I saw Antoni didn't come in today," Maria said, bringing Zofia back to the present. "That's unusual, isn't it?"

"It's been an odd day. First, with the prisoners coming in so late, and then Antoni not showing up," Zofia agreed.

"Do you think something is wrong?"

Zofia didn't answer immediately. She knew life in the camp was unpredictable, given its predictability. Antoni had told her about the daily routine, which sounded dreadful. And then they had to deal with the constant threat of the *Kapos* and the SS. The SS she knew all about, but the kapos were the worst, Antoni had told her. They were Jews put in charge by the Germans to police their own people. For most of them, the power had gone to their head, and they were cruel, eager to impress.

But the unpredictability in their behavior was the worst. A break in the routine usually meant something was wrong. Antoni told her about entire work details disappearing from one day to the next. They would be there at roll call in the morning, only to be replaced in the evening. She didn't want to think that had happened to Antoni.

"He could simply be reassigned for the day, or he might have fallen sick," Zofia said with little conviction.

Maria picked up on her friend's worries. "Perhaps I could ask Wojciech if he knows anything?"

Wojciech was an inmate whose carpentry skills secured him tasks doing odd jobs in the registration office and other offices, and he'd become good friends with Maria. He was a source of news they all appreciated.

Zofia nodded. "That's a good idea. Is he in today?"

"Yes, he's working on the door in the old library. I can make up an excuse to talk to him. In fact, one of my filing cabinets has a loose handle, which should be fixed."

"Great—I'll come to see you at the end of the day, then. Thanks."

Maria waved her hand dismissively. "Anything for you and the Sosienki."

Zofia was restless for the rest of the afternoon. She considered going to Maria's office before the end of the day but decided against it. She didn't know who was in her friend's office, and she'd spotted a pair of SS men patrolling the hallway earlier and didn't know if they were still in the building. They would undoubtedly question her if they found her in Maria's office. She didn't need that kind of attention.

When the clock struck six, a bell rang in the hallway. Deni looked at her in surprise.

"That's the end of the day for you, I'm afraid," she said. "The guards are here to take you back to the camp."

Deni's face fell. "Already?"

"Look, you've done an excellent job. They'll ask me how you've done because they always do. I'll tell them we'd be happy to have you back anytime." She smiled at him reassuringly. "I don't know how many Hungarians are in the camp, but I fear your services will be required again in the future. Did you finish all of today's transports?"

He nodded. "I did—they're all over there." He pointed at a thick ledger on the corner of his small desk.

"Then we'll leave it there, and I'll tell the Germans you've finished your work for today but that I'd love to have you back."

He stood up and neatly tucked his chair in before holding out his hand. "It's been a pleasure working with you today, Zofia. Even if this is my only day outside the camp, I'll treasure it. I haven't eaten this well in a long time, so please thank Olga for me."

Zofia swallowed hard and shook his hand—it felt bony, and her heart broke for the young man. "Take care of yourself, Deni."

He stepped out of the office to the hallway, where an SS guard barked at him to hurry up. She waited for silence to return to the hall before hurrying to Maria's office, who stood waiting for her.

"Did you speak to Wojciech?"

Maria nodded. "I was lucky—there was no-one else in the library."

"And? Did he know anything?"

"He said there was an incident in one of the barracks near him yesterday, and it meant some of the work details were changed."

Zofia's heart sank. "What kind of incident?"

"Some people returning from work in the evening were too late for the dinner round. Apparently, some of them tried to break into the kitchen to steal food. A kapo saw it and called the SS."

*That doesn't sound like something Antoni would do. He's too careful.*

"Was Antoni involved?"

Maria shook her head. "As far as Wojciech knew, he wasn't, but some of the people in his barracks were. As a punishment, all of them were shut into their barracks today, without any food or water."

Zofia breathed a sigh of relief. Although a day in the barracks was tough punishment, Antoni would be fine. His extra rations from his office days would see him through.

"He might well be back tomorrow then," she said.

Maria stood up and motioned for Zofia to follow her. "Yes, but for now, let's get out of here. My parents will be wondering what's keeping me. Do you want to walk home with me?"

Zofia shook her head. "I have a quick errand to run. I'll see you tomorrow."

As Zofia entered the small tavern, the air was thick and had the familiar smell of tobacco and stale beer. The establishment consisted of four rooms—the largest dominated by the bar with its large tap handles.

She scanned the room and recognized all the regulars—an older couple sitting in silence and a man lost in his newspaper. She didn't spot Marian and found a quiet spot in one of the smaller rooms to wait for him—she preferred some more privacy. Piotr, the bartender and owner of the tavern, set a glass of water in front of her.

"The usual for you, Zofia," he said with a smile. "Everything well at the administration?"

"Busy as always, but we'll manage. I'm just glad to have something on my hands to do. I know a lot of people are less fortunate." She looked around the room.

Piotr nodded. "Some of them come in when I open and don't leave until closing time. And they have no money to spend, trust me. I think most people simply want someone to talk to."

Zofia smiled. "And then they find you."

He chuckled and then was silent for a few seconds before continuing: "Are you waiting for Marian?"

"Yes, he should be here any moment."

Piotr leaned a little closer. "Anything I can help with?"

"Just letting us sit here in the back is help enough, Piotr. With some of your clientele, I know that's dangerous enough as it is." She looked at him fondly. "We appreciate your help."

The bell at the door announced new customers. Piotr looked over his shoulder and pulled a face. "Looks like I'm serving some more of those."

The sound of loud clacks on the wooden floors was unmistakable, and a hush descended over the room as four SS officers entered. They went straight to the bar, and Piotr rushed back to help them.

Zofia heard them order in German. *Typical. Anywhere they go, they think they own the place.*

Most of the regulars didn't understand them, but Zofia's German was good enough to hear the derogatory comments about them. She slumped in her seat, hoping they wouldn't notice her.

She kept her eyes on the door.

*What's taking him so long? Did he run into these louts—or did they get suspicious about him?*

She calmed herself down and took a sip of her stale, lukewarm water.

*Keep it together, Zofia. He'll be here soon.*

The Germans sat down at one of the tables in the middle of the main room, much to Zofia's relief. She and Marian needed their privacy. She tapped her foot and caught herself drumming her fingers on the table.

The doorbell rang again. Marian scanned the room and pretended not to notice the Germans. Zofia knew better—she saw him flinch momentarily, but he recovered immediately. He spotted her, and she gave him a quick smile.

Marian was at least ten years her senior, she thought. She didn't know much about him, but he was probably in his late twenties, although his dark hair and beard gave him an older appearance. They never spoke about their private lives—the only thing that mattered was the Sosienki cell they were both members of.

He sat down without greeting, his face flushed. He took the corner seat so he could keep his eyes on the Germans in the other room.

"Did you run over?" Zofia asked, spotting a small dribble of sweat coming down the side of his face.

He took out a handkerchief and dabbed his face. "Maybe a little. I was late, and I know you hate tardiness." He took off his simple jacket and draped it over the chair next to him. "I see we have friends present. Did they just come in?"

Zofia nodded. "They're on their first round, so I'm afraid they'll be quite a bit longer."

"They hate us, but they love our taverns, don't they?" His face was neutral, but his eyes spat fire.

Piotr came over and placed a small glass in front of Marian. "They just ordered food, so I don't think they're going anywhere anytime soon," he said.

Marian nodded. "Thank you, Piotr."

The bartender left without another word. Marian took a sip and smiled faintly. "We might be in dire straits, but at least we still have our vodka."

"I'm glad you've got your priorities straight," Zofia said, raising an eyebrow. "You think now is a good time to drink?"

Marian shrugged. "Now is as good a time as any. Might be dead tomorrow." He took another small sip as if to reinforce his point.

Zofia sighed, although she knew he was right. Men like Marian were the unsung heroes of the war, taking risks every day. If he wanted to have a drink, she had no right to question it.

"You're right—I'm sorry."

They sat in silence for a while, listening to the boisterous sounds coming from the German table.

"They're louder than when I came in, aren't they?" Marian asked.

"They're on their second beer now, and I think Piotr gave them a couple shots of vodka as well."

"Good—maybe they'll get drunk faster and won't pay us any attention."

Zofia glanced sideways and saw one of the men take out a deck of cards. He had a fat face, his skin glowing. "I don't think we have to worry too much about them overhearing us."

The others took out their wallets and placed some coins on the table.

"They don't speak Polish anyway," she added.

"Now you're doing exactly as they do. Never assume they don't understand us. Never underestimate them," Marian chided. He looked disappointed.

She cast her eyes downward.

There was a scuffle in the other room. The Germans had tucked into the food but were calling Piotr back to the table.

"Sounds like he's not happy," Marian said as he finished his vodka.

The German gestured wildly, loudly proclaiming how bad the food was. Zofia felt bad for Piotr, who simply stood and took the verbal beating.

The other officers enjoyed the spectacle, and one of them joined in complaining. It seemed he was just doing it to make Piotr's life harder. He wasn't as harsh as the initial complainer, who pushed his plate away, then threw his cutlery on the table with a loud clang and pushed his chair back.

"I'm not going to be poisoned in this rat hole," the German said, his face red with indignation.

The faces of the other men changed, and that's when Zofia realized he was the highest-ranking of the group. He wasn't joking, and they hurried to get up with him.

"And you can forget about us paying for anything as well. You're lucky if we don't shut this place down," the officer scoffed as they marched out. The door shut with a loud bang, and for a moment, all eyes were on Piotr, still standing at the table.

"Well, that's that, then, isn't it?" he said with a smile as he started clearing the plates.

The regular hum of conversation returned to the bar.

"I'm not sure I'd be able to stay that calm if that happened to me," Zofia said.

"He's used to it. The Germans are here every day, and they always find something to complain about."

Piotr walked by, and Marian ordered another drink. He spread his hands on the table.

"Now, Zofia. We need to talk about the operation."

She sat up. The Germans had delayed their meeting for long enough.

"Did you speak with Antoni today?" he asked.

She shook her head. "That's what I wanted to tell you. He didn't show up for work."

Marian raised an eyebrow, and she quickly continued:

"I was worried about him, too, but then we spoke to Wojciech. He told us there was a small riot in the camp last night, and people from Antoni's barracks were involved. They kept everybody in there without food or water for the entire day—as retribution."

"So we don't know if he's in trouble," Marian said, looking thoughtful.

She nodded. "Antoni has shown up every day without fail. I'm sure this is just a glitch."

Marian looked at her intently. "I hope you're right. Let's see if Antoni shows up tomorrow. When he does, ask him about the uniforms."

"Of course. I can't wait to receive them so we can move forward with the operation." She moved to get up.

Marian held up his hand. "Hang on; there is one more thing."

She sat back down in surprise.

Marian leaned a little closer. "We have a new member joining us from the Warsaw cell."

Zofia's expression didn't change. It was highly unusual for people from other cells to move. It was risky, and people preferred to recruit close to home, often referred by friends. Moving almost halfway across the country was new.

"But that's not all," Marian said. He paused for a moment, then shifted in his seat. "He's not Polish."

"Where is he from?" she asked.

"He's a German Jew."

"We're bringing a German into our cell? That's crazy, Marian!"

He held up his hands.

"Do you think we can trust him?" Zofia leaned forward, her hands on the table.

Marian nodded. "My contacts from Warsaw say they've never seen someone more determined. He's even led a few missions. He kept asking about making the journey here."

Zofia lifted an eyebrow. "He asked to be sent to us?"

"Yes, he was determined to come here."

*Most people want to get away from here.*

"When is he joining?" she asked.

Marian avoided her eyes and looked uncomfortable for the first time that afternoon. In fact, she couldn't remember the confident man wavering before—certainly never in her presence.

*There's something he's not telling me.*

She cocked her head. "What is it?"

"Well, that's the thing," Marian said, pausing. He appeared to be looking for the right words before looking her straight in the eye. "I need a place for him to stay."

"You want him to stay at our house."

"I know I'm asking a lot, but it's perfect. You live outside town, so it'll be easy for us to bring him there without raising suspicion. And you have plenty of space in the cellar. We can easily hide him until we're ready to execute the plan."

"Mama won't like it," she said. "You know our history. It's dangerous to hide someone."

"I know, I know—I'll admit there's a risk, but it's such a long time ago that happened. I'm sure you're no longer of any interest to the Germans. Especially since you've been working in the administration for —what—over a year now?"

"Two years," Zofia corrected. Two years before, her mother, Anna, supplied the prisoners working in and around town with extra food and supplies. When the Germans found out, they gave her a month in the camp. They interrogated her numerous times, but she didn't tell them anything. She was eventually released, but she was dismissed from the registration office—though they were willing to take Zofia in her place.

"Exactly. And your mother has been an upstanding citizen since then. You haven't had any SS visits for a few months now, right?"

"I guess you're right," she said hesitantly as she looked around the tavern where a few people were getting ready to leave. Piotr was already cleaning the bar. It wouldn't be long until darkness fell, and everybody would have to be home. The Germans took the evening curfew very seriously. At night, the town was completely blacked out. Being outside in the darkness was both frightening and asking for trouble.

"How about you talk to your parents about it tonight? It would only be for a few nights. Once we've carried out the mission, he would be on his way."

Her interest was further piqued. "What's in it for him?"

Marian shrugged. "They haven't told me yet. But my contact in Warsaw said he insisted on joining us."

"Is he aware of the danger? This is a small town—people talk."

"He knows. He's been told what to expect. That's why we need to keep him out of sight."

"There's no way to prepare someone for Auschwitz if they've never seen it before," Zofia scoffed.

Marian reached out over the table and lightly brushed Zofia's hand. "Trust me. If there's anyone who knows that, it's me. Once he's here, I'll make sure he knows all there is to know about the camp."

"I'm sorry. I didn't mean to—"

He raised his hand. "No need to apologize. You speak the truth, and you're right to be cautious. All I ask is you discuss it when you get home."

"I will."

Marian stood up. He looked relieved. "Thank you. I'll see you here tomorrow, same time? I hope Antoni is back at work so we can find out what's going on in there."

As he walked away, she felt nothing but admiration. He put his own life on the line every day, and she didn't want to let him down. Convincing her parents to take in a German fugitive would take all her powers of persuasion. She wouldn't let the resistance down. She stepped out into a dimly lit street and hurried home through the narrow streets.

# CHAPTER FIFTEEN

Zofia awoke to darkness. It took her a few moments to find her bearings before realizing she was in her bed. She fumbled on her bedside cabinet for the small clock. It was a little before six in the morning—she didn't have to get up for another hour. It wasn't unusual for her to wake up a couple of times in the night, but something felt off.

She thought she heard something outside and pricked up her ears. With the curfew and living away from town, the only sound she sometimes heard was the low hum of the engines of the odd German car—this was different.

She heard muffled voices close to her second-floor window, open to the fresh air. Zofia lay still on her bed, unsure what to do. The only people who would be outside now were Germans. Was it another raid? Her mind went back to the time they came for her mother. It had been many years ago since they had broken down the front door. She remembered the sound of boots stomping on the wooden floor downstairs, the harsh voices shouting at her mother to come with them. She remembered the protests of her father, her little sister crying, unable to understand what was going on.

She shivered under her covers and felt a cold sweat forming on her back.

But then she thought she heard a faint knock. She sat up to listen.

There it was again, a little louder. Somebody was at the front door.

The Germans wouldn't knock. They would break down the door.

*Maybe they're lost?*

Her anxiety made way for curiosity as she swung her legs out of bed and tip-toed to her door. She listened carefully at the top of the stairs.

After a few seconds, she heard the knock again—louder this time— whoever was on the other side was getting impatient.

She pulled a robe around her and walked down, careful to avoid the creaking floorboards.

At the bottom of the stairs, she heard muffled voices outside speaking German.

She paused and considered her options—if they were SS, they wouldn't wait patiently. Zofia took a deep breath and opened the door.

Two silhouettes stood in the darkness.

One of them stepped forward, revealing his face.

"Sorry for waking you, Zofia, but I'm afraid this couldn't wait."

*Marian.* She let out the breath she didn't know she was holding.

The four sat at the kitchen table, a small candle providing the only source of light. They kept the black-out curtains closed. Zofia poured four cups of watery tea. Anna sat next to Zofia, Marian and the stranger opposite. Zofia handed him a cup—which he took with a weak smile. She studied the man, who looked to be in his late twenties. His eyes were soft, his face hidden behind a small, unkempt beard. He looked tired, his hands clasping around the mug, keeping it close to his face. It seemed to calm him.

She turned to Marian. "So, you're a bit earlier than we agreed, aren't you?"

They all looked at the big man, who calmly took a sip of his tea before answering. "Again, I'm sorry for waking you. You too, Anna"— he looked at Zofia's mother with apologetic eyes.

She brushed it aside with a wave of her hand. "Please tell us what you need, Marian. Jan has an early shift today, but we discussed your plan earlier, and we've agreed to take him in. It would just have been nice to be a little better prepared."

Zofia's father, Jan, worked at one of the nearby coal mines. Zofia looked at the stranger. He followed the conversation alertly, but he kept quiet.

*Does he understand us?*

Marian's troubled expression eased, the relief evident on his face. "I'm so glad to hear that. Having him here makes a massive difference to the success of our plan. And we don't think there's a safer place for him than here with you."

He turned to the stranger and switched to German. "They just said you can stay here."

The man nodded. "I understood that much," he replied in heavily accented Polish. He faced Anna and Zofia. "I really appreciate you taking me in. I promise I won't be a problem, and as soon as we've finished the mission, I'll be on my way."

*His Polish is not that bad. I wonder how long he's been here.*

His voice was soft and, despite the accent, he spoke confidently. He held out his hand. "My name is Jacob, but friends call me Jaco."

"You'll need to stay out of sight as much as possible. And you need a shave," Zofia said, looking to break the ice as she took his hand.

He scratched his beard and smiled for the first time. "Oh, you mean this? I'd be happy to get rid of it. I've been traveling for days now. There is no safe passage from Warsaw down here."

"How did you get here?" Anna asked as she sat up.

Jacob struggled for words as he tried to explain his journey through back roads.

Marian interrupted. "We all speak German, Jacob. If it's easier for you, we can switch. It will be good practice for us."

Jacob looked grateful. "It was hard to get out of Warsaw without papers. The German army has checkpoints all over the city, so I waited until nightfall. As you know, that only made it riskier. The Warsaw resistance smuggled me out through the sewers. I almost got caught, because just as I climbed out into the open, a German patrol passed. I ducked and they missed me."

"You must've traveled the entire way on your own?" Zofia asked.

He nodded. "I walked, keeping away from the main roads and often cutting through forests. But the route is well-traveled. There are many safe houses along the way, and I slept outside for just two nights."

"How long did it take you?"

"A little over a week."

Anna looked concerned. "You must be exhausted."

Jacob smiled. "I am, but I'm relieved to be here. I knew it would be dangerous, and I'm grateful to you for opening your door at this hour. I'm not sure I would've done the same."

Zofia smiled back at him. "You'll find there are some amazing people in the Sosienki. We might not be as big as the Warsaw cell, but our work is just as important."

"You won't believe the size of the camp or the state of the people there. Helping them is some of the most rewarding work I've done in my life," Marian agreed.

Jacob's face turned serious. "I don't doubt it. I've experienced camp life first-hand in the Netherlands. It can be brutal."

Anna shook her head. "I don't think you've seen evil like what we have down the road." She paused. "But first, you need to recover from your journey. Let me show you to our cellar. It's not going to be the best bed you've slept on, but it's a safe place to put your head down."

Jacob stood up and followed her. "I would sleep on the floor at this point."

As Anna took Jacob down to his hiding place, Marian and Zofia stayed at the kitchen table. It was still dark outside, though it was close to seven in the morning. Zofia would have to get to work soon. It brought her back to another crucial element in their plan.

"I hope Antoni shows up today," she said as she took the empty mugs from the table.

Marian nodded as he grabbed his coat. "You know Antoni—he's strong. Even if they interrogated people in his barracks, he'd be fine." He paused for a moment. "What do you think about Jacob?"

*He seems nice.*

She put the mugs in the kitchen sink. "Can't really tell yet. He seems determined. Walking all the way from Warsaw is tough. Staying off the main roads and avoiding the Germans is even harder."

"Just imagine if they caught him. You heard his Polish—they would've made him as soon as he opened his mouth. He would have had a hard time explaining what a German was doing wandering the woods of Poland."

She smiled. "Do you think we can trust him?"

"I have no doubt. After he walked down here on his own, I'm sure of it. The only thing I still don't know is why he was so determined to come here." He looked at her intently. "Perhaps you can have a chat with him and try to find out. He'll have plenty of time to talk, stuck in your basement."

"He doesn't quite grasp how dangerous the camp is, which concerns me – I feel it's right we tell him."

Marian walked to the door. "It might be. Thank you for keeping him here. I know I surprised you, but he just showed up, and you know we can't keep him at my place."

Marian was right. There was no way Jacob could've stayed in Marian's small flat in the center of town. *Too many curious eyes.*

He opened the door. "I'll see you tonight for an update on Antoni. Hopefully, we can move the plan forward." He slipped outside and softly closed the door.

Zofia sat at her desk. After Marian had left their house, she had quickly changed and made her way to the office. Her mother would stay at home and look after Jacob.

She checked the clock on the wall—it was almost eight. It would be another hour until the prisoners from the camp arrived. On a typical day, she enjoyed the silence in the office in the early hours, but now it merely gave her mind a chance to come up with a million thoughts.

Despite Marian's confidence, she still had her doubts about Jacob. He was the first foreigner to join their cell and a German at that. Of course, he was Jewish, so that made her feel a bit better about it all. But still, his motivation for joining them intrigued her. The thoughts kept gnawing at her as she tried to get some work done. She would speak with him later that night and hear his story. She desperately wanted to trust the man in their basement—he added enormous potential to their cell.

It felt like an eternity until she heard sounds in the hallway as her colleagues started their days.

The familiar sound of a truck's engine rumbled through her open window, and her heart leaped. Would Antoni be back today? She had to control herself not to run to the front of the building. If Antoni were here, he'd be escorted to her little office within a few minutes.

It wasn't long until the SS guards stomped through the hallway. It was the same ritual every morning as they delivered the prisoners to different offices.

Zofia heard them tick off their lists. Her office was one of the furthest down the hall, and Antoni was always the last prisoner to arrive. She heard them approach and held her breath.

Two young guards in freshly pressed uniforms filled the door opening.

"Prisoner 613, delivered to the office of Zofia Zdrowak," one of them said as he checked off something on a piece of paper.

Zofia breathed a sigh of relief as the familiar little man walked in. Antoni looked tired and a bit paler than usual. He winked at her as he passed the guards and sat down at his desk without a word. Zofia knew he would wait for the guards to leave before speaking—it was the quickest way to get them out of the office.

The youngest guards had other plans as he eyed Zofia and smiled at her.

*Oh no. What do you want?*

"I've never seen you before," he said, as he walked into her cramped office, putting his hands on her desk. "Are you new?"

Zofia stayed in her seat. *Can't you just leave me alone?* It wasn't the first time one of them had tried to get her attention.

"I've worked here for a while now," she answered noncommittally. She grabbed a folder from the side of her desk and opened it, pretending to study the papers inside.

"Are you from around here?" he asked. He leaned forward a little, his hands pressing down on the desk. *This one is persistent.*

The desk wobbled a little, and she gently leaned on her side to keep it balanced.

"Born and raised in Oświęcim," she said, emphasizing the Polish pronunciation of her city's name. She continued to thumb through the papers in the folder.

The other man in the door opening rolled his eyes and tapped his foot. "Come on; we need to deliver some of the others in the truck as well," he said.

The guard flirting with Zofia wasn't deterred so quickly and ignored his colleague. "What's your name?"

"Zofia."

"That's a beautiful name. My name is Hans."

*What a terribly stereotypical German name.*

"That's a nice name; I don't think I know anybody else called Hans."

Her sarcasm was lost on Hans, who beamed back at her.

She flashed a fake smile. "Hans, I'm terribly sorry, but I have a lot of work to do. You know how many people are coming into the camp these days, right? I'm sure you have important work to do as well—a serious soldier like yourself?"

The goofy smile remained on his face, and he even blushed a little. "You're absolutely right, Zofia. We're responsible for all the prisoners working in this building today, and we have to take a few more to the factory at Monowitz."

"That sounds important for the war effort," she said. "Better make sure they're not late, right?"

He nodded enthusiastically. "You really understand how important our work is."

The other guard was losing his patience. "Come on, Hans. Time to go. We don't have time to flirt with the locals."

Hans continued to ignore him. "Zofia, would you like to go out with me sometime? I can take you to a nice tavern. We have access to some food that you can't get anywhere else, you know?" He winked at her.

*Never in a million years.*

"That sounds lovely, Hans. Maybe we can talk about it when you're back later?"

The other guard had had enough and pulled Hans out of the office. "I'm not going to risk getting in trouble because of you," he said sternly.

"I'll be back later, Zofia," he said as he was dragged out, still smiling.

As Hans and his colleague stomped down the hall, she turned to Antoni—he looked at her with a curious expression.

"What?" she asked.

The sound of boots faded, and the truck engine roared to life in the distance.

Antoni started laughing and slapped his hands down on his thighs. "You're quite the actress, Zofia."

She looked at the small man rocking on the chair opposite her. His laugh was contagious, and she couldn't help but smile.

"Well, that German was just an idiot. What did he expect from me? I'm not going out with a Nazi." She pulled a face.

"Plenty of girls inside would kill to be in that position," Antoni said as he recovered his composure. His face turned serious. "In fact, many do. It's a way to survive."

Zofia stood up. "Enough about him—I'm so happy to see you're okay. I heard there was some trouble in your barracks."

"It was nothing. Some of the younger ones thought it was a good idea to try to raid the kitchen. They were ratted out and are no longer in our barracks. I doubt we'll see them return."

She let that pass quietly. They both knew what he meant. She got up and checked the hallway—it was empty. They were lucky the guards had an extra assignment today. They wouldn't be disturbed, but she still needed to be careful. Even in this building, the walls had ears.

"You're not going to believe what happened in the past two days." She told him about Jacob's arrival.

Antoni listened without interrupting, his eyes focused on her. She liked that about him—most people couldn't wait to interrupt or tell her what to do, but he always gave her his full attention.

"And now he's sleeping at our house," she finished. "What do you think?"

Antoni took a moment to gather his thoughts before standing up and grabbing a new folder from the cabinet across the room. He opened it and looked up at her, his dark brown eyes shining brightly.

"Anyone who comes recommended from Warsaw is going to be an asset," he said. "If this German wants to be part of our cell, let's put him to good use."

Zofia was relieved to hear Antoni was optimistic.

"How are you doing with the uniforms?" she asked, lowering her voice.

"It wasn't easy to get them. The SS are very attached to their uniforms, and they're all marked as soon as they're handed out. But they still need to be laundered, and they definitely won't do that themselves."

He paused for a moment, Zofia looked at him. "And?"

Antoni smiled. "So all of the guards, bar maybe a few, will bring their uniforms to the laundry area. And of course, this is operated by prisoners. We do all the jobs in the camp, so this is no different. The problem is, if a uniform is lost, they'll go crazy. I've seen them beat someone half to death because they claimed they lost a few of the buttons during washing. I've yet to see someone lose a uniform, but I wouldn't be surprised if that meant a direct trip to the gas chambers."

Zofia shuddered. "So, you're saying it's impossible?"

"Not impossible. Very hard. Thankfully, I have many connections."

*Get to the point, Antoni.*

"The other day, a new shipment of uniforms was delivered. These were unused, straight from the factory. That meant they didn't have any numbers printed on them yet. The numbers are printed only when they're assigned. One of my contacts smuggled two out before that. They're complete but for the boots, which we'll need to steal once we execute the plan. Boots are too big to hide, anyway."

Zofia had trouble containing her excitement. "That's amazing, Antoni. When do you think you can use them?"

He shook his head. "There's something I need before we can do anything."

"What is it?"

"These uniforms don't have any badges. They're plain uniforms, but we'll need officers' badges for our plan to work. It's the only way we can go everywhere in the camp without being questioned. If we're just plain guards, the chances somebody starts asking questions are too high."

"And you won't be able to get those in the camp itself?" Zofia asked, even though she knew the answer.

"Unless we overpower two officers and take their badges—but that's too risky. They're too strong, and even if we did, the chances of someone finding out before we get out are too high," he said, still shaking his head. "I need someone on the outside to get them. I was hoping you'd be able to do this, working in the administration."

She thought about it. "Our cell is quite resourceful. I've never heard of us obtaining officers' badges before, but I guess there's no harm asking around."

He nodded. "Whichever way we get them, we need to make sure we don't arouse any suspicion in or around the camp. If we want the plan to work, we need to catch them completely off-guard."

"We're a non-violent cell, but Marian will have connections with other cells that might be able to help. I'm sure he'll have an idea." She looked at Antoni defiantly. "Leave it to me—I'll get you those badges one way or the other. Just make sure you're ready to go at any moment."

He looked at her with admiration. "For someone so young, you really have no fear. The Sosienki are lucky to have you, especially sitting in this office and able to work from the inside, without the Germans noticing."

She blushed. Even though she knew he wasn't exaggerating, she enjoyed being appreciated.

"Today is better than tomorrow," he continued. "Everything can change in an instant, and I would like to be out of there before they decide I'm no longer of use to them."

Zofia understood what he meant. She'd heard of many prisoners disappearing from one day to the next. Some of the men working in the very building they sat in showed up on a Monday, only to be replaced without explanation on Tuesday. There was no time to lose.

"Don't worry—I'm meeting Marian tonight. He'll know what to do."

# Chapter Sixteen

The light streaming in through the small window woke Jacob. The air smelled musty in the cellar, and there was a large damp spot on the ceiling above him. But it was better than he'd known recently. He didn't know how long he'd slept, but the bed was surprisingly comfortable, and he felt refreshed.

He got up and rubbed the sleep from his eyes, then mounted the small set of stairs and reached for the door handle.

He jiggled at it—it didn't give way.

*Why am I locked in?* Jacob thought but then remembered it was for his own safety.

He pressed his ear against the wooden door and heard the sound of cutlery on plates mixed with muffled sounds of high-pitched voices. Women's voices. The people on the other side of the door were eating— his stomach grumbled in protest.

*Should I knock on the door? Is it safe?*

After a few minutes, he decided it was safe to knock.

The voices on the other side of the door stopped abruptly. Quick footsteps approached, and a key rattled in the lock.

The door swung open, and he saw the smiling face of the girl he had met the night before.

*I thought she was older.* His memory must've played tricks on him, given his exhausted state. Despite her youth, she had a confident look about her, looking him straight in the eye as she invited him to join them.

"You must be starving," she said, as she pointed him to an empty chair.

Three other people sat at the table—he recognized Anna, the mother who'd brought him down to the cellar. Jacob sat down next to a young girl who was playing with the vegetables in her broth—she looked up and flashed the same smile Zofia had. At the head of the table sat a man about the same age as Anna.

"Jacob, meet my father Jan—and that's Emilia, my sister."

The man studied Jacob for a moment and nodded before returning his attention to the bowl in front of him.

"I hope you like watery soup with potatoes," Anna said, handing him a bowl. "I'm afraid it's the best we can do."

He took the bowl gratefully and let the warmth spread through his hands. He held it close and let the steam bathe his face. His first spoonful of the soup only further reminded him of how hungry he was.

He finished his soup within moments, and Anna gave him a second portion. It didn't take long for Jacob to finish that bowl, either.

Zofia and Anna sat opposite him—both smiling.

"Now, Jacob, I hope you've regained enough strength to tell us more about the man we've let into our house," Anna said. "All we know is that you're German and that the Warsaw Home Army only had good things to say about you."

Out of the corner of his eye, Jacob saw the man sit up.

"—And that you've specifically asked to be assigned to us," Zofia added. "That is perhaps what puzzles us most. Nobody asks to be assigned to Oświęcim."

He told them about his journey from Berlin and his life in Wester-bork while they listened without interrupting. When he got to the part in the train where his father died, he paused. He swallowed hard, and Anna took his hand.

"That's when I decided I needed to jump from the train," he continued. He cleared his throat. "When I lost my father, there was no-one left to take care of. So I did."

As he thought back to the car, he could almost smell the stench from the bucket.

"When I jumped, I had no idea where I was. All I knew was that I was in Poland. But I didn't think about that, I just ran. I heard the shots behind me. I was sure a bullet would hit me, and it would all be over."

"But you escaped," Zofia said. There was admiration in her eyes.

*She seems nice.*

He nodded. "I got to the tree line and just kept running. I no longer heard the guns, but I didn't know what they were doing back on the train. For all I knew, they'd stopped and were now chasing me on foot. So I ran until I thought my lungs would burst."

He paused for a moment—he was back in the dark forest.

"What about—um—Bertho? Did you meet up with him again?"

He shook his head. "The last thing I remember was him struggling to get through the window. I hope he made it, but I couldn't wait for him. It would've been impossible to find him in the woods. I'd like to believe he escaped."

"What happened after? It must've been cold, and you hadn't eaten anything for days."

"When I couldn't run anymore, I stopped and listened for soldiers chasing me. I was certain they wouldn't let me escape—I expected to hear those heavy boots pounding through the forest every moment. I hid near a large tree for a long time. They never came. I think the train simply continued without me. That was when I realized I needed to find people. All I saw were trees and not a single trace of civilization. There were no paths, no trails or broken branches, even."

He took a sip of water. The smell of the pine trees in the forest came back to him.

"I still had a little chocolate in my pocket. I never knew when I would find food, so I took it in small bites. It gave me the little boosts of energy I needed to go on. By now, it was light, and I couldn't hide forever. At first, I thought there would be a German soldier behind every tree. But after a while, I realized there were none. I spent most of the day walking west, keeping the sun as my compass. I knew there were villages along the train tracks, and I figured moving away from the east would make sense. As dusk fell, I started to worry about sleeping in the forest that night. The nights were cold."

Zofia sat up in her chair and leaned closer. "What about water?"

"Thankfully, there were streams in the forest, so I drank from those. I think that really saved me. I hadn't realized how thirsty I was after jumping from the train. Just before it got dark, the trees thinned out, and I walked into a field. Then I saw a farmhouse and a large barn. There were lights on in the house."

"Did the people welcome you?" Anna looked at him with a puzzled look.

Jacob looked up. "I wanted to knock on the door and hoped that the people would take me in. But then I realized I wouldn't be able to talk to them. I spoke no Polish. How would you respond to a German knocking at your door in the middle of the night? So I waited for darkness to fall and sneaked into the barn. I spent the night there, and in the morning I went to the front door of the house. I had to take a chance."

Anna refilled their glasses. Everybody was quiet and listened intently —even though Jan didn't speak, his eyes never left Jacob.

"An older woman opened the door. She didn't say a word, but she pulled me into the house. She spoke to me in fast Polish, and I held up my hands, indicating I didn't understand what she said. I must've looked a mess because the first thing she did was direct me to the bathroom. When I saw myself in the mirror, I understood why I frightened her. I washed and took the clothes she gave me. When I got back, she fed me, and we tried to communicate. I didn't want to speak German, so I pretended to speak only Dutch. She didn't understand a word I was saying, but for the first time in weeks, I felt safe."

"How did you get from there to Warsaw?" Zofia leaned closer to him.

"The woman was called Sascha. She helped me regain my strength, and I stayed there for a week. It was a very remote area, but somehow she had contacts in the Home Army. I guess it's not that easy these days to move someone who doesn't speak Polish. One evening she handed me a small bag. A man waited outside, and he took me into the woods. I didn't know where we were going, other than that he said 'Warsaw.' We traveled by night and slept during the day, stopping at safe houses along the way."

He looked at Zofia and Anna. "The resistance movement in Poland is a lot bigger than you think. People are helping out in almost every other village. After a week, we arrived in Warsaw, and they took me to a large building with lots of flats. I was hidden in the basement, which I was used to now." He smiled. "Bartek, the man who'd taken me there, told me to wait. He returned to wherever he came from."

"And that's how you ended up joining the Home Army?"

"It was my first contact. At this point, I was just happy to be free. I waited in the basement for a day before someone came. They gave me water, bread, and some cheese. It was the best meal I'd had since leaving Sascha's farm. The man bringing the food spoke some very basic Dutch. He told me I would stay there, hidden from the Germans. I asked him what they did, but he didn't tell me anything more. He didn't even tell me his name."

Jacob paused.

"I stayed in that cellar for two weeks, regaining strength. Every day I counted the hours until someone would come down. It was the loneliest I've ever been in my life."

Zofia looked at him curiously. "I'm surprised you managed to stay sane down there for two weeks. I would go crazy."

"Oh, trust me, I almost did. It was tempting to peek outside. But I knew it was not worth it. What if a German patrol saw me?" He shook his head. "It was safer to stay put. And my waiting was rewarded."

"Did they move you somewhere else?" Anna asked.

He shook his head. "The same man who brought me food the first night was back. In some bizarre coincidence, he was a trader who used to travel to the Netherlands quite often, and that's where he picked up the language. He told me I was with the Home Army."

Anna sat up. "What did you talk about?"

"He asked me where I came from. I told him about Westerbork and how I escaped from the train. I also told him I was about to go crazy in the cellar. I asked if I could make myself useful in any way. He said it would be hard, but he wanted to know if I had any special skills. I told him I had some medical knowledge and that I spoke German."

"Was that enough?"

"He said he would discuss it with the others. He brought me Polish children's books and a German-Polish dictionary when he came back a day later. He told me to pick up as much of the language as possible. I spent the next two weeks learning as much Polish as possible."

Jacob stood up and walked around the table. His legs ached, and he peered outside. It was getting dark, but he saw the small road that ran past the house. This was the perfect hiding place. The only people getting close would be on their way out of town, or they would have a business on the outskirts. He turned back to the table.

"That's when I met Bór. I didn't know it at the time, but he leads the Warsaw Resistance."

Zofia gasped softly and quickly put her hands before her mouth. "Bór's a legend."

Jacob nodded. "He asked me all the same questions about how I got there and wanted to hear about the escape from the train. His German was rather good, and it didn't take him long to pinpoint my accent. That's when he asked if I was really from the Netherlands."

Jacob sat back down.

"There was no point in lying about it, and I told him I was originally from Berlin."

Zofia's eyes went wide. "Was he angry about you lying?"

"He's a strong man. If he wanted to hurt me, there was nothing I could do."

He paused, his thoughts going back to the moldy Warsaw cellar. Bór had terrified him.

"But when he reached me, he held out his hand. He said I could be extremely useful. That's when we shook hands, and he lifted me out of my chair."

He folded his arms and leaned back a little, feeling a bit at home with the rapt audience.

"After that, I spent my time in Warsaw joining missions. We did things for the community—like finding extra rations—but we also attacked German soldiers and transports."

Across the table, Zofia's eyes lit up. "Were you ever in danger?"

"Every mission was dangerous," Jacob said. "We operated in small groups, to draw as little attention as possible. And the fewer people who know about it, the less chance you have somebody finds out about it. We had some hairy moments, but thankfully I've never seen anybody get left behind."

Anna changed the subject: "So, is Agnes the reason you asked to come to Oświęcim?"

Jacob shook his head. "After she stepped on board the train, I hoped to receive news—any news—from her. Even when I was on the train myself, I clung onto the hope I might find her there."

He felt a sharp pain in his chest and struggled to continue. "But when I brought it up in Warsaw, they told me what was really going on in Auschwitz. We always believed people were relocated to work camps. We didn't know about the systematic murder."

Jacob stared at the table for a few seconds before looking up.

"Agnes would've followed her sister anywhere. She would never abandon her, even if it meant her own death."

A heavy silence hung in the air as Jacob's words sank in.

Jacob broke the silence. "When I jumped from the train, I left my best friend behind. I know he was on the train to Auschwitz-Birkenau. We promised each other we would always look out for each other. He's the reason I'm here."

Zofia, for the first time, averted her eyes, studying a stain on the tablecloth. Anna returned his look; there was sadness in her eyes.

For the first time, Jan spoke up:

"I don't want to get your hopes up," he said as he sat up. "But you're saying he arrived at the camp almost a year ago. The conditions in the camp are horrible, the prisoners are fed poorly, and disease rages through the camp. The chances of him being alive are very slim."

*No, Ethan would have found a way to survive.*

"I have to believe Ethan is still alive," Jacob said.

Jan looked back at him, compassion in his eyes. "The odds are against him, but it is still possible he's alive. The conditions in the camp decimate even the strongest men, but I agree—there is a chance he's still alive if he's been smart."

Jacob turned to Zofia. "Is there any way you could look up whether he's still in the camp?"

Zofia stood up and walked across the room. The floorboards creaked as she stared out the window before turning around.

"After we've processed the incoming transports, the files are taken by the Germans. That's the last we see of them."

He looked at the young woman. Her eyes were soft, but her mouth was drawn in a thin line, her hands on her hips—she appeared confident.

*Did I make a mistake coming here?*

Anna pushed her chair under the table and leaned on the back of the chair. "Jacob, listen. We can't promise you anything. Things in the camp change daily and very little of it reaches us. There are too many people, and the Germans are too good at keeping their organized chaos. You know this—you were in a camp yourself."

Jacob nodded.

"But Zofia does have her connections in the camp" She looked at her daughter, who gave a barely perceptible nod. "Maybe they can ask around about Ethan. If he's survived for a year, he must've made some friends in the camp. And I agree, if he's been smart and strong, he could still be alive. But you need to be patient."

"I understand," Jacob said, also getting up. He felt restless. He wanted to be useful. "But at least let me help you with your next mission. If I have to spend another week hiding in the cellar, I will go crazy. From what I was told in Warsaw, you're trying to break people out of the camp. Let me help you. I'm sure it's going to be dangerous, but I'm used to that."

He looked at them pleadingly. Zofia walked back and leaned over her chair. She looked at him with her clear brown eyes. "The plan is in motion. I think you could play an instrumental role in it. Your German is without accent. You could be our back-up when we run into your countrymen."

He interrupted her. "They may share my nationality, but I couldn't feel less connected to them."

She waved away his interruption. "I know, but I'm sure you're the only person in town that speaks German like a German. Nobody will ever suspect you being part of the Sosienki. You're a valuable asset."

He looked at her with admiration. *Is she really only sixteen years old?*

"So, how can I help?"

Zofia thought for a moment. "I don't know yet. Let me talk to Marian tomorrow. I still need to take care of some of the details."

Jacob understood. They weren't going to tell him everything. The less he knew about the details of the mission, the better.

Anna walked to the stove and picked up an iron kettle from the fire. Large plumes of steam escaped as she poured four large mugs. From a cupboard, she took a small tin and added scoops of black powder to the mugs. The sweet scent of coffee filled the room, and Jacob couldn't remember the last time he'd had any.

She handed him a mug and, as he took it, almost burned his hands.

"Careful," Anna said with a smile. "It smells like coffee, but it's a substitute. We haven't had proper coffee since the Germans invaded, but this is as close as it gets."

"We save it for special occasions," Zofia added. "And someone walking all the way from Warsaw to join our cell definitely qualifies." She raised her mug.

Jacob, Jan, and Anna followed suit.

"To the unexpected," Zofia said, her eyes darting around the table. "And to a successful mission."

They clinked their mugs in the air, and Jacob lifted his to his lips. The steam entered his nostrils, and he savored the moment. He looked at his surroundings, and for the first time in many months, he felt at home. He blew a bit into his cup and took the first sip. As the almost-coffee made its way down his throat, he felt energized and ready. He was going to be the best asset the Sosienki had ever had.

Jacob sat at the kitchen table and checked the clock on the far side of the room for the umpteenth time. The Roman numerals showed it was almost three in the afternoon.

He was alone in the house. Jan was at the coal mine, and Anna was out visiting a nearby farm for the night's dinner. He knew it would probably be another soup with potatoes and vegetables, but he looked forward to it, nonetheless. She worked miracles with their limited supplies.

He got up and looked out of the window to find the road deserted.

*What's taking her so long?*

Zofia had promised she would be back for him in an hour or two. She had a rare day off as the Germans inspected the registration offices, and she wasn't allowed to be there. It was a lucky break, according to Zofia. She needed to run an errand in town and then check on something in the woods. She hadn't told Jacob what, exactly, but he suspected it had to do with the escape.

At first, she'd refused to let him join. Marian and Zofia had decided they needed more time to prepare, and Jacob had spent another three days in the cellar. They'd given him more Polish books, and he'd already finished the first. His Polish was improving remarkably, and he enjoyed reading and learning a new language.

However, he'd made sure Zofia knew he needed some fresh air. Besides, going into the woods wouldn't be any more dangerous than walking here from Warsaw, he'd argued. In the end, she relented.

It was now a little past three, and he was getting worried.

*Has she gone without me? Was she caught at something?*

Just as his mind started to race toward all kinds of horrible pictures, Zofia came into sight. She had a spring in her step and looked confident.

Jacob smiled. It would be good to get out of the house.

She opened the door and flashed a smile. "Were you looking out for me, Jacob?" She asked in Polish.

"I thought you were standing me up," he responded in the same language, looking at the clock.

Zofia waved her index finger at him. "We can work on your pronunciation, but that wasn't bad." She reached into her jacket and took out a small bag. "Now, as for standing you up, why would I want to do that? I feel a lot safer going into the woods with a strong German than all by myself."

He smiled. "So, where are we going?"

She looked him up and down. "Before we're going anywhere, you need to have the right clothes. We're foraging mushrooms, so let's get you looking the part."

He'd borrowed some clothes from Zofia's father, and he agreed his outfit of formal brown pants and a button-up shirt was utterly inappropriate for foraging.

Zofia was already upstairs, and he heard her rummaging through her father's closet. Within seconds, she stormed down the stairs with more casual attire for work.

He inspected himself in the mirror. The worn pants and a simple sweater made him look every bit a forager. Zofia handed him a hat and a pair of gloves. They were full of holes, but it would have to do.

She caught his look. "It's not that cold outside, so you don't actually need gloves, but it makes sense if we're picking mushrooms. Let's go."

Zofia was already outside, and Jacob followed. He took a deep breath of cold autumn air and felt better already. After spending almost a week indoors, it felt good to be outside again.

She walked ahead of him, and he had to speed up to keep up with the petite Polish girl as they followed the road further away from town.

"When I got here, I didn't take much notice of the surroundings," he said, small plumes of vapor coming from his mouth as he spoke—it was colder than he'd expected. "I was so focused on getting to your house that I didn't see anything but the ground directly ahead of me."

Zofia didn't miss a step. "I know—this is quite a nice area of our country. Too bad the Germans picked our city to create that camp over there."

Jacob looked in the direction and saw the darkened sky Zofia's father had spoken of earlier.

The sky in the other direction was a lot clearer. "We're not talking about just one or two crematoriums, right?"

Zofia didn't respond right away. She picked up her pace, walking out in front of him. He struggled to catch up with her. She stopped abruptly and turned. Her eyes were damp.

"No, they have at least four. The chimneys are always spitting out black smoke. Day or night, it doesn't matter. The sky here is darker than anywhere else in Poland. Even our rain is black. Nobody knows how many people are burned every day, but if I were to guess, I'd say it's in the thousands."

She looked at him defiantly, her arms at her side. "We dry our clothes indoors. On a bad day, when there is no wind, you can taste the ash in the air."

Jacob didn't know what to say. He saw the pain in her eyes. It was the first time he saw a crack in her confident exterior.

They walked along in silence as Jacob thought about Ethan. Was he still alive, or was he part of the ashes? The plumes of smoke on the horizon made it all very real.

Zofia had stopped and gave him a small poke, interrupting his thoughts.

"Do you hear that?"

He stopped and pricked up his ears. A low rumble came from the road ahead.

"It sounds like an engine."

They were exposed between two parts of the forest. Whoever was coming their way would see them soon enough.

Jacob looked to Zofia. "Should I be worried? I have no papers."

She shook her head. "Just leave it to me. Whoever it is, I can handle it. If anything does go wrong, we run."

He turned back and checked the tree-line—it was at least two hundred meters away. If the people in the car were SS soldiers, he hoped they were poor shots.

Zofia read his thoughts. "Just relax, Jacob. We're not doing anything wrong—we're allowed to be here. It's nowhere near curfew yet. Just let me do the talking."

The sound grew louder, and an army jeep appeared on the horizon.

"Just keep walking and ignore them," Zofia said. "Let's not give them any excuse to stop."

The jeep approached, and Jacob saw two men chatting away. They were about the same age as him and wore SS uniforms.

*Must be on their way to the camp.* He averted his eyes as they passed.

The sound of the engine slowed, and the breaks squeaked. He heard them speak in German, and the jeep reversed with a low whine.

Zofia stopped walking; there was no sense pretending they hadn't seen them. Jacob's heart raced as the car pulled up.

"What are you doing out here?" asked the man in the passenger seat, in German. His arm hung loosely out of the window as he addressed Zofia. His face was passive but not unfriendly.

She smiled at him and answered in broken German: "We're heading down to the forest to see if we can find some mushrooms. They should be in season by now."

He gave her an amused look. "You do this yourself?"

She nodded, keeping the smile. "It's the only way to get the best ones. Also, we can't afford to go to the shops and buy them there."

"I see," he seemed to lose interest in their plans. "I like your accent. Are you from around here?"

Jacob felt the air change and glanced to his side to see Zofia tense up a little. Did the soldier notice it as well?

Zofia quickly recovered and bent her left knee—her posture now inviting and a little flirty. "I practice my German every day. I think it's a beautiful language."

Both men smiled approvingly before the soldier behind the wheel looked at Jacob. "Who are you?"

Jacob wanted to answer, but Zofia beat him to it. "He's just my brother, making sure I'm safe in the forest. You know, it's not so safe. We don't have you everywhere to keep us safe."

The soldier behind the wheel wasn't convinced yet. "Can't he speak for himself?"

A trickle of sweat ran down Jacob's back.

"Of course he can," Zofia said, a nervous laugh escaping from her mouth. "But he doesn't speak any German. He just works on the land near our house."

The man studied Jacob's face and mumbled something in a heavy accent. The other soldier laughed. He turned back to Zofia.

"We need to get going, but I would love to see you some other time."

Zofia smiled. "I will be picking mushrooms here a few times a week at this time for the next month. Maybe we'll run into each other again?"

"I was thinking you'd like to meet me in the city sometime?" He looked disappointed.

"Now, where's the excitement in that?" Zofia said with a cheeky smile. "You know girls like to be surprised."

He looked puzzled, but his colleague settled the matter by starting the engine again.

"If I can't find you here, where will you be?" he asked as the car shifted into gear.

Zofia pointed toward the city. "I live there, so if you look carefully, you might find me walking around there."

The car rolled forward, and the soldier waved.

Zofia waited for them to disappear out of sight before spitting on the ground in disgust. "It's the same with all of them. They're always trying to take me out somewhere."

Jacob smiled. "You seem to be good at letting them down easy. I wonder how many are walking around thinking about you."

"They try this with all the girls, so I don't feel too special. I've heard there are even romances in the camp between soldiers and prisoners. Can you believe that?"

"It was the same in Westerbork," Jacob said. "It's survival instinct kicking in, I think."

"I doubt it helps much."

They walked for another ten minutes, then Zofia stopped. The road cut through a forest. "We're here."

Jacob didn't see anything unusual. He would've walked straight past whatever had triggered Zofia.

She stood still and listened carefully. When she appeared satisfied they were alone, she quickly walked into the forest.

There was no trail, but Zofia navigated through thick branches and bushes.

"Where are we going?" Jacob asked as he avoided a branch swinging his way.

"We're going to check on the bikes we will use to get Antoni to our trail," she answered without breaking stride. "They'll use the Babinicza trail to get away. It's a well-trodden path to send messages and people along the resistance network."

They crossed a small clearing and Jacob struggled to keep up with her—Zofia kept a quick pace and seemed eager to get to the bikes.

"Where does the trail go?" Jacob asked.

"It goes through the forest where we have several bunkers for them to hide in if anything goes wrong. The journey takes a few days, and it's possible to run into German patrols. There is a small church at the end of the trail, and that's where other members of the Home Army will meet them."

"When we get to the bikes, what will we do?" Jacob asked.

"We need to make sure they're in good shape so they can be used right away. It's the fastest way for them to get onto the Babinicza trail and away from the city and camp."

"How far?"

"About twenty minutes by bike, if you can stick to the small paths through the forest." Zofia snapped a branch off one of the trees in front of her.

They took a few more turns before she stopped abruptly.

*Something is wrong.*

Zofia looked lost. "The bikes are supposed to be here, hidden under these branches."

She pointed at a pile of branches and leaves at her feet. It was too small to hide three bikes. Jacob walked around the area, searching for them.

"Maybe they were misplaced the last time?" he said, peeking behind a large oak tree.

Zofia hadn't moved—she stared at the pile.

"The only people who know about these bikes are in our cell. There is no way they would hide them somewhere else. It would be impossible for us to find them that way." She shook her head. "Someone else took them."

Jacob wasn't about to give up so quickly and kept looking. It seemed unlikely that anybody would come all the way out into the forest and stumble upon these bikes.

Zofia sat down on a tree stump. "Jacob, there's no sense looking. We're going to need a different way to get the prisoners away from here."

He sat down next to her. "If it's twenty minutes by bike, it will take them about two hours walking, right?"

"Something like that, maybe a bit longer, considering their condition. They'll be exhausted."

"So let me get this straight—we'll meet them at the bridge, which is the riskiest part, right?"

"The Germans patrol the area around that bridge. If they find out Antoni escaped, the bridge will be one of the first places they'll look." She turned to him. "Why do you ask?"

"We'll need to get them away from there as quickly as possible. Is there no other way to get new bikes? Maybe borrow them from people in the city?"

She shook her head. "No, we had a hard enough time getting these. The Germans have stolen most of the bikes. People who have bikes keep them hidden and use them only sparingly."

Jacob stood up and paced around. Zofia remained seated, her eyes focused on the trees. She was deep in thought, and Jacob left her to it.

She looked up at him. "If they can't use the bike trail, they'll need to take a different path."

"What do you mean?"

She took a stick and knelt in the sandy area—she drew the outline of the river, the bridge, and a circle a distance away from it.

"This is the bike route heading to the Babinicza trail, which is slightly cleared." She used the stick to draw a semi-circle from the bridge to the trailhead.

Jacob studied the crude drawing. "Okay, so can't they just walk the bike trail?"

She shook her head. "Without bikes, it makes more sense to take the direct route through the forest." She drew a straight line from the bridge to the circle. "This will take them right to the start of the trail."

Jacob scratched his head. "But why don't you simply always take this route?"

"Because it'll take longer, and it's more strenuous. There's a steep incline, and you need to know where you're going. There is no logical path—there are no markers."

"Why do you think this is a good option now?"

She smiled. "Because Antoni has been working in my office for months, and I've been supplying him with extra rations. He's in a much better state than most other prisoners. And I can brief him on the path to take when he comes into the office."

"What about the other escapee?"

"I'll have to ask Antoni, but at least he'll know what's expected of him." Zofia looked relieved. "It's still a risky plan, as we've never done this before, but I think it's the only way."

Jacob realized it was getting darker in the forest, and the sun would set soon. "Let's head back before we're caught outside in the dark."

She got up and wiped the sand drawing with her foot. "Let's take the forest route back, just to be sure. Maybe we'll be lucky and find some mushrooms on the way back."

Jacob smiled. "That would be quite the treat."

# CHAPTER SEVENTEEN

Zofia walked through the empty hallway, greeting the early starters as she made her way to her office.

She carried a small linen bag. It contained some potatoes and carrots and was no bigger than a regular grocery bag anybody in the village would use. As she walked into the office with it, the bag felt extraordinarily heavy, and she set it down behind her little desk. She opened the curtains and window and enjoyed the fresh morning air streaming in. She took a deep breath, and her anxiety eased a little.

Zofia rubbed her palms. They were a little sweaty, and she wiped them on the sides of her skirt. She took out a ledger to shift her thoughts.

*I can't wait to tell him.*

She spent the next two hours documenting new arrivals from the west. Belgian, Dutch, and French prisoners had arrived on the previous night's transports. She scanned the names and often found the same surnames, which made her wonder how these whole families ended up on the trains. She tried to picture how they felt arriving in the middle of the night when the doors opened in a foreign place.

The sound of the truck arriving outside interrupted her thoughts, and it didn't take long for Antoni to walk in. She was relieved to see

Hans wasn't one of the men escorting him—she was in no mood to handle him today.

The guards left, and Antoni looked up at her with a twinkle in his eye.

"You look different," he said. "Any news?"

Her eyes shifted to the bag of potatoes. "Actually, yes. Marian managed to get the officers' badges."

"Can I see them?" He got up, and she handed him the bag.

Just as Antoni reached into the bag, a face appeared in the door opening.

"What's going on here? Why aren't you at your desk?"

Zofia's heart sank as she looked up to see one of the SS guards.

*Damn it. I should be more careful.*

The guard walked in, making the small space feel even more constricted.

Antoni turned around, still holding the bag. The three of them looked at each other, the guard's eyes shifting between Zofia and Antoni before settling on the bag.

"What's in there?" The guard's face was stern, his arms crossed.

Despite her fear, Zofia found herself answering: "It's my bag, I brought some groceries into the office this morning. I know I'm not supposed to, but I wanted to give Antoni a little extra food. It helps him focus when he's working here." She forced an awkward smile.

The man didn't return the smile as he took two steps toward Antoni and took the bag from him.

"Sit back down," he barked at Antoni, who did as he was told.

The guard sat on the corner of Zofia's desk before reaching inside the bag.

*Please don't find the badges.*

He held up a potato and scowled at her. "You're giving this prisoner extra food? You think he doesn't get fed well enough?"

She didn't know how to respond as she tried to control her shaking hands. If the guard inspected the entire bag, it would all be over.

"Did you lose your tongue?" The guard dropped the potato back in the bag before setting the bag down on her desk. He planted his palms on her desk and leaned toward her. His face was very close, and her knees felt weak.

*Think, Zofia, think.*

"I'm so sorry. I know you feed Antoni and all the other prisoners very well. I just wanted to give him a little extra, and I have little else to share. He's been a great help to me."

The man's eyes focused on Zofia, his piercing stare further unnerving her. She averted her eyes. For the first time, a smile formed as he turned to Antoni.

"So you're doing such a good job that the locals are giving you extra food, huh?"

*Is he mocking him?*

On the other side of the office, Antoni looked composed. If he was scared, he certainly wasn't showing it.

*He must be used to them speaking to him like that.*

"I just do my best, sir," he said. Antoni's expression was blank, his face passive and devoid of emotion. Zofia struggled to keep her trembling hands under control as she fumbled with her skirt.

The German picked up a ledger from Antoni's desk and flicked through some of the pages. "So this is your work?"

"I process new arrivals coming into the camp." Zofia noticed he refrained from using the word "prisoners."

The guard nodded, put the ledger down, and turned back to Zofia.

"I don't want to see him leaving this building with a sack of potatoes tonight. We feed them well enough inside the camp. I could take that bag from you right now, but I think you can use the food yourself, right?"

She nodded. *Is he going to let it go?*

"If you want to give him extra food, make sure he gets it while he's here," the guard said as he walked toward the door.

Zofia didn't know what to say and kept her lips firmly pressed together. She hoped he would just walk out without another word.

Instead, he turned in the door opening. "You're lucky I'm in a good mood today. If this happens again, you'll both lose your jobs over this."

His footsteps echoed in the hallway, and Zofia felt the air returning to her little office. She looked across to Antoni, who sat in the same position with the same blank expression on his face.

They sat in silence until they heard the sound of the truck's engine sputtering to life outside.

Only then did Zofia relax somewhat as she let out a deep sigh—her throat felt dry.

Antoni looked up.

"That was way too close," he said with a nervous smile. "We need to find another way to smuggle the badges into the camp."

Zofia stood and looked up and down the hallway. It was all quiet, but for the sound of papers ruffling in the office next door. The Germans had left.

"We were lucky," she said. She didn't sit down but stood near the door opening instead—she was still shaking.

Antoni turned in his chair. "So how are we going to do this? I can't wait to get out of the camp."

Zofia leaned against the doorpost. "The longer we wait, the bigger the chance somebody finds the uniforms."

"They might look into the papers and stock a bit more carefully, and then who knows what they'll do to find them," Antoni said.

"Missing uniforms would be a good excuse to ransack all the barracks," Zofia said in agreement. She rummaged through the bag. Antoni's eyes followed her closely.

She felt the soft fabric of the badges between her fingers.

"I don't want to think what would've happened if that guard had searched a little more carefully," she said as she pulled out the badges and handed them to Antoni. He inspected them, turning them around in his hands. He brushed the collar patches, which had three squares running diagonally from left to right. He looked up approvingly.

"These are perfect, Zofia," he said as he held one up. "Do you know which rank this is?"

She shook her head—the lightning bolts and dark colors all looked the same to her.

"These badges identify us as *Untersturmfuhrers*, the most junior squad leaders in the camp."

"I don't know what that means," Zofia said. "Is that a good thing?"

Antoni slid the badges under the ledger on his desk before answering. "These are the officers that transfer prisoners between the two camps, or even escort them outside the camp."

She understood. "So, nobody would ask questions if you were to walk out of the camp?"

Antoni nodded enthusiastically. "Exactly! The rank is high enough for the officer to go anywhere inside or outside the camp, but common enough not to attract too much attention. It's the perfect cover."

Zofia felt the adrenalin in her body fading as she slowly started to calm down. Her hands were no longer shaking, and she inspected the badges. Apart from the collar badges, there were two pairs of shoulder straps.

"These look very ordinary," she said. The straps had a dull grey button, without any fanfare.

"It doesn't matter. The plainer we look, the better," Antoni said, taking the straps back from her. "Marian did a great job getting these. I don't suppose you know how he managed?"

She shook her head. "I don't ask too many questions. The less I know, the better."

Antoni slid his chair back and walked to the window. "I think I can hide these in my shoes. This uniform doesn't have any pockets, so that wouldn't work."

He slid the badges under the inner soles. Putting his shoes back on, he took a few steps. He looked up happily. "I can hardly feel them. I won't need to take them out until the very last minute."

"Which brings us to the final part of the plan," Zofia said. She leaned against her desk as Antoni sat back down. "When are you going to do it?"

His expression turned serious. "Is everything on the outside ready?"

"Yes. We're ready to take you to the escape route—I checked yesterday." She hesitated and fidgeted with a pen on her desk.

Antoni picked up on it. "But—?"

"Well, you'll need to take a different route than the one we discussed before." She explained about the stolen bikes and the more strenuous route to the trail.

He listened silently. When she was done, he placed his hands flat on the desk and straightened his back.

"Zofia, with everything you, Marian, and the rest of the Sosienki are doing, I think taking a slightly tougher route to the trail is a small price to pay. We've all taken so many risks up to now; I think we can manage a bit of a hike."

She sighed. "I know you'll be able to make it, but is your friend also strong enough? You won't have any time to rest until you're well on the Babinicza trail. If something goes wrong, chances are the Germans will find you one way or another."

Antoni bowed his head. "He'll make it—don't worry. It's all we've both thought about for weeks now. We'll get to the trail."

"Okay, so when?"

He answered without hesitating. "Tomorrow after evening roll call. I've thought about it, and there will be no better opportunity to have this much time without anyone noticing us missing. We can walk out of Birkenau, saying we need to inspect something in Auschwitz. This wouldn't be out of the ordinary—officers are constantly going between camps. The patrols there are limited, and we can escape from there."

"It will be very dangerous once you're on the outside," Zofia said. She worried about the evening curfew on her side. "If they see us moving after dark, we won't be able to meet you at the bridge, and you'll never find the start of the trail. Even with your uniforms, it will be hard to explain what you're doing there in the dark, or the early morning."

"So make sure you're well in place before curfew. Our roll call is at seven. Once that's done, everybody goes to their barracks. We're all too exhausted to do anything else. This is when we will pick up our uniforms and make our escape. If all goes well, we can be at the bridge well before midnight."

Zofia calculated the time frames. It meant she and Jacob would have to be in place by half-past four at the latest, close to sunset. It would be a long and cold wait, but she knew where to hide. She didn't worry about patrols noticing her if everything went according to plan. If they found out before he was on the trail, she had bigger problems to worry about.

"Alright, tomorrow evening it is."

She sat back down, leafing through the ledger in front of her. She tried to focus on her work, but her mind was racing. It was going to happen. She was excited and terrified at the same time. So much could go wrong, but if they pulled it off, it would be a big boost to the resistance. Previous escapes had never been this calculated or well prepared. She'd heard the stories of people attempting to climb the electrified fences in their desperation—very few people made it past the perimeter, and even fewer lived to tell about their attempts.

She looked up to see Antoni looking at her, pen in hand. He had an odd expression that she couldn't place.

"What is it?"

He put the pen down and grinned. "We're going to do it, Zofia. We're going to escape from Auschwitz-Birkenau."

# CHAPTER EIGHTEEN

Jacob and Zofia lay in the bushes overlooking the Sola River. The soft wind carried the sound of water rushing under the bridge below. Other than that, the only sound was when a sudden gust of wind rustled the leaves in the trees hanging overhead. The sky was clear, and the moonlight illuminated the river.

He looked at Zofia, whose eyes were fixed on the bridge. He'd told her to take a quick nap earlier, but she'd simply looked at him with a look of disdain. They'd been in the same spot for over five hours, and his legs ached.

He softly poked Zofia with his elbow. "Nature's calling—I'll be right back."

She nodded. "Don't go too far—they'll be here any minute now."

His legs protested as he got up. Even though they'd brought thick blankets and wore several layers of clothing, the cold had seeped into his bones, and he relished the short walk.

Jacob found a spot and listened to the sounds of the forest. He never realized there was so much going on at night outside of a city. Despite the soothing sounds around him, he was anything but relaxed. When Zofia had told him they were meeting the escapees this night, he'd been excited. This was what he'd come down to Oświęcim for, to help the resistance. But as the dangers of the operation sank in and the time to leave approached, he became more anxious. If anything went wrong, they would be in great danger.

Zofia had made it very clear that the SS knew the bridge was an essential part of any escape. The Sola had to be crossed to get away from Oświęcim and onto the escape trail. The river was easy to find, and Antoni had been told to look for the first bridge upstream. The plan was brilliant, as it was almost impossible for Antoni to get lost.

Jacob walked back to their hiding spot, making sure he didn't trip over any branches. Zofia hadn't moved—she kept her eyes peeled for any movement on the bridge. He handed her a flask, and she took a small sip of water.

"Are you worried something might've happened to them?" He kept his voice low. "It's taking a long time, don't you think?"

Her face was calm. "As long as the roads are quiet and we don't hear anything happening in the town below, we wait for them."

"How will we know if they didn't make it?"

"If they're not here by dawn, something went wrong, and we'll make our way back to my house. Either way, we're not going anywhere before daylight. It would be too risky, even though the chance of a random German patrol this far from the camp is unlikely."

Her calm exterior did little to comfort him. During previous missions in Warsaw, he'd become accustomed to taking action. Waiting in a cold, dark forest was new to Jacob.

"How many times have you done this before?" He kept his voice low.

"This is the fourth time I've waited for escapees here," she said. "But it's the first time we're trying something this well-organized."

"What do you mean?"

Zofia sat up, still shielded from view by the bushes. She stretched out before answering.

"We've attempted many escapes. We've tried arming prisoners with weapons and tools to break out of the camp. We've tried to intercept them closer to the camp and get them to the escape trail that way. It never worked. There was always a reason why we failed. We've lost many members and prisoners this way."

Her eyes were sad in the moonlight; her hands clenched into fists.

Jacob sat up and rearranged one of the blankets to put under him on the cold forest floor. "But you've succeeded in getting people out as well, right?"

"We realized we couldn't use this direct approach. The Germans simply increased their patrols and security around the camp after some of the failed attempts. It's now impossible to get anywhere near the camp without drawing attention, even at night." She took another sip from the flask. "So we changed our plans. Half a year ago, one of the prisoners managed to hide in a crate which was heading out of the camp."

"He must have had help doing that. There's no way you can pack yourself in a crate, right?"

Zofia nodded. "Two other prisoners helped him. One of our contacts in the camp told us about the plan, and we waited for the truck to drive through town. As you know, most of the trucks will drive through Oświęcim before heading north. We ambushed the driver just outside of town. He simply stopped when four men in the middle of the road waved guns at him."

Jacob shifted his weight, his limbs protesting. "Were you part of the ambush?"

"No, I was waiting here while Marian led the operation. Once they opened the truck, it was easy to find the crate with the escapee. The people in the camp made sure it was the last one loaded."

"How was he?"

Zofia smiled faintly. "Very uncomfortable, as you would expect after spending a few hours curled up in a crate. Marian then instructed him to get to this bridge."

Jacob was surprised. "Marian didn't bring him here?"

She shook her head. "That would be too big a risk. Once they'd freed him, they left the driver tied up in his truck, and they disappeared. Once you're out of the camp, you're on your own. We never move in groups."

That was how it had been for Jacob, too, coming from Warsaw. He nodded.

"Did he make it?"

She nodded. "He crossed the bridge, and I sent him on his way. This was when we still had bikes. The Germans found out about the ambush many hours later. By then, I was back home, and the escapee was on the trail."

Jacob saw pride in her eyes. "Do you know what became of him?"

"All I know is that he made it to the end of the trail in the south. I'm sure he joined up with the Home Army there."

They sat in silence for a few minutes. Zofia seemed lost in thought.

Crackling sounds in the distance abruptly disturbed the silence, and they turned in the direction of the sound.

"Were those shots?" Jacob asked although he knew the answer.

Zofia raised her hand to silence him and closed her eyes. The wind carried the sound of more shots from the other side of the river.

"It's coming from south of the city," Zofia said, opening her eyes. "That's highly unusual."

Jacob's throat constricted. *It's happening.* He strained his eyes to make something out in the darkness across the water.

"What should we do?" Jacob asked.

Zofia crouched down below the bush. Her knees were on the blanket. Her eyes fixed on the river.

"Nothing. We'll stay here and wait for movement on the other side. If something went wrong, we need to make sure no Germans see their escape path. If they do, all our future operations will be in danger."

Jacob felt frustrated. "We're just going to sit here and wait until they might show up?" He felt a vein in his neck stand up.

She turned to him briefly. "There is nothing we can do. We have no weapons. If they're really being chased, we can only hope they can shake off the Germans before they get here. We can't compromise the trail."

Despite the darkness, Jacob saw the determination in her eyes.

He nodded and crouched down beside her. "We wait."

The sound of the gunshots died as abruptly as it had started.

*I hope they shook off the SS.* He knew what awaited them if they got caught.

Jacob started counting in his head. When he reached sixty seconds of silence, he relaxed a little. Whatever happened, the absence of gunshots meant there was a breakthrough.

Zofia spoke first. "If they made it, they should be here within the hour. Even with the wind carrying the sound, the gunshots weren't far from here."

"And if they didn't? What are the chances of them getting caught and giving away the position?"

She shook her head. "Even if they're caught alive, they'll be taken back to the camp."

Jacob wasn't convinced, and he thought he detected a hint of uncertainty in Zofia's voice. But there wasn't much else to do but wait and hope for the best. They weren't going anywhere tonight.

The wind died down, and the sound of the river faded. The moon illuminated the bridge brightly, its light reflected in the river. Jacob suddenly felt very exposed.

They lay low for what felt like hours, and then Jacob saw something moving on the far side of the bridge.

Zofia nodded—she'd seen it too.

Jacob held his breath. Shadows danced between the bushes on the other side of the river. Whoever was there was careful not to be exposed.

"How many are they?" He whispered to Zofia.

"It's hard to tell. They're well hidden. But it should just be Antoni and one other man," Zofia said, her eyes straining.

Jacob was restless. *What if our plan fails? What if the SS guards are waiting in ambush?*

"Do we need to let them know they're at the right spot? Is there some kind of code?"

Zofia shook her head. "They're too far away. I need to see their faces."

"So, we wait until they cross?"

She nodded. "That's what we agreed upon. Antoni knows this. If it's them, they'll make their way across."

Jacob looked across the water. The shadows disappeared, and for a moment, he thought they'd gone. But then he saw movement on the bridge.

He pointed toward the movement.

"Smart crossing," Zofia said. "He's careful not to draw any attention."

"Do you think it's Antoni? If they were Germans, they probably wouldn't be this stealthy about it, right?"

Zofia looked unsure. "Never underestimate them. If they're looking to draw us out, they'll pretend to be the escapees."

She leaned forward, her hand slightly above her eyes as she tried to focus on the person crossing the bridge.

"It's definitely a man, and he's wearing a uniform. Probably an SS uniform, but I can't see his face."

"Where would he go next? Is there a better place for us to see his face?"

Zofia pointed to a spot left of the bridge. "They'd cross the road there and head into those bushes. There is a spot where they can climb up. They know to walk up to that oak tree over there," she nodded to a large tree close to where they sat. "There, they will wait for us."

Jacob drew the path in his mind. Once they crossed the bridge and went into the bushes, the men would disappear to them until they reached the oak tree.

"It sounds risky just to approach them when they're there," he said, his face scrunched up a little.

Zofia nodded. "It is, but that's where we have the secret signal. If they don't respond in the right way, we'll make our way out of here. You didn't think this was going to be without risk, right?" She gave him a nervous smile.

"Look, a second person is crossing!" Jacob pointed to the bridge.

The first person had almost crossed, and a second shadow stalked toward their side. He was shorter than the first person, and he wore the same uniform.

"That's Antoni," Zofia said, excitement in her voice. "I can tell by his walk."

The man hunched over to make use of the cover of darkness as he briskly made his way across. He met up with the other man, who crouched beside the bridge. They were now quite close, and Jacob heard their hushed whispers.

"Do you recognize his voice?" Jacob asked.

Zofia shook her head. "I can't even tell what language they're speaking."

Jacob strained his ears, but couldn't make out the words, either.

The two shadows stood facing the bridge—their backs to Jacob and Zofia.

*Something's not right.*

"What are they waiting for?" Jacob frowned.

Zofia looked just as puzzled. "I have no idea—they should be coming up toward us."

Just as she finished speaking, they got their answer. One of the men whistled sharply.

On the far side of the bridge, two shadows emerged from the bushes. They were less concerned with keeping cover as they sprinted across. It took them less than ten seconds.

*Two more men?*

"We weren't expecting them, were we?" Jacob looked to Zofia. She looked alarmed and didn't immediately respond. She was focused on the men—now four of them—on their side of the river. They turned and now faced them while one of them pointed up and turned left.

She smiled. "Those other two aren't wearing SS uniforms."

Jacob couldn't tell in the darkness. The men disappeared into the bushes.

"They wore striped uniforms," Zofia continued. "Like the ones worn by the prisoners in the camp. It looks like they somehow saved two extra prisoners."

*That would be a massive achievement for the Sosienki.*

"But we're still not sure, right? You didn't see Antoni's face?"

Her face was serious, but her eyes twinkled. "You're right; we need to be careful. I'm almost certain it was Antoni, but we'll stick to the plan and move to the oak tree to know for sure."

She sat up. "Follow me—it will take them a few minutes. Let's make sure we're in position."

Zofia crouched toward the tree line. Despite the darkness, she knew where she was going, and Jacob made sure not to lose sight of her. It took them half a minute to get close to the oak tree. They kept their distance, sheltered by thick bushes, and had a perfect view of anybody approaching from the riverside.

Zofia sat down. "It shouldn't be much longer. If they take the route straight up, they'll appear from there." She pointed to a pair of low bushes nestled between some smaller trees.

Jacob felt nervous. Although Zofia was confident it was Antoni, he still felt the sliver of doubt he had had all evening. They were well hidden, but the distance between the oak tree and their position was close enough for a trained soldier to cover quickly. If the men were SS, they would be armed, and Jacob did not look forward to running from gunfire.

*We've come this far, and she's convinced it's Antoni. She knows what she's doing—she knows what she's doing.*

He looked at Zofia, her face set in sharp lines. She must've felt him looking because she turned and gave him an encouraging smile.

They heard them before they saw them—the soft crunch of branches and rustling bushes betraying their approach. Jacob's eyes fixed on the source of the sound. Before long, one of the men's faces appeared between the bushes. He was silent and looked around until he spotted the oak tree. He tentatively stepped into the open and signaled for the other men to follow. Jacob now saw them; he'd never seen the striped uniform before.

Jacob was shocked by the man's appearance. As he stepped into the moonlight, Jacob noticed his ghoulish face, cheekbones exposed. His eyes appeared to hover in their sockets.

The other men arrived and gathered around the tree. One of the men in SS uniform approached the tree; his face turned away from Jacob and Zofia.

Jacob turned to Zofia. *Is it them?* He mouthed the words.

She held up her hands. "I don't know any of the other men, and I can't make out their faces," she whispered in his ear.

The men sat down, the ones in SS uniforms with their backs toward Jacob and Zofia. They whispered among themselves, but they were too far away for Jacob to make out what they were saying. Some of the words he thought he recognized—they didn't sound German. But then he also knew heavily accented German didn't sound anything like what he was used to in Berlin.

Zofia turned to Jacob. "I think it's them. I'm going to whistle something. If they return it, it's them."

"And what if they don't?" Jacob sat up a little, using his elbows for support.

"We run." She looked at him, her bright eyes shining. "But hopefully it's them, and we can get them on their way. Are you ready?"

Jacob nodded, and Zofia sat up, still shielded by the bushes. She put her fingers to her mouth and whistled a tune.

He didn't recognize it. Her whistle was soft, and he doubted the men heard it.

They didn't respond right away.

But then, one of them moved. He stood up and looked around. It was the tall man in the SS uniform, and Jacob's hopes rose. *Is it Antoni?*

The wind carried Zofia's tune and made it hard to pinpoint the source.

*All the better.*

Zofia whistled a little louder while keeping her eyes fixed on the men.

The other men stood up, and Zofia abruptly stopped.

For a few seconds, all that could be heard was the faint rustling of the leaves around them. Then the silence was broken by a lower version of the same tune. It was hummed by one of the men in the group under the oak tree.

"And then they came to Bethlehem," the man sang softly, loud enough for Zofia and Jacob to hear.

Zofia burst through the bushes. Jacob was surprised to see her this excited. She ran up to the group of men and hugged the man in the SS uniform.

Jacob followed suit, a little more cautiously. Zofia beamed as she softly spoke with the shorter man in the SS uniform. He was smiling, as were the other men under the tree.

He approached slowly—feeling like an intruder—until Zofia turned to him with a big smile.

"Jacob, meet the men who just escaped from Auschwitz."

Jacob shook their hands. Their grips had no strength, and their arms were bony.

Antoni turned to him and spoke in broken German. "We appreciate your help in this mission, Jacob."

He smiled and answered him in Polish: "I'm just happy to help. Let's get you into some different clothes."

Jacob brought a duffel bag from their hiding spot and pulled out several garments. The men happily stripped out of their filthy camp garments and new SS uniforms. They were a strange sight in the dark forest.

"It's a good thing we have some extra sweaters in there because we didn't know the exact sizes. We weren't expecting four of you," Jacob said to the men wearing the prisoner uniforms—they took the clothes gratefully but silently.

"Yes, how did you manage to take two more out of the camp?" Zofia asked Antoni.

"It was pure luck. After we changed into our SS uniforms, we headed for the exit, and that's where they were waiting. I announced to the guard we were going to Auschwitz. I've been practicing my German for months, and I was worried they might pick up my accent, but instead, he asked if we were sent to escort these men. That's when we decided to take them with us."

Jacob was impressed by Antoni's bravery. *Those two were the luckiest men in Auschwitz.*

"What about those gunshots?" Jacob asked.

"We heard them, too, but they weren't shooting at us," Antoni said while pulling on a pair of worn slacks. "We left the camp on schedule, right after roll call. The gunfire was from the other side of the camp, as far as we could tell. It only encouraged us to get to the bridge faster."

They finished changing, and Zofia took the filthy prison garments and uniforms, checking the SS badges before stuffing them all in the duffel bag.

Dressed in ordinary clothes, the men almost passed for civilians despite their haggard appearances. Antoni looked to be the strongest of the four. Jacob hoped they were ready for the week-long hike ahead.

Zofia handed a smaller bag to Antoni. "Here are some supplies for the first two days. You won't reach the first shelter before that, so ration well. Do you remember the route?"

Antoni tapped the side of his head. "It's all here. Just show me the starting point."

"Good—there's no time to lose," Zofia said, heading into the forest.

Jacob caught up with her as the men followed.

"Can you ask them about Ethan? I would ask myself, but they appear to speak only Polish, and I'm not sure I'll be able to get my questions across."

She nodded. "We still have about five minutes until we reach the trail."

Zofia fell back and asked Antoni if he knew anybody fitting Ethan's description. Antoni asked the other men. The first man shook his head.

"This one says he was in a block with gypsies, so he had no contact with any German prisoners," Antoni translated. He looked at the second man in line, who also shook his head.

Jacob's hopes fell. Perhaps it really was impossible in a camp of tens of thousands of people to find out about his best friend. He looked to the fourth man, and the man was looking at him curiously.

The man spoke in Polish to Antoni, who nodded.

"He's asking if you were transferred from the west, from a camp in the Netherlands."

*How would he know about Westerbork?* Jacob felt his heart beat faster.

Another stream of words came from the man's mouth. Antoni listened as they walked on, nodding.

"He says he's pretty sure he worked with your friend. Whenever someone speaks of him, they tell the story of how you both got on the train, but you never arrived. Nobody knows what happened to you, because when he arrived, he immediately rushed to your train car and didn't find you nor your body. People said you had jumped from the train."

Jacob felt a surge of adrenaline rush through his veins. *Is it possible Ethan is still alive?*

"Can you ask him when he last saw him?" Jacob asked Antoni with his heart thudding in his throat.

The man nodded and held up two fingers.

"Two days ago, when they worked the coal mines together. He says that's the work detail your friend is on. They're escorted to the coal mines just outside the city every morning and evening."

*Ethan is alive!* Jacob felt renewed energy and a spring in his step. *I must find a way to find Ethan.* If these men escaped, so could Ethan.

Zofia interrupted his thoughts. "We're here."

They had reached a hill with dense vegetation, and she pointed up.

"This is where you'll start your climb. It will be tough, but once you get to the top, you'll be safe. There are no roads up there, and the Germans know nothing about this route. You will be the first ones going this way. Keep heading south until you get to the first marker, an old altar in the woods. That's where you'll find the first supplies. This will take two days."

She looked at Antoni. "All the best. When you get to the end of the trail, people will be waiting for you. I hope I'll see you again."

Antoni hugged Zofia. "I owe you everything, Zofia. I'll never forget this, and neither will they," he said and pointed to the men.

"Just get there in one piece," Zofia said, her eyes a little damp.

Antoni signaled for the others to follow him. As they passed Jacob, they shook his hand. Within seconds, they disappeared in the bushes; the sound of crunching leaves ebbing away as they started their ascent to safety.

Zofia looked at Jacob with a knowing smile. "I know what you're thinking, Jacob, and the answer is yes. We're going to find a way to get Ethan out of there."

Without another word, she turned and walked back toward their hiding spot. He followed, his mind racing. He didn't know how they were going to do it, but if Zofia had the confidence to say it could be done, he didn't doubt they'd find a way.

On the horizon, the first rays of sunlight appeared, casting a faint orange glow around the town below.

# CHAPTER NINETEEN

The sun crept its way over the horizon as Jacob walked through the fields outside town. He inhaled the crisp morning air as the frosted grass crunched softly under his feet.

He'd had an early breakfast and had waited for the first rays of light to filter through the kitchen window before heading out. After crossing the last field, he now hiked a small hill overlooking the road below. It gave little cover, but Zofia had told him there would be a small shed in the middle of the pasture. She said sheepherders used it during the season, but he didn't have to worry about that now. There were no herders nor sheep left.

He got to the top and looked down. The dark brown wooden shed was easy to spot, and he jogged down the hill.

The shed was unlocked—the door opened with a loud creaking sound, and he stepped inside to the smell of moldy wood. He sat down on a wobbly stool and peeked through a small crack in the wall. It offered the perfect view of the road below, and he settled in for the wait.

It didn't take long before he saw a host of men came marching down the road. A German army jeep led the way, followed by a sea of men wearing the camp's striped uniforms. Guards flanked them on either side.

Jacob studied the group, which was too far away for him to make out any faces. It reminded him of the many marches he'd supervised from Hooghalen train station to Westerbork. The difference between the men was striking, though. In the Netherlands, the people from the trains wore their own clothes, carried suitcases with their belongings, and didn't know what awaited them. These men all looked the same with their striped uniforms, shaved heads, and ghostly faces.

The number of guards flanking them was excessive. But even if they'd tried to break through the guard, the men wouldn't have had enough energy to escape.

The jeep passed the shed at slow speed, and Jacob saw three officers and a driver. The officers laughed and joked about something. The driver sat stone-faced, his eyes on the deserted road ahead.

Zofia had found out the route Ethan's work detail took to the coal mines. She'd suggested Jacob scout out the group, and had even arranged some forged papers for him.

*How am I going to find Ethan in this group? They're all like the walking dead.*

He tried counting them as they walked by, but the faces blurred into one another. They all looked the same, and even the difference between young and old was hard to determine—camp life added decades to many. Jacob gave up getting an exact count and decided he must've seen at least a thousand men marching past him.

As the last passed, another jeep secured the rear and disappeared over a rise.

Jacob stepped out of the shed—glad to escape the moldy surroundings—and decided to take the same route back to Zofia's house. While he walked through the grass, the sun crept slowly into the sky. Despite this setback, the warmth felt good on his face. He would have to take a different approach to find Ethan. As he peered in the coal mine's direction, he saw the group marching through a small village below.

A thought struck him. They would need to take the same route back to the camp. Instead of going back to Zofia's house, he descended toward the village. He needed to get a closer look.

Jacob sat on a bench in the middle of the village and felt again for the papers in his coat pocket. He greeted some of the villagers walking past in his best Polish—they reluctantly acknowledged him.

He checked the oversized clock on the small bell tower across the plaza—it was almost four. If he'd calculated the march time correctly, the group should start making its way back to the camp around now. He expected them to pass through the village shortly.

Jacob had spent the afternoon walking through the fields and small hills around the village. From his vantage point, he'd located the small square near the church, and he thought he spotted a bench where he could sit somewhat inconspicuously. When he got there, he was glad to find it unoccupied. The village square was quiet but for the occasional passer-by. He hoped the SS guards would be too busy with the prisoners to notice him.

*It's still sunny, so it isn't all that odd for me to sit outside, right?*

While he waited, he went through his cover story again. Zofia had warned him the chances of the SS asking for his papers were quite high —especially if it looked like he wasn't doing anything. The documents she'd forged identified him as Karl Wagner, a German investor looking to capitalize on the coal mining industry in the area. To make him look even more legitimate, Zofia had obtained a fairly recent copy of the People's Observer newspaper from Germany.

*A Nazi newspaper should help.*

He thought about what he would do if he spotted Ethan. He expected his friend would be exhausted from his day in the mines. *Would he recognize me?*

Judging by what he'd seen in the morning, he doubted it—the men kept their heads down, focused on putting one foot before another. He decided merely seeing his friend alive would be enough. Zofia promised they would come up with a plan when he was sure Ethan was alive.

Jacob glanced at the clock again. Almost fifteen minutes had passed, and he drummed his fingers on the bench. He had begun to wonder if they might take a different route back when he heard the rumble of a car —his chest tightened, and his mouth went dry.

The sound increased, and a few seconds later, the jeep he had seen that morning swung around the corner. It drove into town without slowing, and Jacob recognized the officers and grumpy driver. He sat up, quickly took out his newspaper, and casually unfolded it onto his legs. To anybody looking, Jacob was simply a man reading a paper on a sunny day. He hoped nobody cared to take a closer look.

It didn't take long for the first men to march onto the small village square. Despite their large numbers, the group was surprisingly quiet, but for hundreds of feet plodding through the small street—the men didn't speak or look up. Even the SS men escorting them were silent, except for the sound of their boots hitting the cobblestones. Their gazes darted among the prisoners. Even the notoriously cruel SS softened a little with the quiet desperation of the group.

One prisoner lost his footing and stumbled to the cobbles. The other men stepped around him and walked on. It was an odd sight—the neatly formed lines separated past the man, only to go back into formation once he was behind them. The man didn't make an effort to get up, and nobody seemed to have the energy to help him. The guards passed without another look.

Jacob was horrified. At first, he thought it was a mistake—somebody would help the man up soon enough. Or maybe the SS would force him to march on. But nothing happened, and the indifference of the entire group shocked him. However, as he looked closer, he noticed it wasn't indifference—it was compassion. As long as the prisoners closed ranks around him, the man would have his peaceful death in the middle of the street.

Jacob could see that the man's eyes were closed, and it wasn't clear if he was breathing. The occasional prisoner passing by made a small gesture of respect.

When it became clear the man wouldn't get up anymore, Jacob returned his focus to the faces passing by. He needed to find Ethan.

There were too many of them. Old men, young men, and teenagers —their hands and faces pitch-black from the mines. He realized he might be closer to them than he had been in the morning, but the sheer number of identical-looking men made it almost impossible to pick out his friend. Despite that, he kept his eyes glued on the faces.

He was so absorbed by the faces that he hadn't noticed someone standing next to the bench.

"Do you want me to repeat the question?" a fresh-faced guard asked him in German. The expression on his face was stern but not unfriendly.

Jacob looked at him, taking a moment to gather his reply. The young man tapped his foot impatiently.

"I'm sorry, I didn't notice you," Jacob spoke, falling back into the crisp Berlin accent he hadn't used in years.

The guard's eyebrows shot up in surprise. "I asked what you were doing here. But I didn't expect you to speak German. Are you from Berlin?"

Jacob found his composure. The guard didn't look older than very late teens—maybe just turned twenty. *I can handle this youngster.* He made a point of folding his newspaper with the title showing and putting it next to him on the bench.

"Kreuzberg, yes. I work as an investment advisor for the new territories."

"What does that mean?" The guard looked confused.

Jacob tried his most confident smile. "It means I'm sent to new areas of the Reich to assess if we might need to invest money into developing them. That's also why I'm here—to check the potential of the coal mines in the area. We may need to expand."

"Well, these prisoners all work in the coal mines. From what I can see, there's plenty of coal there," the guard chimed in. He looked content with himself, happy to help.

Jacob nodded. "Very well, I appreciate your insights."

One of the other guards shouted something, and the young man turned back to Jacob.

"I will need to see your papers, though, just to be sure," he said, almost apologetic.

Despite Jacob's calm exterior, his heart was racing. He didn't know what they were supposed to look like, and he prayed Zofia had done a good job.

"Certainly," he said, as he reached into his pocket and handed the papers to the guard.

While the man inspected them, Jacob kept his focus on the faces walking by. It was both a way to remain calm while hoping to see Ethan march by.

The guard cleared his throat, and Jacob looked up.

"Something doesn't seem right here," he said, tapping at a line on the document. "It says here you're from Dresden. Didn't you just say you're from Berlin?"

A stab of fear shot through his body. *How did I miss that?*

The guard looked at him suspiciously and held out the document for Jacob to see. "You see? Dresden."

Jacob recovered quickly. "The company I work for is based in Dresden, but I'm originally from Berlin." He laughed nervously. "I'm sorry, I'm so used to saying I'm from Berlin that I always forget my company's headquarters is in Dresden."

The man gave him a hard look.

"With all this documentation these days, it's hard to keep up sometimes," Jacob added, trying to sound convincing.

The guard folded the papers back into place before handing them back. "You should be more careful about that. Papers are everything these days, especially when you're so far from home."

Jacob breathed a silent sigh of relief. "I know, it's clumsy of me—thank you."

The guard appeared happy with his inspection and nodded. "Good luck assessing the coal industry here. We could use some more work for the people in the camp. If possible, do you think you could arrange the mine a little closer to our camp? I hate this walk."

He winked at Jacob and fell back in formation.

Jacob picked up his newspaper and took a moment to calm down.

*That was close, way too close.*

The group moved along, and Jacob tried to scan every face in front of him, but it proved impossible.

*Did I miss Ethan just now?* The inspection had taken only a few moments.

Judging by the number of men from the morning, he was sure he'd only seen half of them so far. The main street in the village was a little narrow, and they couldn't move quite as fast as in the open field. The men were devoid of energy and seemed to appreciate slowing down a little.

Jacob was about to give up when something caught his eye—a familiar gait in one of the men. He sat up and leaned forward to get a better look. It was difficult to focus through the crowd of men in similar uniforms.

One of the men moved to the side, and in a flash, he saw the face he was looking for.

*Ethan.*

His friend walked near the back of the crowd, and Jacob almost didn't recognize him. His face was as gaunt and covered in soot as the others, his arms bony, and he looked years older than he was. He looked frail, but it was Ethan.

Jacob felt a surge of hope. He wanted to shout out to his friend and take him from the group before he quickly remembered his surroundings and controlled himself.

*He's alive!* he marveled.

Ethan walked on with the same beaten-down posture as the other men, oblivious to his surroundings. If he had been alert, he would've seen his friend looking at him, determination on his face.

As Ethan turned out of his sight, Jacob was thinking of ways to rescue him. He knew Zofia would help him—she'd promised as much. He thought about the places where they might be able to intercept him. It would be impossible to ambush the work detail on the way to the mines. Picking Ethan out of the group would be hard enough, let alone overpowering all the guards. He'd counted at least a hundred of them guarding all those men. They would need something more subtle— something that didn't involve violence.

The last of the group turned the corner, and the sound of their footsteps ebbed away. The men would be back at the camp within an hour, just before sunset.

Jacob got up from the bench and walked in the opposite direction, back to Oświęcim. As he passed a garbage can, he tossed the German newspaper into it.

Marian and Zofia sat across from Jacob at the kitchen table. It was late in the afternoon, and dusk was setting in, but Marian didn't seem concerned about the evening curfew.

"You're absolutely certain you saw your friend?" Marian asked.

Jacob nodded. "It was Ethan—no doubt. He looked just as bad as the men around him, but it was him. The way he walked, his face, everything. I would recognize him out of thousands."

"And did he look healthy enough for an escape?" Marian's face was friendly, his eyes soft but alert. "We need to be realistic, Jacob. Escaping from the camp is near impossible, and everything needs to go to plan. We can't ambush that entire group. There are too many of them. We need to be smart."

"I understand," Jacob said while he thought about the question. *Ethan looked exhausted.*

"He's tired, but he'll find the energy to escape. Wouldn't you, if it meant getting away from that place?"

Jacob's eyes went from Marian to Zofia and back. Both of them looked back at him with serious faces. After a few seconds, Marian nodded.

"I would, and if I were in your position, I would do anything to get him out."

Marian stood up and paced around the kitchen. Zofia looked at Jacob with affection. She took his hand and gently squeezed it.

"We'll get him out somehow," she said softly. "Marian always finds a way."

Jacob looked at the man he depended on. He thought about all the things Marian must've seen since the start of the war. Running operations so close to one of the biggest German camps was risky, but he'd successfully done this daring work for almost five years now—if anybody could free Ethan, it was Marian.

"I think I have an idea," Marian said as he sat back down at the table. "But it's going to be even riskier than what we did with Antoni."

Zofia's eyes lit up. "I can hardly imagine anything riskier than walking out of the camp like they did."

"You're right," Marian said and leaned forward. "There is only one thing more dangerous than walking out of the camp."

Jacob looked at Marian, who looked conflicted for a moment. He seemed to reconsider what he was about to say.

"Tell me, what do I need to do? I'll do anything to get Ethan out of there."

Marian sized him up. "You're going to do what no-one's ever done before."

Jacob held his gaze.

"You're going to walk into Auschwitz-Birkenau voluntarily."

# CHAPTER TWENTY

Jacob and Marian stood on the outskirts of town. Both wore the SS uniforms Antoni had used for his escape only a week earlier. This time, Marian had obtained higher ranking officers' badges. Jacob didn't ask him how, but when he looked at himself in the mirror that morning, he saw an SS officer.

Both men looked the part. They were clean-shaven and had had a haircut the night before. Jacob's face almost reflected in his shiny boots.

When Marian laid out his plan, Jacob thought it was the boldest thing he'd ever heard. The efforts they had gone through to get Antoni out had been monumental, and that was just getting them out. Walking in was a completely different thing.

They'd gone through the plan many times in the past days. They'd walk into the camp just after morning roll call. That's when the work details left, and there would be a coming and going of people. Jacob liked the idea, but he worried about finding Ethan in the crowds. Marian agreed, but they decided it was their best chance.

When Jacob said he would go in alone, Marian rejected the idea out of hand. He wanted to be part of the first resistance mission going into the camp—there was no way he was staying behind.

Jacob looked at the man next to him. His back was straight, his eyes focused. He looked confident—every bit an SS officer on a mission—and Jacob wished he felt the same. He was nervous, anxious they wouldn't even make it past the gate.

Marian must have felt his gaze. "Don't worry too much, Jacob. Our preparations went well, and nobody questions these uniforms, remember?"

Jacob gave an uneasy smile. "I just need a little time to get used to this uniform. You seem very comfortable already."

"It's all show. You've got to own it and make them believe you're an officer," he said. He tapped the badge on his collar. "Any guard seeing this will simply salute you and let you walk by. They're not going to question your authority unless you allow them to. With your Berlin accent, you'll be a natural. I'll keep my mouth shut and let you do the talking."

Jacob nodded. He hoped not all the scenarios they'd gone through would have to be executed today. He swallowed hard.

As the gravel crunched under their boots, Jacob thought back to his time in Westerbork. He remembered the SS men, cruel but disinterested as they kept to themselves, and happy to let the Ordedienst do the dirty work. From what he was told, the SS in Auschwitz was more involved. He hoped that would make them blend in easier.

"We're almost there," Marian said as they approached a bend in the road. "Better get your best German officer face on."

They turned the corner, and Jacob saw the camp for the first time. He blinked as it took up the entire horizon. Beyond the high barbed wire fence, there was nothing but rows and rows of barracks going on seemingly forever. At regular intervals, guard towers rose, complete with searchlights—Westerbork paled by comparison to the monstrosity in front of him.

"It's like a small city," Jacob said. He hadn't realized he'd stopped walking until Marian was a few paces ahead of him.

The tall man turned around, his face stoic. "It's bigger than most of the nearby towns combined."

They approached the imposing gatehouse. Train tracks ran through the middle, straight into the camp. To the left, the road passed through an arch. The gate was closed, and Jacob saw the orange flicker of a cigarette hovering next to it. As they got closer, he spotted two guards standing at very casual attention—they were chatting away quite carelessly.

"The guards look relaxed," he said.

Marian nodded. "They have nothing to fear, and as far as they can tell, we are two officers coming back from town. They don't have to worry about anybody coming into the camp, really. It's the other side they need to focus on."

Marian slowed down a little so Jacob could catch up. He talked to him in hushed tones as they neared the gate.

"Now Jacob, you're going to do all the talking. I'll simply nod and defer to whatever you say. Remember, you're an officer. They won't question that—you look and sound the part. Just act natural and be confident, and we'll be in and out in no time."

A shiver ran down Jacob's spine, but Marian was right. There was no reason they wouldn't blend in, especially with the enormous number of people in the camp.

"Let's go and get Ethan," Jacob said, straightening his collar, brushing his hand along the officer's badge.

They fell in line as they approached the building. Jacob rubbed his clammy hands and wiped them on his pants.

The gate was well lit, a bright beacon in a sea of darkness. The guards stood sheltered on the other side. One of them threw his cigarette butt on the sandy ground and crushed the small orange glow with the heel of his boot. The other stepped back into the gatehouse.

The guard faced Jacob and Marian—his eyes were narrow, giving the impression of a constant squint. As Jacob and Marian stepped into the light, the guard's body tensed. He stepped to attention and saluted the officers, his right arm outstretched in front of him.

Marian was quick to respond, raising his arm in similar fashion. Jacob followed with a slight delay. He'd never used the Nazi salute before in Westerbork, and he felt awkward.

*I hope he didn't notice that,* Jacob thought as he lowered his arm.

The guard's eyes scanned Jacob's collar, his eyes betraying surprise at the young officer's rank.

Jacob felt blood rush to his face. His neck tingled, and he hoped the darkness masked his burning cheeks.

The guard's expression didn't change. "You gentlemen are back quite late—or early, I guess."

He stated it as a fact, but the undertone was unmistakable—he was suspicious.

Jacob didn't respond immediately. His palms were clammy again, and he rubbed them together in a reflex. He glanced at Marian, whose face was impassive, but his eyes displayed urgency. *I need to take charge.* He straightened his back and looked the guard in the eye.

"We inspected a suspected breach in the perimeter near the city," Jacob said, pointing behind him.

The guard cocked his head. "I didn't hear about anything like that. Was there an escape?"

Jacob shook his head. "Fortunately, not. But we had intel from some of our informants in town, so we went to meet them under cover of darkness. You know how it is—we don't want the resistance to know that we know."

The guard shifted on his feet. "So, did you find anything?"

"We found nothing substantial. There were no signs of any resistance movements." Jacob paused and looked at Marian while he continued. "I don't think the partisans are very strong in this area. I'm sure we've crushed most of their cell."

Marian's bright eyes looked back at Jacob as he nodded. Marian wouldn't talk unless he absolutely had to. His German was decent but heavily accented. Having him along had been a risk from the start, but Jacob was happy to have the big man with him now.

The guard's eyes shifted between Jacob and Marian, and he seemed to relax a little, but then he appeared to think of something. He knocked on the guardhouse window.

The other guard stepped outside and wrapped his coat around him. "What do you need, Klaus? It's freezing out here."

When he looked at Jacob and Marian, his demeanor changed, and he sprang to attention.

"Did you know about any outside perimeter checks going on this evening?" Klaus asked, ignoring his complaint.

Jacob kept his eyes on the other guard, who looked surprised.

"For tonight? No, there was nothing on the duty sheet," the man said.

Klaus's face lined with suspicion as his eyes returned to Jacob.

Jacob felt Marian's eyes almost burning into the side of his face. He knew he had to do something before these nosy guards compromised the whole plan.

"Look, I can't tell you any more of the details of this mission. I've already told you too much," Jacob said, his eyes now narrowing. He raised himself to his full height and stepped closer to the gate.

Despite the gate between them, Klaus took an involuntary small step back, unsure what to do as Jacob pushed on.

"And, as an officer, I don't like to be questioned when I return to camp. I appreciate you need to be diligent, but you've exhausted my patience."

Klaus averted his eyes from Jacob. Instead, he looked to his partner, who looked ready to slink back into the warmth of the guardhouse.

*He's unsure what to do next. Let's push it.*

"You're going to open the gate, step back into that guardhouse, and hope that I won't write up a report for insolence."

The guard hastily opened the gate, and Jacob brushed past him with Marian in tow. He heard the two men whispering behind him as they stepped back into the guardhouse. Jacob kept his strides long and purposeful.

When they were out of earshot, Marian caught up with him.

"Well done. Let's hope you don't have to pull rank like that again."

"I didn't expect that guard to be so difficult," Jacob said. "We were lucky."

Marian shrugged. "Luck had nothing to do with it. That perfect German will fool anybody here, as long as you're as confident as you were just now."

They took stock of their surroundings. The first slivers of sunlight burst through the sky, the rows of barracks cutting thin shadows across the train tracks to their right.

The high barbed-wired fence behind them hummed softly as they walked into the camp.

"That fence is electrified," Marian whispered as they walked along the train tracks and found themselves in something of a corridor— barbed wire fences lining both sides. To their left, they saw only women.

"That's the women's camp," Marian said. "We'll need to make our way over there instead"— he pointed at a smaller gate about half a mile up the road to their right. It was odd to walk in the no-man's-land along the train tracks, yet be surrounded by people on both sides. In the back of the camp, the train tracks ended abruptly, and the billowing chimneys left no doubt as to what happened there.

*Did Agnes even make it to the women's camp?* Her face flashed into his mind, and he swallowed hard. The women behind the fence looked back at him with hollow eyes. *Even Agnes wouldn't have survived two years in those conditions.* His eyes stung, and he blinked hard.

Jacob shuddered as they turned into the men's camp. It was the most substantial part of the camp, as row after row of neatly-lined barracks stretched across the horizon.

"Looks like we got here just in time," Marian said, nodding at a group of people walking in their direction.

Jacob and Marian stepped out of the way, and the guards leading the group saluted them as the young men marched past them. Two more guards secured the rear, rifles in hand.

"They're already heading out," Jacob said. He looked around and saw most of the people moving about at this early hour congregated around in small groups. Guards stood at the front, calling out numbers as the weary men responded—people were reduced to numbers in Auschwitz.

The amount of human suffering was overwhelming. Everywhere Jacob looked, he saw similar-looking men wearing the same outfit, the same tired look, and—most prominently—shaved heads.

Jacob was distraught. *How am I going to find Ethan in this sea of people?* He looked at Marian. Even the ordinarily stoic Pole looked shocked, his eyes rapidly darting around as he took in the surreal surroundings.

"It's even worse than I thought," Marian said. "Our contacts in the administration building are a lot better off than most of the men here. They're skin over bones, and that's generous."

"They're literally being worked to death," Jacob said as a group of boys passed them. They weren't older than sixteen, keeping their heads down and taking one step at a time. Their worn slippers were torn and could hardly be considered proper shoes for the Polish winter coming up.

Jacob shivered as they walked on. He scanned the faces along the main road.

"How are we going to find Ethan?"

Marian shrugged. "We won't find him just by walking around here. We'll need to ask around."

"Ask who?" Jacob felt his face flush. He'd just recovered from his encounter with the guards at the gate and wasn't looking forward to doing more talking.

Marian looked thoughtful as he scanned the buildings.

Jacob knew what he was looking for. "Are you looking for an administration building?"

The big Pole nodded. "We won't find anyone in here by chance. You'll have to go in and check where to find Ethan's work detail. It's the only way. We'll need to go a bit further—these buildings are all barracks."

They followed the main road through the men's camp. It reminded Jacob of Westerbork. The layout was the same, dusty roads lined with nothing but barracks. The difference was the people. In Westerbork, they looked like actual human beings. Here, the prisoners resembled walking skeletons. The few exceptions were probably new arrivals.

On closer inspection, he saw the differences went beyond just the people. Apart from the barracks, there were no other buildings. There was no school because there were no children, just the sound of prisoners marching to work, prodded along by the SS.

They reached a small open space and Marian nodded toward a building on their left.

"That doesn't look like a prisoner building," he said, as a pair of guards stepped out.

Marian strode toward the building with purpose and looked back at Jacob.

"Come on, no time to lose."

Jacob hurried after him. *Is this really a good idea?*

"Don't you think officers would know where to find their detail?"

Marian didn't stop but answered: "Of course they would. But they wouldn't know every single detail in the camp, right? Just think of an excuse why you need to know."

*How can I make sure I don't sound suspicious?*

They reached the building, and another officer walked out. He held the door for them, and Marian nodded his thanks. He held the door for Jacob.

"Go in there and find out where Ethan is. And be quick about it—who knows how far we'll have to walk to find him!" Marian said.

"You're not coming with me?"

Marian shook his head. "The less I'm spoken to, the better. I'll be right here."

Jacob took a deep breath and entered the building. *Focus! This is your only chance.*

Inside, the room was brightly lit. It smelled familiar to Jacob, and he realized it was very similar to the admin building in Westerbork. The layout was identical. He wasn't surprised—the Nazis liked to build everything using the same blueprint. It was efficient, especially when so much of the same had to be built. He thought back to when Fischer had drawn up the plans for the new barracks in Westerbork—that felt a lifetime away.

The large room was quiet. Rows of men wearing the striped prisoner's uniform sat at small desks, scribbling in large ledgers. They didn't acknowledge Jacob—they were too busy to notice him. On the far side, he saw an open door leading to a hallway. He made his way over and stepped in to find it lined with small offices.

Most doors were closed, but he found one open. There was no sign on the door, and he found a young officer at a small desk.

He looked up and noticed Jacob. "Can I help you?"

*Shouldn't he salute me?* He let it go and cleared his throat.

"I've recently been transferred here, and I'm looking for a particular work detail. I'm meant to inspect the coal mines just outside of town," Jacob said. He held up his hands. "Any chance you could send me in the right direction?"

The younger man looked him over. "Where were you transferred from?"

"Berlin, I did my training just outside the city in Sachsenhausen," Jacob said. He hoped the name would be familiar enough.

The officer's eyes lit up. "Really? I was also at Sachsenhausen."

*Shit.*

Jacob's heart dropped. He hadn't recognized a Berlin accent in the young man's voice. He knew nothing about Sachsenhausen, other than that people from Berlin were sent there.

"Who was your training officer?" The officer stood up, and his eyes sparkled. *He clearly has fond memories of the camp.*

Jacob thought quickly. Sachsenhausen was a big place, and the rotation of officers was high—the chances of the man across from him knowing all of them was near impossible. He and decided to chance it.

"Schröder—great guy," Jacob said. The SS officer's face was still imprinted in his memory.

The young officer looked confused. He scratched his chin as if in deep thought, as he repeated the name.

"Can't remember anyone by that name," he said. "When were you there?"

Jacob cursed under his breath. *Is everyone this nosy in here?*

"Late thirties, so perhaps you weren't there yet?" Jacob surprised himself with his reference to the younger man's age. "But if you don't mind, could you point me in the right direction for that work detail? I saw most of them heading out already. I wouldn't want to miss my assignment."

The officer nodded. "What detail number is it?"

"I'm not sure." Jacob held up his hands. "I was told to report to the largest one, the one to the east of the city."

The young officer stared with little recognition in his eyes, and Jacob felt himself panic.

He was about to speak when the young man raised his hands triumphantly.

"Sorry, I had trouble remembering, but you're looking for detail 57. They always leave as some of the last ones, because they're so big." He smiled at Jacob. "You're in for a treat—the coal mines are some of the biggest I've ever seen. I was assigned to guard duty when I joined the camp. It's quite impressive. And you'll always have some of them drop out on the way back. It's exciting!"

Jacob remembered the man collapsing in the village.

"So, where will I find them?"

"You're actually quite close—let me show you." The officer grabbed a piece of paper and drew the outlines of their surroundings. He traced the outline to an open space a few rows of barracks away from them. "This is where they report."

Jacob barely contained his excitement. *Ethan's close.*

"When do they leave?"

The officer stepped out of the small office and looked at the clock down the hall.

"In about half an hour, so you still have time to get there."

Jacob was already moving down the hallway before turning around. "Thanks for your help—I'll get you a beer in the mess tonight!"

The younger man returned the salute and smiled. "I'll come and find you!"

Jacob stepped out of the building into the rain and found Marian hunched near the door, trying to find some shelter.

"Let's go—I know where," Jacob said, not breaking his stride. He felt energized and confident they were about to find Ethan.

"Now you're acting like the officer you are," Marian said, struggling to catch up. "I take it they haven't left yet?"

Jacob shook his head. "Not according to the man I spoke to. He said Ethan is in the biggest group, and they'll be leaving soon." He pointed ahead to a clearing visible between the barracks.

They stomped on, their boots occasionally getting sucked into the sandy road, which was rapidly turning into a muddy mess. Jacob was glad he had proper shoes, unlike most people around him. Plenty of the prisoners had taken off their shoes and continued barefoot.

They reached the open space and, Jacob stopped in his tracks. Marian looked out wide-eyed as well.

"I thought you said there were a few hundred of them marching to the coal mines," Marian said.

Jacob nodded. "Maybe a thousand, maximum."

At least twice as many men stood lined up in neat rows. They were of all sizes and ages, staring straight ahead—avoiding eye contact with the SS guarding them. The sight reminded Jacob of the roll calls at Westerbork as he scanned the faces in the front rows. He didn't see Ethan.

"We need to get closer before they leave," Marian said in a low voice. "Is there any way I can recognize Ethan?"

"He's tall and has big ears," Jacob said, deep in thought. Apart from that, it would be hard to distinguish any distinct features in this line-up. The men's heads were shaved, and all wore identical clothing.

Marian nodded. "We need to be smarter about this." His eyes went to the front and focused on what appeared to be the detail leader.

"He doesn't look too highly ranked," Marian said. "Even from this distance, I can see he doesn't have more than three stripes on his shoulder. You should challenge him."

Jacob followed his gaze and saw a sulky looking man flanked by two guards.

He turned to Marian. "That's a great idea, but I'm sure he won't know Ethan's name. He's just a number here, and I don't have it. Besides, it would be very suspicious to ask for him."

Marian thought for a moment as the guards in the field continued the roll call. One of the prisoners wavered on his feet, and within seconds a guard was on him, dragging him out of the line-up. The man stumbled after the guard without resistance, barely keeping his balance. The guard took him away from the group, dragging him around the corner. All the other men kept their eyes straight ahead of them. Jacob had no doubt the man wouldn't return to the group.

"We can pretend to help with the inspection," Marian said, taking Jacob back to the challenge at hand. "We'll need a bit of luck, but it's better than nothing."

"It doesn't look like they're quite done yet," Jacob agreed.

"It will take them at least another fifteen minutes at this rate," Marian said, his eyes following a younger guard in the front. "You would find Ethan in that group if you got close enough, right?"

Jacob looked at the faces; he had to believe he would recognize his friend. He hoped Ethan would recognize him as well.

*He might have trouble believing it's really me in this uniform, though.*

"We have to try. I'll talk to the detail leader. Follow me, and once he agrees, we'll search the group for Ethan."

The detail leader spotted them from a way out as they approached. He was even uglier from close-by; overweight and sporting a thin mustache. The man appeared to be in a bad mood, a snarl on his face as they approached. He reminded Jacob of Arthur Pisk. Despite his demeanor, he still had the grace to salute the higher-ranking officers.

Jacob returned the salute. "I see you're almost ready to head out to the mines."

"Are you here to inspect my work, sir?" The man emphasized the last word. His face was ugly, but his eyes showed intelligence.

*Better be careful with this one.*

"Not at all—we're here to transfer two prisoners to the Kapo unit in One. We need reinforcements down the road."

The man cocked his head. "For which part of the kapo's?"

"You know how it is—I'm not at liberty to say. Let's say we have some trouble processing some of the prisoners."

The fat man looked at Jacob, his eyes bearing into him. It felt like he looked straight through Jacob.

"You realize this is completely off protocol, right? I've never heard of work details changed at the last minute. How am I going to explain this to the administration?"

Jacob sighed. *This is going to be harder than I thought.*

The man stood with his arms crossed.

Jacob turned and casually flipped his hand toward Marian. The Pole walked off and started inspecting the men. Jacob turned back to the fat man, whose eyes were following Marian.

"Why don't you help out with the inspection on the far side," Jacob said to the guards next to the detail leader. "That way, we'll be able to leave a bit quicker."

The men saluted him and hurried off, relieved to be away from the officers. Jacob took a step closer to the fat man.

"What's your name?"

The man looked up at him defiantly, the scowl still on his face.

"Pfeiffer," he said, and after a pause—"Sir."

Jacob ignored the insolence and remembered how Schröder pulled rank at every opportunity when a lower-ranking SS guard dared to disagree with him at Westerbork. He kept his eyes on the man and made an effort to even his voice.

"Well then, Pfeiffer. Here's what's going to happen. I'm going to take my time selecting two of your strongest men here. When I've found them, I'll take them from the work detail, and they'll come with me. If you even think of protesting, I'm going to report you to the administration."

Jacob tapped on Pfeiffer's shoulder, making sure he brushed the shoulder pad, indicating he was a low-ranking officer.

"And when that happens, you and I both know what that means for your career," Jacob said. He paused. "Right?"

*I hope this works.*

The scowl had vanished. Pfeiffer's face was passive, but his eyes showed something else. Fear? Jacob wasn't sure, but the man didn't look so confident anymore.

"Sir, please feel free to select any of them, sir," Pfeiffer said with a slightly rasping voice.

Jacob controlled himself as he considered berating him even more, but he needed his time to find Ethan. He turned to the group behind him.

*How am I going to find Ethan? And where is Marian?*

He left Pfeiffer, and his eyes darted along the first line of men. He knew Ethan wasn't there—he'd checked before—but he wanted to make sure.

He spotted Marian on the other side of the field as he'd started his search in the back.

Jacob passed the first row. He considered calling out Ethan's name but decided against it. It would be too conspicuous. He felt Pfeiffer's eyes burning in his back. There was no reason to give the man a chance to doubt his story. He needed to find Ethan before it became too obvious.

He scanned faces in the next row. Their bowed heads made it

almost impossible to distinguish between them. He was about to walk on when he stopped and thought he saw someone familiar on the far side and paced down the row to find a tall man with a slightly slumped posture at the end. He faced downward, staring at the muddy ground. His cap hid his face, and Jacob tapped him on the shoulder.

The man raised his head, and Jacob held his breath.

The eyes looking back at him were not Ethan's.

Jacob cursed inwardly. He didn't have time to inspect all of the men who somewhat resembled Ethan. He left the young man and was about to check the next row when he felt a tap on his shoulder—Marian.

"I think I may have found some good specimens," he said in a hushed tone, his eyes showing urgency.

Jacob followed him to the back of the group. The guards had already finished their roll call here when Marian turned to him.

"We need to hurry up. I can't find your friend if I don't know what he looks like."

Jacob held up his hands in frustration and looked around.

"I know, but how am I supposed to find him in this big crowd? There's no other way but to quickly walk past them and hope I spot him."

Marian shook his head.

"We don't have time for that. It's going to take too long. There are two thousand men here, give or take a few. We need to try something else."

"Any suggestions?"

"We need to call out his name when we pass the groups," Marian said.

Jacob resolutely shook his head. "There are too many guards around. We'll draw too much attention."

Meanwhile, Pfeiffer made his way down the group toward them.

"He's getting impatient," Jacob said under his breath.

Pfeiffer reached them and gave Jacob a curious look, his eyebrows raised.

"We're almost done with our count. Are you having trouble finding the right men, sir?"

Jacob nodded. "These men are in pretty bad shape—we'll need a bit more time."

Pfeiffer looked uneasy. "I have to get them to the mine by eight. That's an hour and a half walk. If we don't get there in time, there will be hell to pay."

"We'll find men soon enough," Jacob said. A thought struck him. He turned to Marian. "Go and inspect on the other side."

Marian walked off, and Jacob turned to Pfeiffer, who still hovered around uncomfortably.

*Let's make use of my rank.*

"It's hard to see all the men as they're lined up like this. It might be more useful for me to inspect them as you head out of this area. How much longer do you need before you're ready to go?"

Pfeiffer ran his eyes over the group and shrugged.

"We should be ready in five minutes."

"Good. Then I suppose you'll go through that opening to the main alley?" He pointed in the direction he and Marian had come from.

Pfeiffer nodded. "We make our way out to the main gate and walk around the city."

Jacob's heart beat faster. The opening to the main throughway was quite narrow. For the men to get through, they'd have to walk four abreast, and Ethan would be easy to spot.

"We'll inspect them as they come through there. It will give me a better view of how strong they are. After all, seeing them on their feet is the best way to check their strength," Jacob said.

Pfeiffer frowned but nodded. "Very well—you're taking your job very seriously, sir. They're just a bunch of Jews."

Jacob bit his lip as the fat man headed back to the front, and Jacob found Marian at the back of the group.

He explained his plan, and Marian nodded approvingly.

"It's smart, Jacob! We'll be able to pick him out easily."

It took less than five minutes for Pfeiffer's men to return to the front. He hastily inspected some papers. It didn't look like he cared too much, and before long, the first men moved through the narrow opening.

Jacob and Marian stood on opposite sides as the group filed out of the field. Jacob had been right—only four men could pass through at a time. The guards made sure nobody slowed down as they hustled and shouted at the men to keep moving.

Pfeiffer came over to Jacob and paused for a moment.

"I'm going ahead. I expect you'll take two of the men and report their numbers to the last guard passing through here," he said, pointing at a tall, young man next to Marian.

Jacob kept his eyes focused on the men passing by and nodded absently.

"I'll let him know. We'll keep the paperwork in order."

Pfeiffer left without another word, and Jacob was happy the man didn't hang around. It was easier to focus without him breathing down his neck.

His head hurt as he strained to focus on the men passing by. He hadn't remembered them walking at quite this pace the other day. He stood there for what felt like an eternity as the faces started to blur. He shook his head and reminded himself to stay focused.

*Have I already missed Ethan? Did I miss my chance?*

Jacob changed his approach. He tried to focus a few rows ahead as spotting the men from a slight distance would be easier. He estimated half of the group had passed, and the clearing was getting empty.

He peered into the distance and saw a flash of a familiar figure before the man disappeared behind another group cutting into line.

Jacob strained his eyes and saw him again. The man walked with the big steps he would recognize out of thousands, even if his posture was more slouched.

Jacob couldn't make out his face, as the man's head was down. He focused on his steps, one at a time, making sure not to bump into the person in front of him. He wore a striped cap, hiding his eyes and most of his face—everything but the big ears pointing out.

*It must be him.*

He was now less than ten rows of men away—rapidly approaching. From the opposite side, Jacob felt Marian's eyes on him, missing nothing.

Five rows away, the man came into view. Jacob looked around, the nearest guard patrolling the flanks was at least ten rows behind him.

*Look up, Ethan. Look up.*

Two rows away. The man in the group kept his head down.

"Ethan!" Jacob heard himself say. He didn't shout, but it was just loud enough for the man's head to shoot up—his eyes went wide, and he looked to where Jacob stood. He locked eyes with Jacob, his face a mix of fear and disbelief.

It was Ethan.

Jacob stood frozen, unable to move. The group forced Ethan to continue walking.

His friend's head was still turned as he marched on.

Jacob was about to bolt after him when he saw a figure break through the group. Marian barged through and grabbed Ethan—now looking even more confused. The slight man in SS uniform hauled Ethan back to the entryway.

Marian looked back at Jacob—who nodded and fought hard to control his emotions. His friend was just a few paces away from him, and he was alive!

Marian said something to Ethan, who turned to the group passing by, scanning the faces. The end of the group was in sight, and the area behind them now almost empty.

Ethan pointed at one of the men approaching. The man's head was already turned toward Ethan, surprise and something else on his face— was it fear? Ethan pointed at him, and Marian waved the man over.

The man was hesitant to step out of the group, and he wavered for a moment. Marian stepped toward him and dragged him out of the group. Ethan said something to him as he stood next to him, and the expression on the man's face relaxed.

As the last of the group passed, the young guard next to Marian looked at Jacob.

"You're taking these two, sir?" The guard's face was neutral. There was no trace of hostility, and Jacob relaxed a little.

He took Ethan's wrist, exposing a crudely tattooed number. Jacob almost gasped but caught himself just in time. Marian shot him a look. The guard scribbled the serial numbers on a sheet of paper and handed the pen to Jacob. He signed at the bottom, and the man hurried off, catching up with the group marching down the main throughway.

Jacob turned to his friend. There were tears in Ethan's eyes, and Jacob felt tears welling up in his own.

"Jaco," his friend said with a weak, husky voice that Jacob almost didn't recognize. "How in the world did you find me?"

"Let's keep the talking to a minimum," Marian warned. "This is not the place to talk. Remember, you're a prisoner escorted by SS officers."

They joined the stream of men headed to the main gatehouse. The sizes of the details varied, but the composition was always the same. SS men led the prisoners to another day of forced labor. In that sense, Jacob's group wasn't all that different, if small. Despite this, Jacob felt on edge. They'd been fortunate. They just needed to get to the other side of the gate.

He looked at Ethan walking alongside him, keeping his head down so as not to attract attention. Now that he was closer to Ethan, Jacob noticed his friend looked very different from the man he'd last seen on the ramp at Westerbork a year before. The prison garments flapped around his bony arms and legs. His hands were covered in soot from the mines. Jacob had many questions, but he fought the urge to ask. If they pulled this off, there would be plenty of time for questions later.

He focused on the task at hand and looked at Marian. The man who'd been with him from the start of this walked with a confident step. He looked every bit an officer, his alert eyes scanning the area.

The large Pole turned to Ethan. "Are there normally any checks at the gate before they let the details out?"

Jacob hadn't thought of that possibility yet and was glad Marian was with him.

Ethan shook his head. "They're too focused on getting everybody out of the camp in time. They want us to get to work as quickly as possible. As long as there are SS escorts present, we should be okay."

"Good," Marian said. "Anything we should know once we get there? Do we acknowledge anyone, do we tell them where to go?"

Ethan considered the question before answering. He rubbed his elbow.

*He's nervous too.*

"I was usually in the back of the group, so I wouldn't see any communication as we got there." His eyes went over Jacob's badges.

"But I would be very surprised if anybody were to question someone of Jacob's rank."

The other prisoner nodded.

They passed a larger group on the side of the throughway. These men were older and frailer than most of the others they'd seen that day. Some of them had simple linen bags slung over their shoulders. Two guards ticked off names on a list, the men raising their hand one by one as their numbers were called out.

Ethan followed Jacob's gaze. "They're no longer useful in the work details. They won't return to the barracks this evening," he said, his eyes sad.

Jacob didn't need to ask where they were going—the chimneys of the crematoriums loomed in the distance. They walked out of the men's camp, passing through the gate without issue. They had another half mile to go until the main gatehouse. As they walked along the train tracks, Jacob saw the women's faces on the other side of the camp. Some of them stood near the fences, silently watching the men passing by.

*I wonder how many of them lost their husbands, fathers, brothers, and sons when they arrived here.*

They slowed down as the group in front of them stopped.

"What's going on?" Jacob looked at Marian, who had a better view.

The Pole strained to get a better look—they still had half the way to go.

"Can't really tell," Marian said. He stepped to the side of the rocky road, looking down the mass of people in front of them.

"Probably a hold-up at the gatehouse," Ethan said softly. "The group going to the mines is the biggest, and it usually takes a while to get through. It's a bit like when we had to squeeze through when we left the assembly point."

Jacob nodded. "Nothing to worry about, then?"

"Nothing too unusual," Ethan said, shrugging. "These things happen in the camp all the time. I've gotten used to waiting and simply accepted I couldn't do anything about it."

Jacob felt his heart ache. Ethan had always been strong, confident, and headstrong. If a year in Auschwitz-Birkenau did this to someone like him, he loathed thinking what it would do to weaker men.

"It might take a little longer, but we'll get there soon enough," Jacob said. He turned to Ethan and the other man. "Just keep your head down and let us do the talking."

There was movement in front of them, and they slowly made their way to the gate. A surge of adrenaline shot through his veins as they approached the main gatehouse Marian and he had passed through earlier.

They walked on in silence, and Jacob wondered how many men had ever escaped the camp. The watchtowers overhead were full of guards with the barrels of their guns pointed down, keeping an ever-watchful eye.

Jacob's heart pounded in his chest as the gatehouse came into view. He kept his eyes straight ahead as the other groups passed without incident. He heard Marian take a deep breath. Ethan and the other prisoner walked between them, their heads down. Marian caught Jacob's look and gave him an almost imperceptible nod.

Jacob calmed himself. Only a few paces between them and freedom. He saw the streams of men on the road outside, going in different directions. Some turned left, toward the mines. Others went right, to the fields that fed the gargantuan camp. A few lucky ones boarded trucks headed further out to places such as Oświęcim's municipal office, where Zofia was surely pacing in her office.

He walked on in a daze, one foot in front of the other, and ran through his cover story one more time, just in case.

The group in front of him cleared, and suddenly he found himself walking through the gatehouse. He felt a shadow as the building blocked out the sunlight. As they passed, they stepped back into the light, clearing the gate and leaving the camp behind. His throat constricted, and he swallowed hard. A weight lifted from his shoulders. He wanted to cry. He wanted to shout out. But most of all, he wanted to hug Ethan. Instead, he focused on keeping his calm and balled his fists to channel his energy.

*We're almost there. Don't lose it now. Focus.*

They walked on slowly and with purpose. The group ahead of them turned left where they continued straight. The road was empty, and they picked up their pace. They were silent, but Jacob felt the change in energy.

He looked at the men walking next to him. As Ethan looked back, his eyes glistened, his face beaming while the other prisoner looked confused and elated.

*He still can't believe his luck.*

At the far side of their small group, Marian walked with his usual stoic expression. Jacob raised his eyebrow as the big man felt his gaze and turned to him.

A smile formed on Marian's face. He tipped his hat.

"Well, that all went exactly as planned."

# Epilogue
## BERLIN, GERMANY. NOVEMBER 1950

Jacob shut the door, lifting the handle slightly to make sure the lock fell into place. He wriggled a bit and then heard the satisfying clunk confirming the door was locked. He pulled at the handle. It didn't budge.

He nodded with satisfaction. The lock was just one of the minor inconveniences of the worn-down building.

He stepped down two small steps and back into the main room of the store. Whoever thought it was a good idea to have these steps placed there obviously didn't have to carry boxes.

Jacob walked past a row of shelves and noticed a small package on the floor. He picked it up—a packet of gauze—and set it back on the top shelf. He remembered the frail old lady who'd come in just half an hour before to buy one of those. She must've been unable to reach the top shelf properly and had dropped one of the packages. He might need to reconsider the height of the shelves or be more aware to help the older people coming in.

Behind the counter, Ethan was restocking drawers. There were open boxes on the counter, and he deftly balanced small packs while opening drawers at the same time.

"Can you hurry up already?" Jacob asked as he leaned on the counter. "I thought you would only be a minute—I'm ready to leave."

Ethan pulled a face while he shut one of the drawers with a loud clunk.

"If you'd have given me the right boxes to start with, we wouldn't still be here." He carried on with a smile. "Or you could help me out, and we'd be done a bit quicker."

Jacob raised the countertop and grabbed one of the boxes. Together, they took less than five minutes to stock all the little boxes.

"Are you up for a quick drink?" Ethan asked as they walked to the front door.

"Sure, it's still early."

"Great, because I'm seeing Julia later. I could use a bit of liquid courage."

Jacob smiled. "Sounds like you two are getting serious. What is this, your third date?"

"Fourth." Ethan grinned. "I really like her. I think we might have a future."

"When do I get to meet her?"

"Soon. You'll like her. She's witty."

"She would have to be if you're still interested after three dates."

Ethan gave him a little jab to the shoulder. "We can't all have what you have, you know."

Jacob had met Angela soon after returning to Berlin after the war. She had survived by hiding in the Polish countryside, and they forged a strong friendship after they both returned to Berlin. They found they had a lot in common, Germans spending part of the war in Poland. It didn't take long for them to fall in love, and they now lived in a small house in Kreuzberg, near Jacob's mother, and were expecting their first child.

Jacob's mother Elsa had somehow managed to avoid every transport list and was still in Westerbork when the Canadians liberated it in April 1945. In what could only be considered a small miracle, Ethan's parents survived Westerbork's selections as well. They lived in a small flat, but they were still trying to get their old house back.

Ethan opened the door, and a little bell clanged distinctively, interrupting Jacob's thoughts. "I'm still unsure about this bell," he said with a frown.

Jacob waved his hand dismissively. "It reminds me of the bell we used to have in the old pharmacy. It's staying."

"Just saying I think we could improve it, that's all. But you're the boss." Ethan shrugged.

They stepped outside, and Jacob closed the door. He felt the weight of the double-bolt lock as he turned it into place.

Ethan stood on the sidewalk and pulled up the collar of his coat. "It's getting chilly, don't you think?"

Jacob turned from the door. He hadn't noticed, but it was a lot colder than when they had come in that morning. The lights of the shops around them illuminated the street.

The sharp clanging of a passing streetcar interrupted his thoughts.

"I think we might have snow coming tonight," Jacob said as he took a breath of fresh winter air.

Ethan smiled. "You and your obsession with snow."

"Let's go. We might still get a seat in the Augustiner," Jacob said.

They crossed the street, carefully navigating the slippery cobblestone streets. Jacob paused as they reached the other side.

"What's wrong?" Ethan asked with a look of impatience.

Jacob fumbled in his pockets. "I forgot my wallet. Give me a minute."

Ethan sighed and found shelter under one of the porches.

As Jacob crossed the street, he couldn't help but smile. The old building was dark but for the ground floor, where light flowed out from the small display window next to the door.

Above the window, they had recently placed a simple signboard—it was white with black letters and had been a bit of an investment, but one Jacob had happily made. Every time he saw it, his heart skipped a beat. It reminded him of everything he stood for.

He turned the key and looked up as he always did.

The sign read *Kagan & Sons Medicine.*

# Author's Notes

Thank you so much for reading *Beyond the Tracks*. I sincerely hope you enjoyed reading my debut novel.

Many of the characters in this story are fictional, but I want to highlight some of the real people that are featured. Of the Polish resistance, Zofia Zdrowak, her family, Marian Mydlarz, and Antoni Wykręt were real people. The Sosienki resistance movement was just one of the many in occupied Poland I encountered while researching possible cells around Auschwitz. That doesn't mean everything they do in the story is historically accurate. The Babinicza trail they used to smuggle people was real. The bridge existed, but I took some liberties with its exact position to fit the story timeline.

Both escapes from Auschwitz—amazingly—happened. In September 1944, a group of Polish prisoners walked out in SS uniforms provided by Zofia and Marian. Two of them, Stanisław Furdyna and Antoni Wykręt, then joined the Sosienki cell. In October of the same year, the same men walked back into Auschwitz, posing as SS officers to successfully free two more prisoners. These men also joined the Sosienki unit.

Zofia and her mother worked in the municipal office in Oświęcim. On December 3, 1944, Zofia and the rest of her family were interned in

Auschwitz, on suspicion of their involvement in both escapes. They were part of the death marches at the end of the war when the Nazis started clearing the camps as the Allied forces approached. Anna and her daughters miraculously escaped during the march. Jan Zdrowak was marched to his death in the Austrian camp of Mauthausen. Zofia died in her hometown of Brzeszcz in 2011.

These people represent the unsung heroes of the resistance. While I've taken creative liberties in writing about them—they are no longer alive—I feel confident they would approve of their roles in this story.

I featured Camp Westerbork for its unique setup and position within the war. Often described as a "comfortable camp"—with facilities no other concentration camp boasted—its sole purpose was to deceive the people transiting through. It was meant to keep them docile and unsuspecting of the horrors they were about to be shipped off to. Despite the superficial comforts of the camp, it was just as much part of the Final Solution as were the more notorious extermination camps.

In the camp, the Dutch and German commanders were real people. The much-detested Arthur Pisk ran the Ordedienst and survived Westerbork and the war. It's believed he escaped to Australia and died there. More importantly, Salo Carlebach, the teacher who voluntarily joined the orphaned children on the first transport, was also a real person. He perished shortly after arriving in Auschwitz, with the children, in September 1942.

Jacob's escape from the train car is a story I couldn't have come up with by myself. A very small number of people escaped from the death trains, and I relied on Tanja von Fransecky's research to get an impression of how they did this. Her (German-language) book, *Flucht von Juden aus Deportationszugen in Frankreich, Belgien und den Niederlanden,* was essential in writing this story, and I thank her for this invaluable research.

I've made a conscious effort to show that not all Germans stood by idly during the violence. Otto Belgardt, the policeman who stops the New Synagogue from getting burned down, did just that during the Night of Broken Glass.

And finally, Jacob is an entirely fictional character. His story could have happened to any Jewish man living in Berlin at the time. Many of the events he encountered happened, and I've done my best to describe them accurately from his point of view.

If you enjoyed reading the story, please consider leaving a review. As an independently-published author, I rely on word of mouth to generate interest in my work. If you'd like to reach out, I'd love to hear from you. You can find my contact details on michaelreit.com. I read and reply to every single message.

All my very best,
*Michael*

# EXCERPT OF "TRACKS TO FREEDOM"

I'm thrilled to be able to share with you the first three chapters of my next book in the *Beyond the Tracks* series, *Tracks to Freedom,* available now everywhere.

With thanks,
*Michael*

# Chapter One

Ciechanów, Poland
April 1942

It was dark when Joel Kozak pulled the sputtering car into the driveway. He stepped out of the car and hurried to open the door for the man in the back.

"Thank you, *Robert*," the man said as he stepped out. "I know I said you could take the car with you tonight, but it looks like you'll need to fix it first."

Joel nodded. "You're right, *Herr* Kesler. I'm just glad we made it back. I'll come in early tomorrow."

Kesler shook his head. "Don't bother, I don't need to be anywhere. You can use the morning to work on the car. Do you have an idea what it might be?"

"Probably a broken clutch; it felt a bit heavy. I can take a look now if you want?"

"No, no. Please go home. You don't want to be out on the streets after curfew." Kesler disappeared inside, and Joel sat back in the car. As he turned the key, the engine made a spluttering sound. Joel tried again, but there was only a soft clicking noise. He got out, opened the hood, and the smell of warm oil entered his nostrils. He shone a small flash-light into the hood and cursed—the motor was covered in oil. *Not just a broken clutch, then.* Joel closed the hood and locked the car—it was no use trying to fix the engine in the dark.

He stepped into the street, closing the gate behind him. Working as a driver for the Germans meant he enjoyed an amount of freedom few people in Ciechanów did. His driver's permit—secured by Mr. Kesler—allowed him to pass through the German checkpoints unhindered.

The streets were quiet, and Joel checked his watch—almost seven. Even though curfew wouldn't be for an hour, he instinctively checked his jacket for his papers. They were still there, and he let out a deep sigh.

He walked on, and large homes made way for smaller houses packed closer together. The pavement narrowed until it merged into the street. Joel walked through the gates of the city center, the sign above him indicating he was now entering the Jewish Quarter. *Quarter*, Joel shook his head. *They should call it what it is.*

He turned the corner to find the street ahead blocked by a dozen people milling about. They had their backs to him, focused on something on the cobblestones. It didn't take long to see what they were looking at; the bodies of two men lay face-down, a dark puddle of blood around their heads—small holes in the back of their necks testament to the execution.

The people crowding around were in various stages of shock. Two women—presumably the men's wives—stood with their hands covering their faces, shaking as they cried. Other people looked on in horror. A man with a determined step exited one of the houses, carrying a set of bed sheets. He put his hand on the shoulders of the two women and gently spoke to them. Through their sobs, they nodded, and he knelt beside the bodies. A lump formed in Joel's throat. *Those poor women.*

"Can you give me a hand?" The man spoke to no one in particular, yet to everybody. When nobody responded, Joel stepped forward. The man looked at him in surprise but quickly handed him the other side of the sheet. Two more men found their courage, wrapped the first man in the sheet, and carried him inside the house.

Two men stood a little distance from the group. Joel's blood ran cold when he saw the glint of the lightning strike shaped *S*'s on their dark green uniforms. A German patrol.

"Well, well, look here." One of them spoke as Joel and the three other men returned. "You'll need to hurry, it's almost curfew." The man looked to be in his early twenties, only a few years older than Joel.

No one responded, keen to finish their gruesome task. Joel knelt and gently lifted the dead man's feet when he felt a presence. He turned and found one of the SS men hovering over him. He met the man's eyes and was dismayed to see a spark of recognition.

"You look familiar," the man said, his brow furrowed as he scanned Joel's face. "But I can't quite place you." His eyes ran over on Joel's arms, and his expression changed from curiosity to suspicious. "Where's your armband?"

Joel's followed the man's gaze. The other SS trooper joined them. "What's going on, Gerhardt?"

"He's not wearing his Jew armband," Gerhardt said, taking a step closer, forcing Joel to readjust his stance to avoid tumbling onto the dead man on the pavement.

"I'm not a Jew." He reached into his jacket and produced his driver's permit. The German inspected it, his eyes narrowing as he read it aloud. "Robert Kozak, a *Volksdeutsche*." Then, a triumphant smile appeared on his face. "So that's why you look familiar. You work for Kesler!"

"I run errands for Mr. Kesler," Joel said, carefully replacing the permit in his jacket pocket.

The German looked more relaxed, but his partner spoke in annoyance. "What are you doing in the ghetto? Don't you know aiding Jews is forbidden?"

Joel stood up, towering over the Germans. "I'm sorry, I was rushing home and didn't realize I was passing through the ghetto. Before I knew it, I ran into this group, and they needed a hand." He waved his hand at the mourners looking at him wide-eyed. "I thought we couldn't just leave these bodies in the street. What would the city come to if we just leave people to rot?"

"I don't care about Jews rotting in the street." The SS man looked at him with a neutral expression. "They should've thought about the consequences before doing whatever they did to get shot."

Joel gritted his teeth. "I understand. I apologize for my mistake."

The trooper was about to say something when Gerhardt spoke up. "Come on, Hansie, let's move on. Mr. Kozak will make his way home and out of the ghetto." He looked at Joel sternly. "We won't see you helping out Jews in here again, will we?"

"Of course not, thank you, sir," Joel said as he turned away from the group. He met the eyes of the man he'd helped carry the first body inside. An unspoken look of understanding passed between them.

As he walked away, he heard the troopers say. "And be careful in the ghetto. Those Jews might just rob you, or worse."

He crossed through small streets, careful to avoid the main thoroughfares. He couldn't risk running into the SS patrol again, even though he was going a different direction. Five minutes later, he reached a small house, a faint flicker of candlelight making its way through the curtains. He turned the key and opened the door with a creak, the homely scent of lavender hitting his nostrils.

"Joel, is that you?" A familiar voice called from the back.

He hung his coat on the rack. "Yes, *Mama*." Before stepping into the cramped kitchen, he opened a drawer and put his papers inside.

"I was worried; you're home so late," she said, giving him a quick peck on the cheek as he sat down at the kitchen table. She placed a steaming bowl before him.

"I'm fine, Mama, it just took a little longer to get home today." He didn't want to bother his mother with the gruesome details.

She sat opposite him as he almost inhaled his soup. "You know you can tell me when something's wrong, right?"

Joel put down his spoon. "I promise I can take good care of myself." He stood, keen to get to his room. "I'm going to make it an early night. Mr. Kesler's car broke down, so I best be in early tomorrow."

His mother remained seated and smiled. "We are so fortunate you've found a job with Mr. Kesler. I'm not sure how we would survive on normal wages. Especially since it's just you and me." Her smile faded slightly, her eyes suddenly a little distant.

Joel's heart ached, as he hugged his mother. "I promise we'll be fine. Mr. Kesler is very pleased, and there is so much work that he'll need me around for quite a bit longer."

"I know, Joel. I just want you to be careful. Every day I worry you might not come back in the evening. Those Germans are so unpredictable."

He broke their embrace and looked at his mother. "Mr. Kesler is different. We can trust him. He wouldn't have arranged those papers for me otherwise."

She nodded, and Joel kissed her forehead. "Good night, Mama."

He climbed the narrow stairs and headed for his room, where he lay on the bed. He closed his eyes. *Those Jews will rob you, or worse.* He opened his eyes and shook his head, the pillow softly crunching as he did. If only they knew.

# CHAPTER TWO

Agnes stood near the bridge. *What's taking her so long? She should've been here fifteen minutes ago.* She tapped her foot, her eyes on the crowded street across the bridge. The sun was out, and it was an uncharacteristically sunny April day for Amsterdam.

The people on the bridge rushed by without notice. A young man caught her eye; late twenties, early thirties, walking purposefully with a straight back and broad shoulders. He wore a suit—no overcoat was needed today—and carried a doctor's bag. He must've felt her looking at him as he looked up and smiled. Agnes returned the smile, then averted her eyes. A few seconds later, she looked in his direction again—he was already halfway down the street.

"Sorry I'm late," a familiar voice interrupted her thoughts. She turned to find her sister standing beside her. "The tram was stuck, and the driver wouldn't let me get off. I swear I left in time," Yvette said, slightly out of breath.

Agnes looked at her younger sister as she stood panting beside her. Relieved, she hugged her. "I was worried about you, it's not like you to be this late," Agnes said.

Yvette Markx, at nineteen years old, was two years younger but a head taller than Agnes. At first sight, it was hard to believe they were sisters. Agnes had a full head of blond curls, whereas Yvette liked to keep her dark brown hair cropped short. It only became apparent when the girls talked that the pair were siblings: their voices were nearly identical.

"Did you get in touch with Johannes?" Agnes asked as they crossed the bridge.

"He should be at the market now; I handed him our coupons yesterday. He said it wouldn't be a problem."

"Where are we meeting him?"

"The southern entrance. We should still be able to make it," Yvette said as she eyed the church clock further down the street."

"Yve," Agnes said, using her sister's nickname. "You sure we can trust Johannes?"

Yvette stopped and turned, frowning. "He's done this for other people as well. We can trust him."

*I'm not going to argue with her.* "Great, then let's go find him."

Since the Germans had taken over, they imposed new restrictions on the Jewish community. Not being allowed to go to markets made it nearly impossible to get fresh produce. Thankfully, Yvette had come up with the plan to ask some Dutch friends of friends to visit the market for them. She hoped Johannes would come through.

Yvette had picked up her pace and turned into the street leading to the market. As soon as she did, she stopped and sighed. Agnes caught up and understood why. Two trucks on either side blocked the street, and green-uniformed men were busy checking papers. The German *Grüne Polizei*—the Green Police—had set up a checkpoint.

"Great, what do they want to check this time?" Yvette said as she reluctantly joined the small queue.

"They're not really checking anything. You know that." Agnes said as she reached for her papers.

The queue moved quickly, and when the sisters stepped forward, the German policeman gave them a friendly smile as they handed him their papers. Agnes returned the smile, Yvette blanked him.

He opened their papers, and his smile vanished. "This area is closed to Jews." He handed back their papers.

"Why?" Yvette's eyes shot fire.

"No Jews beyond this point." He waved his hand dismissively, indicating for them to move back.

"But we need to meet someone just a little farther up the street." Yvette didn't move, and Agnes' throat felt constricted. *Come on, sis, don't push your luck.*

The policeman cocked his head. "What for? For getting illegal produce from the market?" Yvette blinked hard, and he smiled. "We know you're getting Dutch people to get food from the market for you. Well, not anymore." He pushed Yvette back. "Now get out of here before I decide you're a real nuisance. We have plenty of space in the back of these trucks."

Agnes grabbed her sister's wrist and firmly pulled her away. "Come, Yve, let's go."

"Mom and Dad are going to be furious," Yvette said. "I gave him all our coupons for the rest of the month."

They stood a hundred meters from the checkpoint, where more people were turned away.

"Come, take a breather," Agnes said as she guided Yvette to a small bench. "I'm sure Johannes ran into the checkpoint and will realize what's happening. He's not going to steal our coupons."

"How long do you want to wait?" Yvette looked up at her with tears in her eyes. *She always pretends to be tougher than she really is. She's still my little sister, and she needs me now.*

Agnes smiled. "As long as it takes for him to show up. Did you agree on a time with him?"

"We were supposed to meet around the entrance now," Yvette said as she looked at the clock across the street. "Hopefully, he'll understand we couldn't make it there."

"If not, you'll be able to find him, right?"

Yvette nodded half-heartedly. "Don't you have class?"

"I can wait with you."

"No, you should go. It was hard enough to get into the classes. Papa won't be pleased if he hears you're skipping them. Let's not both disappoint him today."

It had been more than a year since Agnes was banned from nursing school. But the Jewish community in Amsterdam responded swiftly, setting up small underground schools, as Jewish teachers were fired from their jobs as well.

"Come, Agnes, go." Yvette interrupted her thoughts. "There's no use in us both sitting around waiting for him. If he doesn't, I'll find him somehow. Go and enjoy your class. I know how much you look forward to it."

"Are you sure?"

Yvette groaned in frustration and playfully pushed her away. "Argh, yes, go. I don't want you here any longer. I'll see you at dinner, whatever that may be."

Agnes was panting when she arrived at the school—an old office building on the outskirts of town. The back door was locked, as expected. The rules were clear; whoever was late would have to wait for the break to come in. It meant Agnes had to wait for the good part of two hours. Worse, she would probably miss an exciting lecture. *If I'm going to be told off, might as well make sure I do it properly.* She waited for a few seconds, straining her ears for sounds on the other side of the door before knocking.

Ten seconds later, a muffled voice answered from behind the thick wooden door. "Who is it?"

She recognized her teacher's voice. "It's Agnes, Mr. Klein."

A pause, then the lock clicked. A tall man wearing horn-rimmed glasses perched on his nose opened the door. Mr. Klein looked flustered and relieved. "Agnes, I was wondering what happened to you." He stepped aside. "You haven't missed a single class, never mind being late."

Agnes entered, and let out a deep sigh. "I'm sorry, it was a bit of a mess in the city, and I got stuck on one of the trams." A little white lie she could get away with.

Her teacher closed the door—making sure to lock it—and shook his head. "Well, you didn't miss much yet, so better hurry inside. But Agnes," he looked at her sternly. "Please don't be late again. I get nervous when students don't show up."

She nodded, Mr. Klein risked so much for their little class of ten. She climbed the broad stairs to the second floor, where she was glad to see the other students sitting around in a circle. She greeted them as Mr. Klein entered, leaving the door to the hallway open. The class resumed, and Agnes caught up quickly. Mr. Klein was an excellent teacher, always able to explain difficult material in a way they could all understand. Many of Agnes' friends weren't as fortunate, teaching themselves from old books at home.

Time passed quickly, and when Mr. Klein called for a short break, Agnes was keen to stretch her legs. She found one of her friends, Mario Nacamulli, standing near a window in the hallway.

"Funny how it's so quiet around here," Mario said as she approached. "This area used to be so lively before the war."

"No need for the office workers here anymore," Agnes said. "I'm just glad the owner is letting us use it."

"He's Jewish. Our people are helping each other wherever they can." Mario looked pensive as he stared out of the window.

Agnes stood next to him and watched the abandoned square below. Bike racks stood empty, and the only sounds in the square were a few birds twittering away.

"We need to stick together." She told Mario about the checkpoint earlier that morning.

He looked sympathetic. "I've heard plenty of stories of people approaching strangers to get them something from the market, only to have them run off with their coupons. It sounds like Yvette could trust him, though."

Agnes smiled back, reflecting his optimism. She was about to speak when movement on the square below caught her eye. "Look!"

Mario's ever-present smile vanished. "Oh shit." His face turned a shade paler, and his eyes narrowed.

A dozen men in black uniforms rushed from the road, heading straight for their building. Agnes was dismayed. "How did they find out about us?"

"Someone must've seen us and told the Germans or the police." Mario was already on his way back to the classroom.

They stepped back into the classroom and found Mr. Klein midbite of a sandwich. "What's wrong?"

"Blackshirts are approaching the building." As Mario spoke, there were heavy thuds on the door one floor below. Voices shouted for them to open up, and for a moment, nobody in the room moved. The other students turned to Mr. Klein, fear in their eyes. He calmly stood, adjusted his glasses and said: "Stay here. I'll handle this."

"Are you sure you don't need help?" Mario said. Agnes froze to the spot.

"That won't be necessary. Just keep the door closed and stay quiet. I'm sure I can reason with them."

"I don't think words will help," she said to Mario. The men in the black uniforms were part of the Dutch Nazi Party, the *NSB*. Similar to the Brownshirts in Germany, they brought violence wherever they showed up.

He shook his head and looked around the classroom. "We need to find something to defend ourselves with." The rest of the students looked scared, a few pleading to leave Mr. Klein to handle it.

Mario was adamant and searched the cabinets in the room. "If Mr. Klein's plan fails, we can't just let them come in here and take a beating." He focused his attention on the other two young men in the class. "You're with me, right?"

They reluctantly joined him as the noise downstairs increased. Mr. Klein had reached the door. He was playing dumb, asking the men their business.

"It doesn't sound like they're convinced," Agnes said as she stood by the stairs, ignoring Mr. Klein's advice to keep the door to the classroom shut.

Mario appeared next to her, holding an envelope opener. "Look, Agnes. There are at least ten of them, maybe more. Only three of us, four with Mr. Klein, but I don't know what they'll do to him downstairs. If it comes to fighting, you must take the back door with the other girls, okay?"

She shook her head. "I want to fight."

"No."

There was a tremendous crash downstairs, and Mr. Klein appeared at the foot of the stairs. He looked panicked, his face red as he rushed up the stairs. "They broke down the front door! Get away from the stairs!" His voice sounded unnatural as he used the railing to propel himself up. He had barely reached the top when the first of the Blackshirts followed.

Mario grabbed Mr. Klein's hand and called for the other men to join him at the top of the stairs. "Come on. This is the best place to stop them." The other students were armed with pieces of wood, and it dawned on Agnes that they'd probably smashed a chair to create their weapons. "Agnes, get out of here, and take the other girls!" Mario said. She could see him tightening his grip on the letter opener.

The young Blackshirt paused halfway up the stairs, sizing up the men waiting at the top, hatred spewing from his eyes. *He doesn't even know us.*

Within seconds, the stairway was filled with black uniforms. Agnes counted at least eight on the stairs, with the same number downstairs. "Just come with us now; there's no need to fight," one of them shouted. "You don't stand a chance, anyway, Jew boys." The man's voice boomed through the building, the words landing viciously.

"He's right," Agnes said to Mario. "Come with us. Maybe we can lose them in the streets."

Mario shook his head, focused on the men on the stairs. "I'm so tired of these thugs. It's time to fight back."

"This is not the time," Agnes said. *He's going to get himself killed.*

He turned to her, and as she looked into his eyes, she saw a determination that she knew no words of hers would weaken.

"Take the other girls, Agnes, and run. We'll hold them off as long as we can. Don't worry about me. This isn't my first fight. Now go!" *He's willing to do whatever to get us out.* Mario turned his face back to the Blackshirts, who were now moving up the stairs, one step at a time. They had fallen into something resembling a battle formation.

Agnes turned to find the girls shaking and crying, and realized Mario was right: there was no sense in all of them being beaten, arrested, or worse. She swallowed hard as she stepped away. "Follow me," she said to the girls, taking quick steps toward the back entrance.

She opened a window and guided the first girl onto the fire escape stairs. She quickly climbed down; they were only on the second floor, after all. When the second girl climbed out, there were screams from the other side of the hallway. Agnes turned to see Mario and Mr. Klein lashing out viciously at the first Blackshirts. The third and fourth girl hurried out. Another roar as one of the Blackshirts tumbled down the stairs. *Maybe they can hold them off, after all?*

The last girl climbed through the window, pausing to see how the men were doing. At that moment, Mr. Klein fell backwards onto the floor. Mario and the others tried to close ranks, but they were too late. Two Blackshirts broke through and were now at the top of the stairs. Mario's small legion was surrounded. They tried as best they could, but soon more Blackshirts poured upstairs, and Agnes reluctantly climbed outside. As she looked back, two Blackshirts descended on Mario like rabid hyenas. As he tumbled to the ground, their eyes met. The last thing she heard was him roaring. "Run!"

# CHAPTER THREE

S amson Tarski was exhausted as he carried his small toolbox. His legs protested as he placed one foot before another, moving almost mechanically as his group entered the city. *Only another kilometer left.*

The day had been like any other, and he'd almost gotten used to the grueling work of sorting scrap metal in the yard outside Kraków. As one of the largest men in the detail, Samson was always picked to push the heavy carts of metal from one side of the depot to the other and help load the trucks.

"Keep moving, you dogs! I want to be home in time for dinner!" Jerzy—an especially vicious Volksdeutsche—boomed from the front of the column. Samson detested the Poles who had discovered some distant bloodline making them *part German*, and thus qualifying as Volksdeutsche. It meant a slighter better treatment by the Nazi occupiers, resulting in higher food rations and jobs overseeing people like Samson.

The work detail trotted through the city, and soon crossed the Vistula river. The walls of the ghetto loomed, and the front of the column entered through Lwowska Street. The Jewish Police, wearing long jackets and hats, was especially vigilant at the gate that evening. They picked out people walking by, interrogating them and then— depending on the answers—let the men pass or direct them to wait near the wall. The latter was not a good omen. Samson was still a way from the gate when he felt the gaze of one of the policemen on him. He looked back, trying to look as composed as possible, but there was no doubt: the officer was focused on him. *What does he want?*

He was still a good fifty meters away when the uniformed man started making his way toward him. Samson gripped his toolbox tighter.

Set up to keep order in the ghetto, the men wearing the badges of the *Ordnungspolizei*—Jewish Police—had taken to the task with a zeal that required little German involvement in making the ghetto a frightening place. They were keen to impress the Gestapo and SS, favoring them over their own people in the Jewish council. Samson kept his head down as he approached the gate, praying he had mistaken the man's gaze.

A strong hand gripped him by the shoulder. "Come with me." Samson was hauled to the side, the other men of the work detail averting their eyes.

"Is something wrong, officer?" Samson said, biting his tongue as he emphasized the last word.

"Shut up unless I tell you to speak." The man spoke in a thick Krakówian accent. "You missed a day's work yesterday."

The suggestion was as ludicrous as it was untrue. Samson had been at the yard for seven days in a row. He was scheduled to have a day off tomorrow, although that was hardly a certainty. He opened his mouth, then remembered he hadn't been given permission yet.

"You know the penalty for missing scheduled work? I'll have to write you up and report you to the council." As he spoke, a smile appeared on his face. He then looked as if he suddenly remembered something. "And to the Gestapo, of course. They'll be very interested in speaking with you."

Samson could no longer hold his tongue. "What are you talking about? I haven't missed a day's work in over a week now."

In a flash, the policeman smashed his baton into Samson's groin. He winced and stifled a groan as he bent forward, dropping his toolbox with a clang. A wave of nausea rose but he managed to suppress it just in time. Some of the men passing by looked up in shock, then—realizing what was happening—quickly looked the other way.

"Are you calling me a liar?" The policeman barked at him, using the tip of his baton to lift Samson's head. "If I tell you you've been missing work, that's what's happened, you hear me?"

Samson looked up at him, his vision clouded. He controlled the anger building up inside. Slowly, he straightened his back and looked at the man opposite him. He was half his size, but the unexpected blow had knocked the wind out of Samson. His vision cleared and he looked the man in the eye. The policeman faced him challengingly, and Samson realized he couldn't win this argument.

"What will happen when you write me up, sir?"

"You'll need to report to the council, if you're lucky. More likely, the Gestapo will come and have a word. You can forget about this job in the future, that's for sure," The man looked gleeful as took out a small notepad. "Now, name."

Those last two words confirmed what Samson suspected; the man had no idea who he was. He was just randomly picked. He'd heard about this happening before, although he'd never seen it happen. Samson looked around and suddenly realized it was an organized effort by the Jewish Police. All around him, men were stopped and interrogated in the same way. They all had been selected; they were strong, healthy-looking men like himself. *Selected for what, though?*

"Have you lost your tongue?" The officer poked him in the ribs with his baton. "Your name, Jew."

Something in Samson snapped. Had this man completely forgotten his background? He looked the officer up and down, a foul taste appearing in his mouth. The officer wore an armband; white with the letters OD, reserved for the Jewish Police. A little to the side, however, on his right breast pocket, he wore the same insignia Samson had. A yellow star of David. He was no less Jewish than him, yet only one of them had sold their soul to the Nazi devil, betraying their own people.

The officer's patience had run out, for Samson saw him raise his baton again. Before he could bring it down, Samson reached for the man's arm, grabbing his wrist. The officer's eyes registered surprise, and then Samson squeezed with all his might. The policeman let out a shriek, dropping the baton. Without another thought, Samson snatched it mid-air with his free hand. He pulled back his arm and—surprising himself—smashed it into the man's face with all the force his tired arms could muster. The man's eyes rolled back into his sockets as his legs gave out, and he fell down on the cold pavement with a dull thud.

Samson looked at the man on the floor and dropped the baton. It had become eerily quiet around him. The monotone drone of hundreds of feet passing in the background had ceased. The procession had come to a standstill. All eyes were fixed on him. Their expressions ranged from dismay to fascination—he had done what many of them had only dreamed about, but had thought better of at the last minute. *Oh shit. What have I done?*

Samson didn't get a chance to ponder his actions, the next thing he heard were heavy footsteps approaching. As he raised his hands and slowly turned around, all he remembered was a ferocious blow to the side of his head and the sky turning black.

# ABOUT THE AUTHOR

Michael Reit is an independently-published author. That means he likes to do everything himself, but he doesn't identify as a control freak. If you're reading this, you own the first version of his first-ever novel. An avid fan of history and historical fiction, and intrigued by WWII, Michael spent years researching lesser-known events, locations, and people to produce Beyond the Tracks. He intends to release his second book a little quicker than the first. Born in the Netherlands, he now lives in beautiful Vienna, Austria, with his partner Esther, daughter Bibi, and Hungarian Vizsla Maggie.

Connect with Michael via his website:
www.michaelreit.com

Or via Facebook:

facebook.com/MichaelReitAuthor

# ALSO BY MICHAEL REIT

**Beyond the Tracks Series**

1. Beyond the Tracks

2. Tracks to Freedom

3. The Botanist's Tracks

**Orphans of War Series**

1. Orphans of War

2. They Bled Orange

3. Crossroads of Granite

**Stand-alones**

Warsaw Fury